TWENTY YEARS BURIED

An absolutely gripping crime thriller with a massive twist

MICHELLE KIDD

DI Jack MacIntosh Mysteries Book 4

Previously published as *Hangman's End*

Revised edition 2023
Joffe Books, London
www.joffebooks.com

First published in Great Britain in 2021
as *Hangman's End*

This paperback edition was first published
in Great Britain in 2023

This book is a work of fiction. Names, characters, businesses, organizations, places and events are either the product of the author's imagination or are used fictitiously. Any resemblance to actual persons, living or dead, events or locales is entirely coincidental. The spelling used is British English except where fidelity to the author's rendering of accent or dialect supersedes this.

Cover art by Nick Castle

ISBN: 978-1-80405-805-3

CHAPTER ONE

Time: 12.30 a.m.
Date: Wednesday 21 May 2014
Location: London Bridge, London SE1

Charlie Somerville unclipped Zac's lead and watched the Labrador scamper away over the shingle and silt-laden mud-flats. The sky was more or less clear, only the occasional tardy cloud still lingered to mask the emerging moonlight. The bridge itself was quiet: just the random rumbling of a London night bus left to disturb the peace.

Charlie sighed and smothered a yawn. He'd been on his feet for much of the day and his muscles ached. The night carer came on at 10 p.m. and afforded him that small window of luxury — time to himself. And, although tired, he welcomed these short walks along the banks of the river. It was often the only chance he had to truly let his mind wander, to allow himself to think of things other than medication routines, feeding schedules, and turning patterns to prevent bed sores. But he didn't begrudge his day-to-day life — not one bit. He'd loved Alice from the moment he'd laid eyes on her at the Roxy Picture House in Edmonton all those years ago — and the harsh cruelty of advancing dementia wasn't going to rob him of that.

They'd met in late 1974, and little did he know that the girl in the cinema ticket booth would one day become his wife. He'd gone to see the new James Bond film, *The Man with the Golden Gun* — but he'd spent the entire time in the foyer talking to Alice, so drawn was he to her dazzling smile and infectious laugh. From that moment on, they'd been inseparable.

And although he often chided himself for enjoying his night-time walks so much, with just himself and Zac for company, he knew Alice understood. The disease might be ravaging her brain, slowly but surely consuming more of her as each day passed, but the real Alice was still in there — Alice from the Roxy Picture House.

Zac had almost disappeared out of sight, heading for one of the arches beneath the bridge. Charlie could just about make out the Labrador's wagging tail as the dark night enveloped them. The sound of the dog's grunting and snuffling floated towards him on the gentle breeze.

As he continued along the shingle bank, he noticed Zac darting towards a dark mound that sat almost directly beneath the first arch. From this distance it looked like a large rock, something uncovered by the receding tide. As he got closer, Charlie noticed Zac had started to run around in a crazy, circular way — first in one direction, then the other — his tail wagging furiously.

And then the barking started.

"Shush, Zac. Stop that racket. You'll wake half of London."

But the dog's barking continued.

As he neared, Charlie saw the Labrador had his nose to the ground, sniffing and yelping with every step — his barks becoming more frantic.

"Zac? Come here, boy." Charlie tried to grab hold of the dog's collar, but the Labrador ducked out of his grasp and scampered away. Despite the dark, Charlie could see the agitation in the dog's eyes.

As Zac continued to gallop excitedly around in circles, sniffing and snorting in the damp mud, Charlie crouched down to take a closer look at what had got the dog so worked up. He instantly recoiled as the pungent aroma hit his nostrils. Whatever it was, it didn't smell too fresh.

What cloud cover there had been overhead now parted, letting moonlight fall onto the riverbed. Charlie frowned. Now illuminated, he could see the mound he'd thought was a rock looked more like a bag — a suitcase.

Glancing over his shoulder, he looked to see if there was anyone else about, anyone who might be missing a rather untidy-looking piece of luggage. But there was nothing and no one; the banks of the river were deserted.

Charlie raised his gaze to the bridge overhead. Had it fallen from above?

Zac continued to jump up and down by Charlie's side, barking excitedly. "Shush, Zac. It's OK, boy. It's OK." Charlie reached out once more to grab the dog's collar, managing to get a hold of him this time. Quickly snapping the lead back into place, he brought the dog to a standstill. "Sit, Zac. Sit."

Although clearly agitated, the dog obeyed the command and sat down on the muddy riverbed, tail wagging behind him.

"Good boy, good boy." Charlie turned his attention back to the suitcase. And the smell. He tried to place the aroma. Before Alice's illness had taken hold, he'd worked at Billingsgate Market and then later at a local butcher's shop. He was familiar with the fruity smells that both places could create.

But this wasn't quite the same.

Winding the dog's lead around his wrist, he leaned in closer. The suitcase was fastened by a rusting zip which kept the contents, whatever they turned out to be, securely inside.

Charlie hesitated, wondering if he should call someone. But who would he call? And what would he say? He'd found a bag on the riverbed? With the amount of fly-tipping that went on these days, who knew what rubbish lay at the bottom of the river at any given moment. Maybe things like this washed up all the time and he just didn't know.

Grabbing hold of the handle, he pulled the suitcase forwards. It felt heavy. He started to pull on the zip with Zac whining at his side — the dog's paws clawing at the damp ground.

"Easy, boy. Easy." The zip caught, and needed a firm tug to set it free.

It was then that the smell intensified and Charlie started to gag.

Flipping the lid of the suitcase open, he promptly turned to the side and vomited.

* * *

Time: 12.40 a.m.
Date: Wednesday 21 May 2014
Location: Monument Underground Station, London EC4

He hadn't hung around for long, leaving the bridge almost as quickly as he'd arrived. He was pretty sure no one had seen him — or if they had, he was inconspicuous enough not to raise even the smallest of eyebrows.

And the gods had been looking down on him for once — the bridge itself had been deserted.

Settling into a vacant seat on the District Line, he glanced at his watch. The dog walker should have found her by now. The evening was clear and calm, so there was no reason to suspect the man and his dog would deviate from their usual routine. Night after night he'd observed them — appearing when the tide was out, as regular as clockwork. What breed the dog was he didn't know and didn't much care. He wasn't really an animal person. And, if truth be told, he didn't like humans all that much, either.

But the dog seemed to enjoy the trips out across the riverbed — scampering away to explore the sights and smells that the departing waters always left behind. He didn't really know why he'd started watching them, but you could never tell when things like that might come in useful.

Such as tonight.

The Tube rattled into Mansion House station and ground to a halt. The doors hissed open but at this time of night there were few people making their way around the capital. Nobody got on or off and the doors soon slid shut once again.

He sat with his hood up and a scarf wrapped around the lower part of his face — leaving only his eyes visible. Facial recognition software was on the increase, whether the public were aware of its use or not. He wore nothing distinctive, nothing to stand out, or to be particularly memorable.

And as well as knowing where the CCTV cameras would be, he also knew where they were not. Once he'd completed his journey, he would quickly melt into the night.

He glanced once again at his watch. Yes, the dog walker would almost certainly be there by now. And judging by how this particular dog delighted in sniffing and exploring everything in its path, he was sure that the suitcase wouldn't lie undiscovered for long. He was too far underground to hear the police sirens — but he could almost imagine them ringing in his ears, playing his tune.

The Tube ramped up speed and hurtled along the tracks towards the next stop. He had another three to go before it would be time to slip quietly away. To pass the time, he pulled out a set of earphones from the rucksack at his feet and plugged himself into his favourite playlist.

The bag was heavy and cumbersome but, unlike the suitcase, at least it wasn't smelling too much yet.

* * *

Time: 2.30 a.m.
Date: Wednesday 21 May 2014
Location: London Bridge, London SE1

The call had come in at a little after two o'clock. Detective Inspector Jack MacIntosh hadn't been asleep and it'd taken him all of two minutes to pull on some clothes and run out to the car. The details had been fairly brief but the urgency, even at this time of night, wasn't lost on him.

The streets were quiet and Jack soon arrived at the entrance to London Bridge, parking at the side of the road by Monument Tube station. That was as far as he could get — the outer cordon already established. He could see the bridge was littered with patrol cars, plus one ambulance standing idly by. The road had been blocked off at both ends, no traffic allowed on or off the bridge.

As he stepped out of the Mondeo, Jack spied a vehicle he recognised. As he made his way on foot across to the south side, where the majority of activity was centred, he picked out the balding head of the Force's forensic pathologist, standing a good foot or so above everybody else.

Dr Philip Matthews stood close to the edge of the bridge, peering over into the shallow waters below.

"Evening, Doc." Jack approached the pathologist's side and followed his gaze. "What've we got?"

Dr Matthews hesitated before tearing his eyes away from the activity beneath them. A tired smile crossed his face. "Good morning, Jack. Hope we didn't wake you."

Jack gave a quick shake of the head. "Not at all." Chance would be a fine thing, he wanted to add.

The pathologist turned to look back down towards the river. "It's an unusual one, Jack. I'll say that much. I've only been here a few minutes myself. They're still establishing the scene down there, so I expect we'll get the nod shortly."

Jack saw the familiar figure of Elliott Walker, crime scene manager, below them on the shingle-covered banks. Even with his protective suit on, Jack recognised the tall, lithe figure instantly — getting a glimpse of his smooth, shaven head before the investigator snapped the elastic hood back into place.

"First indications?" The message Jack had received had been patchy to say the least. A body found beneath London Bridge — that had been the extent of the information divulged that tore Jack from his pitiful attempt at sleep. He joined the pathologist in peering over the edge of the bridge once more, his eyes searching for the body on the banks below. A jumper, surely. It had to be a jumper. But despite scanning the area several times, Jack couldn't see anything resembling the poor unfortunate soul who'd decided tonight was the night to jump.

"Dog walker found it a couple of hours ago." Dr Matthews nodded towards the riverbed. "Concealed in a suitcase."

Jack's eyebrows shot up. "A suitcase?" That piece of information had been absent from the earlier brief phone call.

Dr Matthews nodded, gravely. "That's all I've been told so far."

Just as Jack opened his mouth to comment, he spied Elliott raising a hand in their direction. "Looks like that's our cue, Doc. Let's get down there."

An inner cordon had been set up around the immediate location of the suitcase. Once down on the riverbed, both Jack and Dr Matthews donned their protective clothing and signed the official attendance log, then ducked under the tape and made their way towards the commotion.

Arc lights were already erected, illuminating the area in a harsh, artificial light — and the metal stepping plates, set at regular intervals, helped guide them across the silt banks. Jack slowed down as they approached the scene. "Elliott? What've you got for us?"

Elliott Walker turned around, and Jack could immediately see the concern in the man's eyes. As an experienced crime scene manager, Elliott had attended many a distressing scene, but his eyes told Jack that this one was bad. Really bad.

"Jack. Dr Matthews." Elliott nodded in greeting, stepping to the side to allow both of them to move closer.

Jack hadn't really known what to expect.

But it definitely wasn't this.

"Discovered at approximately twelve-thirty, the suitcase contains what we believe to be a torso, plus both arms and legs. No head, hands, or feet located at this stage." Elliott paused and Jack noticed, even in the dark, how the seasoned crime scene manager's face had paled. "I'm no medical professional, but it looks to me like a child."

CHAPTER TWO

Time: 3.45 a.m.
Date: Wednesday 21 May 2014
Location: London Bridge, London SE1

The night air was eerily still, with only the sound of the arc light generator humming in the background. The river, what there was of it at this point in the tide cycle, slid quietly by. It was as if this part of the capital had come to a brief but complete standstill — maybe out of respect at what had just emerged from its silent waters.

Jack was still reeling from the revelation of the contents of the suitcase. No matter how many dead bodies he saw during the course of the job, each one still had the power to shock. He'd taken only a brief look — thankfully nothing more was required at this stage — seeing the small torso wedged into the confines of the tiny case, legs and arms tucked around the side. It was a macabre and deeply unsettling view.

Jack stepped away, melting into the background. There wasn't much more he could contribute to the scene, and if he hung around too long he'd only get in the way. Dr Matthews had performed a rudimentary examination, so it wasn't really necessary to prolong the process. Life was clearly extinct, and you didn't need a medical degree to see that.

The dog walker had been removed from the scene — the fewer people to contaminate whatever evidence might be lying on the muddied banks, the better. He'd clearly been shocked by the discovery and had to be checked over by the waiting paramedics on the bridge above. After a brief statement taken by one of the first officers on the scene, the man was allowed home. Jack would catch up with him when the details of what he'd just uncovered had begun to sink in.

Alongside the illumination from the temporary arc lights above, the sky looked to be showing signs of the forthcoming dawn. And with the dawn would come the water.

Elliott Walker made his way across to where Jack was waiting. "We'll need to start pulling out soon. The tide's rising and this part will be covered in water before we know it."

Jack nodded. "Of course."

It was an unusual crime scene. Usually, scenes could be locked down for hours, days, even weeks if necessary — while the meticulous crime scene investigators gathered every possible scrap of evidence they could. But this one was different. Mother nature was handing them a completely different set of criteria to work with. As time ticked by, whatever evidence there was could be washed away and returned to the sea, or at least masked from view until the next low tide.

"We'll take the body *in situ*. Take samples from the area in which it was found. We'll examine as much as we can before the tide comes in." Elliott nodded towards the team of white-suited investigators already doing just that. "We've got a video of the scene, and photographs. We'll come back again at the next low tide — see what else we can find." He paused, concern still etched onto his face. "It's a difficult one, Jack. I won't lie. But we'll do our best."

Jack nodded his thanks and watched the crime scene manager return to rally his troops. Using the metal stepping plates, Jack started to walk back towards the bridge. Despite the number of bodies going about their work behind him, the scene was eerily quiet. And although the poor soul in the suitcase was beyond their help, the investigators were treating the discovery with as much dignity and respect as the challenging circumstances would allow.

Jack felt a shiver ripple down his spine as he pulled out his phone. Despite the late hour — or early, depending on your viewpoint — he knew it was time to alert the team.

* * *

Time: 4.00 a.m.
Date: Wednesday 21 May 2014
Location: Flat 3a Ash Road, SE Soho, London

Flicking the switch on the kettle, he felt the familiar flutter at the base of his stomach. He fancied something stronger, but the empty vodka bottle on the draining board told him he'd have to wait until the shops opened.

Tipping some coffee granules into the bottom of an unwashed mug, he waited for the water to boil. He'd tried to sleep after getting back home but his body was far too wired, his mind still buzzing from the night's events. Sleep was futile. He smothered a chuckle and poured the boiling water into the mug. Steam rose and the aroma of cheap coffee flooded his nostrils.

He'd earned his money this time, no question about that. Thinking on his feet — that's what he did best. That's what they paid him for. People didn't call him 'The Fixer' for nothing.

Dawn was yet to break, but it wouldn't be long before streaks of orange and pink would be flooding the sky outside. Reaching across the sink to the only window in the kitchen, he adjusted the blinds to snuff out any signs of the coming daybreak. He wasn't quite ready for the new day to begin. He still had things to do.

Turning his attention to the rucksack sitting by his feet, he pulled out two ASDA supermarket bags from inside and set them down by the side of the vodka bottle. He could see the congealed blood already collected at the bottom, visible through the thin, non-biodegradable plastic. This was no 'bag for life', that was for sure.

"Bag for death, more like," he chuckled, immediately giving himself a swift whack to the chest as the laugh threatened to transform itself into a hacking cough. Dislodging the mass of phlegm clogging his airway, he turned and spat into the sink.

Shovelling three teaspoons of sugar into the coffee mug, he sniffed the remnants of the milk in the carton before deciding to risk it. Once stirred, he took a mouthful of the burning liquid, enjoying the scorch as it made its way down his gullet. He needed sleep, he knew that. He'd been awake for much of the last thirty-six hours, sorting out the suitcase mainly, and then clearing up the mess. But he knew he couldn't rest until the final job was done. After that, he could sleep for a week.

Placing the coffee mug back down, he picked up the first ASDA bag. It was surprisingly heavy and he knew that the cheap, flimsy plastic wouldn't hold it for long. He'd need to double-bag – maybe even triple-bag. Hell, he'd quadruple-bag to be on the safe side. He placed the bag in the sink, on top of the phlegm-covered dirty dishes.

Reaching into the cupboard beneath the sink, he brought out a further bundle of used supermarket bags. He always kept them — you never quite knew when they'd come in handy. There was talk of charging you for them in the shops soon — five pence or something like that, maybe even ten. He looked down at the collection in his hands. On that reckoning, he had at least a tenner's worth here already. He put the collection of bags down next to the kettle and turned his attention back to the sink.

As he pulled down the sides of the ASDA bag, the first thing he saw was a pair of eyes staring back out at him. He had to admit, they were beautiful eyes. It was one of the first things he'd noticed about her; that and her infectious giggle. But he soon got tired of that and irritation had quickly set in.

But the eyes didn't look quite so beautiful now. They'd lost that vivid lustre that only life could bring. Now they just looked empty and lost.

Pulling a fresh bag from the collection by the kettle, he shook it open. With his other hand, he grabbed a handful of the girl's blonde curls and pulled her out of the ASDA bag. Congealed blood still clung in strands from the base of her head where it'd been crudely severed from her spinal cord and vertebrae. It wasn't particularly neat, but that wasn't his problem.

Depositing the head in the fresh plastic bag, he repeated the process until the bundle was inside four new bags. He tested the handle — it seemed strong enough now to take the weight.

And at least the smell wasn't too bad. The girl's torso had been the worst. Even after only a few days, she'd begun to emit a nose-wrinkling stink.

He then repeated the process for the little girl's hands and feet. Without the head and hands, it might take the police that little bit longer to put a name to her — but it wouldn't delay them by much. Little girls, especially those as beautiful as this one, were usually missed when they didn't come home for tea. And even without her head and hands, he knew that identification wouldn't be too far behind the grim discovery.

And then the fun would start.

With everything wrapped up securely in almost a pound's worth of plastic bags, he turned towards the fridge-freezer by his side. He'd treated himself to a new one not so long ago — bought it on the 'never never' from a mate that owed him a favour or two. Pulling open the freezer compartment, he selected the meat drawer — well, it seemed apt in the circumstances. He smiled to himself as he removed a packet of Cumberland sausages to make way, pushing the bag containing the severed head inside. Moving some lamb chops out of the way, he did the same with the bag containing the hands and feet.

Satisfied, he closed the compartment and shut the freezer door. They'd be fine in there while he decided what to do with them. He'd probably end up tossing them in the Thames in the same way he had the rest of her — or maybe he'd put them out for the bin men on Friday.

He hadn't quite decided yet.

Eyeing the packet of frozen sausages sitting on the countertop, he found his stomach beginning to rumble. With a quick glance up at the kitchen clock, he decided to go for a lie down before going out in search of some breakfast.

He was The Fixer.

He'd earned it.

CHAPTER THREE

Time: 8.00 a.m.
Date: Wednesday 21 May 2014
Location: Metropolitan Police HQ, London

Jack leaned back in his chair to adjust the blinds at the window, cutting out the low-lying spring sunshine that was playing havoc with his computer screen. As he did so there was a gentle knock at the door, and DS Amanda Cassidy's head appeared around the door frame.

"He's here, guv." Cassidy tucked a strand of her jet-black hair behind her ear, her dark eyes sparkling. "And he looks really well."

Grabbing his jacket, Jack followed Cassidy out into the corridor and then into the office next door. Inside, DS Chris Cooper was sitting at his desk munching on his customary bacon sandwich, a blob of tomato sauce spotting the ginger stubble on his chin. Cassidy made a beeline for her own desk by the window, taking time to squeeze the shoulders of the man sitting in her chair.

"Daniels," greeted Jack, a genuine smile crossing his face. "Good to have you back."

DC Trevor Daniels grinned from beneath Cassidy's clutches. "It's good to be back, boss."

"We're all so thrilled," squealed Cassidy, almost unable to contain herself. "I got us all a posh coffee from that new deli around the corner to celebrate." She plucked the cardboard tray from her desk and began handing out the drinks. "We've still got our milk thief on the loose, you know. I bought a pint of semi-skimmed just yesterday and it's disappeared already." She grinned in Jack's direction as she selected his plain white coffee. "Don't worry, just a basic one for you. I know you don't like anything fancy." She handed Jack the cardboard takeaway cup. "It's so great to have the whole team back together, isn't it?"

Jack nodded and took a tentative sip of his drink, eyeing the recently returned detective constable. "You sure you're all right to be back, Daniels? You've been signed off as fit to work?"

Daniels accepted his cappuccino and nodded. "All fit and raring to go. Can't wait to get started. What've we got on?"

"Well, you've come back at just the right time. These two here have already been briefed as to what's happened overnight, but I'll take you all through it again now." Jack took another sip of the milky coffee — not enough caffeine for his liking, and too much froth. "Last night, at approximately half-past midnight, a dismembered body was discovered in an abandoned suitcase beneath London Bridge. Due to the tide, only a limited amount of the scene could be processed. I'm meeting Elliott back down there again at lunchtime — we'll see what else the scene can give us then."

Jack took another mouthful of froth, still waiting for the caffeine to hit. He'd gone home after leaving London Bridge but hadn't bothered going back to bed. There wasn't much point. At a little before six o'clock he'd made his way back into the station. Although used to a night without sleep, Jack was beginning to feel the strain. Just then, one of the desk phones began to ring.

DS Cooper swiped up the handset, swallowing his mouthful of bacon before answering. "Cooper." Wiping the tomato sauce from his chin with the back of his hand, he picked up the rest of his sandwich, preparing to take another bite. "Uh huh. He's right here in front of me as it goes." Sandwich dangling tantalisingly in front of his mouth, Cooper handed Jack the receiver. "It's for you, boss. The mortuary."

Jack took hold of the phone. "Jack MacIntosh." Silence followed while Jack listened to the voice on the other end of the line. "OK, I'll send someone across." Jack returned the handset to its cradle and glanced up at his team, noting Cooper was about to take another bite out of his greasy breakfast. "You might want to toss the rest of that sandwich, Cooper. Before it comes back to haunt you."

Cooper's hand hovered in front of his mouth as another globule of tomato sauce dripped onto his desk.

Jack flashed an apologetic half-smile in Cassidy's direction. "I need some volunteers to attend the post-mortem."

* * *

Time: 9.00 a.m.
Date: Wednesday 21 May 2014
Location: Niko's Café, Sunderland Street, London

Although the Cumberland sausages were defrosting on the worktop back home, he decided to go out for breakfast. His growling stomach had prevented him from getting any meaningful sleep — so he'd got up and made the short walk to Niko's.

It was a rundown, backstreet kind of place — not your usual Soho establishment — offering the usual variety of grease-laden fried breakfasts. But Greek-born Niko Georgiades seemed to be doing all right for himself; the place was never empty, day or night. He'd even branched out into supplying some outdoor seating — a few rickety, plastic chairs that had seen better days and a couple of rusting picnic tables.

As the day had dawned bright and clear, he decided to take a seat outside and watch the world go by — nodding at Niko to get him his usual. His body was craving grease — and that was exactly what he was going to get.

While he waited, he looked around for Gina, quickly noting that she didn't seem to be working this morning, which was a shame. He could do with seeing that shapely figure inching its way between the tables. He knew she was off limits, but it didn't stop him from daydreaming.

Interrupting his thoughts about Gina, a battered Ford Transit van pulled up by the kerb and disgorged four shabbily dressed workmen. The lettering on the side described them as '*artisan builders of quality and distinction*' — but judging by the beer bellies that were only partially contained within their paint splattered overalls, their only speciality looked to be in the consumption of Niko's famous all-day breakfasts.

He'd seen this particular troupe before — they were regulars at Niko's, often stopping off on their way to whichever unlucky building site they'd been allocated to that day. And more than likely stopping off on their way home, too.

Gina was fortunate not to be working today. He'd witnessed this particular band of brothers taking enormous pleasure in singing the Gina G Eurovision song, 'Ooh Ah — Just a Little Bit', whenever she passed by — together with all manner of undesirable hand gestures and suggestive catcalls to accompany it.

Although broad-minded when it came to women, he felt a little bit of sympathy for Gina, watching as she tried her best to avoid their wandering hands. And Niko was no use — if anything, he encouraged it.

Huffing and puffing, the man himself appeared — armed with an oversized plate of grease. Throwing a set of barely washed cutlery down on the table, he left with a grunt and headed back inside to where the gang of builders were seated by the window.

Picking up a fork, he stabbed one of the fat sausages and stuffed it into his mouth. He was ravenous. The little girl had taken up far too much of his time over the seven days they'd had her, and he'd barely had time to eat a thing. In some ways, the sausages that lined his plate reminded him of her pudgy little legs. He grinned through the grease and gristle and scooped up a forkful of tepid baked beans.

He'd enjoyed it more than he thought he would — seeing the little girl's limbs hacked from her body. He hadn't really known what to expect, but it had given him an oddly unexpected thrill. Stabbing his fork into the centre of a congealed egg, he watched the slow trickle of pale yellow yolk seep out. It was overcooked but he wasn't all that fussed. He piled it into his mouth along with a chunk of bread and butter.

Noticing that one of the builders seated at the window was reading a newspaper, he cocked his head to the side and saw it was the *Daily Star*. The headline was something to do with UFOs and a donkey.

Last night's escapade didn't seem to have made the news yet — or at least not in the *Daily Star*. He'd probably have to wait until later today or tomorrow morning to see his handiwork on the front pages. The thought excited him.

He speared another sausage and rammed it into his mouth. The food was lukewarm and greasy, but he needed the fuel. Watching the builders slurping their mugs of dishwater-like tea, he ran the last of the bread and butter around the plate, mopping up the rest of the beans and egg yolk. Shoving the last of his breakfast into his mouth, he slipped a five-pound note under the salt shaker and headed home.

* * *

Time: 9.15 a.m.
Date: Wednesday 21 May 2014
Location: Metropolitan Police HQ, London

The incident room had been set up just how Jack liked it. Plenty of whiteboards on the walls, and his own trusty cork pin board on wheels. Warily, he eyed the interactive whiteboard that took centre stage, giving it his customary look of quiet disdain. New technology was part and parcel of the job these days, but he was getting used to it — slowly. Hell, he even owned an iPad now.

Jack pulled out a chair from one of the nearby desks and sat down. At present, all the whiteboards were empty and the mood in the room was sombre. Murder investigations, on the whole, weren't joyous occasions — but this one had an added layer of revulsion running through it. Because this one involved a child.

"Amanda— I need you to take Daniels to the post-mortem at midday. Dr Matthews is expecting you both." He saw the expression on DS Cassidy's face and gave her an apologetic look. "Sorry — I need Cooper with me. We're going to see the dog walker."

Cassidy merely nodded and pushed away her cup of peppermint tea. "Of course, guv." Post-mortems were her worst nightmare. Just the thought of it made her stomach lurch.

"Daniels." Jack turned towards the newly returned detective constable. "You think you're up to attending the post-mortem?"

DC Daniels sat up straight and nodded, enthusiastically. "Absolutely."

Jack liked Trevor Daniels. Their paths had first crossed eight months ago when the quiet and unassuming newly qualified detective had helped Jack in the hunt for the serial killer dubbed the Bishop. With a brain like a sponge and an obsession with the paranormal and outer space, Daniels was often pigeonholed as the station nerd. But Jack had come to see a different side to the bespectacled officer and Daniels quickly proved his worth.

Although the detective constable looked well enough on the outside, passing his return-to-work fitness test with flying colours, Jack knew that the real damage was all too often hidden from view. He found himself slowly nodding. "Good man. But if at any time it gets too much, then step away. It'll be a brutal one — there's no escaping that. There's no shame in stepping outside."

Jack's eyes flickered towards Cassidy and she gave the briefest of nods in response.

"We'll be OK, boss." Daniels inched his chair closer to Cassidy and gave her a friendly nudge with his elbow. "We make a good team."

Jack didn't doubt it. They both lived in the same block of flats and Jack had it on reliable authority that Amanda had been taking care of Daniels, clucking round him like a mother hen the moment he'd returned from recuperating at his family home on the South Coast. "All the same, look after yourselves — both of you."

"Will there be any overtime, boss?" Cooper started to hand out a fresh set of notepads on each table. "I could do with the cash."

Knowing Cooper had recently set up home with Jenny Davies — one of the senior lab technicians heading up Central London Laboratories — Jack felt the flicker of a smile cross his lips. "More than likely, Cooper. Fill your boots."

Jack turned back towards the blank whiteboards. "We need a name for our victim — as quickly as. Before you both head off to the mortuary, start checking the Missing Persons database. Look for any recently reported missing children. Start with the immediate area and work outwards. And pull a list of recently released violent offenders — you know the drill. And request any CCTV and fixed camera footage from London Bridge and surrounding streets."

Both Cassidy and Daniels started to pull their chairs towards their desks to switch on their computers.

Meanwhile, Jack continued to stare at the blank whiteboards. There was something perversely thrilling with the beginning of a new case — wondering what they were going to find and what would be uncovered. But Jack already knew this investigation would be like no other. Since returning from the scene in the early hours, he hadn't been able to get the vision of the suitcase and, more particularly, its contents out of his head. He'd seen dead bodies before, too many to count, but nothing quite like that. He flashed Cassidy another apologetic look, anticipating that the post-mortem wouldn't be an easy one — if there ever was such a thing.

Just then, Jack felt his mobile vibrate in his pocket with an incoming message. A quick glance at the screen was followed by a frown, and an all-too-familiar feeling squeezing his insides. The message was from DS Robert Carmichael.

'We need to talk. It's about James Quinn.'

Quinn.

The man Jack was convinced had murdered his mother.

Pushing the thought from his mind, and the phone back into his pocket, Jack shrugged back into his jacket. "Come on, Cooper. Let's go and see a man about a suitcase."

CHAPTER FOUR

Time: 10.30 a.m.
Date: Wednesday 21 May 2014
Location: 17 Drinkstone Road, Southwark, SE1

Charlie Somerville showed Jack and DS Cooper into the immaculately-kept front room of his modest semi-detached home on Drinkstone Road. A vase of fresh lilies sat in front of the window, the curtains drawn back to let the warm mid-morning sunlight spill inside.

"Can I get either of you a drink? Tea . . . coffee?" The man's voice was light and welcoming, but Jack detected a faint tremor and his face looked drained of colour.

He shook his head. "No, thanks. We're both fine, Mr Somerville. We'll try not to take up too much of your time."

Charlie Somerville nodded for the two detectives to take a seat. "I'm guessing this is about last night?"

Jack eased himself onto one end of a floral three-seater sofa, Cooper the other. "I'm afraid it is. How are you coping? It must've been a shocking thing to find."

Charlie Somerville's skin seemed to pale even further. "It certainly was a shock — you're not wrong there." The tremor remained in his voice, but he tried a faint smile. "I'm sure you guys are far more used to that kind of thing than me."

Jack shook his head. "It's always a shock, Mr Somerville. No matter how many times you witness it. Do you have enough support here at home? Is there anyone we can call for you?" Upon entering the room, he'd taken a quick look around and noticed several framed photographs gracing the walls. Most depicted Mr Somerville with a similarly aged woman with greying hair and a sparkling smile. "You live here with your wife?"

Charlie Somerville hesitated and then nodded towards the pictures. "Yes. That's my Alice. Been married thirty-eight years now, we have. Love of my life, she is."

"Well, that's good to hear."

Just then, the door to the front room swung open and a small woman of indeterminate age bustled in, heading over to a pile of boxes beneath the window. Jack caught sight of her identification badge as she passed. Jessie O'Halloran of the Carnegie Care Company bent down and retrieved a box of incontinence sheets before turning to smile at Charlie.

"Alice is asleep now. So, I'll just replenish these supplies and get on my way."

Charlie Somerville raised a hand in acknowledgement as Jessie backed out through the door. He caught sight of Jack's inquisitive gaze. "Vascular dementia," he said simply, his eyes beginning to cloud over. "My Alice. We do what we can for her here, at home. But she's essentially bedbound now. The carers are a godsend — I couldn't do without them. Young Jessie there should've clocked off at eight, but she stayed on to help me this morning after . . . you know . . . what happened last night." He paused a little, then sighed. "It's not easy, but we do what we can."

Jack now understood why the relatively sprightly sixty-year-old looked so tired. "Then we'll try not to keep you," he replied. "Could you just walk us through what happened last night?"

Charlie Somerville's eyes took on a haunted look. "It was just like any other night. When the tide is out, me and

Zac like to go down by the river. He likes to run around under the bridge." As if on cue, a black Labrador nudged the door open and came lumbering in, settling down at Charlie Somerville's feet. Charlie bent down to pat the dog's head before continuing. "It was Zac who found it. I hadn't seen it — wasn't wearing my glasses, you see, and the moon wasn't out at the time. He started running around in circles, yapping at what looked to me like a big rock."

"No one else around?" enquired Jack.

Charlie Somerville shook his head. "Nobody. We had the place to ourselves." He paused and gave a shaky breath. "I didn't realise it was a suitcase, not till I got up close. And then . . ." He broke off and swallowed, the paleness of his skin now etched with a tinge of green. "And then, the smell when I opened it . . ."

Jack could very well imagine. "You say that you often walk along that stretch of the river. When was the last time you were there?"

"That would've been about midnight, the night before," replied Charlie. "Low tide again, you see."

"And the suitcase definitely wasn't there then?"

Another shake of the head. "Definitely not. I would've seen it. Or, at least, Zac would've." He bent down and gave the dog another pat and scratch on the head. "Always hunting and sniffing, this one. If it'd been there, he'd have found it."

"You walked to the bridge from here?" Jack's question received a nod in response. "Did you see anyone walking away when you arrived?"

Charlie gave another shake of the head. "Sorry — the walk there is a bit of a blur. But I'm pretty sure there was nobody about. It was a really quiet night."

"What was the position of the suitcase when you saw it?"

"Flat, on its back. I wondered if it might've toppled off the bridge above."

"Did you move it before you looked inside?"

Charlie hesitated. "Not really. I maybe pulled it towards me a little before I unzipped it."

"And definitely nobody else around?"

Charlie gave a firm shake of the head. "No. I did look — once I saw it was a suitcase. I mean, it's not something you expect to see washing up after the tide's gone out. We see some odd things, Zac and me, but nothing like that."

"No problem." Jack flashed a look at Cooper and got to his feet. "We'll be on our way now, Mr Somerville. But if you think of anything else — please don't hesitate to give me a call." Jack slid a business card out from his pocket as he made his way to the door.

"Who would want to do that to someone?" Charlie Somerville followed Jack and Cooper out into the hall. "I mean, I didn't get a good look but . . ." The man's voice hushed to almost a whisper. "I didn't see a head."

Jack paused by the front door and cast a glance back at the dog walker. "I don't know," he sighed. "But we'll move heaven and earth to find out who did."

* * *

Time: 12.30 p.m.
Date: Wednesday 21 May 2014
Location: Westminster Mortuary, London

Dr Philip Matthews pulled the overhead light down towards the steel examination table, glancing up towards the two pairs of eyes trained on his every move.

"Welcome back, DC Daniels." The pathologist smiled at the young detective. He'd only met the man once before but remembered him well. "I see they're dropping you into the thick of it straight away."

DC Daniels nodded, standing a little straighter with his shoulders back. "Thank you, doctor. It's a pleasure to be here."

A smile tickled Dr Matthews' lips. "I'm not so sure pleasure is the correct turn of phrase — especially for the poor, unfortunate occupant of my examination table today — but I appreciate the sentiment."

Daniels' cheeks reddened a little, but his eyes maintained their inquisitive sparkle. He'd only managed to attend one post-mortem before the Bishop had put him in hospital, minus a spleen, but the enforced break hadn't dampened his enthusiasm. Nudging his spectacles a little further up his nose, he took a tentative step forward.

DS Amanda Cassidy's expression was somewhat different. Not a lover of seeing a dead body on the pathologist's mortuary slab at the best of times, she already felt decidedly queasy. Everything about the place turned her stomach. Even walking through the front door made her shiver, and not because of the chilled temperature inside. No matter how upbeat and friendly the mortuary receptionist was — and how chirpy her enquiry into how well Cassidy's day was going, and how much she liked her hair — she couldn't quite see past the fact that this was a mortuary. And a mortuary was where dead people were. It was an aspect of the job that she would never get used to, no matter how hard she tried.

And then there was the smell. It was completely unique — like nothing else on earth. It wasn't possible to accurately describe it — nothing ever quite sounded right. There weren't enough words in the English language to do it justice. Whenever anyone asked her, which admittedly wasn't often, she always told them to imagine a heady mixture of rotten meat, mould, and decay, plus a cloying scent of bleach.

But it still didn't quite hit the mark.

Cassidy swallowed, her mouth already turning dry in the chilled air of the examination room. She didn't follow Daniels in taking a step closer to the steel table — in fact, if she could she would have taken several steps in the opposite direction, but the bench behind her prevented her retreat.

Dr Matthews sought out her gaze and gave a slight nod accompanied by a smile. He was well aware of DS Cassidy's aversion to post-mortems, but felt nothing but admiration for her as she still stoically attended when asked to do so. Clearing his throat, he decided not to prolong her agony. Turning towards the body on the mortuary slab, he began.

"Today is Wednesday 21 May 2014 and we have a Caucasian female." The pathologist paused, his eyes trained on the mortuary slab. Before them was the bloated torso of a white female. The dismembered arms and legs lay by the side, minus the hands and feet. Disturbingly, there was no head. Dr Matthews cleared his throat once more and continued.

"Due to the bone length and the absence of breast bud development in the upper torso, I would estimate the age range to be between seven and ten years of age. There are no outwardly distinguishing marks on the torso or either arm. On the back of the right thigh we have a birthmark measuring approximately eight millimetres in diameter."

Dr Matthews stepped to the side while the mortuary technician took several photographs of the torso and limbs.

"Tissue and blood samples will be taken for routine analysis. But there are no outward signs of injury other than the obvious decapitation and removal of limbs." The pathologist paused again, motioning for both Daniels and Cassidy to step closer.

Only one of them did.

"You will see here, DC Daniels, that the skin around the dismemberment sites is somewhat ragged. And the bones beneath are chipped and uneven." Dr Matthews pointed with a gloved finger towards the top of the victim's left arm. Daniels dutifully peered more closely. Cassidy remained where she was. In addition to the usual cloying smell of death and decay that clung to the air, this body was giving off an even more revolting aroma.

The torso was swollen and bloated, the putrefaction process having begun in earnest. It added another unique layer of fragrance to the room.

Once again, Dr Matthews made way for photographs to be taken before continuing. "The ragged nature of the skin and subcutaneous tissue at the dismemberment sites, such as here at the top of the humerus, suggests that a somewhat blunt instrument was used. Similarly, the jagged and splintered edges of bone would suggest a particularly rudimentary attempt was made at dismemberment."

"So, they didn't know what they were doing?" Daniels stared intently at the dismembered limbs. "An amateur?"

A smile tickled the corners of Dr Matthews' mouth. "A possibility, yes. You could be dealing with a particularly inexperienced assailant — or he could just have used the wrong implement for the job."

"Could they have rushed the disposal?" Daniels' eyes flickered up towards the pathologist. "Ran out of time and hurried?"

A further smile danced onto Dr Matthews' lips. "Well, that would be more of a question for yourselves, I think, detective. It's not something I can answer from this table."

"And how long do you think she's been in the water?" Daniels returned his gaze to the bloated torso and limbs.

The pathologist hesitated, the faint shadow of a frown on his brow. "I can't say for sure. I'll be running some more tests, but we can see that putrefaction has clearly started. Decomposition does take place more slowly in water, however I'm not entirely convinced that she's been submerged in water for any length of time. If at all. There is no observable damage from marine life, although the suitcase within which she was found would have afforded some protection in that regard. I can already see that the skin has yet to start separating and there's no sign of shrinkage — both of which would indicate time spent in water. I'll be able to give a more accurate time of death and details of any immersion in water once the test results are back."

With the external examination complete, Dr Matthews proceeded to make his first incision. Cassidy felt the all-too-familiar sensation of bile encroaching on the back of her throat. She'd thought the absence of a head might make the body seem less human to her, and maybe her usual feelings of intense nausea would be lessened. If she could distance herself from thinking of the body as being a person, and merely look at it as a series of body parts, then maybe she would escape. But it was to no avail. Head or no head, it was still a human being. And, heartbreakingly, it was a child at that. With her knees starting to weaken, Cassidy took a fortifying grip of the steel bench behind her.

Averting her gaze, she instead cast her eyes to the floor. She didn't need to look to know that the pathologist would be opening up the chest cavity first, starting just below the collar bone. One incision on each side, drawn together to the midline and then all the way down to the pubic bone, creating the perfect 'Y' shape. She'd seen it too many times before.

The sound of the rib cutters told her that Dr Matthews was now exposing the organs beneath. A brief glance up confirmed that Daniels was still standing in pole position, thoroughly absorbed in the post-mortem process.

"Heart and lungs in excellent condition. No signs of injury or disease." Dr Matthews placed each organ into separate steel bowls. Examining each lung in turn, he looked up at Daniels' expectant face. "I think it's rather a moot point, but there are no signs of water in either lung, confirming that death occurred prior to any submersion in water, if indeed that did occur."

The build-up of gas from the putrefaction process had, by now, escaped into the air of the post-mortem room. Cassidy did her best to hold her breath, but she knew it was futile and accepted the familiar feeling of nausea as it started to spread.

Dr Matthews moved on to expose the abdominal cavity. "Evidence of an appendicectomy— otherwise the small and large intestines are intact, and show no signs of injury or disease."

Skilfully removing the stomach, the pathologist placed the J-shaped organ into another steel bowl for the technician to weigh. Upon its return, he caught DC Daniels' eye. "I'm sure you will remember, detective, the aroma from opening the stomach can be somewhat unpalatable. Fair warning."

Daniels took the smallest of steps backwards but remained transfixed.

Slowly slicing the organ from top to bottom, Dr Matthews continued. "The stomach contents are mostly acidic. The lack of undigested food suggests this poor soul met her death some time after her last meal." The pathologist proceeded to take samples from the liquid contents of the stomach for later analysis. "No obvious water content in the stomach, suggesting there was no ingestion of water before death."

The rest of the post-mortem proceeded as expected, after which time Daniels returned to Cassidy's side, his eyes still sparkling. "Fascinating, don't you think?"

Cassidy gave a wan smile, her cheeks still showing a tinge of green. "If you say so, Trevor. If you're done, can we get out of here?" She still had a grip on the stainless-steel bench behind her when Dr Matthews caught her eye.

"Tell Jack I'll have the preliminary report over to him by the end of the day. I've taken some samples for DNA but with someone so young, I doubt they'll appear on your DNA database." A sad look entered the pathologist's eyes. "I guess a head would help."

Cassidy nodded. "It would indeed."

"You have any idea who she might be?" Dr Matthews stepped back from the table and extinguished the overhead light.

"Not yet, no."

"Well, the DNA sample will be fast-tracked. And I can also tell you that, in addition to having had her appendix removed at some point in the past, the pre-examination X-rays have shown an old break in the right distal radius. It's healed, but there's a metal plate still *in situ*."

With another grateful nod, Cassidy led the way out of the post-mortem room in a desperate search for fresh air.

Dr Matthews sighed as he watched the detectives depart and turned back towards the examination table. Death at any age was a sad event, but when it was a child, and taken so barbarically, there was a particular part of him that ached. No child should ever end up on the sharp end of his scalpel — that was not how things were meant to be.

Placing the scalpel back into one of the waiting stainless steel trays, the pathologist took another step back from the mortuary slab. His work here was done — for now. If they somehow managed to find the poor girl's head, hands, and feet then he may have to re-examine her. But for now, he would let her rest in peace.

With a deeper sigh than usual, Dr Matthews gave a sad bow and swept out of the room.

CHAPTER FIVE

Time: 5.15 p.m.
Date: Wednesday 21 May 2014
Location: Metropolitan Police HQ, London

"We've got three potential identifications from our trawl through the Missing Persons database." Cassidy picked up a marker pen and approached one of the whiteboards. In red letters, she wrote three names. "First, we have Leona Grace. Aged ten. Missing for five weeks from her foster parents' home in Sidcup. Has a previous history of running away. The second is a Maisie Lancaster. Aged eight. Reported missing on 14 May. Disappeared from her own front garden. The third is Francesca Darville. She's a little older than the other two at twelve and has been missing from her home in Wimbledon since early April." Cassidy snapped the lid back on the marker pen. "I guess we should check these three out first, then widen the search if needed."

Jack let Dr Matthews' preliminary report fall back on to the table. "It should be easy enough to eliminate them, based on the doc's findings so far. Two are definitely in the suggested age range, but check out all three. See if any had their appendix removed and also fractured their wrist at some point in the recent past."

"Will do, guv." Cassidy took a seat back at her desk. "Anything more from the scene?"

Jack shook his head. "No. Cooper and I swung by the scene on our way back from Charlie Somerville's. It's approaching high tide again now, so whatever evidence there was, I hope they got to it in time. Elliott says he'll probably do a final sweep tomorrow."

"Are we thinking she entered the water there, at London Bridge, or someway upstream?" DS Cooper woke up his computer monitor and activated the interactive whiteboard. "I've been looking at the tide information for that stretch of the river."

"That's still a little unclear at this stage, Cooper. It could be either. The lab is analysing the suitcase, so we'll see if that throws any light on when, where, and if it entered the water."

Cooper clicked the mouse and the whiteboard was flooded with the tidal times for London Bridge. "The tide was at its lowest last night at 00.22, where it would've been down to just half a metre average depth. The previous high tide was at 17.53."

Jack cast his eyes back down to the draft post-mortem report. "Well, the doc isn't convinced the body was in the water at all — and if he's right, then whoever dumped it did so sometime after the last high tide at just before six last night. We know Charlie Somerville didn't see it on his walk the previous evening, and he's pretty sure he would have, or at least his dog would. But if the doc's wrong and it *was* dumped upstream, with the current bringing it as far as London Bridge, then I'm afraid our crime scene just widened." Jack sighed and rubbed his eyes, feeling their grittiness beneath his fingers. He needed coffee. Or alcohol. Maybe both. "Cooper, get onto the lab again and get them to fast track the tests. We need to know for sure how that suitcase got to where it did."

"I'll give Jenny a ring."

"Dr Matthews confirmed no water was found in the lungs or stomach," added Cassidy. "He's working on the time of death."

Jack nodded. "I think we can be pretty sure that the poor girl didn't drown. She was killed, dismembered, and then dumped. Daniels — chase up the requested CCTV and fixed camera footage for the area around the bridge — that should've been with us by now."

Daniels nodded. "Will do. Did you get much more from Charlie Somerville?"

"Not a great deal." Cooper closed down the tidal information on the interactive whiteboard screen. "He told us pretty much what's already in his statement. He was out walking along the riverbed — does it most evenings when there's a low tide. He's adamant he didn't see the suitcase when he was out walking the night before." Pulling out his notebook, Cooper flicked forward several pages. "He described seeing an object in the shadows, which he first thought was a big rock. The light wasn't too great and he wasn't wearing his glasses. But as he got closer, the dog started going mad. It was only when he got up close that he saw it was a suitcase. He unzipped it but didn't disturb the contents. Once he'd finished vomiting he dialled 999."

Cassidy felt her cheeks pale at the thought of poor Charlie Somerville's discovery. Visions of the headless torso from Dr Matthews' mortuary slab filled her head, the bile in the back of her throat starting to rise once more.

"You OK, Amanda?" Jack raised his eyebrows towards Cassidy's wan face.

"I'm fine," she lied, staring at the cup of herbal tea going cold in front of her. "I just want to find the maniac who did it."

Jack nodded. "Our first priority is to get an identity for our body. So split the three possible names between you — take one each. Ask the families as delicately as possible, but follow up with obtaining medical records to be sure. See who we can eliminate straight away. If we end up eliminating all three, then we start again."

Jack wearily pushed himself up out of his seat and headed for the door. "I'll be in my office if anyone needs me. And to give you all the heads up — Cooper and I spotted a few hacks when we were out at the bridge earlier. It doesn't take them long to smell a story. I'm sure they'll be jumping all over this like a pack of hungry wolves, so beware. The press office will put out a brief statement later tonight, but you can be sure the hounds will be embellishing that for their headlines tomorrow. It's already filtering onto the online sites." Jack reached the door and turned back to face his team. "But as with any investigation, we say nothing. *Nobody* speaks to *anybody* — press or otherwise. There'll probably be a press conference tomorrow, but until then we keep it zipped."

* * *

Time: 5.30 p.m.
Date: Wednesday 21 May 2014
Location: Flat 3a Ash Road, SE Soho, London

Staring at his mobile phone, he willed it to ring. His last three messages had gone unanswered, and it was starting to worry him. He was still owed his money — a significant amount of money — and the silence just made his stomach tighten all the more.

Something was wrong.

He dropped the phone back on to the draining board, knowing he only had enough credit for one more message until his benefits came in. At that precise moment, he had the princely sum of £2.46 in his pocket. Maybe spending a fiver on one of Niko's greasy breakfasts had been a bit extravagant — but he'd felt like he'd earned it.

On top of that, his cupboards were bare — except for some out-of-date noodles and packets of soup in a cup. But it wasn't the food that bothered him so much — he desperately needed to replenish his vodka stocks. All he had was a couple of cans of high-strength lager to see him through the night.

He thought about ringing his brother for a loan — but quickly dismissed the idea. It'd just be a waste of his final bit of phone credit.

Instead, he needed to be patient. He'd get his money eventually. Nobody crossed The Fixer and kept their knee-caps intact. That's the rumour that circulated, anyway, and he was more than happy to let people believe it. In reality he'd never kneecapped anyone.

No — he just needed to wait.

It was his own fault in a way — agreeing to instalments. He should have stood his ground and demanded payment in full up front. He was the one taking all the risks, after all. You couldn't just sweep kids up off the street these days — not as easily as you could before. With CCTV everywhere you looked, you couldn't move without somebody, somewhere, watching you.

He took one look at the defrosted sausages on the work-top and decided he didn't fancy them right now. Niko's breakfast was still making its way through his insides. He picked the packet up and placed it in the fridge, then grabbed one of the two cans of lager he had left and ripped it open. Maybe a drink would steady his nerves.

Sitting back down at the kitchen table, he reached for his tobacco tin and started rolling a flimsy cigarette with the last of his tobacco.

He had a feeling it was going to be a long night.

Once he'd downed half the can and lit his last cigarette, he pushed himself to his feet and grabbed the phone from the draining board. His patience was wearing thin and the alcohol was just making him more jittery. Deciding he might as well use up his last remaining credit, he tapped out the same message as before.

'*Where's my money?*'

* * *

Time: 6.00 p.m.
Date: Wednesday 21 May 2014
Location: Metropolitan Police HQ, London

Jack pushed the Bishop investigation files to the side — the case was as prepared as it was going to be. With the trial starting soon, everyone was busy ensuring every 'i' was dotted, and every 't' had its cross. *Nothing* could be left to chance. With the Bishop being one of the most prolific serial killers to have emerged in recent years, there was no way they could allow him to roam free again.

Massaging his temples, Jack could feel a headache brewing — but a knock at the door stirred him from his thoughts.

DS Robert Carmichael's head appeared around the door frame. "Now a good time?"

Jack waved him in. "As good as any, Rob," he sighed, doing his best to ignore the rest of the paperwork piling up in his in-tray. "Pull up a seat — this about Quinn?" Jack remembered the message Rob had sent him earlier.

Carmichael dragged a chair over from the other side of the room and sat down. He had that familiar look of crumpled sleeplessness about him: a look Jack was well acquainted with. Carmichael nodded. "Tell me about him, again, Jack. Quinn. I need to square things off in my head."

Jack felt the familiar squeeze of his insides. Just hearing the man's name did that to him. He kept one eye on the door. Apart from Dr Matthews, Rob Carmichael was the only other person who knew anything of Jack's suspicions surrounding his mother's death. After she'd been found hanging from a light fitting in the family home when Jack was four, the coroner had ruled the young mother's death as a tragic suicide.

But Jack had recently learned otherwise. Obtaining a copy of his mother's post-mortem report, Jack found reference to tissue beneath her fingernails — tissue later analysed and confirmed as belonging to a man called James Quinn.

"My mother didn't kill herself, Rob — she was murdered. Quinn's skin was found beneath her fingernails, and there were signs of a struggle. Her face was bruised. He did it. I know he did. I just have to find him."

"I see there's a warrant out for his arrest — for that murder of a City banker down in Surrey last year? I've got a contact down there — you want me to have a bit of a dig? See if I can find out if they've heard anything?"

Jack ran a hand through his hair, feeling his headache intensifying. His scalp felt as though it was on fire. He felt exhausted and thinking about James Quinn wasn't making it any better. "I guess it wouldn't hurt, but my hunch is he's long gone."

Carmichael tried to catch Jack's eye across the desk. "What aren't you telling me, Jack?"

The question hung in the air like an executioner's noose as Jack felt his friend's eyes boring into him. He would trust Rob Carmichael with his life but, like many things in Jack's life, sometimes trust wasn't enough.

Before he could come to a decision on how much to divulge, the sound of Carmichael's mobile chirping cut through the strained silence.

Glancing at the screen, Carmichael grimaced and silently cursed. "Sorry, Jack. Have to dash." Pushing himself up out of his chair he made his way towards the door. "I'll catch up with you later. I'll give my contact in Surrey a call — find out the latest on Quinn."

Jack watched his friend and colleague disappear out into the corridor and silently considered which was going to test them the most — finding the killer of the child in the suitcase or finding the elusive James Quinn.

CHAPTER SIX

Time: 7.10 p.m.
Date: Wednesday 21 May 2014
Location: Kettle's Yard Mews, London

Jack passed his brother a fresh can of Budweiser and slumped down on the sofa. "Sorry I wasn't here when you arrived, Stu. Big case landed on us today."

"No worries. I let myself in and opened your beer." Stuart 'Mac' MacIntosh held up a half-finished can in greeting. 'Mac' was the name everyone had called him since his teens — a gang tag that had still stuck long after the gang itself had gone their separate ways.

Everyone, that was, except Jack. To him he would always be Stuart. *Stu*. His baby brother.

Jack spied several empty cans littering the coffee table. "So I see." He gave a tired smile and picked up a beer, resting his head back against the sofa while he closed his eyes. His team were still at the station — all three families were being contacted and their backgrounds checked. Jack couldn't begin to imagine what those conversations would be like, but he'd had to drag himself home before he collapsed, exhaustion having finally got the better of him.

He'd wanted to stay — the first twenty-four hours of a case was the most important — but he'd be no use to anybody the state he was in.

"And I took the liberty of ordering us a takeaway. Unless you were planning to cook?"

Jack opened one eye. "Cook?" He glanced back towards the kitchen where last night's pizza box was still sitting on the draining board. Out of sight, in the bin, were the foil trays from the Indian he'd picked up on the way home the night before. "Nah, I'll give myself the night off from cooking. Takeaway sounds like a good plan. What are we having?"

"Chinese." Mac swigged a mouthful of beer and suppressed a chuckle. "The one round the corner that you have an account with. I stuck it on your tab."

Jack playfully punched his brother on the arm. "Thanks. And there was me thinking you might've treated your big brother for once."

"Next time," grinned Mac, his eyes shining. "I promise."

Jack swallowed his own laugh with another mouthful of beer. As he did so, he felt the familiar wave of protectiveness swell within him. His brother had come back into his life just recently, after they'd both been separated as young boys following the death of their mother. The foster care system had swallowed them up, separating them at a time when they needed its protection the most, and then spat them out the other end. Stuart MacIntosh had spent much of his youth in a children's home — with an approved school, and then youth detention, following on quickly behind. Jack had fared somewhat better, finding a loving foster family and then joining the Metropolitan Police as soon as he was able.

They'd each followed vastly different paths, but those paths had now crossed, and Jack kind of liked having his kid brother around again.

"How are the legs? Isabel says you've got a new physiotherapist?"

Mac nodded. "He's amazing. An ex-footballer — played for Chelsea in his day. Now specialises in sports physio. He's working miracles. I feel as good as new."

Jack knew that his brother's legs, so horrifically burnt in a fire just over a year ago, would never be 'as good as new' — no matter how fantastic the physio was. But the fact that he was so happy and positive was a welcome sign of progress. He'd been lucky to get out of the fire alive if truth be told — and, at one point, Jack thought he hadn't.

"Well, that's good to hear. At least you can walk yourself down the aisle now, and I won't have to give you a piggyback."

Mac stifled a laugh behind his beer can. "Don't even joke about it. There was a time when I thought that might actually have to be an option."

"And how are the preparations coming along?" Jack hated weddings and couldn't think of anything worse than having to organise one.

"Isabel's in control of all that. Her and Sacha. I'm keeping well out of it."

Jack didn't blame him. "So, you've finally decided on a venue? You're cutting it a bit fine if not." Isabel wanted to get married on what would have been her own parents' wedding anniversary, which was only ten days away. The couple had been very tight-lipped as to exactly where the nuptials were going to take place — just telling everyone to 'save the date'.

"All sorted. So long as you don't mind a bit of a trek, we've booked the Tannochside B&B. Willie McArthur's bent over backwards to get the licenses all sorted in time. I think we're good to go."

"Great idea." Jack approved of the Tannochside B&B, having spent time there himself not so long ago. Set in magnificent countryside, just a stone's throw away from a beautiful loch, the Scottish B&B was a haven of peace and tranquillity.

"And Margaret's agreed to do the food!"

Jack held up his beer can in approval. Margaret McArthur produced the most wonderful meals at the B&B. Jack could almost taste her succulent roast lamb just by thinking about it. The wedding would be in more than capable hands.

"How's the best-man speech coming along then, bro? And my stag night?" Stuart MacIntosh gave his brother a grin. "I hope you've started working on them both!"

Jack groaned inwardly but plastered a suitably sarcastic smile on his face. He hated any form of public speaking — his performances at the police press conferences were legendary to any who watched. Therefore, standing up at a wedding, with everyone's eyes upon him, wasn't something he was looking forward to. In fact, Jack would rather stick pins in his eyes than do a best man's speech. But this was his brother. And if he couldn't do a speech at his own brother's wedding, then what kind of man was he? Not a best one that was for sure.

"I'm working on it," lied Jack, avoiding his brother's gaze. "And I've passed the stag night arrangements on to Rob. He's much better at things like that than me."

"Tell him he doesn't have long — stag night's Sunday." Mac crumpled his beer can in his hand and tossed it on to the coffee table to join the others.

"What time did you order that Chinese for? I'm starving," demanded Jack.

Right on cue, Jack's door buzzed and he went out to meet the delivery driver in the stairwell. Bringing the takeaway back inside the flat, Jack stacked the foil trays on the coffee table, grabbing two plates from the draining board in the kitchen on the way. He nodded at the food.

"Dig in. Looks like there's enough to feed an army."

* * *

Time: 7.30 p.m.
Date: Wednesday 21 May 2014
Location: Isabel's Café, Horseferry Road, London

Isabel Faraday collapsed on to her sofa and closed her eyes. Exhaustion had finally won and sent her upstairs to her flat for a rest. The day had been non-stop from the minute they'd opened that morning, but it wasn't just the café that was to blame. The wedding was taking over her life — occupying her thoughts, both day and night. So much so that, if she were lucky enough to drop off to sleep, all she dreamt of were dress fittings, flower arrangements and seating plans.

She'd left the café downstairs in the capable hands of Sacha Greene and her son, Dominic — both of them hard at work getting the café shipshape for the morning.

After taking on the lease for the café two years before, Isabel had landed on her feet when a shy lad had walked through the door with his sister for a milkshake. It hadn't taken long for her to offer him a part-time job, and Dominic Greene quickly became one of the family. With his mother, Sacha, being an expert baker, the café was never short of sumptuous cakes, biscuits and pastries to tempt the passing Westminster trade.

Dominic lived his life by way of routine — never seen without his trusty notebook where he noted down important aspects of his day-to-day life. Dates and times, names and addresses, people and places: everything had its place. Now attending a business studies course in the evenings, Isabel could see a bright future for the lad.

As she lay back against the cushions, she fiddled with the engagement ring on her left hand. Her heart fluttered. Sometimes she had to pinch herself that it was actually happening. That she was actually *getting married*.

Mac was slowly moving into the flat — spending only one or two nights a week away at his own place in Islington. But it was a big step. And they were both treading carefully.

Tonight, Mac was visiting his brother and would more than likely stay over, so Isabel had the evening to herself. She wanted nothing more than to run a hot bath with plenty of bubbles and pour herself a large glass of wine.

Livi, Isabel's tabby cat, jumped up on to her lap and instinctively, she began to rub the cat beneath her chin, smiling at the audible purrs that vibrated towards her. Isabel hadn't been sure how Livi would react to another human living in the flat — although she seemed to have taken to Mac quite happily, giving him the customary once-over and then ignoring him completely unless he came bearing food.

Isabel smiled as she remembered Livi's first days in the café. Rescued from a local stray cat charity, the anxious seven-month-old had hidden for the first twenty-four hours, coming out only when she was too hungry to conceal herself any longer. Scared of her own shadow, it'd taken many months of coaxing to persuade her to even venture downstairs. But over the next two years, she'd been transformed — mingling with the customers in the café, winding herself between people's legs as they sipped their coffee, and making herself at home on the sagging sofas.

Livi was as much a part of the café as the coffee and cake they served.

After a few more rubs behind the ears, Livi jumped down and trotted off in search of her food bowl. Isabel stretched her legs out along the length of the sofa, enjoying the last few moments of her enforced break. Leaning her head back once more against a soft cushion, she let her tired gaze fall on the bookcase opposite. Rammed full of her most prized possessions — books — it was also home to a selection of treasured photographs.

One photograph, in the centre of the bookcase, always took pride of place. She'd bought a new silver-edged photo frame in a local thrift shop around the corner and found that it fit perfectly — as if it was meant to be. She didn't possess many pictures of her parents, but the ones she did have she treasured above all else.

And this one in particular was her pride and joy.

Taken on her fifth birthday at their home in Surrey, five-year-old Isabel grinned out towards the camera while astride her brand-new red tricycle. With both her mother and father standing by her side, she often thought how happy they looked that day. The perfect family.

It was the last picture she had of them all together.

As well as bringing a smile to her face, the picture often nudged tears from her eyes. She couldn't help it. With everything that had happened, she couldn't look at the photograph without feeling her heart squeeze.

They would have been so proud — not just with her opening the café, but how she had managed to make something of herself. How she had overcome everything that life had thrown at her.

And now she was getting married.

Isabel's eyes focused on her mother's smiling face in the photo — a faint dusting of icing sugar on her cheeks from making the birthday cake. She would have been so thrilled at the wedding — Isabel could picture her buying up every single wedding magazine in the shops and dragging them both around each and every wedding fair she could find.

But, instead, Isabel had been planning her wedding alone. Sacha had offered to help, but Isabel felt it was a journey that she needed to make solo. She did, however, take Sacha up on her offer of making the wedding cake. Her best friend was the finest baker this side of the river – how could she refuse?

Her father would most likely have kept himself out of much of the organisation, Isabel was pretty sure of that. But there was one duty he would make sure was his — and his alone. It brought fresh tears to her eyes.

There wouldn't be much of an aisle at the Tannochside B&B, but Christopher Faraday would have been the proudest man on earth to walk by her side and give her away. But it was an occasion that he was destined never to see, a duty he was destined never to fulfil.

Tears dripped from Isabel's cheeks. Wedding days were moments for families to come together — but neither she nor Mac had much of a family to be united with. She'd toyed with the idea of asking Jack to give her away, and part of her could think of no one better. But Jack was already Mac's best man, and she didn't want to step on anyone's toes.

In the end, there was no decision to be made at all. She knew *exactly* who would be perfect for such an important role.

There could be no one else.

Smiling to herself, Isabel brushed away the thoughts of her parents, together with the tears from her cheeks, and got to her feet. Descending the narrow stairs down to the café beneath, she couldn't help but let her smile widen. The radio was on, its tinny sound wafting around the deserted café, with Sacha singing along to Clean Bandit's 'Rather Be'.

The whole café looked spotless — chairs were neatly tucked underneath the tables; cushions plumped and straightened on the comfortably battered sofas. Books and magazines had been returned to the bookshelves, and the air smelled of lemon-scented floor cleaner.

Entering the kitchen, she saw Dominic emptying the last load from the dishwasher and Sacha busily stocktaking the contents of the fridge.

"We're almost out of cream cheese," muttered Sacha, her head hidden behind the fridge door. "And double cream. Can you add them both to the order tomorrow, Dom?"

Dominic pulled a laminated card across the worktop and made the additions.

"All looking good in here?" Isabel stepped forward to be met with a warm smile from Sacha as she slammed the fridge door shut.

"All good to go." Sacha wiped a hand across her forehead. As she fanned her face with a tea towel, she caught Isabel's eye, noticing how exhausted her friend looked. "Let's lock up — you look like you need an early night." Sacha touched Isabel lightly on the forearm.

Isabel nodded — she wouldn't say no to an early night, but there was one thing she needed to do first. "I need you to do something for me, Dom — before you go."

Dominic closed the dishwasher door and let a frown trickle over his forehead. He consulted his notebook on the worktop. "I think everything's done for the day. I'm putting the food order in at six o'clock tomorrow morning — unless you need me to do it now?"

Isabel shook her head, her smile broadening. "No, the morning's fine, Dom. It's not that."

Dominic's frown deepened. He took another look at the notebook – he was pretty sure he'd completed all his tasks for the day.

Isabel couldn't keep the young lad in suspense for much longer without bursting out laughing at his serious expression. Taking him by the hand, she pulled him back out into the café. "We need to practise."

"Practise?" Sacha joined them both on the café floor, the frown on her own forehead matching that of her son's. "Practise what?"

"For our walk down the aisle — when Dom gives me away."

CHAPTER SEVEN

Time: 9.00 p.m.
Date: Wednesday 21 May 2014
Location: Kettle's Yard Mews, London

He'd seen Jack arrive home some two hours ago — parking his car by the kerb, the detective inspector had dragged himself out of the driver's seat, not even bothering to lock it before heading towards his front door. No quick glance behind him; not even a scant scouring of the shadows that graced both sides of the quiet, cobbled street. If he had, he might have noticed the car parked opposite — a car that wasn't usually there.

And then he might have seen the shadowy figure inside of James Quinn.

Quinn smiled at his good fortune.

He knew which window of the mews-style flats belonged to Jack. It was surprising what you could find out if you spent enough time looking. He also knew the detective lived alone — apart from the odd work colleague and takeaway delivery driver, Jack MacIntosh appeared to have little or no visitors.

But he hadn't been alone tonight.

About an hour before Jack pulled up in his Mondeo, he'd seen the lone figure strolling along the length of Kettle's Yard Mews and then disappearing through the communal door. Only when the door swung shut did Quinn feel a vague tug at his memory.

He hadn't seen Stuart MacIntosh since the boy had been in nappies — but the long stride and sloping shoulders was too similar to his elder brother's to be anyone else.

He spent the rest of the evening watching.

He hadn't contemplated both brothers being here, and the thought filled him with a mixture of anticipation and caution. Could he really end the MacIntosh line in just the one hit? It wasn't part of the plan — if you could call it a plan — but now he couldn't stop thinking about it.

He saw a young lad on a scooter come and go — from the slogan emblazoned across the back of his jacket, he was from the China Garden restaurant around the corner.

The thought of food was now starting to make his own stomach rumble. He noticed the curtains at the second-floor window flicker — and then the faint sound of a movie theme tune filtered out through the open window.

Quinn licked his lips, feeling their dryness beneath his tongue.

He couldn't stop thinking about it.

Both brothers.

Together.

Maybe it was time to reassess his plan.

* * *

Time: 9.15 p.m.
Date: Wednesday 21 May 2014
Location: Kettle's Yard Mews, London

They ate in silence, scooping generously sized helpings of special fried rice, chicken chow mein, and crispy duck on to their plates. Jack had switched on the TV, picking one of those Fast and Furious films that his brother usually liked — but neither of them were really watching it. After a while, Jack noticed that his brother was toying with his food, pushing it around the plate with a glum expression on his face.

"You OK, Stu?" Jack helped himself to another serving of rice. He surprised himself as to how hungry he felt. Seeing the contents of the suitcase up close on the banks of the Thames that morning had more or less killed his appetite for the rest of the day — even Cooper had dispensed with his usual bacon-themed snacks.

But now he felt like he could eat a scabby dog.

Mac pushed his plate away and reached for a fresh beer.

"Your parents are meant to be there when you get married, aren't they?" Mac's words hung emptily in the air. "That's how it's supposed to be."

"There's no 'supposed to' about life these days, Stu." Jack shovelled more rice into his mouth. "That's not how it is anymore."

Mac took a swig from the can. "Do you think Mum would've liked her? Isabel, I mean? If she was still around?"

Jack put down his fork. "I'm sure she would've loved her, Stu."

"So, what was going through her mind when she . . ." Mac broke off, his throat thickening — unable to finish the sentence with the words 'killed herself'. Instead, he took another swig of beer.

Jack returned his plate to the coffee table and edged closer to his brother. "I'm not sure anyone really knows."

"Do you think she realised that she'd never see us grow up — never see us get married, or have kids of our own? Did none of that go through her mind?" Mac's voice cracked. "'Coz I really struggle with that some days, Jack. Everyone tells me how devoted she was to us, yet . . ." He broke off and stared down at his beer can. "If we meant that much to her, why did she choose to leave us? I just feel cheated, Jack."

Jack rubbed his eyes. Tiredness from the day was catching up with him fast and his body was crying out for sleep. And the food had only made it worse — and possibly the beer, too. "Things are never that black and white, Stu."

"But she chose to kill herself, Jack." Anger edged Stuart MacIntosh's tone and his eyes took on a fierce look. "She *chose* to leave us. She *chose* to never see any of those things."

Jack saw the raw pain etched deeply into his brother's face. The loss of their mother was still affecting him, that was abundantly clear. It had affected Jack, too, but in a different way. He had his nightmares to keep him company; Stu had nothing.

The all-too-familiar feeling of guilt started to flicker once more. Jack knew he could help his brother — right here, right now — just by telling him the truth. Or at least the truth as he suspected it to be. That their mother didn't choose to die — didn't choose to leave them alone.

But Jack did as Jack had always done. He kept his mouth shut and decided to keep his suspicions about James Quinn to himself.

"I'm sorry, ignore me." Mac gave an apologetic half-smile and Jack noticed the anger that had been piercing his brother's eyes had now disappeared, almost as quickly as it had descended. "I get a bit like this when I've drunk too much beer. This bloody wedding's on my mind all the time. I just want it over and done with."

"It's to be expected." Jack gathered up the plates and took the uneaten food back to the kitchen, placing the foil trays in the fridge — at least that was dinner sorted for the next couple of days.

It was getting late, and Jack knew he would have to at least pretend to get some sleep. Thoughts of the body in the suitcase were already starting to surface once again. The relaxing effect of the alcohol was wearing off, replaced by a dull headache. He turned and threw a spare blanket at his brother.

"I take it you're staying?"

Mac stretched his legs out on the sofa and nodded.

"Well, I'll be out early in the morning. I'll try not to wake you." Jack headed for his bedroom, passing Mac the TV remote control as he went.

If he'd stopped by the window, he would have seen an unfamiliar dark coloured car pull away from the kerb and disappear into the night.

CHAPTER EIGHT

Time: 8.00 a.m.
Date: Thursday 22 May 2014
Location: Flat 3a Ash Road, SE Soho, London

Still having the Cumberland sausages to eat, he decided to give Niko's café a miss this morning — taking the short walk to the Spar around the corner instead. His benefits were in, and he desperately needed to stock up. He picked up two four-packs of cheap lager and two bottles of own-brand vodka, placing them into his basket. He then added a tin of beans to go with the sausages and, because he was feeling flush, a family-size packet of biscuits. Standing in the queue for the till, his eyes caught sight of the newspaper racks.

He usually bought the *Daily Mirror* for the racing pages, but this morning it was the headline that caught his attention.

'*Horror find beneath bridge.*'

If he'd had any doubt that the man and his dog had been for their usual evening stroll, then the *Mirror's* front page blew that out of the water.

She'd been found.

Picking up a copy of the newspaper, he couldn't help but let his eyes skim the brief front page article. It contained nothing by way of detail or substance — they didn't even say it was female. And certainly no name. That part would take a while, but it would come. A pretty name to put to a pretty face. . . a face that was still languishing in his freezer compartment back home.

He fought hard to contain the chuckle rising up at the back of his throat. The last thing he needed to do was draw unwanted attention to himself. Tucking the folded newspaper under his arm, he stepped forward to pay, adding tobacco and another bottle of vodka to the bill. And more credit for his phone.

Back home in the kitchen, he set himself up with a couple of inches of neat vodka and sat down at the table. Spreading the newspaper out in front of him, he saw the story continued inside on page three — but it still didn't contain much by way of fact. There were the usual calls for witnesses to contact a dedicated hotline number or to call Crimestoppers anonymously with any information.

But that was it.

The police wouldn't have made the link with the suitcase yet — but he knew that they would — eventually. And when they did . . .

A smile tugged at his lips and he rewarded himself with a slug of vodka. Yes, the suitcase had been a clever touch. An added extra.

Placing the newspaper to the side, he slipped his newly topped-up mobile from his pocket. There were still no replies to any of his messages, and that concerned him. He wanted the rest of his money. He *needed* the rest of his money. He'd kept his end of the bargain. In fact, he'd gone above and beyond what'd been expected, so in essence he deserved a bonus. The thought made him chuckle again.

He stared at the empty screen. He'd give it another twenty-four hours, and then maybe a personal visit might be in order.

Pushing himself up out of his chair, he pulled open the fridge door and grabbed the sausages. Hunger clenched at his insides, and he knew he could make a better job of it than Niko. Before closing the fridge door, he felt his eyes straying towards the freezer compartment and his thoughts turned to what lay inside. Another smile teased his lips as he reached for the frying pan.

* * *

Time: 8.30 a.m.
Date: Thursday 22 May 2014
Location: Metropolitan Police HQ, London

Jack had stepped into the sanctuary of his office a little after eight o'clock. It would have been earlier but exhaustion still wracked his body. With the knowledge that the body in the suitcase was that of a young girl, aged no more than ten according to Dr Matthews, he'd been unable to sleep and spent the night pushing away images of the girl's headless torso.

Who could behead a child? And then dismember them?

The thought left a distinctly unpalatable taste in his mouth.

And then there'd been Quinn.

His brief chat with DS Carmichael yesterday had left him feeling unsettled. He hadn't been entirely honest with his friend and colleague, and he was pretty sure Rob was aware of that. The man wasn't stupid.

'*What aren't you telling me, Jack?*'

Rob Carmichael's words echoed inside his head.

Collapsing into his chair, Jack surveyed the carnage that was his desk and pushed the thought of both James Quinn and Rob Carmichael out of his tangled mind. He needed to focus on the job in hand. And today that job was identifying the poor child who had washed up in a suitcase early yesterday morning.

He briefly considered visiting the vending machine for some coffee. Although not the greatest tasting coffee in the world, it was better than nothing. Or he could head to the incident room where there was a stash of better tasting coffee granules — although apparently still no milk. Unless DS Cassidy had apprehended the milk thief overnight and made them replenish the stocks.

Deciding he didn't have the energy for either, Jack rubbed his eyes and tried to focus his attention back to his in-tray.

Before he had a chance to reconsider his coffee choices, the office door flew open and Cassidy burst in. "I think I've got her, guv. It's Maisie. Maisie Lancaster."

Jack's weary eyebrows hitched. "You're sure?"

"As sure as I can be without, you know, the rest of her." The glint that had been in Cassidy's eyes dulled. "Her parents confirmed she had her appendix out when she was six. And she fractured her right wrist ten months ago — had a plate inserted at St Thomas's."

"You've spoken to them?"

Cassidy nodded, her face grim. "Only very briefly — late last night. They were already aware of yesterday's find. It's been all over the internet. Something told them it was her. So, in some ways, they were expecting our call."

Jack hadn't seen today's papers yet, but he would bet his last pound that the discovery under London Bridge had already made the headlines. Every national newspaper — tabloid and broadsheet — would no doubt lead with the grim discovery. The papers wouldn't have a lot to go on, but that didn't usually stop them speculating — and a full press conference wasn't scheduled until later that day. Jack couldn't wait.

"I've organised a liaison officer to go round and be with them." Cassidy received an appreciative nod from Jack. "But . . ." She lowered her voice. "If we don't, you know, find the rest of her . . . could we get the mother's DNA — see if there's a match that way?"

Jack nodded. "Yes. We'll do that anyway. I don't want to leave any room for doubt on this one. But let's just see what else today brings. Elliott's due at the scene again as soon as it's low tide, to see if anything else has cropped up overnight." By 'cropped up' Jack meant the poor girl's missing body parts, in particular her head. "I'll check in with him later."

"Could we show them the photos from the post-mortem? Not the graphic ones, obviously, but the ones with her birthmark?" Cassidy shuddered once again. "I didn't want to mention it to them over the phone. They were distraught enough as it was, and I wasn't sure they were taking in much of what I said."

Jack rummaged around on his desk, locating the preliminary report from Dr Matthews underneath the morning's post. Flicking through the pages, he came to rest on the series of colour photographs that accompanied the conclusion. He flicked to the final photograph, confirming an eight- millimetre birthmark on the back of the right thigh.

"Good idea. I'll go out to see them later today — show them the photograph. If they confirm that Maisie had a birthmark like this, then I think we can pretty much conclusively say we have an identity."

"And the DNA?" added Cassidy as she turned to leave.

"We'll do that, too. Just to be sure. Can you let me have their address, and we'll swing by once I've caught up with Elliott?"

"Sure. I've got it here. 21 Lambert Grove, EC1."

Cassidy watched as the colour instantly drained from Jack's face.

CHAPTER NINE

Time: 10.45 a.m.
Date: Thursday 22 May 2014
Location: 21 Lambert Grove, London EC1

For Jack, it was like stepping back in time. The makes of the cars parked nose-to-tail along each side of the road may have changed, but essentially the street looked exactly as it had done twenty-five years ago — which was the last time Jack had walked its path.

His eyes flickered momentarily towards number 30, sitting a little farther along the street. It looked exactly as he remembered, even down to the rickety wooden gate at the front — which still hadn't been repaired, and hung limply from a single rusty hinge.

But they weren't here to revisit Jack's memories of number 30.

Leaving the Mondeo parked at an angle across the short drive, he led Cassidy towards the front door of number 21. The post-mortem report burned, uncomfortably, in the inside pocket of his jacket.

The door was opened by DC James Anderson, a family liaison officer who Jack knew well. Nodding in greeting, DC

Anderson stepped back to allow Jack and Cassidy into the carpeted hallway.

The first feeling that Jack experienced as he stepped inside was an overwhelming one of familiarity. The second feeling that enveloped him was the unmistakable sense of sadness. It was as if the house itself was grieving. Grief had no sound, but it was deafening just the same.

Anderson opened the door that led through to the living room where the feeling of sorrow only intensified. It was a typical Victorian-style front room — square with a high ceiling, and a large three-sided bay window to the front. Every inch of the room seemed to be packed with furniture and toys. A large, wooden dolls house hugged one wall, a box of games and puzzles sat by the side of the TV.

Russell and Sara Lancaster were seated on a pale blue, two-seater sofa facing the window. They'd kept the curtains closed, not wanting to face the rest of Lambert Grove just yet. Two high-backed armchairs flanked each side of the sofa, and as Jack edged further inside, followed by Cassidy and DC Anderson, the front room felt even more cramped.

Both Mr and Mrs Lancaster looked up as Jack came into view, their eyes telling the story of a sleepless night — or more likely a series of sleepless nights. With their daughter missing for over a week, Jack was sure they wouldn't have slept a wink in between. Sara Lancaster clutched a photograph in her hands, her grip so tight her fingers were turning white. Her husband sat motionless by her side, his face pale and drawn.

Jack perched awkwardly on the arm of the nearest armchair, taking a swift glance around the room as he did so. A display cabinet behind them was crammed full of all manner of knick-knacks, from china dolls to presentation trophies. In among the haphazard arrangement of trinkets, several framed photographs stood out — and even from this distance, Jack could make out the happy, smiling face of a blonde-haired, blue-eyed girl.

His hand went instinctively to the inside pocket of his jacket where the photographs from Dr Matthews' post-mortem were tucked away. Was the girl grinning out from the pictures behind the glass of the display cabinet now lying on a cold grey slab at the Westminster Mortuary? Jack knew there was really only one way to find out for sure.

"How are you both bearing up?" Cassidy's voice was soft as she leaned in towards Maisie's mother. "We spoke yesterday on the phone. I'm DS Amanda Cassidy." She glanced up at Jack. "And this is Detective Inspector Jack MacIntosh."

Jack was grateful for Cassidy taking the lead. Ever since the words 'Lambert Grove' had spilled from her mouth earlier that morning, he had virtually lost the ability to use his tongue. Just being here, merely doors away from number 30, he felt his blood pressure beginning to rise, his palms hot and clammy.

With pressure mounting for him to say something, Jack fumbled inside his pocket for the photographs. As he did so, his eyes caught sight of a copy of the *Daily Mail* sitting on a low-rise coffee table. Although folded, the headline was plain for all to see. And the look on both Mr and Mrs Lancaster's faces told Jack that they'd both seen it. He didn't need to ask.

"Thank you for seeing us." Jack pulled the paperwork from his pocket. "We won't take up too much of your time." Clearing his throat, he tore his eyes away from the newspaper headline. "As you know, a body was found early yesterday morning on the banks of the river beneath London Bridge. We are, at present, trying to identify that body."

"It's her, isn't it?" Sara Lancaster's voice was barely audible. "It's Maisie."

Jack paused. "At this stage, we're unsure. But yes, it's a possibility." There was no sense in lying or prolonging the family's agony.

"It's her," repeated Mrs Lancaster, fresh tears streaming down her already saturated cheeks. "I know it is. I can feel it in here. She's gone." She placed a trembling hand to her chest. "It's our Maisie."

Russell Lancaster placed a hand on his wife's shoulder. "The body that was found — you told us last night they'd had their appendix removed and a fracture treated with a metal plate." He swallowed, his face blanching as the words formed in his mouth. "Maisie had both of those."

Jack gave a slow nod. "I know. It's still not conclusive evidence, but . . ." He broke off and turned to the photographs in his hand. Knowing he couldn't put it off any longer, he selected the picture showing the birthmark. "Does Maisie have any birthmarks, at all?"

The silence in the cramped room deepened before Mrs Lancaster replied. "She has one just below her left eye." As soon as the words escaped her mouth, she buried her face in her hands and sobbed — the sound not unlike that of a wounded animal.

A birthmark to the face wasn't going to help identify the body in the suitcase. The newspapers that morning had been particularly graphic in their description of which body parts had been found — and, more importantly, which had not.

Russell Lancaster's grip on his wife's shoulder started to tremble. Jack could see from the man's expression that he was barely holding things together. Outwardly, he was trying to demonstrate a resoluteness, a strength from within for his wife's sake — but inside, he was clearly a mess. Clearing his throat, Maisie's father looked up with watery eyes. "She has another one on the back of her right thigh." His voice cracked beneath the strain. "In the shape of a butterfly."

Jack's eyes lowered to the photograph he held in his hand before handing it across. "I understand how distressing this must be. But could you please take a look at this photograph?"

Russell Lancaster took the picture with a shaking hand and instantly his eyes flooded with tears. Unable to speak, he merely nodded.

Jack took the photograph back and slotted it away inside his pocket. Nobody needed to see it anymore. Mrs Lancaster continued to bury her face in her hands, rocking back and forth on the sofa, her wailing cries growing in intensity.

Jack flashed a look towards DC Anderson who was hovering by the door. "Is there anything else we can do? Anyone we can call?" Jack acknowledged the shake of the head from the family liaison officer.

"Mrs Lancaster's parents are already here, supporting them." Anderson's eyes drifted towards the ceiling. "They're upstairs. And the family doctor called round earlier this morning, too."

Jack nodded, relieved that at least the family weren't alone in their grief. Knowing there was nothing further he could do or say that would make the situation any better, he started to head towards the door. Just as he reached it, the door flew open, almost colliding with his face.

And in the doorway stood a man Jack hadn't seen for a quarter of a century.

"Get out of this house!" the man thundered, eyes blazing. "Go on. Get out!"

"This is Mr Foster — Mrs Lancaster's father," began DC Anderson, instinctively moving towards Jack's side. "Maisie's grandfather."

"I know who he is," replied Jack, his tone neutral.

"Too bloody right you do!" Derek Foster took several steps forward, fists clenched into balls by his side. "And I don't want the likes of *you* anywhere near my family. So get out! *Now!*"

Jack remained where he was, mostly because the exit from the room was blocked by the man's hulking frame in the doorway. Standing just shy of six feet, Derek Foster looked as though he still kept in shape, despite his advancing years.

"We were just leaving, Mr Foster." Jack raised his eyebrows in the direction of the door. "If you would be so kind as to move out of the way."

Derek Foster stayed where he was, his face flushing a bright shade of crimson. Beads of sweat began to pop out along his brow, spit gathered at the corners of his mouth. "Don't you dare come back here — not *ever*. You've caused enough trouble along this street, you and your cronies. Don't think I've forgotten what you did!"

Jack edged closer to the doorway. He could almost feel the heat emanating from Foster as the man's temperature continued to rocket. But before he could take another step, Foster lunged forwards and grabbed Jack's tie and collar in his sweating hands. The force almost swept Jack off his feet and it was only the quick-thinking DC Anderson stepping between them that prevented Maisie's grandfather's hands from closing in around Jack's throat. Instead, there was the sound of ripping fabric.

With the doorway now clear, Jack leapt towards the safety of the hallway. Cassidy followed, her face a mixture of shock and bewilderment.

"I mean it, MacIntosh," thundered Derek Foster, his voice carrying from the front room. "Stay away!"

* * *

Time: 11.00 a.m.
Date: Thursday 22 May 2014
Location: Metropolitan Police HQ, London

DS Robert Carmichael bit the inside of his lip, keeping one eye on the door. This was one phone conversation he didn't particularly want to share. Although his office was tucked away along a rarely used corridor, walls still had ears. And eyes.

Satisfied the coast was clear, he continued the conversation. "I just wondered if you had anything further on the whereabouts of James Quinn?"

"The trail's gone pretty cold here," confirmed Surrey Police's DI Tim Fletcher. "He's literally disappeared. No one's seen or heard from him."

"From what I gather, he's pretty good at that. Disappearing."

"Indeed. We'll keep looking for him — we've a warrant out for his arrest for the murder of Roger Bancroft. Plus, there's a number of unsolved burglaries going back some years that other forces want to talk to him about. You heard about the murder, right?"

Carmichael hesitated and swapped the telephone over to his opposite ear, checking once more that no one was listening. "Only in passing. Remind me."

"Roger Bancroft was a retired City banker — only recently moved to Surrey when he was shot dead in his own home. Died from a single gunshot wound to the chest. We've forensic evidence that Mr Quinn was at the property, plus a rental car in Quinn's name was seen travelling to and from Surrey that night. It was later found close to Quinn's house in London with traces of Roger Bancroft's blood inside."

"Sounds pretty conclusive."

"You'd think so, wouldn't you?"

"And you don't?" Carmichael could detect a hesitancy in DI Fletcher's voice. "You don't think Quinn killed this Bancroft fella?"

Fletcher paused again, a degree of intrigue entering his tone. "Why are you so interested in our Mr Quinn, anyway?"

It was a question he'd been expecting and Carmichael had his answer prepared. "Quinn's name popped up once or twice in one of our own enquiries. Plus, there's the burglaries you mentioned." The lie tripped off Carmichael's tongue with ease. "We'd like a chat with him if he ever surfaces again."

"I'm about to head into a strategy meeting. Let me call you back later. There's a lot more to this one than meets the eye." DI Fletcher hung up, leaving Carmichael clutching an empty receiver.

There's a lot more to this one than meets the eye.

Carmichael was left wondering just what that might be.

And what it might have to do with Jack.

* * *

Time: 11.05 a.m.
Date: Thursday 22 May 2014
Location: 21 Lambert Grove, London EC1

"Are you going to tell me what the hell just happened in there?!" DS Cassidy clipped her seatbelt into place and stared, open-mouthed, across to Jack in the driver's seat. "You *know* these people?"

Jack gripped the steering wheel, but left the keys hanging in the ignition. His heart was thumping. Although he'd known coming back to Lambert Grove would dig up some memories, most of them unpleasant, he wasn't quite expecting that.

He wasn't expecting Derek Foster.

Fighting to get his breathing under control, Jack's grip on the wheel tightened. After Cassidy had informed him that they were heading for Lambert Grove, he'd put it down to an unhappy coincidence that the Lancasters happened to live on the same street. But now . . . ? Now he'd seen Derek Foster again, his memories from twenty-five years ago came flooding right back.

"Seriously, guv," continued Cassidy, her eyes still wide in shock. "What in God's name just happened?"

Clenching his jaw, Jack half-turned in his seat. "Do you remember our little visit to Essex to see DCI Hobbs last year? Part of the Bishop investigation?"

Cassidy's eyes widened even further. "The bloke dressed like a clown?"

A smile twinkled at Jack's mouth. "Indeed, yes, the bloke dressed like a clown."

"What's he got to do with whatever the hell it was that just happened back there?"

Jack opened his mouth but then shook his head. "It's a long story, Amanda. I'll fill you in another time. We should be getting back to the station."

CHAPTER TEN

Time: 11.30 a.m.
Date: Thursday 22 May 2014
Location: Isabel's Café, Horseferry Road, London

It wasn't somewhere Gina would usually choose to go — from the outside it looked expensive and being in Westminster it probably was. But her feet ached like mad and she needed to sit down. She'd left her bedsit just before eleven, unable to stand being cooped up any longer. She'd been kept awake most of the night by the couple on the floor below — if it wasn't the arguing that penetrated her paper-thin walls it was the non-stop drum and bass. And then the baby on the floor above had started screaming.

Despite her tiredness, she'd pulled on her trainers and hit the pavement. She wasn't much of a runner — more of a Sunday jogger at best — but today she just felt like putting one foot in front of the other and not looking back. After a few circuits of the local park, she headed down towards the river and ran along the embankment. After a while, she slowed down to a walk. Neither her trainers nor her legs were capable of much more.

But as she didn't want to go back home, she kept on walking — which was how she ended up outside Isabel's Café, her feet aching and her mouth parched. The smell was intoxicating, and she had no option but to obey her senses and walk inside.

Gina was immediately greeted by a welcoming smile and shown to a comfortable-looking sofa. Collapsing into it, she instantly felt as though she were being given a virtual hug. To top it off, a soft, furry tabby cat wove in and out of the nearby table legs and then hopped up next to her, curling up against a plump cushion.

"Let me know when you're ready to order." The woman with the beaming smile reappeared by Gina's side and handed her a laminated menu. "We have some specials on the board, too."

Gina smiled and inhaled the wondrous mix of coffee and sweet pastry. She settled back against the soft cushions, stretching her legs out underneath the table. Her muscles reminded her that occasional Sunday joggers didn't cover half of London in a pair of clapped-out trainers, especially when fuelled by just a cup of black tea.

"Oh, and if Livi becomes a pest, just nudge her out of the way!" The woman nodded towards the tabby cat who had now settled down to sleep next to Gina. "Sometimes she acts like she owns the place!"

"Not at all, she's gorgeous." Gina gently gave the tabby cat a stroke, feeling the rhythmic purrs beneath her hand.

As the woman turned away to head back towards the counter, Gina brought out the assortment of coins she'd stuffed into her pocket before leaving her bedsit. She didn't often treat herself — hence the clapped-out trainers — and certainly not to coffee and cake from a swanky café in Westminster. She instantly felt a flash of heat warm her cheeks. Where had she gone wrong? She was thirty-nine years old and still counting pennies to see if she could afford a slice of cake with her cappuccino.

It wasn't the life she'd planned.

Looking at the meagre collection of coins in her hand, Gina felt herself starting to well up. She looked towards the door and began debating how she might be able to slip out unnoticed. But before she could make a move, the woman reappeared at her side.

"Hi, I'm Isabel." The woman held out a hand. "And this might sound really odd, but could you do me an enormous favour?"

* * *

Time: 11.30 a.m.
Date: Thursday 22 May 2014
Location: 21 Lambert Grove, London EC1

"I'm so sorry." Sara Lancaster's shoulders heaved as she rested her head on her husband's shoulder. "I've not seen him lose his temper like that in a long time."

DC Anderson seated himself on one of the armchairs. "No need to apologise. Emotions run high at times like these. It's understandable."

"No it's not." Maggie Foster came to sit next to her daughter, her face pale and her eyes red-raw. "There's no excuse for his behaviour — he's just a brute. He should be supporting us all at a time like this, not . . . not picking fights with the police."

"I can hear, you know." The door to the front room burst open and Derek Foster's heavy-set frame filled the gap. "I'm not deaf."

"Just go away, Derek." Maggie's eyes brimmed with tears. "You're making things worse."

"Me?" Derek Foster cast a contemptuous look towards DC Anderson. "It's his lot that're making things worse, trust me. But I don't hear you calling for them to be thrown out on to the street."

"Mr Foster." Anderson rose to his feet. "I can assure you we're working flat-out on this — and I'm here to support you all in any way I can. Losing your temper isn't going to help."

Foster took another few steps into the room, coming within inches of Anderson's much slimmer and smaller frame. The young FLO barely flinched and stood his ground. With the colour in Maisie's grandfather's cheeks crimson once more, he made a grab for Anderson's shirt collar, pulling him close. He then leaned in with his mouth millimetres from the detective's ear.

"I won't say it again. I want you gone from my house."

"The problem is, Mr Foster, this isn't your house." DC Anderson's tone was cool and measured. "I'm here on the authority of the Metropolitan Police to support your daughter and her family — and if you don't remove your hands from me, I'll be arresting you for assaulting a police officer."

Derek Foster's grip on Anderson's shirt momentarily tightened, but eventually he stepped away. "I'll be watching you," he snarled, as he made his way towards the door. "I'll be watching your every move."

"And I'll be watching you too, Mr Foster. Make no mistake about that."

* * *

Time: 11.45 a.m.
Date: Thursday 22 May 2014
Location: Isabel's Café, Horseferry Road, London

Isabel had noticed Gina's tatty trainers the minute she'd walked in — and when she'd handed her the laminated menu, she'd seen hands that belonged to someone who scrubbed tables, floors and dishes for a living. It was a look Isabel knew well.

And the woman's eyes had such a pained look to them, and not just from whatever it was she'd been running from — because she was definitely running from something — but a hollow look of deep despair. A look that said, '*my life is worthless and I don't expect it to get much better*'.

Something within Isabel stirred. Maybe it was the way the woman stroked Livi — so tenderly and full of care — or maybe the way she sighed when at last she could take the weight off her feet. Whatever it was, Isabel felt an instant connection.

And when she saw the woman surreptitiously counting out her coins, Isabel's mind was made up.

"Are you sure?" Gina's eyes widened in disbelief.

"Absolutely — you'll be doing me a massive favour." Isabel set the first mug of frothy coffee down on the table. "With this new coffee machine, my head barista over there hasn't had a chance to try out all the new gadgets. A friend of mine was meant to be helping me out today — to be my guinea pig — but she can't make it."

Gina eyed the smooth, caramel-scented coffee, her mouth starting to water. "You really want me to try out all your coffees — for free?"

Isabel nodded enthusiastically, her smile broadening. "That's about the size of it, yes! Dom here will keep you well supplied! Just let us know what you think of each one."

Isabel left Gina to start sampling her first coffee of the day and worked hard to hide her grin as she slipped back behind the counter.

"You didn't really have someone coming to test the coffees today, did you?" asked Dominic, already preparing Gina's second drink.

"Nope," whispered Isabel, smothering a giggle. "But let's keep that between you and me. It's our little secret, Dom. Just keep the coffees coming — and maybe throw in a muffin with the next one. She looks like she could do with it."

Just then, Sacha emerged from the kitchen armed with a fresh batch of warm croissants, a smile on her face. "I heard what you did just then." Sacha nodded towards Gina, who was leaning back against the soft sofa cushions, her eyes closed. "You really are an angel."

Isabel shrugged, her cheeks starting to colour. "It's no biggie. Just a few coffees. The poor thing looked like she could do with a bit of good fortune. And we do need to try out this new coffee machine."

Both Isabel and Sacha watched as Dominic slid a double chocolate chip muffin on to a plate and placed it next to Gina's second coffee.

"It's not just that — it's everything you do for Dom. You really are something special, Isabel Faraday. I hope Mac appreciates what an absolute angel he's landed himself with."

Isabel's cheeks flushed even more. "Stop it! Dom's a hard worker — I'm not doing any favours here. He's earned his place in the café, fair and square."

"I know, but you gave him a chance when everyone else didn't. Mention the 'A' word and suddenly doors start slamming in your face."

"Dom's here on his own merits, Sacha. He's doing brilliantly at night school — one day he'll end up running this place on his own, you just watch. Have his name above the door and everything."

Sacha looked shocked. "You're not thinking of leaving, are you? Please say you're not."

Isabel hesitated for a fraction of a second, then grinned at her best friend. "Of course not! Where would I go?"

Sacha smiled with relief and returned to the kitchen, leaving Isabel with her thoughts.

She watched as Dominic wiped down the coffee machine, humming to himself as he worked. Was she thinking of leaving? Packing up and moving on? Not really, but who knew what the future held for anyone? With her and Mac getting married, and now she had the family home in Surrey again, maybe there would come a time when they would want to branch out, see more of the world.

But for now . . . ?

For now, the café was the only place she wanted to be.

* * *

Time: 1.15 p.m.
Date: Thursday 22 May 2014
Location: London Bridge, London SE1

With the tide now on its way out, Elliott Walker knew they had just a small window of opportunity. The area where the suitcase had been discovered early yesterday morning was again hastily marked out with tape and a fresh round of investigations were underway. Elliott wasn't sure what else of note they could possibly find — not after goodness knows how many cubic feet of Thames river water had submerged the scene in the intervening hours. But rivers were funny things – sometimes they kept hold of their secrets.

With the head, hands and feet of the victim still missing, there was a grim determination reflected in each and every one of the investigator's faces. It was a silent and sombre job.

Elliott retraced his steps along the metal plates that guided him over the muddied banks. From what he could gather, the favoured explanation was that the suitcase had been dropped from the bridge overhead when the river was at low tide — although tests on the suitcase were still ongoing.

He held a hand up to his brow, filtering out the sunshine that now streamed across the bridge. He let his eyes scour the exposed riverbed along the whole of the south side. If the killer had tossed the head, hands and feet out separately, then they could be anywhere by now. The hands and feet were light enough to be transported away on the tide — and, if that was the case, then it was unlikely they would ever be found.

But the head.

They needed to find the head.

Sighing, Elliott started walking back towards the shore. He hadn't got far when he heard a shout.

"Here!"

Elliott turned to find one of the investigators crouching down low to the ground, waving a hand in the air. Even from this distance, he could see immediately what had been uncovered.

Another cordon was quickly placed in position, and fresh stepping plates were brought over from the van. Bob Snowden, an experienced investigator with over twenty years' service, was still kneeling down on the muddied riverbed, taking a series of photographs. Another investigator was already preparing the video camera to record as much detail as possible before the tide turned against them.

The tide.

Elliott looked at his watch. They had a while yet — but not as long as he might like. He considered calling Jack, but by the time the detective inspector managed to get away they might already have had to move out. He put a call in anyway and left a message on Jack's voicemail.

He then scrolled down to another familiar number and placed a further call. This one was answered on the second ring.

"Dr Matthews?" Elliott took another look at the skull embedded in the silt of the riverbed. "I'm back at the scene under London Bridge. You might want to come down and have a look at this."

CHAPTER ELEVEN

Time: 2.00 p.m.
Date: Thursday 22 May 2014
Location: Metropolitan Police HQ, London

Jack looked up as DS Cooper and DC Daniels entered the incident room.

"House-to-house is getting underway again along Lambert Grove, boss." Cooper went to pull open the only window in the room. "And the CCTV. We should be able to view something later today."

"Good." Jack got up from his seat and headed for his beloved pin board.

"How did you get on at the Lancasters? Did they identify the birthmark?"

"They did, indeed, Cooper. We can be pretty sure our body in the suitcase is Maisie Lancaster." Jack pinned a photograph of the eight-year-old to the centre. After their rather unceremonious exit from Lambert Grove, DC Anderson had obtained a recent photograph of Maisie and emailed it through to the incident room. "We've left Anderson doing the follow-up DNA samples, but I don't think we expect it to be anyone else."

"And you'll never guess what else happened!" Cassidy looked up from her computer monitor, her eyes shining. "He only went and got himself thrown out!"

Jack sighed. "I did not get myself thrown out, we were leaving anyway." He smoothed down the collar of his ripped shirt self-consciously.

"Who threw you out of where?" Cooper was unsure whether to laugh or be concerned. Daniels merely looked baffled.

"No time to explain. We've had a development." Jack turned towards the whiteboards. "Elliott's called in. They've found a head at the scene — well, a skull to be precise. Buried in the silt just a few metres away from where yesterday's suitcase was located."

"A head to go with our headless torso?" Daniels' eyebrows hitched as he took a seat.

"A head yes," replied Jack, "but it can't possibly be Maisie. This is a skull and has obviously been there for some time. Elliott says they've also found some additional bones, which may or may not be related. Dr Matthews will be examining the remains later today — he's prioritising it above everything else. I'm heading over later to see what he has. The site will be processed as best as it can be before the tide comes back in. They'll do another sweep in the early hours when the waters recede again."

"A second body or a second killer?" Daniels voiced the question that was on all their lips.

Jack paused. "That remains to be seen. But let's not get ahead of ourselves — we'll wait to see what Dr Matthews has to say about the new discovery before we start hypothesising. For now, we run them as separate investigations." Jack glanced towards his team. "And now we have an ID for the first body, I want you to focus on the Lancaster family. Find out everything you can about them — liaise with DC Anderson. And go over any last known movements and sightings we have of Maisie."

"Pippa rang while you were out." Cooper waved a Post-it note in the air. "She said to let you know the press conference is at five o'clock. And don't be late."

Jack silently groaned. "Thanks. Any more good news?"

Cooper grinned. "Not yet. But you can't show up on national TV looking like that." He nodded at Jack's torn shirt collar. "You'll have to borrow one of my spares."

* * *

Time: 4.30 p.m.
Date: Thursday 22 May 2014
Location: Darwin Hotel and Conference Centre, London

"And so, ladies and gentlemen — I thank you once again, most profusely, for the invitation to speak to you today. It has been one of the most enthralling and captivating events that I've ever had the good fortune to be involved in." Professor Leon Kaufman gave a small bow, the light from the overhead chandelier bouncing off his scalp. Gone was the head of thick hair from his youth — the years were advancing on him just like everybody else and there was little he could do, or indeed wanted to do, to halt its journey.

Age was what made the world what it was: what made the universe what it was. In comparison, he was only just born. From the moment human beings took their first breaths, everyone was on a steady decline towards ageing — and death. It was a process that could never be stopped, not entirely. It could be delayed by any manner of lotions, potions and expensive medical procedures, but the eventual destination could not be avoided. Despite what the back-street quacks might tell you.

And age was what had brought the professor to London on this Thursday afternoon. 'Forensic Anthropology — Through the Ages' was also what had drawn the ninety-seven attendees to the Darwin Conference Centre. At least Kaufman hoped it was. Maybe the free set-lunch and complimentary sparkling wine had something to do with it, too.

The forensic anthropology community were a tight-knit and intriguing bunch. Not content with ordinary pathology, this section of the profession liked them old; and the older the better. A bit like a fine wine — except the bodies they examined very rarely improved with age in neither taste nor aroma.

There were two more speakers due to take the stage during the rest of the afternoon session, and Professor Kaufman was already hoping for an early escape when he spied a familiar figure lurking by the exit. He left the podium amid a smattering of applause, shaking hands with the occasional seated guest as he made his way towards the back of the conference room. The smile on his face widened as he finally reached the gatecrasher hovering by the door.

"My goodness, Philip!" The smile turned into a heartfelt grin. "I haven't seen you in many a year! What brings you to my select gathering this afternoon?" The professor swept an arm out towards the seated guests who were already gearing up for the next speaker — a Dr Fleisch from Leipzig who was about to talk to them all about mineral deposits.

Dr Philip Matthews accepted the hearty handshake offered to him. "Good to see you, too, Leon. It's been a while."

"Indeed it has, indeed it has." Professor Kaufman glanced around, finally nodding towards a small table at the side which was unoccupied. "Shall we? You've missed the lunch I'm afraid, but I can get us a bottle of something nice — we've so much to catch up on!"

The professor started to take Dr Matthews by the elbow, guiding him in the direction of the empty table. Feeling the eminent pathologist resist, the professor cast him a surprised look. "No? Don't tell me you've given up the good stuff?"

Dr Matthews shook his head. "No, nothing quite so alarming. But, do you mind?" The pathologist nodded towards the double doors that led back out into the foyer.

"If you have a few spare minutes, could we find somewhere quiet to talk?"

Professor Kaufman allowed himself to be led out of the conference room and, once out of the glare of the chandeliers, he noted the deep concern etched into his old friend's eyes. They might not have seen each other in the flesh for something in the region of fifteen years, maybe more, but it was a look that he recognised.

"I wonder if I might call upon your expertise, Leon." Dr Matthews led the pair of them towards a quiet alcove next to the reception desk. "A rather interesting case has landed on my slab."

"Of course, of course. Fire away. I'm not speaking any more today — my time is yours. What's on your mind?"

Dr Matthews hesitated, seeing the confused look on the professor's face deepen. Then he made a decision. "Actually, would it be possible for you to come to my examination room at the mortuary? I have something I need your advice on, but I think it needs to be in person, so to speak. Words won't really do it justice."

Intrigue replaced the confusion on Professor Kaufman's face. He began to nod, fervently. "Of course. Lead the way, my friend."

Dr Matthews glanced towards the door that led back into the conference room. "But I don't want to drag you away from anything important. If it's not convenient . . ."

"Nonsense." Professor Kaufman had already begun to stride towards the revolving doors that led out on to the street. "Best excuse I've had all day. To be honest, Philip, these things bore me to tears. You know what it's like. You can't really turn down the invitation to speak at these events — it always looks good in the academic publications — but they can be intensely tedious things."

They arrived on the pavement outside the Darwin Conference Centre and the professor immediately sprang forward to flag down a black cab. "You must have attended your own fair share over the years, Philip."

Dr Matthews felt himself nodding. "One or two, Leon. One or two." He knew exactly what his friend was talking about. He'd had to endure many a lecture in his time, most of them tedious enough to turn you to stone. So much so that Mrs Matthews now refused to accompany him to any such gatherings. She said she'd rather walk barefoot across hot coals than sit through another talk on the effect of temperature on rates of decomposition. He jumped into the back of the taxi that had stopped by their side. "so long as you don't mind."

"Not at all." Professor Kaufman pulled the door shut behind them and turned towards the driver. "Westminster Mortuary, please, young man."

* * *

Time: 5.00 p.m.
Date: Thursday 22 May 2014
Location: Metropolitan Police HQ, London

Pippa Reynolds, the force's head of PR, adjusted Jack's microphone and gave him a knowing smile. "I'll keep the questions to a minimum at the end — less chance for the circus to degenerate."

Jack nodded his thanks and reached for a glass of water. He could already feel his blood pressure skyrocketing and they hadn't even started yet. He ran a finger around the inside of his shirt collar — the top button a little too tight for his liking. But it was either wear DS Cooper's spare shirt, or be presented to the capital's media looking like he'd come off worse in a bar brawl.

As if on cue, Cooper slipped into the vacant chair beside him. Behind them, the enlarged computer screen flickered into life, depicting the Metropolitan Police logo.

It didn't take long for the room to fill — Pippa manning the door to greet a stream of newspaper and other media reporters. The chairs at the front filled up first, latecomers resigned to standing room only at the back. Jack took another sip of water and scanned the assembled faces — searching for one in particular.

It wasn't long before he found it.

Having crossed swords with Jack on plenty of occasions in the past, Jonathan Spearing wasn't about to miss an opportunity to repeat the process. Jack locked eyes with the casually dressed *Daily Courier* crime correspondent, noticing the playful gleam in the man's eyes even from his position at the back of the room.

Jack ran another finger around the inside collar of his borrowed shirt, feeling the material pinching his skin. He loosened his tie a little. He'd spied Jonathan Spearing at London Bridge yesterday lunchtime, sniffing around with the other hacks, trying to squeeze out a story from the tight-lipped crime scene investigators.

A hardened reporter, Spearing was good at his job. And, to be fair, his articles were, more often than not, based on fact. But DI Jack MacIntosh was his Achilles heel. A clash of personalities was putting it mildly. Not one to shirk away from saying exactly what he thought, Spearing often portrayed Jack in a less than favourable light: something Jack was all too aware of.

Holding Spearing's gaze for several more seconds, Jack then caught Pippa's eye as she closed the conference room door.

Let the battle commence.

Keep it brief, Jack, he muttered to himself, taking one last sip of water and clearing his throat. Keep it brief and get out in one piece.

"At approximately 12.30 a.m. on Wednesday 21 May, several body parts contained in a suitcase were discovered beneath London Bridge." Jack kept his eyes lowered to the front row of reporters, seeing a multitude of digital recording devices angled in his direction. "A murder investigation has been launched and enquiries are continuing."

"Do you have a name?"

And so it began.

Jack shot a look up towards a gum-chewing Jonathan Spearing, who was lounging against the back wall in his Arctic Monkeys T-shirt, tape recorder in hand. "Enquiries are continuing as to the victim's identification . . ."

"But you have an idea?" Spearing continued to chew, his eyes locked to Jack's. "You have a name?"

Jack had no intention of divulging Maisie Lancaster's name to Spearing or anyone else. He stared into the *Daily Courier* reporter's eyes, challenging the man to take it one step further. Did Spearing know about the Lancasters? It was possible. The Metropolitan Police was no less leaky than any other ship in the country — and pieces of information, no matter how confidential they might be, had a habit of jumping overboard.

But Jack didn't think Spearing had anything substantial on the victim's identity — if he had, he would have said so. He was nothing if not direct.

"I repeat — identification has not been made at this time. Enquiries continue."

Jonathan Spearing gave a curt nod and resumed his chewing. Jack took another sip of water.

"If anyone was in the vicinity of London Bridge on the evening of Tuesday 20 May, and the early hours of Wednesday 21, please contact the information hotline. Similarly, anyone driving in the vicinity who may have dash cam footage, please get in touch."

That was all Jack was prepared to say. Short. Succinct. Nothing that could upset the bigwigs upstairs.

"What about the activity under the bridge earlier today?" Jonathan Spearing's lazy tone rang out once again. Several heads turned in his direction, their digital recorders primed for any tasty new leads. "Did you find any more of the missing body parts? I saw the cordons were still up."

Jack felt Cooper shift slightly in the chair at his side, maybe anticipating Jack's rise in blood pressure.

Keep a lid on it, Jack. Keep a lid on it.

Jack clenched his jaw muscles, clamping his teeth tightly shut. Beneath Cooper's stand-in shirt, Jack felt patches of sweat clinging to his back and the collar tightening around his neck.

Thankfully, Cooper decided to step in.

"As DI MacIntosh said earlier, our investigations are continuing into the identity of the victim. Our forensic investigation team will remain on site for as long as necessary." Cooper flashed a quick look sideways at Jack. "For now, we repeat our appeal for anyone in the vicinity of London Bridge on Tuesday evening and the early hours of Wednesday to get in touch. If you saw anything unusual, or out of character, no matter how small, please use the dedicated information hotline."

Pippa Reynolds started to move forwards, silently mouthing her thanks to DS Cooper. Crisis averted.

Or so she thought.

"What about the internal enquiry into the arrest of the Bishop?" Jonathan Spearing wasn't giving up; he had the floor to himself and saw no reason to waste it. "Are you competent enough to lead another high- profile investigation, DI MacIntosh?"

Jack could feel the blood boiling beneath his skin.

"You put a man in hospital, detective inspector. Reports say he was in a coma for four weeks. And one of your own team nearly died." Spearing paused, swapping his gum from one side of his mouth to the other. "Are you the best person to lead such a difficult case?"

Jack shot out of his chair at exactly the same time that Pippa Reynolds took command of the small stage.

"Thank you for coming, ladies and gentlemen. All details plus photographs are on the website, together with the hotline number." She stared pointedly at Spearing, letting him know that this particular part of the show was definitely over. "If you would like to make your way outside."

As people began turning towards the door, Jack jogged down the platform steps and strode towards the exit. If he didn't get away from Jonathan Spearing, he wasn't quite sure what he might do. In his current mood and state of sleeplessness, just about anything was on the cards.

At that moment, Jack's mobile chirped with an incoming message. A quick glance at the screen dashed his plans for a quick exit.

"*When you've a moment. Come to my office.*"

CHAPTER TWELVE

Time: 5.30 p.m.
Date: Thursday 22 May 2014
Location: Metropolitan Police HQ, London

If the tiredness on Jack's face was evident, Chief Superintendent Douglas 'Dougie' King didn't mention it. "Sit down, Jack. Take the weight off your feet."

Jack did as he was told and watched his senior officer pour two mugs of coffee from the machine behind his desk. If there was one thing that Jack looked forward to when summoned to the chief superintendent's office, it was the coffee. None of that vending machine muck they otherwise had to suffer or the overpriced froth from the new deli around the corner — this was *proper* coffee.

With two steaming mugs in his hands, Dougie King eased himself back behind his mahogany desk and passed one of the drinks across to Jack.

"Tell me about your body under the bridge."

Jack relayed the salient points about the discovery of the suitcase beneath London Bridge — and the headless torso within.

"And where are we on a possible identification?" The chief superintendent leaned back in his swivel chair, the leather creaking beneath his ample frame. "I'm guessing with no head, hands, or feet, that could be a challenge?"

Jack inclined his head while taking a sip of the too-hot coffee. He didn't mind the burn; he needed the caffeine hit too much to worry about scalded lips.

"We're pretty sure the victim is Maisie Lancaster — eight years old. We're waiting on DNA results, but it's pretty conclusive."

"I see you chose to keep that piece of information from the press conference earlier." Dougie King's greying eyebrows raised a fraction. "Probably a wise decision."

Jack nodded. "We need to give the family some time to come to terms with it before unleashing the world's media on them. But I suspect the tabloids will find out one way or another — they usually do."

"And today? I hear there was more activity under the bridge?"

Jack gave another nod. "A skull — plus several other bones. Discovered in the immediate area of where we found the suitcase. I'm due to attend an examination at the mortuary later."

"Coincidence?"

Jack paused and caught the chief superintendent's quizzical gaze across the rim of his mug. Dougie King was no more a fan of coincidences than Jack was. "We'll see," was all he would commit to.

"Any further forward on the retirement to the sun, sir?" Jack nodded towards a photograph on the chief superintendent's desk — a picture of his late parents' home on the beach at Kingston, Jamaica. "Still not tempted?"

"Oh, I'm tempted every day, Jack." Dougie King raised his bushy eyebrows at the piles of paper that swamped his desk and no doubt the bundles of red-tape contained within each. "Tempted each and every day. So, never say never."

After taking another swig from his mug, the chief superintendent pulled out an official-looking letter from his in-tray. "But this was the real reason I wanted to see you, Jack."

Jack eyed the letter suspiciously from his side of the desk. "Is it?" Jack had learned to be wary of official-looking correspondence — especially when they were in the hands of a senior officer.

Chief Superintendent King noted the trepidation on Jack's face and suppressed a chuckle. "No need to worry, Jack. You're not in any great trouble . . . *this time*. It's just the formal findings from the enquiry into the events surrounding the arrest of the Bishop last September. I take it you're already aware that no action is to be taken regarding your conduct that day?"

Jack nodded. "And my whacking a suspect over the head with a breeze block and putting him in a coma . . ."

"And that," added the chief superintendent, his dark eyes sparkling. "This just rubber stamps it — brings it all to a formal conclusion. That's all."

Dougie King handed the letter across the desk and Jack took a quick glance before handing it straight back. It didn't tell him anything he didn't already know. The outcome of the enquiry was irrelevant as far as he was concerned — if faced with a similar situation again in the future, he'd do exactly the same in a heartbeat. Maybe he'd even throw the breeze block a bit harder next time. Or find a bigger one.

"And how's young DC Daniels? I believe yesterday was his first full day back with you?"

"It was, yes." Jack was grateful for the conversation being steered back to safer ground. "He's looking well. Keen to be back."

"Well, that's good to know. He excelled himself that day, Jack — and for a new member of your team that's even more commendable. Putting his own life on the line like that, you should be proud of him."

"He's a good lad," admitted Jack. "He'll go far."

Jack swallowed more coffee and began to feel the welcome effect of the caffeine hit. Despite his tiredness, he was intrigued to be summoned to the Westminster Mortuary and was looking forward to hearing what Dr Matthews had to say about the most recent find. He glanced at his watch as he ran a finger around the collar of his too-tight shirt and loosened the top button.

"New shirt, Jack?" The chief superintendent's eyes retained their sparkle, and Jack wondered whether news of his earlier run-in at Lambert Grove had reached the upper echelons of the building. By the look on Dougie King's face, that was entirely possible.

"Borrowed," replied Jack, downing the rest of his coffee. This was one conversation he didn't want to get into right now. And luckily he had a 'get out of jail free' card. "If that's all, sir, I really need to get to the mortuary."

* * *

Time: 6.15 p.m.
Date: Thursday 22 May 2014
Location: Westminster Mortuary, London

"Thank you for agreeing to come. It's much appreciated."

Professor Kaufman held up a hand in acknowledgement and followed Dr Matthews into the chilled post-mortem room, their rubber wellington boots squeaking on the newly polished floor tiles.

"It's no trouble. The conference will be winding down before long — they can certainly do without me. And from what you've told me, this is an intriguing case."

While they'd waited for the examination room to be prepared, Dr Matthews had brought his old friend up to speed on the bizarre discovery. As he described the findings beneath the bridge, he had watched the old professor's eyebrows hitch higher and higher.

Now the room was ready, the pathologist led his colleague towards the steel examination table where the most recent finds from the banks of the River Thames looked stark beneath the bright, white light from overhead.

During the hurried excavation, completed just before the waters of the Thames started to reclaim the silt banks, Elliott's team had discovered —in addition to the skull — a perfectly intact femur, plus both the tibia and fibula of the lower left leg.

Dr Matthews waved Leon Kaufman forwards. He'd been delighted to find out that the professor was in London speaking at the Darwin Conference Centre — feeling that it must be a sign. Whoever it was that turned out to be lying on the mortuary slab before them, they needed the best. And as far as Dr Matthews was concerned, the best came in the form of Professor Leon Kaufman.

More used to seeing the deceased encased in their customary coverings of skin and subcutaneous tissue, seeing only the skeletal remains of what used to be a living human being sent an odd feeling through the pathologist.

And the smell was different, too.

Absent were the usual nose-wrinkling aromas that would ordinarily accompany one of Dr Matthews' post-mortems — the fetid stench of death; the sometimes eye-watering odour of the gases that built up within, released only under the incision of a carefully placed scalpel. Stomach contents, as Dr Matthews always warned his spectators, could release all manner of nausea-inducing aromas.

But there were no such smells in the examination room this evening. Instead, there was an earthy aroma, somewhat musty and stale. Nothing too unpleasant, if the truth be told.

As the professor got to work, Dr Matthews stood back and observed. The work of forensic anthropology fascinated him just as much as his own discipline did. The pair of them had met and studied briefly together in Austria, where the young and inexperienced Dr Matthews was on a student exchange programme. Kaufman was London-born, but his parents — themselves eminent medical professors — originally came from Salzburg, and it was to that city he headed to complete his training. Hitting it off immediately, they'd stayed in touch, and when Kaufman landed back in London during the 1980s, Dr Matthews sought him out. He hadn't been surprised to learn that the professor had branched off into the world of forensic anthropology — the man was a genius.

As Professor Kaufman bent over to take a closer look at the skeletal remains, the door to the examination room swished opened and Detective Inspector Jack MacIntosh hurried inside. He held up a hand as he edged around the perimeter of the room.

"Sorry I'm late, Doc. Press conference. Thanks for the call."

"No problem, Jack. We're just getting started." Dr Matthews nodded towards the table.

Like Dr Matthews, Jack was used to seeing putrefied and bloated flesh, open wounds, blood, and other bodily fluids on the examination table — but seeing just bare bones, their blanching whiteness reflected in the harsh lights above, was oddly fascinating. He edged a little closer.

Leon Kaufman went about his examination in a fastidious manner, inspecting and reinspecting all aspects of every single inch of each of the bones in turn. He spent a great deal of time examining the skull, leaning in closely, taking all manner of detailed measurements and bone samples. Neither Dr Matthews nor Jack even dared to take a breath, plunging the post-mortem room into a deathly quiet.

After an hour the eminent professor turned around to face his captivated audience. "Well, I can tell you with a decent amount of certainty that we're looking at a female, approximately eighteen to twenty-five years of age, in the region of 165 centimetres tall."

"You can tell that, just from what we have here?" Jack looked incredulously towards the partial skeleton.

"The skull tells us a lot, Inspector. I only have to look at the temporal line here . . ." The forensic anthropologist pointed towards the skull which was sitting upright on the table. "Plus, the size and angle of the eye sockets. Both are good indicators of whether a skull is male or female. As is the supraorbital ridge and mastoid process."

Jack was impressed. "And it's definitely female?"

"Without a doubt."

"And the height?"

"That comes from an examination of the femur, just here." Professor Kaufman tapped the longer and larger of the bones on the table. "It's a fairly simple calculation and surprisingly accurate."

"And you estimate under twenty-five?"

The anthropologist nodded. "There are a number of skeletal indicators here. Although I cannot be exact, there are enough to point towards this being a young woman. Certainly below the age of thirty-five — due to the lack of fusion of the sagittal suture. Then the epiphyses at the ends of the tibia and fibula, here . . ." Professor Kaufman pointed towards the two slighter thinner bones next to the femur. "This gives another clue that the person was at the younger end of the age bracket. The teeth are still well preserved, surviving decomposition. And there are two partially erupted wisdom teeth. This leads me to believe the female in question is under twenty-five. I've taken various bone samples to check for bone density and demineralisation. You should also be able to extract some DNA from the femur which may, or may not, help you with identification."

"Wow." Jack shook his head. "I never knew so much could be gleaned from so little."

The professor smiled. "The human body is a wonderful thing, Inspector."

"You wouldn't have any idea as to the cause of death?" Jack was expecting a negative response but asked the question anyway. He was pleasantly surprised by the answer.

"In this case, that would be fairly easy to determine." The forensic anthropologist beckoned Jack to step closer. "You'll see a fracture here to the frontal bone — certainly evidence of some form of blunt force trauma to the front of the skull."

"Enough to kill?" Jack saw the obvious dent and damage to what would have been the victim's forehead.

Professor Kaufman paused and gave a small shrug. "Possibly. But there is another fracture to the base of the skull here." The anthropologist carefully turned the skull over. "The occipital bone at the back has a large fracture line — consistent with another severe blunt force trauma. This one would almost certainly have been fatal due to its close proximity to the brainstem."

"Hit over the head," mused Jack, nodding as the professor replaced the skull on the table. "Twice. Thanks — that's really helpful. Can you tell how long they've been in the water?"

"That is a little more difficult to determine, but there are some further tests we can do. We'll do some carbon dating and see if we can pin it down a little. Could be up to thirty years, but at this stage I would say at least ten."

As Jack watched the professor return his examination equipment to the trolley, he caught Dr Matthews' eye.

"Another difficult one for you, Jack." The pathologist glanced at the bleached-white remains. "I think dental records might be your best bet at an identification. We've already taken X-rays."

Jack started to move towards the door. "I think you could be right, doc. Thanks."

Leaving the mortuary technician to finish up, Jack followed the professor and Dr Matthews out into the corridor. But not before he took one last look at the partial skeleton on the table and made a silent vow to find out who she was.

And how she came to be at the bottom of the Thames.

CHAPTER THIRTEEN

Time: 8.45 p.m.
Date: Thursday 22 May 2014
Location: Kettle's Yard Mews, London

Pouring another two inches of Glenfiddich into the tumbler, Jack returned to the sofa. The TV was on, but the sound was turned down. He didn't really know why he had a TV — weeks could go by before he even switched it on. It was only really when Stu came round that they'd watch the football, or some high-octane car chase movie his brother liked.

Taking a swig of the amber liquid, Jack caught the scrolling headlines on the muted 24-hour news channel. The discovery of Maisie had a small section at the end of the 'news alerts', but nothing more than that. The name had still not formally been released, but this was likely to be the last night the family had before everything hit the fan tomorrow. Their lives from this moment on would never be their own — they would be captives of the press, and the public would scrutinise their lives from every possible angle. Jack gave an involuntary shudder.

And, so far, there was no word about the skeletal remains found earlier today. Even Jonathan Spearing seemed to be keeping his mouth shut, which was a first.

Instead, the TV channels were all full of the run-up to the World Cup in Brazil. A news reporter was following the England team in their preparations, asking the age-old question of whether this time England could do it and finally bring it home. As much as Jack wished they could, he doubted it would happen. After a few minutes he turned his attention back to Maisie. The images of her dismembered limbs and headless torso were still at the forefront of his mind — and he'd only seen the photographs. He wondered how Amanda was doing, knowing how difficult she found post-mortems at the best of times. Part of him felt guilty for asking her to attend something so graphic in his place. He had no such qualms about DC Daniels. The new recruit to the team reminded him of Cooper in many ways — both sharing an almost childlike enthusiasm for something as macabre as a post-mortem. He made a mental note to catch up with Cassidy first thing in the morning — maybe buy her one of those weird chai tea things she was always drinking.

Jack pulled out the preliminary post-mortem report on Maisie Lancaster once more. The details were already etched into his brain, but he went through them again anyway. The same chill ran up his spine as he read the pathologist's account of the inexpert dismemberment. He took another mouthful of whisky to dull the sensation and found his thoughts drifting to the skull and bones he'd seen in the mortuary just a few hours before.

Were they really looking for one killer here? Or, instead, two crazed individuals? Although there would be plenty in London who fit that description, two landing on his patch at the same time made Jack nervous.

Pushing the report and photographs of little Maisie Lancaster's dismembered remains to the side, Jack pondered food. There was leftover Chinese in the fridge but his appetite had now been lost. Just the thought of eating churned his stomach.

Running a hand around the side of his neck, he could almost feel how close Derek Foster had got to throttling him.

In those few heated moments, he'd seen the same hatred and rage in the man's eyes that had been ever present twenty-five years ago.

And with the thought of Derek Foster inevitably came thoughts of Raymond Dixon. The fact that the Lancaster family lived only a few doors away from number 30 Lambert Grove left its own bad taste in Jack's mouth.

For Jack had never forgotten little Carrie-Ann.

An unsolved case that would forever haunt him, no matter how much time had passed.

* * *

Time: 12.30 p.m.
Date: Monday 3 July 1989
Location: 30 Lambert Grove, London EC1

Thirty Lambert Grove sat in the full glare of the midsummer sun, but inside it felt as cold as ice. The newest detective on the team, Detective Constable Jack MacIntosh, stood awkwardly in front of the main bay window, watching Detective Inspector Graham Hobbs trying to console Raymond and Kelly Dixon. With less than two months on the job, even he could see that the boss wasn't comfortable — like the proverbial fish out of water.

The senior officer's voice was clipped, lacking any form of sincerity or compassion, his gestures empty and stilted. Empathy looked to be a vastly alien concept.

"We're doing everything we can to find your daughter, Mrs Dixon." Hobbs' nasal tones grated in the suffocating air. "Let me assure you of that."

All the windows were closed at number 30, despite the soaring temperatures outside. Jack was starting to sweat profusely. He shifted his weight from one foot to the other, desperate to move out of the way of the piercing rays searing through the window behind him.

"And what exactly *is* that?" Ray Dixon's voice was taut while his wife sobbed uncontrollably by his side. "What exactly *are* you doing? Because, from where I'm sitting, it looks like sweet FA."

DI Hobbs visibly bristled. He didn't take kindly to his competence being questioned — especially by people like the Dixons. Here they were, dressed in their fake designer his 'n' hers tracksuits, chunky fake gold jewellery around their necks — and with a top of the range TV and surround-sound cinema system taking up most of the space in the cramped front room. All probably paid for by benefits. The Dixons screamed 'tacky' at him from all available angles.

And from what information had been gathered so far, it seemed as though they let their daughter run riot. Eight years of age and they had no idea where she was most of the time. Not at school that was for sure.

With blaring music, questionable acquaintances coming and going at all hours of the day and night, everyone arguing like cats and dogs — suffice to say, the Dixons weren't the most popular residents of Lambert Grove.

And now they had the cheek to ask *him* if he was doing his job properly, if *he* was making enough effort to find their wayward daughter — someone who they'd systematically failed to keep an eye on for themselves.

DI Hobbs peered down his narrow nose, fixing Raymond Dixon with a cold, contemptuous look. "As I said, we are doing everything we can to locate your daughter. Are you sure you can't think of any places she might go to play, or to hide? Any other friends that you've not told us about?"

Hobbs was sure that the amount of man hours they were wasting on this investigation would eventually result in the girl being located at a friend's house, or merely hiding out somewhere to escape her family. Anything to delay returning to the shabby mid-terrace house along Lambert Grove. Hobbs couldn't really blame her for that.

Not waiting for a response, or maybe not caring if one were provided or not, he rose to his feet. "Well, if there's nothing else, we'll be on our way." He nodded in the vague direction of Jack. "We're done here."

With the door to number 30 firmly shut behind them, DC MacIntosh followed the detective inspector back along Lambert Grove towards their waiting car.

"Don't you think we should be searching the house, sir?" Jack slipped into the passenger seat as Hobbs rammed the keys into the ignition. "There's something about the father that I don't trust."

Hobbs' hand hovered over the ignition. He turned and fixed the young detective with a hardened look. "Not you as well. When I want your input, MacIntosh, I'll ask for it."

"But she's been missing five days now. And she's only eight. What if he's got her in the house somewhere? What if he's killed her? You hear about this type of thing all the time."

The steely expression on the DI's face was accompanied by a snarl. "You were recommended by Detective Superintendent Reece to join my team, MacIntosh. And, at this point in time, I'm starting to question why that was. Tell me, how much experience do you have in being a detective?"

Jack's cheeks coloured.

"Come on, tell me. Don't be shy."

"Two months, sir."

"Two months. And suddenly you're an expert in how to conduct an investigation?" Hobbs twisted the keys and fired the engine into life. "I've been in the force thirteen years, and a DI for the last five. I do not expect to have to listen to mind-numbingly incompetent suggestions from the likes of you. One word from me and you're back in uniform. Got it?" Hobbs swung the car away from the kerb and thundered to the end of the street. "You keep quiet and do as you're told. That way we'll get along just swimmingly."

Jack nodded. "Yes, sir."

* * *

Time: 9.00 p.m.
Date: Thursday 22 May 2014
Location: Kettle's Yard Mews, London

Jack poured himself another generous measure of Glenfiddich. Eight-year- old Carrie-Ann Dixon's body had been discovered in the attic at number 30 some five days later. Jack had fought long and hard to forgive himself over the next twenty-five years.

If only I'd pressed harder.

If only I'd insisted on a search of number 30.

If only I'd had the balls to stand up to Hobbs.

But he'd done none of those things. Instead, he'd done exactly as he was told and kept quiet.

The post-mortem evidence had revealed that little Carrie-Ann had been alive for some time in the attic, although a precise time of death was unable to be given. But Jack couldn't shake the thought that if DI Hobbs had acted on his suggestion to search the house sooner, then the eight-year-old might well have been discovered alive.

It was something no one would ever know for sure.

But there was one thing that Jack *was* sure of — from that day on, his loathing for Graham Hobbs was born and did nothing but deepen as each day passed. The man didn't even have the decency to admit his mistake: in the subsequent internal inquiry he maintained that proper procedure had been followed at all times. The inquiry predictably found in his favour and Hobbs was free to continue his slapdash ways. Nothing changed. No lessons were learned.

But Jack didn't buy it then, and he sure as hell didn't buy it now.

Carrie-Ann Dixon died because of them.

And that hadn't been DI Hobbs' only mistake. The entire case was littered with them.

When eventually the evidence, such as it was, pointed in the direction of Raymond Dixon being involved in his daughter's disappearance and murder, Hobbs had given him enough time to concoct an alibi. An alibi that would later cause him to walk free from court, the case against him for the murder of his daughter dismissed. And the one piece of forensic evidence they *did* actually have, Hobbs had obtained unlawfully — by not following correct procedures. As soon as it was presented in court, the defence barrister gleefully applied for it to be thrown out. The judge had no option but to agree, and the case against Dixon collapsed.

From that moment on, the young Detective Constable Jack MacIntosh vowed to be a better officer — a better detective than the one person he was meant to look up to.

DI Hobbs applied for a transfer to Essex not long after the collapse of the Dixon trial and Jack, for one, was not unhappy to see the back of him. How the man had subsequently made DCI he could never quite fathom.

After Hobbs' departure, Jack's own career had flourished — but he never forgot Carrie-Ann.

As Jack contemplated pouring another generous splash of whisky into his glass, he heard a knock at the door. Glancing at his watch, he noted it was late, but pushed himself up from the sofa and went to see who it was. Before he got there, he heard DS Carmichael's voice.

"It's me, Jack. You got a minute? I've got something more on Quinn."

CHAPTER FOURTEEN

Time: 9.30 p.m.
Date: Thursday 22 May 2014
Location: Kettle's Yard Mews, London

DS Robert Carmichael accepted the glass tumbler without a word and sank a mouthful before speaking. "You do know your door's still bust downstairs? That lock doesn't work. Anyone could just walk in."

Jack nodded. "It's been reported. Several times." He poured himself another measure of Glenfiddich. "You said you had something more on Quinn? Any news where he might be?"

Carmichael shook his head, taking another sip of the fiery whisky. "Nothing like that. This could've waited until tomorrow but . . . I thought you'd want to know. They're looking into it again — the shooting of that banker down in Surrey."

Jack felt a familiar jolt in the pit of his stomach, not helped by the neat whisky. "Looking into it how?"

"Sounds like they're not convinced he was murdered. Or if he was, then they're not convinced it was Quinn who did it."

"Not convinced it was Quinn? I thought there was evidence at the scene that Quinn was there."

Carmichael placed his glass down on the coffee table and fixed Jack with a concerned look. "It's a whole bunch of things, Jack. I just got off the phone with my contact down there. For one, they're looking into his mobile phone records again. Looks like he was home on the night of the shooting."

Jack shrugged in response. "So what? His phone was at home. Doesn't mean he was."

"Maybe. Maybe not. But the phone was used — a call was made at 10.45 p.m. from the handset."

Jack gave another shrug. "Maybe he got someone to use his phone to make it look like he was home. It's the oldest trick in the book, Rob. Surely they're not falling for that one? Any decent detective would see right through it."

"All the same — they're now throwing more resources at it. And then there's the trajectory of the bullet. You know what these ballistics experts are like. Something about the angle of the gun and the entry wound."

"So, what are they saying happened instead?" Jack tried to keep his voice from rising a notch. His throat felt dry, so he took another swig of whisky.

"Apparently the post-mortem showed the victim was riddled with cancer. So maybe it was suicide — which has a knock-on effect for our Mr Quinn."

"It does?" The whisky continued to swirl, uncomfortably, in Jack's stomach. "How so?"

"Well, if this Bancroft fella *did* shoot himself — who was there to make it look like a murder? Can't have been Quinn because why would he frame himself? It makes no sense. Someone else had to have been involved."

"Maybe Bancroft did it himself — set the scene up to frame Quinn before he pulled the trigger."

"Maybe." A smile crept on to Carmichael's lips. "Look, I couldn't care less either way, Jack. It makes no odds to me what happened to him. It's not our case. It's Surrey's problem. But there's one thing that keeps niggling me."

Carmichael paused to pick up his tumbler again and take a sip, eyeing Jack over the rim. "This Roger Bancroft. He dies, and suddenly leaves everything he owns to Isabel Faraday — your soon-to-be sister-in-law. And the guy in the frame for his murder — this James Quinn — is the man you think killed your mother. I don't need to be a detective, Jack, to know that there's more to this than a happy coincidence."

It was at that precise moment that Jack knew the end of the line had been reached. He'd spent much of his working life vowing never to make the same mistakes as Graham Hobbs — priding himself in striving to be an exceptional police officer. There would never be another Carrie-Ann — not in a million years. Not on his watch.

And exceptional police officers didn't lie.

Robert Carmichael was the closest Jack had to a true friend — and the man deserved the truth.

Warts and all.

"Let me top you up, Rob." Jack reached for his best friend's glass. "This could be a long night."

* * *

Time: 8.45 p.m.
Date: Saturday 28 September 2013
Location: The Glade, Church Street, Albury, Surrey

Jack pulled up outside the Glade and switched the engine off. He'd done as instructed, avoiding the main roads as far as possible.

Geraghty had been quite clear on that.

The hire car had tinted windows, and Jack had dutifully worn the baseball cap tugged down low over his eyes. But probably the most alarming instruction, and one that Jack knew he should have questioned at the time, was the wearing of gloves and covering the seats in plastic sheeting before setting out.

And leaving his mobile phone at home.

He sidelined the creeping disquiet that had intensified throughout the ninety-minute journey. Finding James Quinn was more important. How Joseph Geraghty knew of Quinn's whereabouts, he wasn't quite sure — but Jack had long ago stopped trying to second-guess men like Geraghty.

He had never visited Isabel's childhood home, although he'd seen it in photographs. The house was set back from the small, single-track lane and nestled in among mature trees and gardens. A gravelled garden path led up to a wooden front door beneath a shady front porch. On all sides, the house was concealed behind tall, leylandii hedges.

Perfect for hiding behind, mused Jack, as he left the hire car parked by the gate and made his way up the garden path. As he approached, he could see the front door was already open. Hesitating only momentarily, Jack pushed it wider and stepped inside the dimly lit entrance hall.

About to announce his arrival, Jack noticed a movement up ahead. A connecting door swung open and the doorway was filled with the imposing presence of Joseph Geraghty.

"Detective Inspector." Geraghty took several steps forward and came into view. He looked pretty much as Jack remembered him — perhaps a little thinner in the face. His hair was light, with flecks of grey — but whether that was his natural colour, who could ever tell? The man changed his appearance as often as others changed their socks.

What hadn't changed, however, were his piercing eyes. Coloured green this time, from what Jack suspected were tinted contact lenses. His true eye colour was anyone's guess.

As Geraghty continued towards Jack, he noticed there were lines around his eyes that hadn't been there before. The man's cheeks looked a little sunken, his skin tone looking pale even in the dimness of the hallway.

If Jack didn't know any better, Joseph Geraghty looked unwell.

"Do come in." Geraghty waved Jack into the house, gesturing towards a connecting door to the right. "I'll get us some refreshments."

Geraghty led the way into a light and airy living room. It was sparsely furnished, with just the one three-seater sofa and one armchair surrounding a low-level glass-topped coffee table. The room opened out on to a generously sized patio area, where Jack could see pieces of wicker furniture and a brick-built barbeque. The patio doors were open and a cool evening breeze was wafting in from the garden.

Jack removed his baseball cap and felt a thin line of sweat sticking to the inside of his collar. The drive down had been warm and sticky, with no air conditioning in the car and the strict instruction not to open any of the tinted windows. Geraghty had already brought through a tea tray laden with a china teapot and two cups with saucers.

"Tea, Inspector?" Geraghty picked up the teapot and Jack noticed a slight tremble in the man's hand. "Or do you require something a little stronger?"

Jack accepted the cup of tea that he didn't really want and went to sit on the edge of the sofa.

"Let's sit outside." Geraghty headed towards the patio doors. "It seems a shame to waste such a beautiful evening."

Jack frowned a little but followed the man out into the darkness that was now enveloping the garden. The motion-sensitive outside lights sprang into action as Geraghty settled into one of the wicker chairs. It was at that moment that Jack could clearly see the waxen appearance of Geraghty's skin.

As if in response to the question that hadn't yet been asked, Geraghty raised his gaze to meet Jack's.

"I'm dying, Inspector."

Jack's tea cup hovered in front of his mouth. "I'm sorry to hear that."

Geraghty gave a small laugh. "I don't think we need to pretend. I've been a thorn in your side for far too long for any false pleasantries. You're probably thinking, and not without foundation, that karma has finally caught up with me."

Jack sipped the lukewarm, weak tea and took a seat in one of the other wicker chairs.

"Pancreatic cancer," continued Geraghty. "Stage four. It's inoperable. Already spread to my lungs, liver and bones — so it's only a matter of time now."

Jack placed his tea cup on to the wicker table and looked across at Geraghty's pale face. "I don't understand why I'm here. You said you had information on James Quinn."

Geraghty nodded. "And indeed I do, Inspector. But all in good time. Before I impart to you my knowledge about the elusive Mr Quinn, I need you to understand something. Something about this house. And something about Isabel."

Hearing Isabel's name spoken by the man who had caused her such grief made Jack's neck prickle. "Why bring her into this? She has nothing to do with Quinn. Haven't you caused her enough heartache already? I have grounds to arrest you right here, right now."

"I know you do, Inspector." Geraghty paused and took a sip of his tea. "And if that's the course of action you wish to take, I'll not stand in your way. But . . ." Geraghty's pale green eyes hardened slightly in the muted light. "I will then take my knowledge of James Quinn with me to the grave."

Jack gave a slow nod. He knew he was breaking numerous police procedures with just his presence here, but something told him he needed to hear what the man had to say. He could always arrest him afterwards, couldn't he?

"As I said, I'm dying. There's no escaping that fact. My diagnosis was made in Cuba last year — a doctor friend of mine gave me the good news. The paperwork will never see the light of day, so my disease is only known to myself and my doctor. And now you." Geraghty paused. "I took out a life insurance policy a few months ago — but it won't pay out if there is any suggestion I didn't disclose the full extent of my diagnosis — which of course I made no mention of when I applied."

Jack's frown increased. "I still don't . . ."

Geraghty held up a hand. "As I said, Inspector, let me explain. The life insurance has one beneficiary — Isabel Faraday. And in my will, everything I own goes to her.

Including this house." Geraghty paused. "And indeed her parents' trust fund money that I misappropriated."

"Don't you mean stole?"

Geraghty let the comment slide. "Upon my death, everything will go to her. I made a promise to her parents and I intend to keep it."

"You've got very strange loyalties." Jack watched for Geraghty's reaction. "You killed them. I've seen the accident report — you were there."

"I've done many things I'm not proud of, Inspector. But I never wanted to hurt Isabel. I've always tried to protect her."

"Is that why you've been stalking her?"

"Stalking is a harsh way of putting it."

"You've been watching her at the café."

Geraghty took another sip of his tea. "I needed to see what had become of her. How she'd fared in adult life. I can see she's grown into a remarkable young woman, with a thriving business. She deserves to have everything returned to her."

"Look, where are we going with all this?" A tinge of irritation entered Jack's voice. "I came here because you said you had information on James Quinn."

Geraghty nodded. "And I do, but just bear with me a few more minutes. As I say, cancer is consuming my body. It's eating away at me every single day. I don't know precisely how much time I have left, but I know it's not long. And, let's just say, it's not the way I wish to die."

It was then that Jack spied the gun hidden behind the vodka bottle on the wicker table. "So, you want to kill yourself?" He shrugged. "Why do you need my help?"

"Why do I need your help, Inspector?" Geraghty reached into his pocket and brought out a folded piece of paper which he passed across the wicker table towards Jack. "My insurance policy."

Jack took the document and unfolded it. He nodded as his eyes scanned the details. "And this is the name you're going under now, is it? Roger Bancroft?"

Geraghty managed a thin smile. "Yes. I'm a retired banker."

Jack scanned the rest of the policy and nodded. "Isabel is your sole beneficiary in the event of your death. You already said that."

"Indeed. But look at the clauses at the bottom — the exclusions."

Jack's eyes scrolled to the bottom of the paper.

"You'll note how the policy is void if I die by my own hand. Suicide."

Jack began to nod.

"I cannot die from cancer, Inspector. Although I've covered my tracks as best I can with regard to my diagnosis, it's a risk I cannot afford to take. And I cannot die by suicide. The policy will be null and void either way."

Jack's eyes flicked towards the handgun. "You're not asking me to . . . ?"

Geraghty gave another small laugh. "No, no — nothing quite so abhorrent, Inspector. Although I'm sure that there's a small part of you that might relish the thought of pulling that trigger. No — I need you to do something else for me. For Isabel." Geraghty paused. "I need you to stage a murder."

* * *

Time: 10.00 p.m.
Date: Thursday 22 May 2014
Location: Kettle's Yard Mews, London

"Geraghty planned it all. He planted Quinn's DNA in his house — hairs, fingerprints on a pint glass — and hired a car in Quinn's name. I was just the pawn to bring it all together." Jack slugged back another mouthful of whisky. "I helped him set the scene, then drove the car back to London, parking it close to Quinn's home address."

Jack could see the questions piling up inside Rob Carmichael's head.

"I needed justice for my mother, Rob. Quinn killed her and he's got away with it for over forty years. This way, at least, he'd go down for something."

"And what did Geraghty get out of it?" Carmichael's glass was empty and he helped himself to another measure, emptying the bottle. "This elaborate plan of his?"

Jack hesitated. Geraghty's motive was becoming less clear. All he could do was shrug. "I guess he just wanted to die."

"Did you pull the trigger?" It was a question Jack had been expecting. "Or just set the scene?"

The bottle of Glenfiddich stood empty on the coffee table. The enormity of what Jack had just disclosed warranted another bottle, but neither of them had the energy to move. Sometimes the truth sapped your strength.

Pinching the top of his nose with his thumb and forefinger, Jack closed his eyes. "I think the less you know the better, Rob. Neither option paints me in a very good light."

Carmichael had to concede that that was probably a fair point. Jack had crossed the line — it was just a question of how big a step he'd taken.

"You think this hunt for Quinn could come back and bite you? If Surrey are looking into it again, you think they might discover Quinn was nowhere near Surrey that night? That his alibi might stack up?"

Jack exhaled, his eyes glassy from a combination of the effects of the whisky and lack of sleep. "I honestly don't know. I'm more worried about Isabel, though. The insurance company's already coughed up on the basis it was murder."

Carmichael leaned forward loosening his tie. He sank the rest of the whisky in his glass. "I need you to level with me, Jack. I don't particularly want to know what happened, but please tell me there's nothing out there to link you to the scene? Nothing to put you in Surrey that night? You did cover your tracks, right?"

Jack hesitated. Was there anything? Eventually, he shook his head. "No — everything was taken care of. Geraghty planned it to perfection. I was careful. I'm clean."

"Well, that's something, I suppose." Carmichael rose from the sofa, glancing at his watch. "Leave it with me. I'll keep an ear to the ground. Let you know what else I hear."

Jack nodded his thanks and walked with Rob to the door.

"Just don't do anything stupid."

Jack gave a half laugh as Carmichael crossed the threshold and stepped out on to the landing. "When do I ever do anything stupid, Rob?"

With a deep sigh, Carmichael jogged down the stairs and disappeared out of sight. Jack lingered for a few moments, listening for the communal door opening and closing below before he stepped back inside his flat.

'Tell me there's nothing out there to link you to the scene?'

Carmichael's words echoed as Jack made his way towards the kitchen in search of that second bottle of whisky.

'Nothing to put you in Surrey that night?'

Jack hadn't been entirely truthful in his answer.

He still had the gun.

CHAPTER FIFTEEN

Time: 7.00 a.m.
Date: Friday 23 May 2014
Location: Metropolitan Police HQ, London

Jack hid his bloodshot eyes behind his coffee mug. After Rob had left, he hadn't really slept — instead he'd opened the second bottle of whisky, sat by the open window in the living room, and watched the world waking up before heading into the station before sunrise. As he took a fortifying mouthful of the strong black coffee, he still couldn't get Carrie-Ann Dixon out of his mind.

Yesterday's trip back down memory lane, or Lambert Grove to be more precise, had been somewhat unexpected — and distinctly unwelcome. Jack didn't need any reminders about his shortcomings that day. People could tell him over and over that it wasn't his fault — that his senior officer made the decisions, not him — but he felt responsible all the same. You pulled on the uniform, metaphorically speaking, and that made you responsible. There was no way Maisie Lancaster was going to become another Carrie-Ann. Not if he had anything to do with it.

And right now, Maisie deserved the team's undivided attention.

Clearing his throat, Jack took another mouthful of bitter black coffee and eyed his team. It was an early start, but no one seemed to mind. "Overnight, we had a result on the DNA taken from Sara Lancaster — confirming a mitochondrial match to the body parts in the suitcase. Therefore, we're as sure as we can be that this is Maisie Lancaster. What we don't know, however, is how or why she met her death. Or who was responsible. Her name is likely to be released to the media sometime today — we can't hold off much longer. DC Anderson remains in place at the Lancaster's house to ward off any press intrusion." Jack paused and glanced towards DS Cassidy. "How do you both feel after yesterday's post-mortem? It can't have been an easy one."

Cassidy, nursing the cup of chai tea Jack had bought her from the expensive deli around the corner, managed a weak smile. "I just want to find the monster that did it."

Jack nodded. "Talk me through the Lancaster family tree."

Cooper brought up a picture of Maisie Lancaster on to the interactive whiteboard, matching the photograph Jack had already tacked to the cork pin board. "Initial enquiries into the family confirms Russell and Sara Lancaster as the parents. Sara is twenty-five years of age — having had Maisie when she was seventeen. Her husband, Russell, is a little older at twenty-nine. Maisie was their only child. Both sets of grandparents are still alive. Mrs Lancaster's parents live here in London — Derek and Maggie Foster. They live just a couple of minutes' walk away on the next street. Mr Lancaster's parents live in South Wales. Sara Lancaster has one sister, living in Kent, and Russell Lancaster has two brothers, both of whom live in Watford."

Jack gave a slow nod. The first whiteboard had already been annotated with details of the Lancaster family tree. No one needed to mention that statistics showed a high proportion of child murders were committed by someone they knew, often within their own family unit. Jack's eyes settled on the names of Derek and Maggie Foster — Sara Lancaster's parents — and the familiar gnawing sensation started to spread.

Taking another sip of the scalding coffee, he pushed away the image of Carrie-Ann lying in the attic of her family home. Now was not the time. "Well, like it or not, we'll have to speak with each of them." Jack could already visualise the carnage when they started to question family members. Tempers were likely to flare, they always did. Instinctively, his hand went to his neck, still able to feel where Derek Foster's hands had grabbed him.

Jack turned his attention back to his team. "And where are we on the last known whereabouts of Maisie?"

Cassidy opened her notebook. "Maisie was last seen playing in the front garden at her home address on Lambert Grove on 14 May. It's only a small patch of grass enclosed by a low wall, and she could easily be seen from the window of the family's front room. At five o'clock, Sara Lancaster went to call Maisie in for her tea, but she was nowhere to be seen. She initially thought Maisie might've gone to see her grandparents — Maggie and Derek Foster. They live just around the corner on Hartington Crescent, so she wasn't unduly concerned. When Maisie still didn't come home, Sara Lancaster called her mother. Learning that Maisie wasn't there, the Lancasters scoured the road outside, but couldn't see her anywhere. They then called the police."

"Any CCTV along Lambert Grove?"

Cooper shook his head. "None of Lambert Grove is covered, boss. Neither is the road where the grandparents live. It's a complete blackspot. The nearest cameras are three or four streets away."

"Check them anyway — the nearest fixed cameras too. From mid-afternoon onwards. And double check what house-to-house statements are on the system. Somebody must have seen something."

"I made a start on some of the house-to-house last night, guv." Cassidy inched her chair closer to her desk, taking a fortifying sip of her chai tea. "Statements were taken from most of the residents of Lambert Grove on the evening of the fourteenth, and several more in the following days. There was one from a Mrs Rita Hamilton, from number twenty-seven, that caught my eye. She says she saw a silver coloured car in the vicinity of Lambert Grove around the time Maisie was last seen. It was driving quite slowly along the street, as if someone was lost. She didn't get the registration." Cassidy paused and looked up from her notes. "I gave her a call last night — asked her more about the car. She managed to recall that it started with a BM — her late husband's initials — and now feels sure it was a Vauxhall. And — this is the good bit — now she's had time to think about it, she's sure she's seen it in the street before. Parked at the side of the road."

"OK, sounds promising. It might be a long shot, but let's check the database and see how many silver Vauxhalls beginning with BM we have registered in the area. And maybe pop back and see her once we know more." Jack paused to drain the rest of his coffee, the caffeine hit finally breaking through the dullness inside his head. His stomach growled with the lack of breakfast and the liquid dinner he'd consumed last night. "Moving on — as you all know, the area where Maisie was found is now also the site of another set of remains. I attended the preliminary examination at the mortuary late yesterday afternoon. The remains belong to another female, aged approximately eighteen to twenty-five. So far just a skull and three leg bones have been recovered. Elliott and his team undertook another excavation of the area at low tide overnight, and I'm told they've found what appears to be more remains plus some kind of metal chain, which may or may not be connected. Everything has been transported back to the lab and is being analysed as we speak — with any luck, we'll get an update later on today."

DC Daniels grabbed a marker pen and stepped up to begin updating the second whiteboard with the details of the second set of remains.

"Do we think this is just an unhappy coincidence — Maisie washing up at the same location?" Cassidy nodded towards the whiteboards as she sipped her chai tea, some colour returning to her cheeks. "They're not connected?"

All Jack could do was shrug in response. "At this stage, we don't know. The second set of remains have clearly been in the water much longer — Dr Matthews and Professor Kaufman estimate it could be anything up to twenty or thirty years, certainly at least ten. For now, we investigate them separately, but we'll keep an open mind. A priority is getting an identification for this second victim. The doc says DNA should be recoverable so we'll just have to wait and see. Our best bet is likely to be dental records, though. Cooper — can you chase that up? X-rays were taken yesterday and the search set in motion last night."

"Boss." Cooper flicked open his notebook. "I'll give Jenny a call. She might be owed a favour or two and get it fast-tracked."

Jack nodded his thanks. "Let's just hope our victim was a regular visitor to the dentist. Start with London-based records, then move out. While you're at it, Cooper, see where they are with analysing that metal chain." Jack then turned his attention to Daniels. "Daniels — start trawling the database again for anyone reported missing in the age bracket eighteen to twenty-five. Start with thirty years ago — so 1984 — and work forwards."

"Boss." Daniels snapped the lid back on the marker pen and returned to his computer.

Jack faced the first whiteboard again — and the Lancaster family tree. "And, like it or not, we're going to have to talk to the Lancaster family. Amanda, can you drop by the family home this morning and catch up with DC Anderson — see if he has anything new to tell us from overnight. Then phone the sister in Kent and the two brothers in Watford. Get some family background. Cooper, you take the grandparents in Wales. But tread carefully everyone. Emotions will be running high."

CHAPTER SIXTEEN

Time: 8.00 a.m.
Date: Friday 23 May 2014
Location: Metropolitan Police HQ, London — Cold Case Unit

Leaving the rest of the team following up leads in the incident room, and DS Cassidy heading out to the Lancaster house, Jack jogged down the final set of steps. There was something to be said about being underground — away from the hustle and bustle of the floors above. Everything appeared calmer, quieter — tranquil, even.

Reaching the bottom step, he glanced at his phone. No signal. To some that would be a problem but, to Jack, it was a welcome bonus. Down here you could be unreachable. Undetectable. And he liked that idea — he liked that idea a lot.

Jack hadn't been down to the basement in a long time. Accessed via just the one set of stairs at the rear of the station, the long-promised provision of a lift never quite materialising, it wasn't generally somewhere you went by accident. But as quiet and serene as the basement was, Jack knew there was nothing serene about the work that went on down here. The unsolved case squad — otherwise known as the Cold Case

Unit — were a tightly-knit bunch that kept themselves to themselves. Like moles, they very rarely popped their heads up above ground level. Which was another aspect of the job that appealed to Jack — especially after his run-in with Derek Foster.

But it was a unit that was held in high regard by all. The tenacity and dedication they showed in finally bringing justice to those that had waited the longest wasn't forgotten by anyone who worked above ground.

Detective Inspector Jane Telford was expecting him.

"Jack," she greeted, holding out a hand as Jack entered the subterranean maze of offices that made up the Cold Case Unit. Her grip was light, and the smile that crossed her face was genuine. "Good to see you. Come on through."

Jack followed DI Telford through a set of double doors and eventually into a medium-sized room with row upon row of metal shelving lining the walls. Every inch was stuffed full of buff coloured folders, lever arch files, and stacks of cardboard boxes. The square room understandably had no windows, and a series of overhead strip lights illuminated their way. Being in a room without natural light or ventilation would be some people's idea of hell, but Jack instantly felt at home. It was somewhere you could be completely separated from the craziness of the world above. He could see the attraction.

"You were asking about the Dixon case?" DI Telford's words brought Jack back to the land of the living. "From 1989?"

"Yes, yes I was." Jack gave a nod and a lopsided smile. "Sorry, I know you must be up to your eyes in other things."

"Not a problem." Jane Telford's eyes shone, and her tone was light. "I've dug everything out for you. Was there something in particular you were looking for?" She nodded towards the stack of boxes and folders littering the table in the centre of the room.

Jack hesitated. If he was honest, he wasn't quite sure where he was going with it himself. Just what was it he was expecting to find? The Lancasters living on Lambert Grove, only doors away from Carrie-Ann, was something that refused to leave his head. But he knew he needed to tread carefully — the Cold Case Unit might be buried deep underground, but word had a habit of spreading. Especially if those words involved Jack MacIntosh. It wouldn't take long for those higher up, in both the building and rank, to get a waft of whatever it was he'd been sniffing around.

"Not really." Jack eyed the boxes on top of the table. "Raymond Dixon was the prime suspect in his daughter's murder, back in the summer of 1989. Do you know if he's still living there — in Lambert Grove?"

Jack knew he could find this out for himself via other means. It was really an excuse to get down here for himself and lay his eyes on the original case evidence. Which was something that wasn't lost on DI Telford. She gave him a mischievous smile and motioned for him to take a seat.

"He is. Sit yourself down and I'll bring you up to speed."

They both took a seat at the large wooden table. "We conducted a cold case review on this not so long ago — you know we have a revolving system that brings up each unsolved case for periodic review?" Jane Telford peered over the top of her wire-framed spectacles. Jack nodded. "Since our last review in 2011, Raymond Dixon has served eighteen months of a three-year sentence for the fraudulent use of a credit card. Convicted in 2012, he was released towards the end of last year and as far as we know returned to live at number 30 Lambert Grove."

Fraud? Jack wasn't sure of the relevance, but tucked away the piece of information anyway. "Does his wife still live with him? Kelly Dixon?" He reached for a stack of folders and began leafing through.

DI Telford lowered her eyes to the paperwork in front of her. "We suspect they may have had a parting of ways after his most recent conviction. She's not been seen at the house for some time."

"And he's still your main suspect for Carrie-Ann's murder?" It was more of a statement than a question.

"I think you already know the answer to that, Jack." The DI's smile continued to twitch. "I'm intrigued, though. What's the real reason you've made the trip down here? It's not for the coffee, that's for sure." She nodded at the ancient vending machine in the corner.

Jack paused, weighing up his options. He'd met Jane Telford many times before, and she was one of the good ones. Quick thinking, yet thorough. With a sharp eye, not much got past her. He had a feeling he could trust her.

"I have a vested interest in the case of Carrie-Ann — you know that already. But I'm investigating the murder of another young girl, Maisie Lancaster — who just so happened to live on Lambert Grove. Only a few doors away from the Dixons."

DI Telford's eyes widened. "The body in the suitcase? And you think Ray Dixon could be your man?"

Jack shrugged. "I'm not sure what I think to be honest. It's unlikely, I know. There's been a twenty or so year gap between offences if it *is* him. And I have no evidence yet that he's implicated, other than living on the same street. But there's something niggling me about it. I had a bit of a run-in with Derek Foster yesterday, which got me thinking."

"Foster? I know that name." Telford rummaged back through the paperwork. "Close family friend of the Dixons at the time, wasn't he?"

"The one and the same. And he also happens to be the grandfather of my current victim."

Telford's eyebrows hitched. "I can see why it rang a bell. Small world."

Jack nodded. "And he certainly hasn't lost any of his animosity towards the police over the years — well, towards me, mostly."

"I can't say that surprises me." Telford tried hard to suppress a grin. She tapped the pile of folders in front of her. "We have it all in here. Accused you and Hobbs of 'fitting up' his best friend — I believe those were the words he used. And harassing the entire family. And failing to catch Carrie-Ann's real killer." A smile twitched at her lips once more. "It makes for quite impressive reading."

Jack didn't need reminding. "You said you'd carried out a recent cold case review? Did you come up with anything new?"

The smile on DI Telford's face slipped a little. "Unfortunately not," she sighed. "The case is rather unique. We know who did it — we just can't prove it. Not to the threshold required, anyway. Without any fresh evidence the CPS aren't interested and our hands are tied."

"No DNA? Techniques were pretty rudimentary back then." Jack knew the answer would be in the negative.

Predictably, Telford shook her head. "We've retested all the evidence preserved from the scene — the clothing she was found in, and the duvet she was wrapped up in. There's nothing new. We never found the clothes she was wearing when she disappeared, though, which was odd. And the one piece of forensic evidence we *did* have — well, you know what happened about that."

Jack did. DCI Graham Hobbs' face swam back into focus.

As if reading his mind, Telford cocked her head to the side and regarded Jack from across the table. "Have you spoken to Hobbs about any of this?"

Jack baulked at the mere mention of the man's name. "No. We don't exactly see eye to eye."

The smile returned to DI Telford's lips. "I heard about your run-in with him last year. I seem to remember the word 'twat' was mentioned?"

Jack's eyes widened, causing the DI's smile to turn into a giggle. "We might be buried someway underground here, Jack, but we still surface for air from time to time."

Jack couldn't help but mirror the broad smile on Telford's face. "Well, he was a twat . . . and still is. He's the reason Dixon walked free back in 89. *And* he's the reason we didn't find Carrie-Ann soon enough." Jack's hatred for his former boss surprised himself sometimes. Twenty-five years may have passed but his loathing for the man hadn't diminished one jot.

"I appreciate what you're saying, Jack. But it is what it is. We can't turn the clock back and conduct the investigation all over again. As much as we'd like to."

Jack knew what she was saying was true — but it didn't make it any easier to swallow.

"Can you keep me up to speed — let me know if anything changes?"

Telford nodded and flashed another smile. "Of course. And likewise — if anything comes your way investigating that poor little girl's murder that implicates Dixon, I'd appreciate the heads up."

"Will do."

"I'll get a summary put together — key facts and evidence on Dixon. His previous convictions, and so on. Maybe a fresh photo if we have one. I'll let you have it as soon as. And don't be a stranger." Telford got to her feet. "You're always welcome down here, Jack. No appointment necessary."

"Thanks." Jack stood up from the table and headed for the door. Part of him wanted to stay beneath ground, safely out of sight — even if the coffee was ropey.

But the floors above were calling.

* * *

Time: 10.00 a.m.
Date: Friday 23 May 2014
Location: Metropolitan Police HQ, London

"They want to see her." DS Cassidy waited for Jack to take a seat. "The Lancasters. They want to see Maisie."

Jack sighed and nodded. He'd been expecting it, but maybe not quite so soon. "It's understandable, I guess. But it's not something I would necessarily recommend." He watched Cassidy's pale face nod in agreement, no doubt still visualising the headless torso from the mortuary slab. "I'll go back and see them myself in due course. Try and persuade them that it might not be the best idea. Anything else useful from your visit?"

Cassidy got to her feet and strode over to the whiteboard where the Lancaster's family tree was annotated. She picked up a marker pen and started to add some more detail.

"I spoke to James while I was there. He's already spoken to most of the family. Sara Lancaster's sister in Kent has MS and is unable to travel without assistance. She's offering what support she can by phone. As for Russell Lancaster's brothers, both have cast iron alibis for the time Maisie disappeared. Derek and Maggie Foster were both at the house during my visit, and I detected a bit of an atmosphere. I didn't feel like I could stay much longer."

Jack gave another nod. "Thanks. Anything else?"

"Russell's parents." Cooper flicked several pages over in his notebook. "I managed to speak to them both. They live in a retirement complex in South Wales, just outside Cardiff. Mrs Lancaster, senior, is essentially housebound with crippling arthritis — her husband is her main carer. They're both in their seventies and don't own a car. I think we can safely cross them off the suspect list."

"Agreed." Jack reached for the fresh mug of coffee by his side, noticing it was still black. He took a sip, grateful for the extra sugar Cassidy had slipped in. "So that just really leaves Sara and Russell Lancaster, and the Fosters. I'll speak with them myself — they could be a little prickly."

"Something else came in while you were downstairs, boss." Cooper handed Jack a print-out. "The list of recently released violent offenders."

Jack skim read the piece of paper. There were nine names — but only one had been highlighted. "What's the relevance of this one here, Cooper? Darren Hughes?"

Cooper pulled the keyboard towards him and woke up the interactive whiteboard. "Well, you'll recall the statement of Rita Hamilton that Amanda mentioned earlier — the woman who saw a silver Vauxhall car in the vicinity of Lambert Grove around the time Maisie went missing?"

Jack nodded.

"Well, I ran a DVLA check like you asked on vehicles in the area starting with a BM . . ."

Jack looked back down at the print-out in his hand. "And you found one registered to this Mr Hughes?"

"I did," beamed Cooper, twirling a biro between his fingers and looking pleased with himself. "A silver Vauxhall Astra. And Hughes was recently released from prison after serving twelve years for attempted murder."

"Tell me more." Jack watched as the image on the whiteboard screen changed to that of a police mug shot.

"Hughes was involved in an altercation on the Delaware Road in Clapham in October 2000. At the time, he was working as a taxi driver. According to the witness statement of the male passenger he had with him at the time, the taxi was overtaken by a blue Ford on the approach to a set of traffic lights. By all accounts the Ford cut him up and almost caused a rear-end collision. The witness recalls Hughes shouting and swearing out of the window as they waited for the lights to turn green. Once on the move, Hughes tailed the Ford, honking his horn and gesticulating through the windscreen. At some point, the car in front slammed on the brakes, causing Hughes to take avoiding action and mount the kerb, almost ending up wrapped around a tree.

"Hughes flew out of the taxi and headed across to the Ford. The witness lost sight of him for a few seconds but recalls seeing him running back towards the taxi with a look of, and I quote, 'the devil' on his face. Hughes went straight to the boot of the taxi, and the witness recalls him emerging seconds later with a spanner. The witness didn't see the attack itself but saw Hughes running back towards the Ford. Hughes then reappeared after about a minute with the bloodied spanner still in his hand. The witness states that at that point he exited the taxi and ran for his life."

"Smart man," commented Jack.

"How the victim didn't die is beyond me, but Hughes got slapped with twelve years for his trouble." Cooper minimised the screen and leaned back in his chair. "And he just so happens to have a car similar to one seen around the time Maisie disappeared."

Jack nodded, not taking his eyes from the image of Darren Hughes for a second. "Good work, Cooper. You can come with me to pay this delightful chap a visit."

"You think he could really be a suspect for Maisie?" Cassidy unwrapped a cereal bar to go with her tea, the colour finally returning to her cheeks along with her appetite. "It seems quite a leap from beating the living daylights out of someone with a spanner to dismembering a small child."

"I hear what you're saying, and I agree. On the face of it, the offences are wholly different. But we'll go and see him anyway, ask him where he was on the day Maisie disappeared. See where his car is. Are we any further on with forensics from the suitcase?"

DC Daniels raised his hand. "Preliminary report came in a few minutes ago. The suitcase was manufactured by a company called Maine and Maine, sometime between 1983 and 1985. The company no longer exists and ceased making this particular style in 1985. Initial tests confirm that the case most likely hadn't been submerged in water — there's no water damage and no significant trace of Thames water in any of its fibres, other than where it came into contact with the riverbed. They're confident that the case must've been dumped on the banks at low tide and not washed up from further upstream. They're sending further samples for DNA testing."

Jack nodded. "So that fits with what Dr Matthews was thinking and narrows the window of opportunity for our killer. High tide was just before six the previous evening, and low tide peaked at twenty-two minutes past midnight. Our dog walker, Charlie Somerville, stumbled across it at around half past midnight. Which means, by my reckoning, the killer dumped it sometime between roughly six and midnight."

Jack folded the print-out of released offenders and slotted it into his pocket. "Right, Cooper, get your jacket. Let's go and see this Darren Hughes. While we're gone, Daniels, keep trawling the Missing Persons database for a name to go with our bones — and Amanda, get the CCTV from the bridge reviewed for the time we think the case was dumped, and carry on reviewing the house-to-house along Lambert Grove. See if anyone else mentions this car."

CHAPTER SEVENTEEN

Time: 11.30 a.m.
Date: Friday 23 May 2014
Location: Flat 3a Ash Road, SE Soho, London

Darren Hughes sat on the edge of the cheap, plastic kitchen chair and continued to roll his cigarette. He'd looked at both Jack and DS Cooper with what could only be described as disdain before grudgingly stepping aside and letting them into the cramped, one-bedroomed, ground-floor flat. Leading them into the kitchen, no offer was made of tea or coffee — which Jack wasn't altogether upset about as he spied the piles of cracked and unwashed dishes in the sink.

A thick layer of grease covered the cooker, and the heavy aroma of chip fat clung to the air. The only window above the sink was welded shut by mould.

Jack stood motionless in the doorway, watching as Hughes rolled the flimsy cigarette paper around what he hoped was tobacco. Something else wouldn't have surprised him, but busting the guy for possession of illegal drugs wasn't part of Jack's schedule for the day, and would only create a mountain of additional paperwork that his in-tray didn't need.

As the empty silence continued, Darren Hughes eventually looked up, licking the side of the paper to finish the job and then popping the sagging cigarette into his mouth. His dry, chapped lips curled up at the corners as he narrowed his gaze.

"My my, it's the Sweeney." Hughes started to cackle at his own joke — a laugh that quickly turned into a hacking cough. Jack could almost hear the man's ribcage rattling. Once the cough had subsided, he lit the cigarette and inhaled sharply. "So, what can I do for you boys? If you could make it quick, I'm a little busy today."

Jack resisted the urge to quip a reply. From the evidence decorating the plastic-topped kitchen table, Darren Hughes was a very busy man indeed. A battered tobacco tin lay open with a line of cigarette papers next to it, waiting to be filled. An open can of premium strength lager rested on the morning newspaper, which was open at the horse racing section with various horses already ringed and starred.

"We'll try not to keep you," he replied, his tone laced with enough sarcasm to earn a grin from Darren Hughes.

"That's what I like to see. A copper with a sense of humour."

"I take it you live here alone, Darren?" Jack felt he knew the answer to that question but asked it anyway.

It earned another crackling cough. "What d'you think?" Hughes swept an arm around the greasy kitchen. "Does it look like I've got a woman with me?"

"Could be a man," suggested Jack, his expression stony.

Another laugh turned into an eruption of chesty phlegm. "My, my — a copper with a progressive outlook. The filth really are being more progressive these days. Well done you."

Jack's patience was beginning to wane. "Do you know the Lancaster family from Lambert Grove?"

Darren Hughes was shaking his head almost before Jack had finished his sentence. "Nope. Don't know 'em."

"Are you sure? Think again."

Hughes narrowed his gaze. "I'm perfectly sure. I've a good memory for faces and names."

"OK, let's try another. Where were you on the afternoon and evening of Wednesday the twenty-first of May?"

"Don't you have to caution me or something?" A crooked smile crept across Darren Hughes' pock-marked face as he drew in another lungful of cigarette smoke. "I'd hate for you to get into trouble."

"We're just having a quiet, good-natured conversation," replied Jack, edging further into the kitchen. "I haven't said we suspect you of anything. Just helping us with our enquiries, that's all." He paused at the edge of the grease-infested table. "If you'd rather come down to the station under caution, then I'd be more than happy to oblige."

Hughes smiled, showing an uneven row of broken and blackened teeth. "I'm just jesting. But no, I don't know them — whoever it was you mentioned. And I was here all day and all night. Part of my licence conditions, you see. I'm a good boy now."

"Anyone who could corroborate that?"

"Nah." Hughes sucked in more cigarette smoke. "Home alone, watching TV."

"Hmmm." Jack's expression remained unimpressed. "When were you released?" He already knew but wanted to keep the man talking.

"October. Last year."

"And you spent how long inside?" Again, it was information Jack already had at hand, but apparently you could tell a lot about a person the more they talked. He remembered that little nugget of wisdom from one of the mind-numbing courses he was forced to attend on occasion. *Progressive Interview Strategies* had it been called? *Waste of Time* was more apt. "What was your sentence?"

"As if you don't already know," laughed Hughes, reaching for the can of lager and taking a swig. "I served twelve years. Let out on good behaviour." He again cackled and coughed at his own joke.

"And how was prison? Rushmore towards the end, wasn't it?"

The question momentarily seemed to stump Darren Hughes, stopping him mid-cough while a frown crept across his forehead. "How was it?" The frown was followed by a shrug. "It was prison. I've been in worse."

"Do you own a car, Mr Hughes?" Jack hadn't noticed a vehicle matching the description they'd been given parked anywhere outside.

Hughes shook his head and took another swig of lager. "Nah. Walk everywhere, me."

Jack and Cooper exchanged a look.

"What about a Vauxhall Astra, Mr Hughes? DVLA still has one, registration number BM12 ONS, registered to yourself at this address." Jack watched as Darren Hughes flicked cigarette ash on to the plastic-topped table before responding.

"Not anymore. Got rid of it ages ago."

"You sold it?" Jack's eyebrows raised a notch. "Who to?"

Hughes shrugged. "Bloke down the pub. Can't remember his name, can I?"

"I don't know, Mr Hughes. That's why I'm asking."

Hughes sucked in a lungful of tobacco. "Nope, can't recall the guy's name. Was a while ago now."

"You do realise that it's an offence not to inform the DVLA of a change of ownership?"

Darren Hughes exhaled, the smoke spiralling up towards the already nicotine-stained ceiling. "So, arrest me. I'll come quietly, I promise!" His face broke out into a grin.

Taking one last look around the dishevelled kitchen, Jack signalled to Cooper that they were done. Before leaving, he slid a business card on to the sticky kitchen worktop. "In case you remember anything after we've gone, Mr Hughes."

Stepping on to the pavement outside Hughes' ground-floor flat, Jack took in a breath of much sweeter London air. Darren Hughes might not be a model citizen, and might live in grime-infested, grease-laden squalor, but they had no reason to suspect him of anything untoward. Failing to notify the DVLA that you had sold your car wasn't exactly the crime of the century. But was he a murderer? The question forming in Jack's mind was mirrored by Cooper as they made their way back towards the Mondeo.

"You think he's our killer?" the young sergeant asked. "Hughes?"

Jack unlocked the driver's door and hesitated, casting a brief look back at the peeling paintwork of flat 3a before ducking into the car. "I'm not sure, Cooper. Are you?"

Cooper slid into the passenger seat. "He seemed kind of normal — well, normal for around here, anyway. Nothing shouted 'killer' at me as I went through the front door. Although public health could probably do with taking a look in his kitchen."

Jack pulled the Mondeo away from the kerb. "They could indeed, Cooper."

"But then again . . ." Cooper gave Jack a sideways glance. "Maybe his conviction for attempted murder was just a practice run. Maybe he got it right this time."

* * *

Time: 12.00 p.m.
Date: Friday 23 May 2014
Location: Flat 3a Ash Road, SE Soho, London

Darren Hughes stared at the door long after Jack and DS Cooper had left.

That had been close.

Too close.

After a while he let a faint smile grace his unshaven face. They'd been standing no more than six feet away from where the little brat's head was stuffed in his freezer — and they had no idea.

He took a swig of vodka straight from the bottle.

Sometimes the coppers couldn't see things when they were right under their pig-like snouts.

Pushing himself up from his chair by the greasy kitchen table, he swiped his phone up and glanced at the screen.

Still no reply.

Where was his money?

He'd virtually spent all his benefits for the week already. And hadn't made any of his loan repayments.

He shuddered, taking one last look at the freezer door.

Maybe it would be his own head in there if he didn't get himself straight soon.

Another shudder.

With another swig from the bottle, he gathered up the racing pages of today's *Daily Mirror* and decided to head to the bookies with his last tenner. Maybe his luck would change.

And at least he had Gina.

* * *

Time: 12.10 p.m.
Date: Friday 23 May 2014
Location: Metropolitan Police HQ, London

Jack and Cooper entered the incident room to see DS Cassidy squinting closely at her computer screen.

"Good, you're here," she announced, looking up. "Bad news on the CCTV front. The cameras at both ends of the bridge were out of action on the night we think the suitcase was dumped."

"Really?" Jack frowned and rubbed his chin. "That's extremely fortunate for our killer."

"You think he knew, or just bad luck on our part?" Cassidy reached for her mug of tea then wrinkled her nose as she realised it was stone-cold.

"Who knows." Jack headed for one of the whiteboards and wrote Darren Hughes' name up in red letters. "Our visit to see Mr Hughes wasn't exactly enlightening. Home alone on the night in question. Nobody to verify."

Cooper unwrapped the bacon roll he'd picked up from the canteen on the way in and slumped into one of the vacant chairs. "When he says he was home alone — don't you think someone like him would've concocted some sort of alibi? If it was really him? He knows the system better than we do."

Jack watched as Cooper wrapped his mouth around the soft white bread, the smell of bacon fat taking him back to the grease-laden kitchen at Ash Road. Jack's stomach growled, but the thought of food was unappealing. "You would've thought so, Cooper. But he doesn't look like the brightest star in the sky. We'll keep him on the board for now. First rule of policing — rule nothing out, rule everything in. Let's run a full ANPR check on that registration. Hughes' explanation about selling the car to a bloke down the pub isn't something we can prove or disprove, but I want to know where it's been — both on the day Maisie was last seen and on the night she was dumped."

In their absence, DS Cassidy had pinned a map to the wall, coloured pins marking various pertinent locations — London Bridge and the discovery of Maisie; Lambert Grove, the home of the Lancasters; Charlie Somerville's home in Southwark; and now Ash Road where Darren Hughes lived.

Jack stepped across to peruse the map. Ash Road was a fair distance from London Bridge, certainly by foot. Could someone really transport a body that distance without being seen? "Let's try and get some CCTV and fixed camera footage from around Ash Road and Soho. See what pops up." He glanced behind him. "And where's Daniels?"

"Still trawling the Missing Persons database," replied Cassidy. "He's down in the Tech Suite — it's cooler there and he's got the place to himself. He's not surfaced for ages." Pushing herself up from her seat, she crossed over to the hot water urn to make a fresh round of drinks. On the way, she stuck a Post-it note on the edge of Cooper's computer monitor. "Jenny rang while you were out. Asked if you could call her back. Something about the dental records. And . . ." An impish smile crossed Cassidy's face as she handed Jack a black coffee. "DI Telford came up to see you — she was disappointed you weren't here. Think you might have an admirer there, guv!"

Jack narrowed his eyes over the rim of his mug. "Did she want anything in particular?"

"Came to give you a photograph." Cassidy handed the picture to Jack. "Said you'd know what it was about."

The man in the photograph looked older than the one Jack remembered — but he had the same harsh, steely grey eyes. And, in Jack's view, they were the eyes of a killer.

With his free hand, Jack turned to pin the image to the cork pin board — next to Maisie Lancaster.

"This is Raymond Dixon." Jack tapped the photograph and fought to keep his revulsion for the man out of his tone. "Twenty-five years ago, his daughter Carrie-Ann disappeared from the family home at 30 Lambert Grove. Ten days later, her body was found in the attic. Dixon was the main suspect and was eventually charged with her abduction and murder. Unfortunately, at his trial, the prosecution was forced to concede the case and offer no evidence after a vital piece of forensic evidence was ruled inadmissible by the judge. As the prosecution had nothing else, and Dixon had a watertight alibi, the case collapsed, and the man walked free."

"And does he still live in Lambert Grove?" Cassidy eyed Raymond Dixon's unshaven and unwashed face. Bloodshot eyes stared out from beneath hooded eyelids.

Jack nodded. "Still at number 30, according to DI Telford. Only a few doors up from the Lancasters — and Maisie."

"You think they know each other? Him and the Lancasters?" Cassidy sat back down at her computer, blowing across the top of her fresh peppermint tea.

Jack nodded and ran a finger around the inside collar of his shirt. "They do — at least Sara Lancaster's parents do. Derek and Maggie Foster, whom we've already met, were friends with the Dixons throughout the 1980s and 90s."

"And you think this Dixon killed his own daughter — Carrie-Ann?"

"I *know* he killed his own daughter." The muscles in Jack's jaw clenched. "The man's a murderer, no question about that."

Cassidy frowned. "So . . . he could also have killed Maisie?"

Jack hesitated. "I'm not sure. I like him for it more than I do Darren Hughes, if I'm honest. But . . ." Eventually Jack had to shrug and took a sip of his bitter black coffee. "Again, it's a different kill method — Carrie-Ann was raped and suffocated, with no evidence of any attempt to dismember." Jack held the image of Raymond Dixon in his gaze. Something was beginning to niggle at him. "But if he did kill Maisie, I'm not letting him get away with murder for a second time. Let's run a check on any vehicles he might have registered in his name. And mobiles. Anything and everything. I want to know if Dixon so much as sneezed around the time that Maisie went missing."

CHAPTER EIGHTEEN

Time: 2.30 p.m.
Date: Friday 23 May 2014
Location: London Bridge, SE1

The tide was on its way out and would be at its lowest in about half an hour. Elliott adjusted the elasticated hood from his protective suit and squinted up at the sky. At least it was clear with no threat of rain — but the sun was unseasonably hot, beating down uncomfortably on to his shrouded head. Trickles of sweat inched their way down his back.

Due to the pack of journalists who had descended on the scene that morning, they had erected screens around the site of yesterday's discovery. But the hacks had soon melted away once they realised the river wasn't giving up any more secrets today — and, for now, the bridge above was quiet.

Elliott hopped across the metal stepping plates, heading towards the edge of the receding waters. Bob Snowden was again crouching down low over the silt banks and, as Elliott approached, he noticed the experienced investigator's posture change a little. With his back and shoulders straightening, Bob raised his right hand.

"Here."

Elliott was by his side in a matter of seconds, kneeling down on to one of the wider stepping plates. He soon saw what had grabbed Bob's attention.

Watching as the investigator carefully continued to peel away more layers of muddied silt, Elliott saw the unmistakable appearance of bleached bone peeking through the mud. As more shingle and silt was scraped away, more bone was exposed.

Elliott jumped to his feet and waved towards where his deputy was standing by the stationary forensics van. They needed a tent. And fast. The media would descend like rabid dogs once they smelled a fresh story.

"Colin!" Elliott cupped his hands around his mouth to help the words travel across the river bed. "We need a tent. Over here. Now!"

Colin Ashman started pulling the equipment from the back of the forensics van, while Elliott pulled out his phone.

* * *

Time: 2.30 p.m.
Date: Friday 23 May 2014
Location: Riverside Café, London Bridge, SE1

Jonathan Spearing had retreated to the pavement café at the entrance to the bridge over an hour ago. He'd been watching the activity beneath the bridge since mid-morning. Something had told him that today was the day for a big story. Call it a journalist's nose, or a hack's intuition — but *something* was going to happen. And Jonathan Spearing was going to be there when it did. But the morning dragged by and slowly all his fellow hacks gave up and disappeared, no doubt heading back to their newsrooms. They didn't have the perseverance that Spearing did — which was what set him apart from the rest, making him a reporter everyone loved to hate — or hated to love, depending on your perspective.

The waitress brought him his second cappuccino. With the sun high in a cloudless sky, he felt a faint trickle of sweat run down his back beneath his faded Nirvana T-shirt. He could go inside, sit in the shade, but then he might miss something.

He pulled his laptop closer. He had an outline for an article in his head but just needed that one, attention-grabbing headline — the one golden nugget that none of the other papers would have.

Just as he opened up the draft article, Spearing heard his phone ring, his editor's name flashing up on the screen. It was the third call so far that day and, as with the previous two, he silenced the call and placed the handset in his laptop bag. He knew what it would be about — instructions for him to delegate the London Bridge story, if there even *was* a story, to a more junior member of the team, and for Spearing to move on to something more important. Namely the phone hacking scandal that had rocked the media industry for goodness knows how long.

But Jonathan Spearing wasn't interested in phone hacking — scandal or no scandal — and had dug his heels in. This story was his — no one else's. He knew it was more than just a body found in a suitcase. The renewed activity beneath the bridge told him that much. And when the story broke, he wanted to be there in the thick of it. Not listening to some tedious phone hacking trial.

Even with the noise from the traffic crossing the bridge, Spearing's sharp ears managed to pick up the sound of a voice. Pausing, his hands hovering over the top of his keyboard, he listened again. The voice sounded as though it was coming from beneath the bridge. Abandoning the cooling cappuccino, he slid his laptop into its bag and raced across the street.

Peering over the side of the bridge, Spearing immediately spotted the crime scene manager, a man he knew to be called Walker, talking animatedly on his phone. Behind him, another investigator was dragging a white tent out of the back of a van. Spearing grabbed the camera from around his neck and quickly reeled off a series of shots.

He felt his stomach flip.

This could be it.

The white tent was quickly and expertly erected, but not before Spearing had managed to get a few close-up shots of the activity beneath. With his zoom lens, he could clearly see that they'd found something buried in the silt. Was it the head? He felt his heart quicken at the thought.

Putting the lens cap back on his camera, Spearing started to turn away — but not before he spied the figure of Elliott Walker staring up at him from the muddied banks beneath. He gave the man a small wave and smothered a laugh. Walker still had his mobile clamped to his ear and Spearing could only guess who he might be talking to.

Jogging back along the street towards the Tube, the journalist glanced at his watch. He had plenty of time to make the evening news deadline.

* * *

Time: 2.45 p.m.
Date: Friday 23 May 2014
Location: Metropolitan Police HQ, London

Jack put the phone down and ran a hand over his chin. He couldn't remember when he'd last shaved — but the roughness beneath his fingertips told him it was at least a couple of days ago. Elliott's call had been short and to the point.

More bones.

Jack tapped his biro against the side of his empty coffee mug. Questions flooded his brain in a relentless procession. Were they looking at the same set of remains as before? Or a new body? Getting to his feet, intending to go and find his team, Jack heard his mobile ring once more.

Thinking it must be Elliott, he scooped up the handset. "Elliott . . . ?"

But it wasn't the crime scene manager this time.

"Detective Inspector, how lovely to speak to you. How are you feeling today?"

The unmistakable tone of Jonathan Spearing's voice filled Jack's ears. He felt his jaw clench. "How did you get this number?"

"Mere details, Jack my friend, mere details. But I'm really glad I managed to get hold of you. I was surprised not to see you down here today — at the bridge. Especially after what they've just found."

Jack's veins turned to ice. "You need to vacate the area, Spearing. Don't interfere. Let them get on with their job."

"Oh, I will Jack. I will. I've got everything I need, for now. I just wondered if you'd care to comment?" Jonathan Spearing's nasal voice paused. "I mean, more bodies? Where will it all end? Just how many people have been buried beneath the bridge, Inspector? Right under your nose. I think the public have a right to know, don't you? Should they be worried?"

Silence hung between them, and Jack fought the almost irresistible urge just to hang up. But Spearing wasn't likely to give up. He'd file his story, with or without Jack's help.

"What do you want to know, Spearing?" Jack wearily slumped back down into his chair. "You've got five minutes."

CHAPTER NINETEEN

Time: 5.25 p.m.
Date: Friday 23 May 2014
Location: Metropolitan Police HQ, London

It had taken most of the afternoon, but at last DC Daniels thought he was getting somewhere. It astounded him just how many missing person reports there'd been, even when applying the parameters of sex, age and location. The sheer volume of names that the search had thrown up had initially daunted him — but by focusing on one year at a time, he started to make headway. By the time he reached 2004, his eyes felt gritty from the glare of the screen.

As he ploughed on through, it became apparent that the vast majority of those reported missing either returned home or were located safe and sound elsewhere in the country. There were some who unfortunately didn't return home alive — but their number was, thankfully, small in comparison. Tiny, even.

But then there were the missing — those that simply disappeared without a trace.

The missing.

Daniels put down his pen and flexed his neck. He'd been sitting in the same position for the last five hours, and his spine was protesting. Stretching his arms above his head, he heard a click. It was some eight months now since the Bishop case, but the after-effects were still very much with him. His body didn't seem to have the same level of stamina as it had before — not that he mentioned that at his return-to-work interview. He tired more quickly and ached each and every morning. He wondered if some of it was simply due to his new role. In the Traffic Division, he was used to being out and about on patrol on a daily basis, but since becoming a DC his time spent behind a desk had increased fourfold.

Which wasn't good for anyone's posture.

He felt a small smile tug at his lips. Maybe he should take Amanda up on her incessant cajoling to increase his activity levels — hardly a day went by without her trying to get him to come to some kind of yoga or Pilates class. Hot yoga — wasn't that the thing she was into now? He hadn't a clue what it involved and was scared to Google it.

After another stretch, he resumed his search. He'd narrowed it down to a handful of women reported missing between 1984 and 2004 — but there was one which stood out over and above the rest. Something in his gut told him she was the one.

Narelle Williams was formally reported missing by her parents on 27 September 1994 — but, in reality, she hadn't been seen since 31 August. She was an Australian national, working her way around Europe for the summer. According to the brief report Daniels had managed to find, Narelle had arrived in London on 27 March, after spending the previous six weeks in Germany. Her only known address was at a block of flats on Connaught Road, and at the time of her disappearance she'd held down two jobs — one in a café, the other in a pub by the Thames.

The file contained very few further details, other than a couple of photographs. It would seem that after the initial standard investigations had been made, the search for Narelle had faltered. As her backpack, clothes and passport were all missing, it had been assumed that she'd merely carried on with her travels. It was only due to her parents' dogged insistence that disappearing without a word was so unlike their daughter, that the case stepped up a gear. But the delay had taken its toll on the investigation — vital time had been lost, and the trail was already cold.

As far as Daniels could tell, the file ended there. The trail, such as it was, had dried up and become stagnant.

To back up his suspicions, he'd searched the online database for newspapers in circulation at the time and very quickly managed to find several articles reporting Narelle's disappearance.

The first appeared in the *Evening Standard* on 28 September 1994, some four weeks after the last sighting of her. It was a small piece at the bottom of page seven.

'*Australian backpacker missing.*'

A small black and white photograph of a young woman accompanied the article.

The next was three weeks later — another small report buried on page nine.

'*Still no sign of missing Australian teen.*'

Then there was nothing.

And no trace of Narelle Williams was ever found.

Daniels checked the date of birth recorded in the file. 21 March 1975. Which would have made Narelle nineteen at the time she went missing. A young girl living in London, in the prime of her life, had literally disappeared into thin air — to all intents and purposes she'd dropped off the face of the earth.

Daniels hit 'print' and listened as the printer spat out what limited information he had managed to glean from Narelle's file. As he went to go and collect the paperwork, the door to the Tech Suite swished open and DS Cooper rushed inside.

"How're you getting on with the missing person files, Trev?"

Daniels scooped up the papers sitting in the printer's out tray and waved them in the air. "Think I might have someone."

Cooper crossed the floor and held up his own sheet of paper. "And I've got a match on the dental records."

The two detectives swapped paperwork and for the next few seconds a heavy silence descended on the Tech Suite. Eventually they both looked up. It was Cooper that spoke first.

"Let's go and tell the boss the good news."

* * *

Time: 5.45 p.m.
Date: Friday 23 May 2014
Location: Metropolitan Police HQ, London

Jack took another look at the towering piles of paper on his desk and sighed. He didn't know why he was so surprised. He hardly ever saw the bottom of his in-tray, let alone the surface of his desk.

As he leaned back in his chair, he felt the vertebrae in the base of his spine crack. Cassidy had suggested he join the Force's five-a-side football team, a suggestion that had been met with a not unexpected amount of laughter and derision from his side. Nobody needed to see him puffing his way around a football pitch, albeit a small one, chasing after a ball that he was never going to catch up with.

He assured Cassidy that, as flattered as he was with her interest in his health and wellbeing, he was happy with his creaking back and stiff shoulders. It was nothing that a good shot of a decent single malt couldn't sort out.

As if tapping into Jack's thought processes, a swift rap at the door was followed by DS Carmichael's head appearing around the door frame. "You fancy grabbing a pint after you're done here? Or maybe something stronger?"

Jack beckoned Carmichael inside. "Sure. I'm just about finished, as it goes." He averted his gaze from the offending files piled on his desk. They had waited this long, they could wait another day. And he could do with a drink. But before Jack could reach for his jacket, the door swung open again.

"Boss, you need to see this." Daniels strode past Carmichael, holding out the sheaf of printer paper on Narelle Williams. "I'm pretty sure I've found her."

Jack took the papers and skim read the details. "Narelle Williams. Disappeared in the summer of 1994, aged nineteen. Lived and worked in London. Sounds promising." He looked up, noticing Cooper hovering in the background. "From the look on your face, Cooper, you've got something to add?"

Cooper's grin widened. "Sure have, boss. Jenny sent this. Dental records found a match and it's the same name. Narelle Williams. Visited an emergency dentist on the fifth of July 1994 for a partially erupted wisdom tooth."

Instantly, Jack heard Professor Kaufman's gentle tone.

'The teeth are still well preserved, surviving decomposition. And two partially erupted wisdom teeth . . .'

"Look, I'll catch you later. Sounds like you're in the middle of something." Carmichael headed back towards the door. "Perhaps a drink at yours? Call me when you're leaving."

Jack nodded as Carmichael departed, his attention drawn to another print-out Cooper was waving in front of his nose.

"I followed up on the metal chains like you asked." Cooper handed Jack several more sheets of paper, one of which contained a series of colour photographs. "Jenny put together a brief preliminary report for us. There's more to come but this is what they've got so far." Cooper paused, letting Jack take in the brief details. "The chain is rusted and corroded, but it's survived the elements, more or less. Initial tests found microscopic fragments of bone embedded in the metal. Preliminary results give a ninety-nine per cent match to the DNA from the skull and femur. They're doing more tests."

Jack studied the photographs. A weathered portion of metal chain sat in the middle of the forensic laboratory bench. Relatively innocuous, if it wasn't for the fact that it had been sufficiently close to the recently discovered skeleton to attract bone fragments. In Jack's eyes there could only be one conclusion.

"I think we can safely assume our victim — whom we now believe to be a young woman by the name of Narelle Williams — was tied up and weighed down by these metal chains, her body sinking to the bottom of the Thames." Jack took another look at the laboratory photographs and sighed. "Where she's been buried in the silt for the last two decades, never to be seen again."

Until Maisie Lancaster turned up in a suitcase.

"They've run some more tests on the skull, too." Cooper nodded towards the report. "More microscopic fragments, but this time they're from some kind of fabric embedded in the bone."

Jack looked up at both of his detectives. "Good work, both of you. But we'll need to tread carefully with this one. Not a word gets out until we're sure. Daniels — get me everything you can find on Narelle Williams. Anything about her disappearance in 1994 and any subsequent investigation. In particular, details of her next of kin. Cooper, get me the dental records confirmation in writing. I need that before I can even think about contacting her family."

Cooper and Daniels headed out of the door and Jack returned his gaze to the forensics report — in particular the image of the skull.

Narelle Williams.

After twenty years at the bottom of the Thames, it looked like the river was finally giving up its secrets.

And, not for the first time, Jack wished that the dead could speak.

CHAPTER TWENTY

Time: 8.55 p.m.
Date: Friday 23 May 2014
Location: Niko's Café, Sunderland Street, London

Gina wiped her brow with the back of her hand and sighed. Her feet ached so much she felt as though she could quite happily sink to the floor and never get up. But the thought of coming into contact with the tacky stains on the aged linoleum kept her upright. There was no telling what bacteria might be glued to its surface.

She'd pulled a double shift, having started at five o'clock that morning, and it was now approaching nine. It was backbreaking work at times, without much more than an occasional five minutes to gulp down some water — but she needed the money.

Niko Georgiades kept his café open twenty-four hours a day — and soon the night-time clientele would be shuffling through its doors. Mostly taxi drivers and the odd shift worker from the nearby hospital, there would be a steady stream of customers throughout the night. She knew she could have offered to work right through — but a triple shift would just about finish her off.

Reaching to collect the last stack of dirty plates, the smell of fried egg and bacon filled her nostrils — along with a heavy stench of cooking oil. It clung to the back of Gina's throat and almost made her gag.

"Gina, stop slacking, girl!"

The sound of Niko Georgiades' voice cut into Gina's tired thoughts. She turned around to see the man himself filling the door frame that led back into the kitchen. His more than ample belly strained at the tightly fitting white apron tied around his waist — well, it had probably been white at the beginning of the day, but was now decorated with every ingredient on the all-day breakfast menu.

Sweat dripped from his brow and trickled down to meet his flabby jowls. Sniffing, he wiped his bulbous nose with the back of his hand and coughed up a globule of phlegm, spitting into an empty paper cup on the side of the counter.

How the place had earned itself a three-star rating for hygiene, Gina couldn't fathom. The kitchen was horrendous — cooking oil and other fats stuck to every available surface, and the walls thick with grease. The dishwasher had packed up weeks ago, so now they had a young kid, who looked no more than twelve, rinsing plates and cooking utensils by hand in lukewarm, dirty water.

And the sink had seen better days, too. Cracked and chipped, a thin layer of grey slime settled over the surface no matter how much detergent was used — which, judging by the rancid smell from the waste pipe, wasn't a great deal.

And as for dishcloths — Gina was certain she had seen the same ragged, grey cloth used for the last six months.

Six months. That was how long she'd been working at Niko's café. Six long, hard months.

But she couldn't complain, not really. Mr Georgiades asked no questions and paid her the minimum wage in cash — which, with her job history, Gina knew was probably about as good as she was going to get.

And it wasn't all bad. She could eat for free — although she'd learned that lesson quite early on and now brought in her own homemade sandwiches — and the hours were good. If you considered working a sixty to seventy-hour week as good.

Gina pulled the stack of dirty plates towards her and headed for the kitchen. Mr Georgiades stepped out of her way, but not until his hulking figure had brushed up against her for the briefest of seconds. Gina swallowed the nausea that threatened to engulf her and pushed past.

The smell of his stale body odour followed her into the kitchen. That, mixed with the lingering aroma of cooking oil, made her stomach churn. Dumping the stack of plates into a sink full of lukewarm water, a film of congealed fat already on its surface, Gina felt her phone vibrate. The accompanying 'ping' told her it was a text message.

The sickness she felt in her stomach, both from the stale cooking smells and Mr Georgiades' body odour, deepened.

Another text message. She knew who it would be from. And what it would say.

Wiping her hands on her apron, she pulled her phone out of her pocket. Her hands shook as she unlocked the screen.

'*Payment tonight. No more excuses.*'

Fresh nausea welled up inside her.

"Gina!" Niko Georgiades waddled into the kitchen, a reproachful look on his flabby face. "No phones on shift. How many times do I have to tell you?"

Gina jumped at the sound of his voice, almost dropping the phone into the slimy water. "Sorry," she mumbled, slipping the phone back into her pocket. She backed away towards the fire exit, illegally wedged open with an ageing fire extinguisher that hadn't passed a safety inspection in years. She grabbed her jacket from the peg by the door. "I'll be going now."

Pulling off her apron, she rolled it up into a ball. She'd take it home and wash it overnight in the bath — it might still be damp in the morning, but it was better than nothing.

Mr Georgiades grunted and went to slap more streaky bacon into a heavy-duty frying pan, with a generous portion of lard. His next round of customers would be in soon, demanding their full English fry-up. Gina suspected that something else went on in the dark confines of the café overnight — not just the consumption of fat-riddled, heart-attack-on-a-plate breakfasts. Card games and gambling, for sure — and alcohol was definitely sold under the table. Maybe worse.

Gina pushed the thoughts from her mind. It wasn't her problem, so long as she got paid at the end of the week. What they did, legal or otherwise, was none of her concern. As she hovered in the fire exit, pulling on her jacket, she turned back to face Mr Georgiades.

"Is . . . is there any chance of an advance on my wages?"

The thunderous look that flashed in her direction told Gina all she needed to know on that score. He'd given her an advance last week, and the week before that. Whatever compassion and goodwill he possessed, which admittedly wasn't much, looked to have been exhausted.

Gina scuttled out into the night. She just about had enough change to get there, but when she turned up empty-handed — again — there was no telling what might happen.

The thought made her shudder.

Turning to vomit in the gutter, she ran the final few yards towards the bus stop.

* * *

Time: 9.45 p.m.
Date: Friday 23 May 2014
Location: Metropolitan Police HQ, London

Jack hung up the phone and sighed. It wasn't news that he would ordinarily deliver over the telephone, but the Williams family lived ten thousand miles away in Brisbane, and a personal visit wasn't on the cards – not on his budget. After delivering the bad news to Gregory Williams, Jack organised officers from the local police force to offer them whatever support they needed. Mr Williams had thanked Jack and indicated that both he and his wife would fly to the UK just as soon as they could book flights.

Jack stressed that they didn't need to rush, but Narelle's father had been adamant. If their daughter had been found after all this time, then they wanted to be there. And soon.

Jack didn't mention the discovery of Maisie Lancaster's remains in the suitcase. The Williams family had enough to process right now. And, in any event, Jack had no reason to believe the cases were connected. Not yet. On the face of it, how could they be?

Rubbing his eyes, Jack noticed the time. There was little else he could do tonight that couldn't be done in the morning. He'd managed to send the rest of the team home for a well-deserved break, but knew they would be back in as soon as the sun rose in the morning. Reaching for his jacket, Jack noticed DS Carmichael reappearing in the doorway.

"Ready for that drink?"

* * *

Time: 9.45 p.m.
Date: Friday 23 May 2014
Location: Flat 3a Ash Road, SE Soho, London

"What d'ya mean you don't have it?" Darren Hughes fixed Gina with a hard stare. "I've already given you a payment holiday, Gina. More than one, if I recall."

"I know, I know." Gina had been sick again, after getting off the bus. The thought of turning up with no money had torn her insides to shreds. "I tried to get an advance on my wages, but . . ." She let the sentence fizzle out as the look on Hughes' face darkened. She was running out of excuses, she knew that. And maybe running out of time, too.

"Gina, Gina. Whatever am I going to do with you?" Darren Hughes' voice took on a softer tone, but Gina wasn't fooled. She saw the way he looked her up and down, his hungry eyes roaming every inch and curve of her body. Mr Georgiades did the same at the café. Neither had touched her yet, but that didn't mean they wouldn't. The thought made her shiver.

"You do know the debt increases each time you turn up empty-handed? I'm not a charity, Gina."

Gina merely nodded.

"When I took on this debt of yours, I did it as a favour. I felt sorry for you. The Carson brothers, they were a nasty lot to get involved with." Hughes stood up and went over to the draining board, pulling two grimy-looking glasses out of the pile waiting to be washed. He brought them back to the kitchen table and proceeded to pour a generous measure of cheap vodka into each. "The Carsons aren't people you want to get on the wrong side of." He held up one of the glasses and nodded at Gina to take a seat. "Your debt is now mine — and they aren't renowned for their patience. You see how you turning up here empty-handed again causes me problems?"

Gina nodded once more. Everything was screaming at her to turn and run. But her legs refused to obey her brain and, instead, she sat as instructed and took hold of the tumbler. "I know, I'm sorry. I'll pay you double next week."

Hughes resumed his seat opposite and swept his own glass to his lips. Judging by his hooded, glassy eyes it wasn't the first one of the day. Or night. "Promises, promises." He gave a stomach-churning wink across the table.

Gina squirmed in her seat. How had her life been reduced to this? A couple of bad decisions and look where she'd ended up. Well, maybe that wasn't strictly true. It had been more than a couple of poor choices — and she only had herself to blame.

But she was trying to get herself straight — get herself out of this godforsaken hole that she'd managed to dig for herself. She owed money — *a lot* of money — but she was determined to pay it off. Determined to come out the other side and get Rosie back.

"How's that daughter of yours?" It was as if he could read her mind. "When was the last time you saw her again?"

Gina felt her cheeks redden and a hot flush envelop her body. Darren Hughes repulsed her. As did Mr Georgiades from the café. But she suffered both of them in the vain hope that one day she would get to see Rosie again.

Rosie was who she was doing all this for. Working all hours in a crappy greasy café — all for the chance of a better life. A chance at a new start with her daughter. She just needed to get rid of this spiralling debt first and get the leeches she'd managed to attract to crawl back into the gutter where they belonged. *Then* she could be free.

"You know, when the Carsons first told me about you, I knew you were something special." Hughes edged his plastic chair closer to Gina, topping up his glass as he did so. Gina's eyes widened in trepidation. He might not appear very strong — a bit weedy looking with thin arms and a narrow waist — but she had no doubt that he could overpower her if he wanted to. People like that always could.

She sat rigidly in her chair, her hand clasped around the glass of vodka, yet she had no intention of letting a single drop pass her lips.

"So, that's why I decided to help you out," continued Hughes. "You owed them a lot of money, and I could see their patience was wearing thin. You needed rescuing. They don't call me The Fixer for nothing, you know."

Gina dropped her gaze to her lap. She wasn't proud of what she'd done. She'd hit rock bottom and got herself mixed up in something she should have known to avoid. But she'd needed a place to stay — and rent was never cheap in London. The Carson brothers had offered her a way out. A regular income, cash she desperately needed to support Rosie. But she had been naive, so very, very naive. No one ever gave you something for nothing, not in this world. The money had come at a price — a heavy one.

Indebted to one of the biggest crime and prostitution gangs this side of the river, Gina was forced to do whatever they asked. And if she didn't . . . the very thought made her feel sick. No one said 'no' to the Carson brothers. Not if they valued their life.

And all the while her debts increased. No matter what she did, she always ended up owing more.

And Rosie had been in the middle of it all. Exposed to drugs, prostitution and worse. It was no life for a child — no life for anyone, but definitely not for a child.

"Go on, then. When was it?" Hughes dragged Gina's thoughts back to the present. "This year? Last? Not exactly mother of the year material, are you?"

Gina felt her jaw clench. Despite fearing what Hughes was capable of, the fire she felt inside when anyone spoke about her daughter was as overwhelming as ever.

"I'm going to get her back." Gina's voice was quiet but firm.

Hughes chuckled, which then turned into a hacking cough which he subdued with another mouthful of vodka. "Well, we'll see about that, won't we. You've got some work to do to get this debt paid off first."

"I told you, I'll pay double next week." Gina had no idea how she would manage to do that, but if she had to work triple shifts and endure Mr Georgiades' roving eye on an almost constant basis then she would. She'd do anything for Rosie. Next week was her sixth birthday. She'd been promised a phone call — not a visit, not just yet, but a phone call was a start. She couldn't afford to mess this one up.

"Forgive me if I don't hold out much hope of that," quipped Hughes, emptying the rest of the vodka into his glass. "I think we need to work out a new payment plan."

The words hung in the stale air like a noose, and Gina's stomach tightened. "I'll get you the money," she whispered. "I'll get it to you next week, I promise."

Darren Hughes brushed Gina's words aside and downed another mouthful from his glass. His eyes sparkled through the alcoholic haze. "We'll see. But in the meantime, let's try it my way. Get yourself back here Sunday night — seven o'clock — I'll have some friends waiting. Wear something short, low-cut."

Ice flooded Gina's veins. She pushed her glass, with the vodka untouched, back across the table. "I don't do that any-more," she croaked. "Please don't make me."

A hardness entered Hughes' eyes, the muscles on his unshaven jaw clenching. "Once a whore, always a whore. You'll do as you're told — or you'll never get to see that brat of yours again."

Gina blinked back the tears that pricked her eyes. "Please," she whispered again. "Anything but that."

"Too late." Darren Hughes pushed himself up out of his chair and threw the empty vodka bottle into the sink. "You've had more than enough warning. Sunday night. Don't be late."

* * *

Time: 10.05 p.m.
Date: Friday 23 May 2014
Location: Kettle's Yard Mews, London

James Quinn was pleased that Jack had decided to live in a quiet street, where the dark descended to a depth not usually seen in central London. Even in the thick of night, London was very rarely truly dark.

But here? Here was different. Here you really *could* disappear.

The car's dashboard clock blinked with each passing minute as he settled down to wait, and the tinted windows afforded him the luxury of invisibility.

Nothing moved, nothing stirred. Kettle's Yard Mews was silently slumbering.

He'd had some time to think since his last visit to Kettle's Yard Mews. Seeing Stuart MacIntosh had momentarily caught him off guard, but the more he thought about it, the more he liked the idea. Both together — it could work. With any luck, the younger brother would call by again tonight.

And this time he would be ready.

A movement out of the corner of his eye caught Quinn's attention. With his own presence obscured by the tinted windows, he turned his head to see a shadowy figure looming into view.

Holding his breath, Quinn slipped his hand into the outer pocket of his coat and gripped the cool metal of the handgun. Even with thin nylon gloves covering his hand, he could feel the gun's texture beneath his grip. His finger rested lightly on the trigger.

He couldn't wait to blast a hole in Jack MacIntosh's head. His brother, too. The satisfaction that single act would bring fed his resolve each and every day. It had been some time since he'd been certain of DI Jack MacIntosh's involvement in Roger Bancroft's plan to frame him. The plan had been ambitious to say the least, some would say foolhardy, but had been well executed – up to a point. And if he hadn't got cold feet at the last minute, and vacated his poky lodgings, things could have turned out very differently.

The old James Quinn would never have fallen for it, never have let himself be reeled in quite so easily. But that James Quinn had been gone a while — out of the game for far too long. The all-too-familiar feelings of anger and frustration bubbled beneath his skin. Well, the old James Quinn was back now. And he wouldn't be making that kind of mistake again.

As he watched Jack move further into view, a fleeting image of Stella MacIntosh flashed into his mind. He'd loved her once — at least, he'd thought he had. It was hard to tell sometimes — the past was often just a heady mix of random memories. But she'd been a beautiful woman — of *that* he was sure. With such exquisite bone structure and poise, she really had been a cut above all the other girls he had employed. He'd known that from the first moment he had laid eyes on her.

But she'd got ahead of herself — thought she was more important than the man who had literally picked her up from the gutter and showed her the finer things in life. *Saved* her. Suddenly, she'd started to have opinions.

Yes, he'd definitely loved her once.

But even Stella MacIntosh had had to go.

Realigning his fingers around the grip of the gun, Quinn silently opened the car door. He'd recently oiled the hinges to ensure it made no sound, and the darkness swallowed him whole as he stepped out into the street. By now Jack was heading towards his front door, obscured by a row of parked cars, and Quinn almost tripped over his own feet in his haste.

He'd been so focused on Jack, that he hadn't seen the second figure following on behind. Just in time, Quinn melted back into the blackness, unseen and unheard. Momentarily thinking that Stuart MacIntosh had accompanied his older brother home, Quinn's hand tightened around the gun. Lady Luck could be with him tonight, after all.

But as he watched both figures enter the building, Quinn quickly saw it wasn't Stuart MacIntosh accompanying his brother home — the second man was taller and broader. He had the unmistakable look and gait of a police officer, even in the dark. Quinn loosened his grip on the gun and slipped back towards the car.

Having already switched off the interior light, he slunk back into the driver's seat and closed the door soundlessly behind him. His hand remained curled around the grip of the gun inside his pocket, his palm thick with sweat inside his glove.

It was still relatively early, but he couldn't sit here forever — all it would take would be one nosy neighbour and his cover could be blown in an instant. Turning the key in the ignition, he fired the engine and pulled out of Kettle's Yard Mews.

Another time, MacIntosh.

Another time.

CHAPTER TWENTY-ONE

Time: 10.15 p.m.
Date: Friday 23 May 2014
Location: Kettle's Yard Mews, London

Pulling two bottles of Budweiser from the fridge, Jack handed one to Carmichael before collapsing on the sofa. The call to Narelle's parents had ended the day on a solemn note. He might have been ten thousand miles away but he knew the sound of grief when he heard it. Taking a swig from his beer bottle, Jack banished the thoughts as best he could.

"Tough day?"

Jack nodded. "You could say that."

"I couldn't help but overhear — you got an ID on the bones found under the bridge?"

Jack nodded again, followed by another swig from his bottle. "Narelle Williams. I just got off the phone speaking to her father — they're in Australia. Flying out first chance they get."

"Must've been a shitty call to have to make."

"You're not wrong there, Rob. You're not wrong there."

"Linked to your body in the suitcase?" Carmichael knew Jack well enough to know how his mind worked.

This time there was no nod and Jack merely stared at the label on the beer bottle in his lap. Eventually he raised his eyes. "You know me Rob. No such thing as a coincidence."

"Just connections you haven't found yet." Carmichael lifted his bottle in the air before taking another swig. "Good luck with it, mate."

Jack gave a rueful smile and decided to ask the question that had been on his mind all day. He didn't want to, but felt he had to.

"You heard any more about Quinn?"

Carmichael gave a shake of his head, draining his bottle in one. "Not much. Surrey still have no idea where he is."

"Well, he's good at staying hidden. We know that already. I'm not holding my breath."

Carmichael shrugged. "That may be so, but the guy's no Houdini. He'll slip up and show his face at some point."

"Maybe." Jack wasn't convinced. Noting his friend's empty bottle, he heaved himself up off the sofa and went to collect two fresh beers from the fridge. Neither of them had spoken about food, but Jack noted the remains of the Chinese from Stu's visit a couple of nights back were still there if they got desperate.

Accepting the fresh bottle, Carmichael snapped the lid off with a bottle opener. "The only thing they did mention was that they were resuming the search for the gun."

Jack took hold of the bottle opener but avoided Carmichael's gaze.

Robert Carmichael knew Jack too well to be fooled.

"Tell me you don't still have it, Jack?"

Jack snapped the lid off his second beer, and wordlessly motioned for Carmichael to follow him. Flicking on the bedroom light, he crossed over towards the solitary wooden chair tucked away in the corner by the window — Stu's battered teddy bear propped up on top.

Jack picked the bear up and turned towards Carmichael. The frown on his friend and colleague's face told him all he needed to know. It was now or never — this was one secret he could no longer afford to keep. And there was no one he trusted more in this world right now than Detective Sergeant Robert Carmichael.

Flipping the bear over to reveal a row of carefully placed stitches beneath the thinning fur, Jack picked up a small pair of nail scissors from the window ledge. Pausing only briefly, he began to unpick the thread.

When the gap had widened enough to fit a hand inside, Jack removed several fistfuls of soft white stuffing together with a plastic evidence bag.

Carmichael's eyes widened. "Is that what I think it is?"

Jack gave a quick nod in response.

Carmichael took a step closer, not taking his eyes from the gun that could be clearly seen through the transparent plastic bag. "And the bullets?"

"Inside." Jack held up the deflated teddy bear where another smaller plastic bag could be seen still nestled in the remaining stuffing.

After what seemed like an eternity, Carmichael merely nodded and went back to the living room. Jack returned the gun to the safety of Stu's childhood teddy bear and joined him.

"No one saw me that night, Rob. I'm sure of it. My car remained parked outside here all night. My phone was inside the flat the whole time. None of the cameras en route could've picked me out. And we cleaned the scene down to remove any trace of me being there. It was textbook."

"That's as maybe, Jack, but why have you still got the gun? Whether you pulled that trigger, or Bancroft did it himself — and I'm not even sure I want to know — that gun ties you to the scene, Jack. And you've got it stuffed in the back of a kid's teddy bear?"

Jack gave an exhausted sigh. "I know. I panicked. I was meant to leave it in the car, but I forgot. By the time I'd got back here, I realised I still had it with me. But there was no time to go back. You rocked up on my doorstep, remember?"

Carmichael did. Images of the bloodstains on Jack's shirt, and the tap running in the sink, filled his head.

Carmichael reached for his half-drunk bottle of beer, not really wanting it but feeling like he might need it. "Well, for now you keep it where it is. And tell no one, Jack. Not a single soul. No one can ever know that you still have it."

CHAPTER TWENTY-TWO

Time: 9.30 a.m.
Date: Saturday 24 May 2014
Location: 21 Lambert Grove, London EC1

"Grieving families can be a volatile hot-bed of emotions, Daniels — keep your wits about you." Jack locked the Mondeo and led the way across the street towards number 21 Lambert Grove. "But they can also divulge many a hidden secret. Eyes and ears open at all times."

"Most child murders are committed by a family member." Daniels followed Jack up the garden path while adjusting his spectacles on his nose. "For all child murders in the year ending March just gone, fifty per cent were killed by a parent or step-parent. Only nine per cent were committed by a total stranger."

Jack looked back over his shoulder, a quizzical look on his face.

Daniels gave a sheepish smile. "I downloaded the crime statistics from the ONS last night. It made really interesting reading."

And that was precisely why Jack liked Trevor Daniels.

Turning back towards the Lancasters' family home, Jack noted curtains still shrouded the windows. The place looked deserted. DC James Anderson again opened the front door and ushered them inside. The same sense of burdensome grief suffocated the air around them as they headed for the open door leading to the front room.

Russell and Sara Lancaster were seated on the same pale blue sofa as before. It looked like they hadn't moved since Jack's last visit. And perhaps they hadn't. Another newspaper sat folded up on the coffee table. With Maisie's identity now released to the press, Jack had no doubt that each and every headline contained her name. Edging around a high-backed armchair, he went to stand in front of the shrouded bay window, while Daniels hovered with the family liaison officer by the door.

It was Sara Lancaster who broke the heavy silence. "Have you caught them yet?" Her voice was barely above a whisper and immediately swallowed by the deafening silence.

Jack gave a soft shake of the head. "Not yet, no."

Tears coursed down Sara Lancaster's cheeks. "I want to see her. I want to see my baby."

It was the question Jack had been expecting. "I wouldn't advise it at this time, Mrs Lancaster. If you wait . . ." He was cut off mid-sentence.

"So, why are you here?" Russell Lancaster's voice was louder than his wife's and edged with suspicion. "You're wasting time with us when you should be out there looking for whoever did this to our beautiful little girl." His eyes were red-rimmed and raw — his thin face contorted by grief.

"I can assure you, Mr Lancaster, that everything is being done to catch the person responsible." The stock phrase was well-oiled and Jack threw it out there as much for want of something to say than anything else. For a horrifying second he thought he sounded just like Graham Hobbs. The thought unnerved him. "We just need to ask some additional questions, that's all. Then we'll leave you in peace."

"Peace? You think we'll ever find peace again, now that . . . ?" Sara Lancaster's voice trembled, as did the hands that flew to her face.

"My apologies," Jack murmured regretfully. "I didn't mean to sound so heartless." More visions of Hobbs filled his head. He silently chastised himself — this wasn't who he wanted to be. "Do you recall any visitors to the house in the weeks preceding Maisie's disappearance? Anyone take an interest in your family that hadn't done before?" Jack paused. "Any unusual phone calls?"

Mr Lancaster gripped his wife's trembling hand. "No," he replied. "Nothing. We've already been through this. Several times."

Jack ignored the edge of irritation in Russell Lancaster's voice. "Had Maisie been anywhere recently — gone to visit any friends? Stayed away overnight? Anything out of her usual routine?"

Russell Lancaster's shoulders shuddered. "No. She always stayed very close to home. The only place she ever went was to her grandparents' house around the corner."

"Was it usual for Maisie to go visiting her grandparents without asking, Mrs Lancaster?" Jack switched his gaze back to Maisie's mother. "You said in your original statement that initially you'd assumed she'd gone around the corner to see them?"

Sara Lancaster lowered her head and Jack spied fresh tears leaking from her eyes. "Sometimes," she whispered, her voice so brittle it seemed it might break. "She thought it was fun — a game. She knew not to step into the road and to keep to the pavement. It's a thirty second walk."

"When did you first discover that Maisie wasn't with her grandparents as you'd thought?"

"I . . . I left it for about ten or fifteen minutes." Sara Lancaster's shoulders heaved with a fresh sob. "I . . . I should've gone out there sooner. I just thought . . ." She collapsed back against her husband and buried her face in her hands once again. "I rang my mother after Maisie didn't appear back, thinking she would be there, badgering her nanny for the homemade biscuits she loved so much. But she hadn't been there at all."

"Unfortunately, there's no CCTV along this street or Hartington Crescent — but we've been canvassing local residents once again to see if anyone has any private cameras or saw anything out of the ordinary."

"And did they?" Mr Lancaster looked up, his bloodshot eyes wide. "See anything?"

Jack gave a sad shake of the head. "Not exactly, but we're following up a sighting of a car, seen on Lambert Grove around the time Maisie was last seen. We'll keep asking." Flashing a look at Daniels, Jack decided to ask the one question that had really brought them back to number 21 Lambert Grove. "At the time Maisie disappeared, can I clarify where the both of you were exactly? I know you'll have covered this in your initial statements, but it would really help to hear it again."

Mrs Lancaster extricated her hand from her husband's grasp. "I . . . I was here — in the front room." Her words caught in the back of her throat as she thought back to the last time she saw her daughter alive. "I was right there, by the window. Just where you're standing now. I was ironing. I could . . . I could keep an eye on Maisie while she was playing on the grass outside."

Jack turned and parted the heavy drape curtains with a finger, noting how Mrs Lancaster would have had a clear and uninterrupted view of her daughter. *If* she was watching.

"And you were there the whole time? Facing the window?"

Mrs Lancaster started to nod, then dropped her gaze to her lap. "I . . ." Faltering, she glanced up at her husband, giving him a pained look. "I . . . may have gone out to the kitchen to check on Maisie's tea a couple of times. And . . . and there was a film on TV I was watching . . . I . . . I don't really remember. It's all very hazy."

"And what about yourself, Mr Lancaster?" Jack turned his attention towards Maisie's father. "Where were you in the time immediately preceding Maisie's disappearance?"

Just at that moment, the door leading back out into the hallway flew open, crashing against the wall next to where Daniels and DC Anderson were standing, narrowly missing them both. Derek Foster once again thundered into the cramped front room, his face verging on scarlet.

"I told you before — you're not welcome here." Maisie's grandfather thundered across the small space in a couple of strides, jabbing a nicotine-stained finger in Jack's direction. Jack instinctively took a step backwards, brushing up against the curtains. "But you just don't stop, do you? Can't you see they're grieving?" Derek Foster swept his arm around towards his daughter and son-in-law. "They've just lost their one and only precious daughter, and you come around here asking about their movements? Asking if they have alibis?"

Jack opened his mouth to speak but was instantly closed down.

"Here you are again — asking pathetic questions when you should be out there hunting for the real murderer — not accusing them of killing their own child!"

"Mr Foster," began Jack, raising his voice to be heard. "No one is accusing anyone of anything. I can assure you of that. These are routine questions we always ask in situations such as this."

"Derek." Maggie Foster had followed her husband into the front room and was hovering in the doorway. Her face looked red and blotchy, her watery eyes sunken. "Please calm down."

"Daniels?" Jack motioned for DC Daniels to take Mrs Foster out of harm's way. Derek Foster's fiery expression was still simmering, and Jack was acutely aware of how quickly the situation had boiled over before — he certainly didn't want to encourage a repeat performance. Instinctively, his hand went up to his neck. He'd escaped with just a ripped collar last time — who knew if his luck would hold again.

Daniels quickly guided Maisie's grandmother out into the hall.

Jack turned to face the advancing Derek Foster. He noted the man's fists were once again clenched into balls by his side.

"Mr Foster. This isn't helping anyone." Jack flashed a look towards the horrified expression on Sara Lancaster's face. "Least of all your daughter. And as I said — these are routine questions we have to ask everyone. Even yourself."

And that did it.

If Derek Foster wasn't yet in a full-blown rage, he was now. His hulking figure lunged forwards, arms outstretched, knocking the small coffee table sideways as he lumbered towards Jack. But Jack was too quick for him this time and easily side-stepped out of the way, sending the man careering towards the window.

Russell Lancaster instinctively pulled his wife towards him and cradled her in a protective embrace.

"This is just the same as last time, isn't it?" spat Foster, regaining his balance. "Poor Ray from number thirty — you hounded him almost into his own grave. Fitting him up for Carrie-Ann like that — and now you're trying to do the same with one of us!"

Jack bristled at the mention of Raymond Dixon's name. "Nobody fitted anyone up, Mr Foster. And that is certainly not what we are trying to do here. We all want the same thing — we want to find your granddaughter's killer. And if I have to ask some upsetting questions along the way, then I make no apologies for that."

"Well, you're not gonna find him in here, are you?!" Derek Foster again lunged in Jack's direction, his hands heading for the throat. Jack quickly slipped around the back of the sofa, conscious that this was one fight he was never going to win.

The only sensible option was to retreat.

* * *

Time: 9.45 a.m.
Date: Saturday 24 May 2014
Location: Flat 4 Ironbridge Buildings, Ironbridge Lane, London

Gina sat cross-legged on the floor of her bedsit and sighed. She'd spent an hour going through all her possessions once again — searching for something, *anything*, that might be worth selling. She already knew she wouldn't find anything — it was a process she'd gone through on more than one occasion. The answer was always the same.

She had nothing.

Although that wasn't strictly true.

Gina's gaze flickered towards the imitation silver photo frame that sat by her bedside. Not real silver, as far as she knew, but it looked nice. Someone might give her something for it.

But Gina knew she could never part with it. She let her finger trace the outline of Rosie's smiling face.

Rosie.

Rosie was the only reason she was doing this — or at least contemplating doing this.

Knowing that she would one day be reunited with her daughter was the only thing that kept Gina going. Making the decision to let Rosie live with her grandparents was one of the hardest decisions she'd ever had to make. But it had been the right one. London, and the circle of people Gina had found herself encased in, was no place for a child. Her parents had been happy to help — but had made it clear that it was only Rosie being offered shelter. If Gina wished to come too, she would need to clean up her act.

As harsh as that sounded, Gina understood. She'd been a mess back then. Still using cocaine too frequently and drinking far too much — she was definitely no role model. She'd been on a downward spiral and about to take her daughter down with her.

Her parents were right — they had to be cruel to be kind.

'Sort yourself out, Gina. Then come home.'

So that was what Gina was doing. Or, at least, trying to do. She'd kicked the drugs into touch a while ago now — and the alcohol. She didn't even smoke anymore. She felt better: had put on weight, and her skin and hair had lost their dullness. She felt energised and positive about the future. And when Darren Hughes had popped up late last year, offering her a way out of her debt, she'd jumped at the chance.

But she didn't blame them — her parents. Not one bit. Instead, she was thankful that they had taken that decision. Rosie was happy and healthy. She was going to school, making friends — doing everything a soon-to-be six-year-old child should.

But Gina's heart ached for her daughter every day. The only thing that got her through each backbreaking shift at Niko's was the thought of seeing her again. She'd spoken to Rosie over the phone a few times now, and every time she burst into tears at the sound of her daughter's voice.

If anything gave her the incentive to turn her life around it was Rosie.

Gina traced another finger over her daughter's face.

"One day soon, Rosie," she murmured. "One day soon."

But the thought of tomorrow night rapidly pushed aside any happy thoughts of a reunion with her daughter.

Tomorrow night.

Gina instantly felt the bile rise up inside her throat. Running wasn't an option. The Carson brothers and Darren Hughes would find her in a heartbeat — people like that always did.

There was no other way. She'd have to go through with it. But if it paid off her debt — maybe she could cope one last time?

* * *

Time: 9.50 a.m.
Date: Saturday 24 May 2014
Location: 21 Lambert Grove, London EC1

"What did I say about it being a volatile hot-bed?" Jack gunned the engine of the Mondeo and flashed a look at DC Daniels in the passenger seat.

"He *really* doesn't like you." Daniels snapped his seat belt into position.

"I think we can safely say that time has not been a great healer for our Mr Foster." Jack pulled the Mondeo away from the kerb and headed out of Lambert Grove. Suddenly the relatively wide avenue felt claustrophobic and suffocating.

"How come he's so wound up about this Raymond Dixon? What did Carrie-Ann's murder have to do with him?"

Jack slowed down as he drove past number 30 and took a long hard look at the front of the house that had haunted him for the last twenty-five years. "He was Dixon's best mate back then. Maybe he still is, who knows. But they were as thick as thieves, back in the day. Never saw one without the other."

"Could it have been him who killed Carrie-Ann? Foster? Is that why he's so angry at you turning up again — thinking you might dig up the truth this time?"

Jack shook his head as they left number 30 behind and headed for the main road. "Cast iron alibi. Definitely wasn't him."

"And you're sure it was Raymond Dixon?"

"One hundred per cent." Jack's jaw clenched. "He calmly sat sobbing his crocodile tears on the sofa, when Carrie-Ann was most probably already dead in the attic upstairs. He was revelling in it. And the thing is, he knows we know — but we just can't make it stick. The case went nowhere after the trial collapsed."

"And Maisie? Do we really think one of the Lancasters killed their own child? I mean — dismembering her like that — and keeping the head . . . ?" Jack saw Daniels shiver in his seat. "Surely no parent could ever do that?"

Jack pulled the sun visor down to shield his eyes from the sun streaming in through the windscreen. "Never say never, Daniels. I'd like to say no parent ever could — but I've been in this job long enough to know that some people's depravity knows no bounds." He swung the car out on to the main carriageway. "And you said it yourself — the crime statistics suggest it's more than possible. In fact, it's quite likely. So, while we're at it, let's add Derek Foster into the digging."

CHAPTER TWENTY-THREE

Time: 10.45 a.m.
Date: Saturday 24 May 2014
Location: Metropolitan Police HQ, London

DS Cassidy picked up the spare marker pen and approached the second whiteboard. "While you've been out, Chris and I have been digging further into what we know about Narelle."

"Go on." Jack pulled his chair closer to the whiteboard, noticing that a small photograph of the nineteen-year-old had now been pinned up.

Cassidy started annotating the board. "Arrived in London on 27 March 1994 and started working at White's café on Whiting Street. The café itself has gone now — turned into apartments — but she lived only a short walk away from there on Connaught Road. Again, her block of flats is no more. The whole area's been totally redeveloped. She then took on a second job at a riverside pub in mid-April. At the time it was called the End of the Road.

"She worked her last shift at the pub on 31 August — after which time she was never seen again. A search of her flat some weeks later revealed that her backpack, clothing and passport were all missing." Cassidy paused and turned to face Jack. "Everyone put it down to Narelle moving on with her travels."

Jack nodded. "And when were her parents first alerted that something might be wrong?"

Cassidy turned back towards the whiteboard. "Narelle phoned home every Sunday evening. So, when she failed to call on 4 September her parents became concerned. They gave it another few days but when Narelle still failed to get in touch they called the pub. They were told that they thought Narelle had moved on."

"But they weren't convinced?"

Cassidy shook her head. "No, not at all. They spent the next week or so trying to locate her. They got in touch with the hostel in France that Narelle had booked herself into for the next stage of her travels, but received little by way of assistance. All they did manage to find out was that Narelle wasn't there."

"What did they do next?"

"By this time, two weeks had passed since Narelle was last seen so they then contacted the Australian High Commission. Although helpful, they didn't find anything concerning about Narelle's disappearance. She was nineteen and not considered vulnerable. Her parents flew over to the UK on 20 September and spent the next week searching." Cassidy snapped the lid back on the marker pen. "They didn't find a single trace of her."

"And reported her missing?"

Cassidy nodded. "Officially on 27 September."

"OK, good work. Mr and Mrs Williams are on their way. They're catching the first available flight out of Brisbane. My guess is they'll arrive at some point tomorrow. I'd like it if you could sit in with me when I talk to them."

Cassidy gave a nod and went to sit back down at her computer. "Of course."

"In the meantime, Daniels — find out where this pub is. The End of the Road, or whatever it's called now. If it's still standing, then I think we should take a trip out and see for ourselves where Narelle was last seen. I doubt there'll be anyone still there who was around in 1994, but we need to tick that box. Let's see if we can't pull together something meaningful to tell Narelle's parents when they get here."

Jack glanced at his watch. "I've got to head off to the mortuary soon — Dr Matthews is examining the latest find. While I'm gone, continue trawling CCTV and any other cameras, and keep digging into both Dixon and Derek Foster. And that silver Vauxhall. I want to know where it's been and where it is now."

* * *

Time: 11.30 a.m.
Date: Saturday 24 May 2014
Location: Westminster Mortuary, London

Professor Kaufman flicked on the overhead lights, the brightness searing into each of their eyes like an overexposed camera. Jack and Dr Matthews followed the forensic anthropologist towards the steel examination table which had already been laid out, their attendance expected. Although dressed in regulation protective clothing, aprons and rubber wellington boots, this morning's examination wasn't going to produce the same blood and bodily fluids as would usually be expected.

The professor snapped on his gloves as he approached the table. "I've already had a fairly detailed look, Philip," he said, pulling down the overhead light to focus a more intense beam on to the remains. "And it's most intriguing."

Yesterday's find beneath London Bridge had been rapidly and expertly retrieved from the silt and shingle banks, then transported to the Westminster Mortuary. Narelle's skull was at the head of the examination table. Next came what now looked like two upper arms, a relatively intact pelvis, several ribs, and both upper and lower legs.

The professor stood at the side of the table, waiting for his audience to assemble. "As you can see, we now have an almost intact skeleton — it's quite remarkable."

"And the bones are all definitely from the same person?" Jack edged closer, his eyes scanning the remains. "One victim?"

The professor nodded. "Yes. All the remains are from the same body."

Narelle.

It seemed inconceivable that this collection of bleached-white bones was once part of a vibrant young woman. Visions of Narelle's laughing, smiling face swamped Jack's head. The treasured photographs that Mr and Mrs Williams had kept, memories they took with them everywhere they went, would now have to last them a lifetime. For all that remained of Narelle now lay on the chilled examination table of the Westminster Mortuary.

Although not ideal, it was a step up from the muddied riverbed of the Thames.

Jack felt an inexplicable pull towards Narelle's remains. It was almost as if her soul was still there, some unseen force giving her life, even if her heart was no longer beating and skin no longer covering her bones.

Who did this to you, Narelle?

Jack willed the bones to speak — to find some way, in this world or the next, to send him a message from the other side.

And right now, Narelle was the only one that held the key to that question: the only one that truly knew the secret she'd taken with her to her watery grave at the bottom of the Thames so many years ago.

Speak to me, Narelle.

"Leon here has uncovered something quite interesting, Jack." Dr Matthews' voice jolted Jack back into the present. The pathologist sounded sombre, nodding at the professor to continue.

"Indeed." Professor Kaufman took another step closer to the table. "The remains found yesterday include the humerus, which is the upper arm, and also the shoulder girdle on both sides. There are also several ribs, and a more or less intact pelvis." The professor took a gloved finger and pointed first to the upper section of Narelle's left humerus. "You'll see here, Inspector, where the humerus meets the shoulder girdle, there is evidence of the joint being cut and the bones forcibly separated — it's the same on both sides."

A cool rush flooded Jack's veins. "Cut? You mean . . . ?"

Professor Kaufman nodded. "It's my professional opinion that this young lady's upper arms were severed from her body by a sharp instrument."

Jack swallowed.

Cut.

Severed.

Dismembered.

The professor continued. "And now that we have the pelvis recovered, I can quite clearly see evidence of a similar severing of the top of the femur from the hip joint. — again on both sides. There's damage to the acetabulum here — can you see these grooves?" The professor pointed to a series of linear indentations. "I had my suspicions when I examined the femoral head before, but this has confirmed it." He nodded gravely at Jack's unspoken question. "Yes, Inspector. Both legs were removed from the body by a sharp instrument."

Two bodies.

Two dismemberments.

Two killers?

Jack eventually found his voice and asked the question that had been unthinkable just twenty-four hours before. "Are you saying we're definitely looking at the same killer here? The same person killed Narelle back in 1994 and now Maisie?"

A sideways glance was exchanged between the two pathologists. It was Dr Matthews who spoke first.

"It would be wrong of us to speculate whether the same person was responsible, Jack. All we can say is that both bodies were dismembered in a very similar fashion. Whether they both met their deaths in the same way, and by the same hand, we cannot say. But." Dr Matthews paused. "The manner in which the dismemberment has been performed again shows evidence of a rather brutal, almost inexpert, method. Similar to that of poor little Maisie. The similarities are subtle, but they're there all the same. Whether the act was performed by the same person unfortunately cannot be answered from this table."

Jack nodded. He heard the cautious tone of the pathologist's words and stared once more at Narelle's bleached-white remains.

The same words floated around his head.

Two bodies.

Two dismemberments.

And, as implausible as it sounded, *potentially one killer.*

CHAPTER TWENTY-FOUR

Time: 1.25 p.m.
Date: Saturday 24 May 2014
Location: The Bridge Public House, London SE1

"Why have I never heard of this pub, Daniels?" Jack let the sat nav guide him away from the station in the direction of the South Bank. "I've been in a lot of pubs in my time but can't say I recall this one."

"It's changed its name a few times over the years. Bought out by one of those big pub chains who tried to turn it into more of a foodie kind of place — it's so close to Borough Market, I guess they wanted to try and cash in on the eating-out scene. But it never took off and reverted back into more of a drinkers' pub not so long ago. Back in 1994, when Narelle worked here, it was called the End of the Road."

Jack couldn't help but think of the sad irony in the name.

The journey took them less than fifteen minutes, the traffic surprisingly light through the capital on this Saturday lunchtime. Jack found a parking space one street away, and he and Daniels walked the short distance back towards the pub's entrance.

It looked like a relatively nondescript public house from the outside — with a brick facade opening directly out on to the street. If you blinked, you could easily miss it. There were two entrances — one to the 'Bar' and one to the 'Lounge' — a common enough set-up for many pubs in years gone by, and whoever had renovated the Bridge had decided to keep with tradition.

In Jack's eyes, it was a nice touch. He pushed open the door to the Bar and stepped inside.

In days gone by, the Bar was for the working classes — with spit and sawdust on the floor, men would stand at the bar in their work clothes, downing a well-earned pint after a hard day's graft. Fast forward to today, and the spit and sawdust had been replaced with a patterned carpet and individual seating booths that hugged the walls.

Tastefully redecorated, the pub felt light and airy. The seating was padded leather, the tables highly polished wood. Laminated menus were propped up along the length of the bar which stretched all the way from one side to the other, curving around out of sight to presumably serve the Lounge area on the other side.

"May I help you?"

Jack's attention was drawn to a voice that seemed to appear out of nowhere. Turning around, he spied a shaved head popping up from behind the row of beer pumps. The skin on the top of the man's head shone from the bright recessed lighting above, and Jack detected several beads of perspiration on his pink forehead. Dragging a crate of bottled beers up on to the surface of the bar, he wiped his brow with a tea towel and smiled.

"Drink?"

Jack was about to decline but then changed his mind. "That would be grand. We'll have two bottles of whatever non-alcoholic lager you might have." He pulled out his warrant card and held it up. "And then a moment or two of your time."

* * *

Time: 1.30 p.m.
Date: Saturday 24 May 2014
Location: Flat 3a Ash Road, SE Soho, London

Darren Hughes stubbed out his drooping hand-rolled cigarette and flicked the butt across the kitchen table. He could feel the jitters starting already, and the nicotine wasn't helping. He chugged down another mouthful of neat own-brand vodka and screwed his eyes shut. The jitters would pass in a few moments — once the alcohol had worked its way into his system.

He'd stepped out early that morning, picking up his usual newspaper and tobacco — and made it back home before the rest of the street awakened. He didn't know why, but he felt like he needed to stay hidden.

Yesterday's visit from the police had unnerved him more than he'd bargained for. He hadn't expected them to call so soon, if at all. He'd covered his tracks well — or so he'd thought. Asking him about the car had thrown him, though. He hadn't realised it was still registered in his name — prison must have dulled the sharpness he'd once had.

He looked towards the worktop and the business card the lead detective had left behind, seeing it propped up against the side of the kettle. *DI Jack MacIntosh.* The man's name had been all over the papers that morning, especially the *Daily Courier* which had run a four-page spread on the finding of parts of a skeleton beneath London Bridge. He'd had a quick read of it while waiting in the queue at the Spar, noting that the journalist — someone named Jonathan Spearing — seemed to have no love lost for the officer in charge.

The *Daily Mirror*, however, was still reporting on the body in the suitcase and, as he unfolded his morning copy, there was no getting away from the headline.

'*Body in suitcase named.*'

Maisie Lancaster's name was everywhere now, and that meant one thing for Darren Hughes. He glanced down at his phone, seeing that he still had no new messages. And he still hadn't received the rest of his money. His patience — such as it was — was wearing thin.

His eyes flickered back to the *Mirror*'s front page. Maisie Lancaster's smiling face stared back out at him. The police had chosen a particularly cherubic picture to give to the media — he recognised the dimples and mass of strawberry blonde hair in an instant.

Letting his gaze wander towards the fridge-freezer, he knew he should have got rid of the rest of her by now — but the contents of the meat compartment drawer would now be too hot to handle, metaphorically speaking. He afforded himself a grin at his attempt at dark humour. He couldn't try to dump her now — not when half of London knew the little girl's name.

Although not exactly part of the plan, he resigned himself to letting Maisie hide out in his freezer a little longer. And to be honest, he had bigger problems to worry about.

Gina for one.

He was well aware how lenient he was with her — letting her off the repayments far too often. He was a soft touch and he needed to toughen up. But her problems were now becoming his — the Carson brothers weren't famous for their leniency.

He glanced back down at his silent phone.

He needed that money.

And he needed it now.

* * *

Time: 1.35 p.m.
Date: Saturday 24 May 2014
Location: The Bridge Public House, London SE1

The barman, who Jack now knew was called Steve, brought over two bottles of non-alcoholic lager to where Jack and DC Daniels had seated themselves in one of the padded leather booths. Jack took a sip. To be fair, despite the lack of alcohol, it wasn't bad.

"So, what can I do for you?" Steve hovered by the side of the booth.

"How long have you worked here?" Jack noted the man looked to be in his mid-twenties, so was unlikely to be of much help.

"Only about three months," replied Steve. "February time."

"Anyone work here who might've been around in 1994?" Jack took another sip from the bottle.

"1994?" Steve's pale eyes widened. "That's going back some. I'm not sure — most of us here are quite young."

Jack thought as much. This area of London always made him feel his age. Borough Market was just around the corner — an area of London that had seen a resurgence in recent years. Numerous cafés, bars and restaurants lined the streets and it was quickly becoming known as 'the place to go'. At night, it would be thick with people, three or four deep on the pavements.

Jack shuddered at the thought.

"So, no one that could tell us anything about what was going on back in 1994?"

Steve frowned, his attention turning to the door as a group of four entered and made their way over to the bar. "The only person I can think of who might've been around back then is our head barman."

"And where might I find this head barman?"

"He's not in today. Day off. But I can get you his number? Otherwise, he should be here first thing in the morning." Steve pulled out a notepad from his pocket and a pen that had been lodged behind his ear. He quickly jotted the name and number down, then ripped the sheet from the pad.

Jack noted the scribbled handwriting. '*Jerry. 07700 900109.*'

"Anything else I can get you?" Steve started to turn back to the bar where the party of four looked like they were ready to order.

Jack shook his head and drained the rest of his bottle. "No, thanks — we'll be on our way. Drink up, Daniels."

Not particularly fond of lager — with or without the alcohol — Daniels grimaced as he swallowed the rest of his bottle and made to follow Jack towards the door. As he did so, he noticed a length of rope in a glass case embedded in the wall above the bar.

"What's that?" he asked, catching Steve's eye as he passed.

The barman glanced up to where Daniels was pointing. "Sorry, no idea. Something about the history of this place, at a guess."

Daniels nodded his thanks and pushed his way out on to the pavement, noticing Jack was already heading up the road, but in the opposite direction of where they'd left the Mondeo. Hurrying after him, Daniels saw that Jack had come to a standstill on the southern side of London Bridge.

Jack turned towards the young officer as he approached. "What do you see, Daniels? Place look familiar?"

Daniels followed Jack's gaze down on to the choppy waters of the Thames. "It's the place both Maisie and Narelle were found," he replied.

Jack nodded. "And do you not find that a little coincidental?" His own gaze was fixed on the exact site where only three days ago he'd been standing a matter of feet away from Maisie Lancaster's dismembered remains. He felt his stomach churn, not unlike the waters below. "Both our victims are discovered a stone's throw away from where one of them was last seen alive. Anything about that strike you as odd?"

Daniels glanced back over his shoulder towards the Bridge. "You think there's a link to the pub?"

Jack gave a small shrug. "You know me and coincidences, Daniels. Let's see if we can track down this Jerry fella. If he was here back in 1994, then he might just know something we don't." Dragging his gaze away from the Thames, Jack started making his way back towards where they'd parked the Mondeo. "You come across that name in any of Narelle's paperwork? Jerry? From the pub?"

Daniels jogged to catch up. "Doesn't ring a bell, but I'll take another look."

"You do that, Daniels. You do that."

As they passed the entrance to the Bridge, Jack couldn't help but feel the sad irony once again.

The End of the Road.

For Narelle, it'd been just that.

CHAPTER TWENTY-FIVE

Time: 4.30 p.m.
Date: Saturday 24 May 2014
Location: Metropolitan Police HQ, London

DC Daniels didn't have time to come up to the canteen much anymore, but whenever he did he liked to sit by the window. The view, if you could call it that, looked out on to the road at the front of the station, and he liked to watch Londoners going about their daily business as he sipped his coffee or ate his sandwich.

DS Cooper slid into the seat opposite and instantly scooped up the freshly prepared bacon roll from his plate.

"I've been looking forward to this all day." Without another word, he opened his mouth and sank his teeth into the soft, white bread — making satisfied noises as he chewed.

Daniels merely smiled and stirred his coffee. Since getting back from the Bridge, he'd been going cross-eyed watching endless reels of CCTV and ANPR footage, tracking the movements of both Derek Foster and the silver Vauxhall registered to Darren Hughes.

Cooper made light work of the rest of his late afternoon breakfast, wiping his mouth with a serviette as he finished.

Taking a glug of milky tea, he turned to gaze out of the window. As he let his eyes roam the street, he noticed a figure standing on the pavement, almost directly opposite the main entrance to the station. A frown crossed his brow as he took another mouthful of tea.

"Isn't that your friend over there?" He nodded through the glass. "That old fella. What was his name again?"

Daniels looked up from his coffee cup and followed Cooper's gaze. The frown that was on his colleague's brow soon appeared on his own.

"That's Arnie. Arnie Miller." Daniels' frown deepened. "What the devil's he doing all the way out here? This isn't his patch."

After abandoning his half-drunk coffee and bounding down several flights of stairs, Daniels rushed through the main entrance and out into the street. A quick glance told him that Arnie Miller was still there.

As Daniels jogged across the road, he could tell by the look on the old man's weather-beaten face that something was on his mind.

"Arnie?" He arrived by the old man's side. "What are you doing all the way out here? Everything all right?"

Daniels had known Arnold 'Arnie' Miller for some years. While he was in uniform, he would regularly see the ageing pensioner as he made his patrols with the Traffic Division, often stopping off to give the old man a hot cup of tea and maybe a sandwich — sometimes even a burger if he had time.

And Arnie Miller was as regular as clockwork. Daniels could always count on seeing him at the same time, and the same place — day after day, night after night. And that place was a million miles away from here.

No one was ever quite sure just how old Arnold Miller was, and that included Arnie himself. Having grown up on the streets, it was the only life that he'd ever known. He had survived living rough for the best part of six decades, getting by on his own knowledge and understanding of how things worked. In particular, he knew where to go, and more importantly where *not* to go. Arnold Miller had his own patch and he stuck to it like glue, never deviating.

Until today.

"Arnie?" repeated Daniels, taking hold of the old man's arm and guiding him towards a wooden bench behind them. "Are you OK?"

Arnold Miller appeared to snap out of his trance-like state and began to nod. "Yes, yes, Mr Trevor. Everything's fine with old Arnie."

"Then what are you doing out here? It's a bit far away from your usual haunt?"

Arnie glanced up at the impressive facade of the Metropolitan Police HQ before him, his brilliant blue eyes wide open in wonder. A small smile flickered beneath his greying whiskers. "You work inside there, son?"

Daniels followed the old man's gaze. "Yes, I do. Why — do you want a guided tour?"

The smile on Arnie's lined face widened into a grin, a row of discoloured and broken teeth now visible. He shook his head. "No, you're all right there, lad." He then fixed the young detective with a sad look. "You found out who dumped that poor wee girl in the river yet?"

Daniels' eyebrows shot up a notch. "You mean Maisie Lancaster?"

Arnie nodded. "Aye. If that's the poor little mite's name, yes. The one in the suitcase?"

Daniels frowned. "We're working on it. Is that what you came here to talk to me about, Arnie? Something to do with Maisie? Did you know her?" Daniels couldn't quite fathom how a homeless septuagenarian like Arnie would ever cross paths with an eight-year-old girl from Lambert Grove.

Sorrow filled the old man's eyes, but he shook his head. "No, nothing like that, son. But I see what they write in the papers like everyone else."

There was another hike of Daniels' eyebrows. "You've been reading the newspapers?"

A chuckle escaped Arnie's mouth. "I can read, laddie. Just enough to get by. You need to these days — won't last five minutes out here otherwise. I use the leftover papers to sleep on — there's a young fella down by Embankment tube station who lets us have a few at the end of the night. Keeps out the chill, you know. Newspaper. That's one of the first things you have to learn out here on the streets. How to keep out the chill."

Daniels gave a slow nod. "OK. So, the newspapers? What's on your mind, Arnie?" He knew the old man well enough to spot when something was troubling him. His blue eyes, usually so vibrant and sparkling with humour, now had a dull sheen — and his already well-lined forehead seemed more creased than usual.

Arnie scratched his rough beard. "As I was settling down for the night last night, I saw there's been another." Reaching into the pocket of his tattered donkey jacket, he pulled out a crumpled piece of paper — yesterday's front page of the *Evening Standard*.

Daniels skimmed the headline. The article beneath it was brief, but contained pretty much everything that had been divulged to the press about the discovery of Narelle Williams. Everything, that was, bar her name. That would come in time — no doubt all too soon for Mr and Mrs Williams.

Daniels handed the press report back to Arnie. "What about it, Arnie?"

Arnold Miller's eyes bore into the young detective.

"Have you ever heard about the Legend of Hangman's End?"

* * *

Time: 5.15 p.m.
Date: Saturday 24 May 2014
Location: Metropolitan Police HQ, London

Jack ducked his head inside the incident room to see both Cooper and Cassidy hard at work, studiously staring at their computer screens.

"Cooper — did Daniels have any luck finding any reference to our Jerry from the pub in any of Narelle's paperwork?" Jack's eyes scoured the room. "Where is he anyway?"

Cooper glanced up from his computer screen. "Nothing about a Jerry, no. There's no answer from the mobile number we were given, either. And last I saw, Trev was downstairs talking to that homeless fella — Arnie."

Jack frowned. "OK, I'll swing by the pub again tomorrow morning, when this Jerry's meant to be working."

Cooper gave a nod and turned his attention back to his computer monitor.

"Anything else coming in from the repeated house-to-house enquiries?" Jack had secured a team of uniformed officers to repeat the house-to-house visits along Lambert Grove in the hope that someone might have remembered something new.

"Not really, but there's one thing that might be useful." Cooper tapped his keyboard and angled the screen in Jack's direction. "An old man living next door to your friend Dixon said that he'd sometimes go to the Lambert Grove Working Men's Club — with Dixon — and often they'd meet up with Derek and Maggie Foster. They'd sit and drink together, play cards or pool. But recently, for some reason, Dixon hasn't been going. The Fosters have been going on their own."

Jack gave a slow nod. "OK. Park it. We might come back to that. Anything else on Dixon or Derek Foster?"

"We're waiting on phone records for them both. Raymond Dixon doesn't appear to have a car registered to him, but Derek Foster does — we're putting the registration through the system to see if it pings anywhere interesting."

"Good. Well, I've an update from the mortuary." Jack perched himself on the edge of the nearest table. "Dr Matthews and Professor Kaufman examined the rest of the bones that were found yesterday. They're sure that the body was dismembered before being dumped in the river. Again, it wasn't particularly elegant or sophisticated."

Jack heard a slight intake of breath from Cassidy.

"So, we *are* looking at the same killer." Cooper's ginger eyebrows hitched. "For Maisie and Narelle?"

Jack gave a shrug. "We can't be sure on that. It's possible. For now, we'll carry on investigating them as separate enquiries, but be mindful. Anything you see that could link to the other case, give me a shout. I'll be in my office if you need me." Jack pushed himself to his feet and started walking towards the door. He hesitated on the threshold. "And while you're digging into Dixon and Derek Foster, add our friend Darren Hughes into the mix. Let's find out where he was in August 1994."

* * *

Time: 6.45 p.m.
Date: Saturday 24 May 2014
Location: Metropolitan Police HQ, London

Trevor Daniels was in his element. It'd taken three mugs of tea and two packets of bourbon biscuits before Arnie finally finished telling his tale. And Daniels had hung on to every word.

Now alone in the incident room, the others busy elsewhere, he'd begun to piece it all together.

History fascinated him.

As well as space exploration and the paranormal, DC Trevor Daniels was a history nerd. At school they'd been reading HG Wells' famous novella, *The Time Machine*, and the teacher had asked them all what year they'd like to travel to if they had the chance. Virtually everyone in the class had wanted to go into the future — but young Trevor Daniels' feet were firmly planted in the past.

The Edwardians.

The Tudors.

The Victorians.

He was spoilt for choice: he wanted to visit them all.

Naturally, his classmates all thought him weird — well, maybe just weirder than they already did. But none of it mattered to young Trevor.

And here he was now — some fifteen or so years later — immersing himself in seventeenth- and eighteenth-century London. Quite what Jack and the rest of the team would make of it, he hadn't a clue. But something told him to press on.

Reaching for the last of the bourbons, Daniels returned his attention to his computer screen.

* * *

Time: 7.45 p.m.
Date: Saturday 24 May 2014
Location: Metropolitan Police HQ, London

Jack leaned back in his chair and closed his eyes. The day felt as though it would never end. So far nobody had mentioned the four-page spread in the *Daily Courier*, but he knew that everyone in the building would most likely have read it by now.

A copy was sitting on the top of his in-tray.

The article had gone way beyond what Jack had been expecting, and he chastised himself for thinking he could control what came out of Jonathan Spearing's mouth . . . or, for that matter, his pen. Their five-minute conversation, during which time Jack felt he'd barely said three complete sentences, had been blown up into a full scale 'inside interview'. Starting off with the discovery of little Maisie Lancaster, it had moved swiftly on to the as-yet-unnamed skeletal remains beneath the bridge. But the article then, alarmingly, changed direction and began to delve into the background and private life of its lead detective — DI Jack MacIntosh.

Seeing himself described as a dogged bachelor in the black and white newsprint had almost brought a smile to his face. *Almost.* He wasn't entirely sure whether to take it as a compliment or not. And if the article had left it there, Jack would have shrugged it off and been happy to see it as tomorrow's chip paper — but Spearing then veered off on an even more dangerous tangent and began to talk about Jack's upbringing in foster care. All leading up to his main focus of the entire article — was DI Jack MacIntosh competent enough to lead such a high-profile investigation?

And then he'd mentioned Stu's time in prison and conviction for robbery.

At that point Jack had stopped reading.

It'd been his own fault. He'd told his team to '*keep it zipped*' — those had been his exact words, if he remembered rightly. And not to talk to *anyone*.

So, what does he go and do?

He'd never trust Jonathan Spearing again, not even if his life depended on it. *Especially* then.

Jack rubbed his eyes and sighed, pulling his thoughts away from Spearing and back to the investigations. Although Maisie's name had now been released to the media, they'd still managed to keep Narelle's identity under wraps — although there was no telling how long that anonymity would last. Only the *Daily Courier* seemed to be making connections between the two cases — fuelled by Jack's 'off the record' chat with Spearing yesterday. But the others were catching up fast and the press office had been inundated with enquiries from almost every newspaper in the country, forcing them to place a recorded message on their main enquiry line. And Jack had lost count of the number of messages he'd tossed into the bin — a good proportion of them from Jonathan Spearing himself.

Just as Jack was about to get to his feet, his desk phone trilled. Still rubbing the tiredness from his eyes, he answered the call. "DI MacIntosh."

"Good evening, Jack."

It was a voice Jack recognised.

"Before you go, pop up and see me."

CHAPTER TWENTY-SIX

Time: 1.00 a.m.
Date: Sunday 25 May 2014
Location: Kettle's Yard Mews, London

Jack tipped coffee granules into his mug and stared at the kettle. He hadn't bothered to try and sleep yet — he already suspected it would be a pointless exercise. After being summoned to the chief superintendent's office, he had decided to call it a night and head home, telling his team to do the same.

Dougie King had predictably seen the *Daily Courier* and was less than impressed, despite Jack's assurances that he'd barely said two words to the journalist.

But what was done was done, and Chief Superintendent King had merely sent him on his way with a flea in his ear and reminded him to stay away from the media. Jack didn't need telling twice. Jonathan Spearing wouldn't get to him so easily next time.

He'd spent much of the evening going over the evidence, such as it was, in his head. The likelihood that the same individual was responsible for Narelle's murder, and then for Maisie's some twenty years later, still made no sense to Jack. But he also knew that, as unlikely as it sounded, it wasn't completely outside the realms of possibility. Stranger things had indeed happened – on more than one occasion. The killer could have been in prison in the interim, or maybe moved abroad. Or maybe he'd continued with his killing spree in the intervening years and just hadn't been caught — and his victims not found.

That last thought brought a shiver to Jack's spine. That there could be more victims lying at the bottom of the Thames was an unpalatable thought.

Jack screwed the lid back on the coffee jar and pushed the mug away. It was after one o'clock and there was hardly any point in trying to sleep now. Dawn would be upon him before he knew it, and in any case he was far too wired for sleep. Instead, he reached for the half-empty bottle of Glenfiddich and grabbed a clean glass from the draining board.

Chugging a good measure into the glass, Jack headed for the sofa and sat down with a heavy sigh. He swirled the amber liquid around the base of the glass before taking a mouthful. He knew it wasn't the best option for calming his nerves — but maybe calm wasn't what he needed to be.

Slugging back another mouthful, he glanced at his watch. If it was one o'clock in the morning here, then it would be eight o'clock in the evening in New York. Late, but not too late . . .

Without further hesitation, Jack reached for his phone and scrolled through his contact list until he found the one he wanted. He wondered if the call might go to voicemail, and if it did what would he say? Just as he was trying to put together a coherent message, the call was picked up.

"Detective Inspector MacIntosh — to what do I owe this pleasure?"

Dr Rachel Hunter's voice was light, and Jack detected an element of humour in her tone. In the background he could hear several other voices and the clinking of glasses.

"Sorry, are you busy? I tried to gauge the time difference — I can call back tomorrow?"

"Don't be silly." Dr Hunter's voice climbed down a notch or two. "Hold on a moment — I'll find somewhere a little more private."

Jack heard rustling and then the sound of a door opening and closing — the voices in the background suddenly disappearing.

"That's better." Dr Hunter's light tone returned. "So, you were saying?"

Now Jack had the forensic psychologist's full attention, he wasn't quite sure what to say or where to start. He took another fortifying mouthful of Glenfiddich. "This really might be better done in the morning," he eventually replied, noting that his glass was empty. He eyed the bottle on the coffee table. "It's late. I shouldn't have called."

"Nonsense," teased Dr Hunter. "The night is young. And to be honest, you're doing me a favour. I've been stuck on a table with the biggest bunch of bores the United States Psychological Society could hope to find. They all talk over me and treat me like some kind of dimwit, just because I'm a woman. I'm finding it all rather tedious and I've been looking for a good reason to escape. So, I'm grateful for the call." She paused, her voice taking on an edge of concern. "So, tell me. What's keeping you awake in the early hours? You wouldn't have called me if it wasn't important."

That much was true. Jack wasn't known for his chit-chat. His monthly itemised phone bill told everyone that much. And his meagre contact list. He shook his head, even though he knew she couldn't see him. "I'm not sure I know where to start."

"Try the beginning." Jack could sense the smile that he was sure would be teasing at the corners of Dr Hunter's mouth right about now. "I find that usually works."

* * *

Time: 11.05 p.m.
Date: Saturday 24 May 2014
Location: The Sycamore Hotel, Central Park, New York City, USA

Despite the late hour, the hotel had been more than happy to loan her the use of their printer. Now sitting on her third-floor balcony with a strong black coffee in hand, Rachel Hunter turned over the first page of the two files Jack had sent over.

She'd seen the online reports about the body in the suitcase — or parts of a body, at least — before she'd boarded the plane for New York on Thursday evening. But there was now a confirmed name to put to the gruesome discovery — Maisie Lancaster.

Such a sweet, pretty name — it conjured up all sorts of happy images of a carefree young girl with a beaming face and freckles. The Maisie that Rachel was imagining in her mind wasn't far from the truth — on the second page of the paperwork Jack had sent through was a photograph. An unruly mop of strawberry blonde hair cascaded around a heart-shaped face, her bright blue eyes blazed towards the camera. Freckles did, indeed, pepper her cheeks and, as she smiled, two dimples popped out on either side of her mouth.

Rachel felt a familiar tug in her heart. Sometimes this job was so painful.

For the next hour Rachel absorbed the case file on Maisie's disappearance — and then the shocking discovery of the suitcase some seven days later on the banks of the Thames beneath London Bridge. She watched her coffee slowly go cold on the table, unable to stomach even a sip as she immersed herself in the grisly findings inside the suitcase.

After she was finished, she turned to the equally heartbreaking story of Narelle Williams. Narelle's parents had waited twenty years to discover what had happened to their daughter, and Rachel could do nothing but admire their courage.

By now it was well after midnight, but Rachel carried on. At two o'clock she was forced to take a nap on the king-sized bed but was up again at first light to see the sun rise over Central Park. Resuming her place on the balcony, Rachel shielded her eyes from the early morning glare, and continued to read.

Her stomach lurched with every sentence she read. Poor little Maisie would never get to see another sunrise, or play on a beach on a beautiful summer day. And from this moment on, neither would her parents. No amount of sunshine would ever be able to lift their hearts from the dark recesses that grief had plunged them into. And as for Narelle's parents — they had already been living this nightmare for the last twenty years.

Rachel let out a deep sigh as she turned over the final page. Despite her lack of sleep, various threads were starting to form in her mind. Her university lecturer had always told her that the mark of a good psychologist was being able to read between the lines — to see beyond the printed words, to uncover what was so often hidden from view, to go beyond the obvious.

She took a look at her watch and grimaced. She was meant to be attending a talk on innovative cognitive behavioural techniques later that morning at another hotel around the corner. It started at ten, which didn't give her much time. Swallowing the dregs of her cold coffee she headed for the shower.

CHAPTER TWENTY-SEVEN

Time: 10.45 a.m.
Date: Sunday 25 May 2014
Location: Niko's Café, Sunderland Street, London

The bright morning sunshine beat relentlessly through the café's grimy floor to ceiling windows, warming Gina's back as she scrubbed hard at the table top. Whether it was the heat, or the remains of the greasy breakfast before her, she felt sick.

Sidling around the end of the table to get out of the glare, she felt a shiver trickle up and down her spine. No matter what she did, she just couldn't get the thought of tonight out of her head.

Tonight.

She'd lain awake most of the night, tossing and turning as thoughts of what Darren had in store for her to pay back her ever-spiralling debt rushed through her head — forcing even the remotest chance of sleep from her exhausted body. Whatever it was, it wouldn't be pleasant. Not for her, anyway.

Her room was on the top floor of the dilapidated block of flats, which had been earmarked for demolition some months ago. It had paper-thin walls and gaps around the windows, allowing each and every noise to penetrate. And the nearby Northern Line meant there was an almost constant underlying rumble, both day and night.

Despite her tiredness, she'd shown up to work at Niko's half an hour before her shift was due to start, unable to stall the day any longer. Before leaving home, she'd gone through all her possessions one more time, desperate to find something she'd missed that would be worth selling. But she had nothing left — everything had either already been sold or was languishing in the pawn shop around the corner.

Part of her wondered whether Darren might show up for breakfast this morning, just to rub it in — and she'd spent the first two hours of her shift nervously watching the door. She wouldn't put it past him to come in and gloat.

"Gina!" Niko Georgiades' thick tone rang out across the café floor, jolting Gina back to the present. She looked up to see him gesturing with a fat finger towards the table opposite, a look of urgency on his sweaty face.

Gina's stomach sank even further — the builders were here again. In no apparent rush to get to their next job, they seemed content slouching in the cheap plastic chairs, poring over copies of the Sunday edition of the *Daily Star*. Plucking her notepad from her apron pocket, she dragged herself towards them. She was immediately greeted by jeers and whistles.

"Morning, darlin'," greeted the eldest builder, wisps of greying hair poking out from beneath the lopsided hard hat on his head. "Come on lads — let's give it to her!"

All at once, the table erupted into loud and very poor singing.

"Ooh, ah — just a little bit — ooh, ah, a little bit more!" Booted feet stamped in time to the beat, dirty cutlery drummed on the sticky table top.

Gina felt her cheeks burn, the sickness in her stomach growing in intensity as she squirmed by the side of the table. Out of the corner of her eye she saw Mr Georgiades' fat face beaming widely.

"I'd give you a little bit more anytime, darlin'," chuckled the eldest builder, his pale eyes raking up and down Gina's body. "You just say the word." More raucous laughter and jeering followed.

"What can I get you?" Gina gripped the notepad, trying to raise her voice over the din. "The usual?"

"Aye — four of your finest breakfasts, my love," replied one of the younger builders seated closest to her. "Made by your own fair hand, I hope."

Gina turned to leave, her legs desperate to ferry her away — as she did so, the young builder slapped her bottom hard as she passed the edge of the table. The resultant cheer that went up bounced off the walls and followed her into the kitchen.

Gina threw the notepad on to one of the grease-laden worktops and rushed over to the open fire exit. The vomit that threatened to leave her mouth subsided, and she merely clung to the door frame, gulping in huge gasps of air.

She needed to get out of this life.

And soon.

* * *

Time: 11.00 a.m.
Date: Sunday 25 May 2014
Location: Metropolitan Police HQ, London

Jack couldn't remember the last time he'd been late for work. After speaking at length to Rachel in the early hours, he'd once again sat by the window and watched the sun rise. He'd tried working on his best man speech, but couldn't concentrate. Thoughts of Maisie and Narelle filled his head, along with the well-deserved dressing down he'd received from Dougie King.

The next thing he knew, he was waking up with a sore neck and pains shooting up through the small of his back. He'd drifted off to sleep propped up on the windowsill, his body slumped against the window pane.

Spending longer in the shower than normal — he'd allowed the hot jets to massage his shoulders and pummel his scalp for over twenty minutes — he stepped out only when the lure of coffee was too great to ignore.

But no one had really noticed his tardy arrival at the station — his team were already hard at work in the incident room, noses glued to their computer screens, so he'd slipped quietly into his office without so much as raising an eyebrow. The thought of tackling the abundance of paperwork that was still swamping his desk wasn't appealing, so he soon decided on an escape.

"Jack. Good to see you again, come on through."

DI Jane Telford held the door open to the maze of basement offices of the Cold Case Unit, and Jack gratefully slipped through.

Instantly, he felt at home.

"It's actually quite good timing." DI Telford showed Jack into the same room they'd been in before — but this time the table in the centre was free from the multitude of files and paperwork. There was just the one slim manila folder sitting next to a half-drunk mug of coffee. "I've just this minute finished putting together that summary on Raymond Dixon for you."

Jack accepted the chair that was offered and sat down. "That's great, thanks. But that wasn't what I came down for — not really."

Jane Telford's eyebrows hitched as she flicked open the thin folder. "Oh?" She peered over the top of her wire-rimmed spectacles. "More developments?"

"Not exactly, but . . ." Jack watched as DI Telford slipped into the chair opposite. "Did you ever consult a forensic psychologist on the Carrie-Ann Dixon case?"

"No." Telford shook her head. "I wanted to — but we just didn't have the budget. The CPS were adamant that we needed fresh evidence. Even if we got a psychologist to confirm that Dixon fit the profile of the killer, it wouldn't have been enough. In their eyes, it would just be money wasted. Why? Is that something you're looking into for your cases?"

"I've made some tentative enquiries — just waiting on a formal report. But . . ." Jack paused. "The pathologists raised the idea that the cases might be linked. Similar method of dismemberment."

Jane Telford's delicate eyebrows raised another notch. "I see. That puts a fresh slant on things."

"You could say that. I'm just trying to get my head around it."

Telford extracted a single sheet of paper from the thin file in front of her. "Well, this is the summary on Dixon, if that helps at all." She slid the summary across the table. "If you need anything else, just give me a call."

"Great, thanks." Jack folded the piece of paper in half and slotted it into his jacket pocket. "I'll leave you to get on."

"I'd offer you a coffee, but . . ." DI Telford nodded towards the murky brown liquid languishing in the bottom of her mug. "I wouldn't risk it if I were you . . ."

Jack merely smiled and, after saying his goodbyes, headed back out into the corridor and towards the stairs leading up to ground level. As he neared the top, his phone sprang into life with a message from Daniels.

'*I might have something.*'

* * *

Time: 12.30 p.m.
Date: Sunday 25 May 2014
Location: Metropolitan Police HQ, London

"So, the current London Bridge isn't actually the original." DC Daniels hitched his spectacles up onto the bridge of his nose and activated the whiteboard. "The first bridge — Old London Bridge as it's known — was built in the thirteenth century, opening in 1209. It would've looked pretty different to the one we know today. There would've been shops like haberdasheries, grocers, textile merchants and blacksmiths all the way along — plus taverns and houses too." An artist's impression of the Old London Bridge filled the screen. "It was the only route across the Thames at that time, and iron spikes at the southern side bore the heads of traitors to the Crown — to serve as a warning to all who crossed the bridge into the city. William Wallace was thought to be the first head on display in 1305. Then people like Oliver Cromwell, and even Guy Fawkes. They would be left on the spikes until they rotted — then they'd be tossed over the side of the bridge into the river.

"During the seventeenth and eighteenth centuries, highwaymen were rife in London. And as the Old London Bridge was the only crossing point, it became a haven for street robbery. A lot of the arterial roads in and out of London at that time also became targets — especially those leading to the south and west. Indeed, Hyde Park was notoriously dangerous after dark due to the threat from highwaymen — so much so that King William the third installed oil-filled lamps to make the route a safer prospect at night."

"As much as I'm enjoying the history lesson, Daniels, is there a point to all this?" Jack took a mouthful of coffee and glanced at the wall clock. "We do have a murder investigation here — two murder investigations, to be precise. And we've still got a lot of ground to cover."

Daniels gave his glasses another nudge and afforded Jack a small smile. "I know. I know. I'm getting to it. Bear with me." Clearing his throat, he clicked the mouse and changed the picture on the screen. "The punishment for highwaymen was death. There was a very famous execution site at Tyburn — colloquially known as Tyburn Tree — where public hangings took place of many a notorious highwayman. The picture on screen is an artist's impression of the Tyburn Tree, and it's pretty much where Marble Arch is today." Daniels paused once more, seeing that both Cooper's and Jack's eyes were, for now at least, still trained on the screen, and Cassidy was hanging on to his every word. He continued.

"However, sometimes Londoners took the law into their own hands and, according to tales handed down through the years, many highwaymen actually met their deaths on the Old London Bridge. There was a particular section of the bridge, close to the south side, where the highwaymen would be tossed over the side and left hanging below for all to see. Another deterrent I suppose you could call it. This particular section of the bridge was known to the locals as 'Hangman's End'. The executioner would arrive on horseback, dragging the condemned man behind him in a noose. Once he reached Hangman's End, the executioner would dismount from his horse and lead the highwayman to the edge of the bridge. Then he'd throw him over the side, leaving the body hanging there for the next three days before it would be cut down and left to fall into the water to rot."

Daniels clicked the mouse to change the image once again. "After the execution, the executioner would lead his horse to one of the taverns that marked the entrance to the bridge and drink a pint of ale — the cost of which was borne by the tavern owner. The tavern was named the Hangman's End, and it stood until the new London Bridge was built.

"Here you can see another artist's impression of the New London Bridge which was opened in 1831 — not quite on the same site as the Old London Bridge, but more or less. Just about thirty metres or so away upstream. You'll see it looked a little different, though." Daniels enlarged the image on the screen. "Gone are the houses and other buildings, no more shops and taverns. It's on the same site as the current bridge we have today."

"Not wanting to sound like a stuck record, Daniels, but . . ." Jack held the young DC in a questioning look. "Relevance?"

Daniels' eyes continued to sparkle, the hint of a smile returning to his lips. "Maisie's body, and also the remains of Narelle, were both found beneath the exact section of the bridge that used to be known as 'Hangman's End'. The exact site of the public executions."

"And you think our killer somehow knew this?" Jack puffed out his cheeks, biting back a snort as he began to slip into his jacket. "He's some kind of history buff?"

"I have no idea." Daniels shrugged, watching as Jack headed for the door. "But that's not all. The tavern — the Hangman's End — it's still with us today. Not quite in the same location as the original, and it has a new name, but it still exists. And we've both been there."

"We have?" Jack stopped donning his jacket and frowned in Daniels' direction. "When?"

"The Bridge. When Narelle worked there it was the End of the Road. But before that, it was called the Hangman's End." Daniels let the information sink in. "Both Maisie and Narelle are murdered and wash up at the exact location of the notorious Hangman's End, and Narelle used to work in the pub that used to be the original tavern. I'm not saying it's relevant, but — you were looking for a link between the crime scene and the pub . . . Well, this might be it."

Jack felt his tiredness dissipating fast as he toyed with the car keys in his hand.

"And you say it was Arnold Miller who told you all this?" Jack had a soft spot for the old man who lived on the streets.

Daniels nodded. "I saw him hanging around outside — which, in itself, was unusual. He doesn't stray far from his patch all that often — if ever."

Decision made, Jack beckoned the young detective to follow him. "Next time you see young Arnold Miller, Daniels — make sure he gets a hot drink and sandwich for his troubles. In the meantime, get your coat. I feel another trip to the pub is on the cards. Let's see if Jerry made it into work."

But before they could reach the door, one of the desk phones began to ring. Cooper made a grab for it.

"Incident room, DS Cooper speaking."

With his hand hovering over the door handle, Jack caught the young detective's eye and he instantly knew what was coming next.

"Boss — Mr and Mrs Williams are on their way in." Cooper replaced the receiver. "They want to speak to you."

CHAPTER TWENTY-EIGHT

Time: 1.00 p.m.
Date: Sunday 25 May 2014
Location: Metropolitan Police HQ, London

Narelle Williams had travelled to London in March 1994, on a gap year, intending to work her way around Europe before returning to Australia to begin a university course. Her parents had last seen their daughter on 12 January, when she'd left Brisbane bound for Europe.

Christine Williams' face was contorted with the same pain Jack had witnessed on Maisie's mother's not forty-eight hours before. The loss of a child, no matter how old they were, was a loss like no other. Jack saw the deep despair in her eyes, her face bearing each and every second of the two decades of not knowing what'd happened to her daughter. Pain aged you like nothing else.

The Williamses had arrived at the station virtually straight from the airport — only depositing their luggage at their hotel reception before heading straight out again. Nothing else mattered. The one and only thing on their mind was Narelle.

"There isn't a great deal I can tell you right now," said Jack, wishing he had better news — if there could ever be good news in a situation such as this. "The investigation is still in its very early stages."

Both Mr and Mrs Williams nodded. "Can you tell us anything about how she died? Or when?" Gregory Williams' voice was strained.

DS Cassidy had dashed out to the deli around the corner and got them all a frothy, and expensive, coffee. Jack sipped his lukewarm flat white, wishing instead he had told her to nip upstairs to the chief superintendent's office and get them all a decent Colombian — or gone further afield to Isabel's. He dismissed the thought and swallowed the weak, tepid liquid. "Again, we don't have a lot to go on at the moment, but my thoughts at this stage would be that your daughter met her death quite soon after the last sighting of her."

"And she's been in the water all that time?" The words caught in Christine Williams' throat. "Under that bridge?"

Jack gave a faint shake of the head. "It's difficult to tell at this stage. My guess is most probably, yes." Pausing, he wondered whether to divulge the next piece of information — but he considered that nothing he said would make them feel any worse than they already did. Or had done for the last twenty years. If it were him, and his daughter had been missing for that length of time, he'd want to know. He'd want to know *everything*.

"We found some sections of metal chain close to Narelle's remains which have been forensically linked to your daughter." Jack paused, his throat constricting with the words he was about to say. Giving a small cough, he continued. "We believe Narelle's body was weighed down when she entered the water. So it's likely she's been in that location ever since."

Mrs Williams stretched a shaking hand towards the cup of cooling takeaway coffee in front of her. She managed a brief smile before her face crumpled. "Thank you," she whispered.

Cassidy stared at the untouched caramel latte in her lap, feeling the tell-tale pinpricks of fresh tears pinching at her own eyes.

Jack considered the other piece of information he had heard only yesterday, during his visit to the mortuary. Looking at Narelle's parents across the table, he saw how completely broken they were. He decided they had enough to deal with right now — hearing about their daughter's suspected dismemberment was something for another time. He pushed his half-drunk coffee to one side.

"If you don't mind, may I ask a little bit more about Narelle? What kind of person she was? What friends she might've had around that time?" Although it was a long shot, and memories often faded over time, he had a hunch that Mr and Mrs Williams' memories of their daughter were as vivid today as the day she'd been born.

"She had a very outgoing personality," replied Gregory Williams, taking hold of his wife's hand. "Always full of fun, full of life." His voice hitched. "She always wanted to see the world. Every day was like a new adventure for her."

"Did she live alone while she was in London?"

Mr Williams nodded. "I think so. She told us about some room she was renting. She seemed content enough there."

"We know from the file that she worked in both a café and a pub. Do you know if she worked anywhere else?"

Mr Williams shook his head. "Sorry. She moved about and changed jobs like the wind. Never one for stopping in one place very long, our Narelle. She moved three times while she was in Germany."

Jack nodded. "And she didn't tell you about anybody she'd met? Any friends while she was here? Or maybe in Germany? No one travelled with her to London?"

It was Mrs Williams' turn to shake her head. "As far as we knew, she'd always travelled alone. I always worried about her, of course. But she was so strong-willed. So headstrong. She always told us that there were so many young people doing it — travelling — and that we weren't to worry." Mrs Williams choked back a fresh round of tears.

Gregory Williams gave his wife's hand another squeeze. "There was only one girl that she mentioned to us. Gina, I think her name was. I don't remember her surname. Narelle worked at the pub with her from what I can remember. I think they were quite good friends. She mentioned her occasionally on the phone and sometimes in her letters home. I don't remember her mentioning anyone else."

Jack's eyebrows hitched a notch. "Letters? Would you be able to make copies for me after you return home?"

"No need, Inspector." Christine Williams' eyes blinked back her tears. "I have them with me. Well, in my luggage back at the hotel I mean. I take them with me everywhere I go. It's all I have left of her, you see." She paused and nodded. "I'll get them sent over as soon as we get back to our room."

"That would be great. Thank you. It's probably nothing, but anything that can help us build a picture of what her life was like while she was here in London — what she did, who she spent time with — it all helps. I'll get them back to you as soon as I can. And if you remember anything else, then please give me a call." Jack slipped a business card across the table towards Mrs Williams. "We'll let you go and check in at your hotel. You must be exhausted."

"Can we see her?" Christine Williams' voice was barely audible above the heavy silence of the room. "Narelle?"

Part of Jack had been expecting the question — much as he had from the Lancasters. But expecting it didn't make it any easier to respond to.

"I can give you the number for the Westminster Mortuary, but . . ." Jack paused and gave both Gregory and Christine Williams a sad smile. "Maybe think about it first. You might want to remember Narelle the way she was when you last saw her." Jack slipped another business card out of his pocket and wrote the contact number for the mortuary on the reverse. "Here. If you still decide you want to, give them a call. They'll make the necessary arrangements."

Jack thanked Mr and Mrs Williams for coming so quickly and assured them he'd be in touch with any further news. After showing them to the exit, he led Cassidy upstairs towards the incident room.

"I don't know how they're keeping themselves together," remarked Cassidy as they approached the door. "I can't even begin to imagine how they feel — after all this time. We really need to find out what happened to Narelle, for their sake."

Jack nodded as he held the door open. "We do — and we will."

After a quick update with the team, Jack beckoned Daniels to follow him. "We're off to visit Jerry at the pub. Amanda, are you following up this Mrs Hamilton about the car?"

Cassidy nodded. "I am. I'll walk downstairs with you."

"While we're gone, Cooper, see what you can dig up on this Gina from the pub that Narelle's parents mentioned. They don't have a surname. Just see if there's any mention of her anywhere in the paperwork."

* * *

Time: 2.30 p.m.
Date: Sunday 25 May 2014
Location: The Bridge Public House, London SE1

Jack sat opposite Daniels in one of the leather-lined booths and sipped his non-alcoholic lager. He was starting to get a taste for it.

"Yeah, so the site of the original tavern is a little bit downstream from where you're sitting right now." Jerry pulled up a bar stool and joined them at the table. "When the new bridge was built, they dismantled the original Hangman's End tavern and rebuilt it here — brick by brick." He nodded towards the bar. "We still have the original wooden bar over there — it's been renovated and repaired over the years, but the original structure easily dates back to the thirteenth century."

"And that rope over the bar?" Daniels nodded towards the rope he'd noticed on their last visit.

"As far as I know, it's one of the original nooses used by the executioner." Jerry's eyes sparkled. "Cool, huh?"

Jack took another long pull on his bottle. "The owners didn't keep the name, then? The Hangman's End?"

The barman gave a slight shrug. "I guess they felt it wasn't in keeping with such a vibrant area of the city. Maybe a bit too 'olde worlde', if you get my meaning. It's all bistros and pavement cafés around here now — no one's really interested in the old days of highwaymen and daylight robbery."

Jack conceded the point. His own preference was for a pub with character – something with a bit of history behind it, rather than a nondescript collection of bricks held together with chrome and fancy artwork.

He put down his bottle. "You know much about the history of the original Hangman's End?"

"Sure do!" The barman's eyes gleamed and a broad smile broke out on his face. "It's a fascinating story. You're familiar with it?"

Jack glanced sideways towards Daniels. "A little, but why don't you enlighten me?"

Jerry pulled his bar stool closer to the table. "Research tells us that the original Hangman's End tavern was built in 1209, during the original construction of the Old London Bridge. Situated right at the south entrance to the bridge, it would've been the perfect stopover for carriages travelling in and out of the city. Back then, it was the only crossing point over the river. The original tavern had stables at the rear, making it a real coaching inn."

"And why the name?" Jack noted the animation in the barman's features. "My detective constable here tells me it was something to do with executions?"

"And he's spot on!" The barman's grin widened.

Hiding himself behind his bottle, Daniels' cheeks began to colour.

"Highwaymen were rife from the seventeenth century onwards. Old London Bridge was a good hunting ground for them, plenty of carriages making the crossing with an abundance of goods and wares on board — and plenty of rich people. If caught, punishment for the highwaymen was death by hanging. Most executions were carried out at a place called Tyburn — but some also took place on the Old London Bridge.

"The executioner would ride a black stallion through the streets, dragging the condemned man behind him. Sometimes, the poor sod could be dragged for miles. Once on the bridge, the executioner would dismount from his horse and disconnect the rope, securing one end to one of the metal spikes at the entrance. Then he would literally fling the highwayman over the side to hang. He'd be left there for all to see for a period of three days. Then, the rope would be cut and the body would be swallowed up by the river. After the execution itself, the hangman traditionally went into the tavern and was stood a pint of ale on the house for his troubles."

The tale was pretty much as Daniels had explained earlier. But as fascinating as it was, Jack was still none the wiser as to how it could fit into the investigation of Narelle or Maisie's murders.

"How long have you been working here, Jerry?" Jack drained the rest of his bottle.

"I've always been here, on and off — started here as a pot washer back in ninety-two. Had a bit of a break when I joined the Army. Then I came back. Been here ever since."

Jack's ears pricked. "Ninety-two? In that case, I don't suppose you'd remember the case of a young woman who went missing in 1994?"

Jerry hesitated, a frown crossing his forehead. "A woman? What woman?"

"Well, I say woman — she was a girl really. Went by the name of Narelle Williams. Australian. Was backpacking around Europe until she disappeared in August 1994. Worked here before she disappeared."

Jerry continued to frown. "Ninety-four? Well, there were a lot of casuals that came and went back then. Australian, you say?" He started to shake his head. "Sorry, doesn't ring a bell."

"What about someone called Gina? Would've been working at the pub around the same time?"

Again, the barman started to shake his head. "Sorry. The memory isn't what it used to be. Oh, hang on a minute . . . Gina, you say?" Jerry tapped his fingers on the table before slowly starting to nod. "Actually, I might remember someone by that name. Tall girl, dark hair."

"Surname?" Jack raised his eyebrows.

Jerry gave a small shrug. "Could've been something like Simmonds. Or Simons. Began with an S anyway."

"OK, does the pub have a head office? Someone who would've dealt with the payroll back then?"

Jerry nodded. "We're part of the Darsten pub chain now. I guess I could get you the head office details if you want? But whether they have what you're looking for, I'm not so sure. Some of us were paid in cash back then, especially the temporary staff. And I'm not sure how long they keep their records for." He gave another shrug. "But I'll see if I can find their number."

Jack watched the barman retreat to a small room behind the bar. With his bottle already empty, he indicated to Daniels that it was time to drink up. He let his gaze drift towards the ceiling just as Jerry came back into view with a piece of paper in his hand.

"Phone number and email there." Jerry passed the folded piece of paper across the table. "Hope it helps."

"Thanks." Jack kept his gaze on the ceiling. "Are there any rooms above? If the original tavern used to be a coaching inn, I'm guessing it had rooms to rent?"

Jerry's gaze joined Jack's as he nodded. "There's a few rooms up there, yes. I guess they might've been let out, back in the day. But it's just used for storage now."

"Any staff live up there? Back in ninety-four?"

Jerry gave another shake of the head, together with a shrug. "Sorry, I've no idea."

Several more people had now entered the bar and were consulting the laminated menus. Jack got to his feet. "Thank you for your time. We'll let you get on."

Daniels didn't bother to finish his bottle this time and hurried out on to the pavement behind Jack. Instead of heading back towards the Mondeo, Jack led them up on to the bridge itself, away from the Sunday lunchtime crowds that were trawling the pavements looking for a vegan wrap and an overpriced coffee. Jack considered that with the prices some of the pavement cafés charged, maybe daylight robbery wasn't such a thing of the past after all. Stopping on the bridge, he gazed once more down to the murky brown waters of the Thames below. The tide was starting to recede, both Narelle and Maisie's final resting places hidden from view beneath the river water.

"Why here, Daniels?" Jack's eyes remained fixed on the river. "Why were both Narelle and Maisie found here? Coincidence?" Jack flicked his gaze back towards the pub formerly known as the Hangman's End. "Or are we missing something?"

* * *

Time: 2.30 p.m.
Date: Sunday 25 May 2014
Location: 27 Lambert Grove, London EC1

Rita Hamilton stood a little over four feet tall in her stockinged feet as she welcomed DS Cassidy inside the entrance hall to number 27 Lambert Grove. She was dressed in a simple pair of linen trousers and a pale blue blouse, with a pair of pink fluffy slippers on her feet. Her cropped white hair sat above a pair of intensely green eyes.

"Come on in, come on in," she breezed, gesturing for Cassidy to follow her along the hall. As she did so, Cassidy noticed every inch of the walls was covered in family photographs.

"I see you have lots of family."

Rita Hamilton's face broke out into a broad smile as she showed the detective into the front room, where even more photographs stood to attention on every available surface. "I do, that. I'm very lucky. I've twelve grandchildren and six great grandchildren at the last count!"

"Wow!" Cassidy returned the smile as she lowered herself into a comfortable armchair by the window. "That's amazing. They must keep you very busy!"

"They do indeed." Rita Hamilton perched herself on the edge of a two- seater sofa and nodded towards a pile of knitting by her feet. "I've always got some kind of knitting on the go — they grow out of things so quickly, you know."

Cassidy nodded, although she had no idea at what rate children grew out of anything. The thought of motherhood and settling down with a family of her own was still a faraway thought — if it was a thought at all. Her gaze flickered towards the window and the street outside.

"So, what can you tell me about this car? When we spoke on the phone you said you'd been giving it some more thought?"

Rita nodded, enthusiastically. "Yes, yes, I have. But first, let me make some tea. You'll have a cup, won't you? And I've baked some shortbread, too." Before Cassidy could decline, the diminutive Rita Hamilton had sprung to her feet and disappeared back out into the hallway towards the kitchen.

With the door open, it wasn't long before the wonderfully buttery aroma of freshly baked shortbread wafted through. Cassidy's mouth began to water at the thought, her stomach rumbling in anticipation. She hadn't had time for breakfast this morning, so this would be a welcome substitute.

Rita soon returned with a loaded tea tray and, once she was settled, she handed Cassidy a bone china teacup.

Resting the teacup on her lap, Cassidy returned to the reason for her visit. "So, the car. Have you had time to think about where you'd seen it parked before?"

Rita took a delicate sip of her tea, a faint tremor in her bird-like hands. Her previous statement had documented her age as eighty-two, but Cassidy saw the sprightliness of a woman half that age. After placing the cup carefully down on the saucer, the old lady nodded.

"Yes, yes, I have. I must apologise to the lovely young officer who came to speak to me first of all, but I was so upset to hear about young Maisie going missing that I don't think I really answered his questions all that well."

"No apology needed, Mrs Hamilton. Do you know the family well? The Lancasters?"

Rita Hamilton gave a sad smile. "Yes, quite well. I'd see little Maisie out and about playing. Her mother would take her to the park at the end of the road quite a lot when she was little, and more recently she's been out on the pavement on her bike. Such a lovely little thing she was." The old lady swallowed and her lips began to tremble. "I can't quite believe what's happened to her. It's all so shocking."

Cassidy took a sip of her tea. It was a little strong for her liking, but welcome all the same. "It is. When you spoke to the officer on 14 May, you mentioned this silver car."

"Yes, yes, I did. And I'm now sure it's a Vauxhall. I've been looking at some pictures, and yes — I'm sure that's what it was. And silver, too. With a different coloured door panel."

"Oh?" Cassidy reached for her notebook. The door panel hadn't been mentioned anywhere before. "What colour was the door panel?"

"It was a darker colour — a darker grey."

"And when we spoke on the phone, you said you were sure you'd seen it before, parked on Lambert Grove?"

More fervent nods as Rita took another sip of tea. "Yes, most definitely. I can see it now, so clearly. It's definitely been parked on the street before, further along in that direction." The old woman raised her hand and indicated out of the window, across the street and to the left.

"And how many times do you think you saw it?"

Rita paused, her already lined forehead creasing further. "Oh, I'm not sure of the exact number of times, but quite a few, I think. I assumed it belonged to someone in the street."

Cassidy placed her teacup back on to the low-rise coffee table and jotted down a few extra notes into her notebook. "That's great, Mrs Hamilton. And have you seen the car since? After Maisie disappeared?"

"Do you know what, I don't think I have — now that you mention it. I think that's why I forgot about it." The old woman gave a little chuckle. "Gosh, it's just like an Agatha Christie novel, isn't it? Putting all the clues together!"

Cassidy smiled. "A little. And you have no idea who the car belonged to? Or maybe which house they were visiting?"

Rita Hamilton paused, her frown deepening. "Well, no, not really. It was often parked in different places along the street up there." Again, she gestured out of the window towards the left. "But I would say it was mostly outside number 32."

Cassidy's eyebrows shot up. "Number 32?"

Rita nodded, enthusiastically. "Yes, more often than not. There's a little parking space just outside. I'm not sure if it was his though — I never saw him driving it."

"And who lives there?"

"That would be Brian. Brian Johnson."

Cassidy closed her notebook. "Thank you, Mrs Hamilton. You've been really helpful." As she rose from the armchair, Cassidy noticed the old lady spring forward and pick up the plate of shortbread.

"You'll take some away with you, won't you?"

CHAPTER TWENTY-NINE

Time: 4.00 p.m.
Date: Sunday 25 May 2014
Location: Metropolitan Police HQ, London

The atmosphere in the incident room was quiet but tense. They had made a fresh round of coffee and devoured the plate of homemade shortbread Cassidy had brought back from Rita Hamilton's.

Jack turned away from the whiteboard where he'd written the words 'HANGMAN'S END' in bold capitals next to Maisie and Narelle's names. "What the significance is, if any, is still unclear." Leaning up against one of the desks, he folded his arms across his chest. "But this pub is connected to Narelle — and, therefore, Maisie too. It's our job to work out why. Amanda? Anything useful from Lambert Grove?"

Cassidy got to her feet, pulling out her notebook. "A little." She approached the whiteboards and took hold of the pen from Jack. "Rita Hamilton lives at number 27 — three doors away from the Lancasters, and knows them pretty well as a family. She was first spoken to on the evening of 14 May but was in such shock at Maisie's disappearance that she didn't quite say everything she could have. Although she's eighty-two, she's as bright as a button and in full possession of all her marbles. A really lovely lady."

Cassidy paused, securing the lid back on the marker pen. "In the days before Maisie went missing, Rita is now certain that she saw the silver Vauxhall parked along the street outside number 32. She mentioned that it was often parked at various points along the road, but mostly outside number 32 — the home of a Mr Brian Johnson. She's now certain it was a Vauxhall and remembered the first part of the registration as beginning with a BM — her late husband's initials."

Jack felt the hairs on the back of his neck prickle. "Outside number 32?" He couldn't help but slide his gaze along to Raymond Dixon's mugshot still pinned to the cork board. "She's sure of that?"

Cassidy nodded. "There's a small parking space outside number 32, enough for two cars. She's certain this car had been parked there on more than one occasion. But, interestingly, she hasn't seen the car at all since Maisie disappeared."

"Brian Johnson?" Cooper clicked his mouse, a frown on his forehead. "Why do I recognise that name? Ah, look, here." Cooper tapped his computer screen. "He's the chap who said in his house-to-house statement that he used to go to the Lambert Grove Working Men's Club with Dixon."

Jack slowly nodded, rubbing his unshaven chin. "So he is, Cooper. So he is. Look, we need to find this car. Pronto. Keep running the plate and checking the cameras and keep tracking those vehicles in and around the bridge on the twentieth. It has to pop up somewhere."

"I knocked at number 32 after I left Mrs Hamilton's, but there was no answer." Cassidy returned to her seat. "I've got his phone number so I'll keep trying that."

"Good work." Jack turned his gaze away from Raymond Dixon. "We need to keep digging into Dixon. With this car seen driving slowly along Lambert Grove only moments before Maisie was taken, and now sighted parked close to his address, I'm even more convinced of his involvement in some way. Where are we on any phone records? And Derek Foster's, too?"

"Waiting on Dixon's to come through, boss." Cooper glanced at his computer monitor. "As far as we know, he's only got the one mobile registered to him. As for Foster, his phone records are in and I'm just going through them now."

"Good. Let me know if you see anything useful." Jack pushed himself away from the table and headed for the door. "Before I go — do we have anything on this Gina now we have a possible surname?"

Daniels tapped his keyboard to wake up his computer monitor. "The original files on Narelle's disappearance don't mention anyone called Gina, but the name Gina Simmonds has pinged on the system a couple of times. And the age looks about right. Some minor drug and prostitution offences a few years ago. There's nothing for a Gina Simons."

"OK. Keep digging into this Gina Simmonds. Sounds like it could be the one. See if you can get a recent address. I'll check with head office."

* * *

Time: 11.00 a.m.
Date: Sunday 25 May 2014
Location: The Old Oak Hotel, New York City, USA

In the end, she'd only been half an hour late for the talk. Nobody seemed to notice as she slunk quietly into the conference room and slipped into a vacant chair. And from the look of it, she hadn't missed much. 'Cognitive Behavioural Therapy: The Future' — it wasn't exactly a crowd pleaser.

Before leaving the hotel, Rachel had ordered herself a fresh coffee from room service, together with a light breakfast. While getting ready, she'd ploughed through both files once more.

There was much less information on Narelle. All Jack had been able to send through was some scant paperwork on the original missing person's enquiry, several statements from her parents, and the initial draft report from Professor Kaufman.

But, even so, Rachel's interest was immediately piqued. She noted that Narelle was last seen on 31 August 1994, and her parents had never given up hope of finding her alive. A hope that had now been so heartbreakingly dashed by the discovery beneath the bridge.

The level of detail in Professor Kaufman's report was astounding. It never failed to amaze her just how many secrets could be unlocked from the bones of the deceased, even after many years had passed. Although it wasn't yet clear how Maisie had met her death, the manner of the dismemberment afterwards was strikingly consistent with Narelle's. The photographs from Maisie's post-mortem were so graphic in their detail that Rachel quickly felt her newly digested croissant beginning to lurch inside her stomach.

Giving an involuntary shudder, she pulled her thoughts back to the present and joined in with a ripple of applause for the departing speaker. She glanced at the agenda on the table and reached for a glass of sparkling mineral water. There were a few more speeches to endure before they would break for lunch.

Although lunch was the last thing on her mind — she needed to speak to Jack.

* * *

Time: 4.15 p.m.
Date: Sunday 25 May 2014
Location: Metropolitan Police HQ, London

Jack's call to Darsten's head office was placed on hold, and his ear was instantly filled with tinny hold music. While he was waiting, he couldn't help but think about Raymond Dixon. Once again, the man's name had thrown itself into the investigation — and it was a coincidence that left him feeling distinctly unsettled. Before he could let his mind wander any further, the tinny music suddenly stopped.

"Thank you for holding. I have the information for you now."

A pleasant-sounding Scottish accent filled Jack's ears. He'd already forgotten the woman's name. "That's great, thanks," he replied. "Fire away."

"You were asking about an employee by the name of Narelle Williams. Employed during 1994?"

"Yes, that's correct."

"I can confirm that the system does show that she was employed from 15 April 1994. Her contract came to an end on 5 September that same year."

Jack remembered that 5 September was the date Narelle had failed to turn up for her shift at the pub. "OK. And the address she was living at back then?"

The pleasant-sounding Scottish voice confirmed the details that Jack had already seen on Narelle's letters home — the squalid bedsit on Connaught Road. "That's the only contact address we have on file."

She then ran through a list of other employees who were working at the pub around the same time as Narelle, none of which Jack recognised — other than Gina Simmonds.

"Do you have a contact address for Gina Simmonds? Anything recent?"

Jack could almost sense the woman shaking her head on the other end of the line. "Sorry, we have nothing after she left us in 1996."

"OK. One more thing. The rooms above the pub — were employees ever allowed to rent them? If so, did Narelle ever rent a room?" Jack thought back to her bedsit address and hoped to God that she did.

"The rooms were sometimes rented, yes," came the reply. "But we don't have anything on record that Narelle Williams rented one. And it would be on the system as the rent is deducted from the employee's wages at source."

“OK, thanks anyway.” Jack replaced the receiver and slumped back in his chair.

At least they now knew that the Gina Simmonds on the system looked to be the right one — but, apart from that, the conversation with the head office hadn’t moved them that far forward.

Sighing, Jack swallowed the remnants of his cold coffee and reached for his jacket. Just as he did so, his desk phone began to ring. He debated whether to ignore it, just in case it was the chief superintendent ready to give him another earful, but dutifully snatched up the receiver while shrugging into his jacket.

“DI MacIntosh.”

Jack listened to the short message on the other end, nodding as he did so.

“I’ll be right down.”

CHAPTER THIRTY

Time: 4.30 p.m.
Date: Sunday 25 May 2014
Location: Metropolitan Police HQ, London

The Williamses had been true to their word and a padded envelope addressed to Jack soon arrived by express courier. Closing the blinds to shut out the sunlight streaming through his office window, Jack seated himself back in his chair and tipped the contents out on to his desk.

A selection of blue airmail envelopes and postcards soon stacked up into a small pile. Turning over the first envelope, Jack noted the post mark was dated 31 March 1994. Taking out the enclosed letter, he saw that it was written on very thin, airmail paper — but the ink was still legible. From a quick scan of the first few lines, it suggested that Narelle had been in London for just a short while.

> *'Hi all! Managing to find my feet in this big old city! I've found a place to stay and a job in a café around the corner. Life is sweet!'*

The rest of the letter continued in the same upbeat manner, with Narelle saying how much she was looking forward to her London adventure. She wrapped the letter up by asking about her baby brother and hoping that no one was missing her too much.

Jack slid the letter back inside the envelope and moved on. The next was dated 30 April 1994.

> *'Hi! Me again! Hope all is good back home. The weather here is getting better but it's nothing like good old Brisbane! But at least it's better than Germany. There it rained the whole time. I can't wait to see you guys when you fly out to see me in France! Don't forget to bring me my Oasis tapes. I've managed to find a second-hand cassette player. I'm still in the same flat as before — it's OK — a bit small but I don't have much! I'm still working in the café, but I've also started a new job in a pub by the river. It's so cool! I can see St Paul's Cathedral from the window while I'm working! It's quite a busy pub in the evenings and I have to work long hours. But I don't mind, as the pay is quite good and I get lots of tips! This whole area is getting a makeover — lots of cafes and restaurants are opening up all the time. It's really cool! And there's a nice girl, Gina, who's showing me the ropes and everything is great!'*

He plucked another airmail letter from the pile, this one dated later on 10 July 1994. It was another letter full of joyful enthusiasm at her new-found freedom, telling her parents how well she was settling into the pub with Gina's help. And she'd even managed to find an emergency dentist to sort out her toothache.

After reading a few more, Jack turned his attention to the stack of postcards. He noted a few were from Germany, but he counted out eight that were from London. Most had only a few lines scrawled on the back — ranging from the classic '*Wish you were here*' to '*I'm having the greatest time of my life!*'. One in particular stood out — it was dated 17 August 1994, only two weeks before the last known sighting of Narelle. She signed off with — '*I never want this to end!*'

Jack selected two more postcards from the pile, both sent only a couple of days before Narelle disappeared. One, dated 28 August 1994, had a picture of the Changing of the Guard on the front — and on the back she'd scrawled '*me and G saw this today! AWESOME!*' The other card had a picture of Buckingham Palace. Jack flicked it over to reveal Narelle's looping handwriting — '*Going to see the Queen with G!*'

Jack slotted the letters and cards back into the padded envelope. Mr and Mrs Williams had given the original investigation a selection of their most treasured photographs. Each one gave the impression of a fun-loving, carefree nineteen-year-old woman — brimming with excitement and adventure. And from the tone of her letters back home, she was clearly enjoying her new life. Each letter was an exuberant description of the perfect backpacker's lifestyle.

Jack stared at the padded envelope and cast his mind back to when he had been that age. *Nineteen.* He couldn't remember being so full of energy, or loving life to quite the extent that Narelle was. Everything she did gave the impression that this was the most amazing time of her life, finding enjoyment in anything and everything — even the most mundane things like shopping and working. Her communications oozed enthusiasm and energy. She even had good things to say about her bedsit which, when Jack saw the address where she'd been living at back in 1994, made him wonder if they'd been talking about the same place.

The truth was, Narelle was living in a crappy part of London and was holding down two equally crappy jobs. She can't have been earning much and, other than the occasional mention of Gina from the pub, there was no indication she had many friends enjoying this supposedly idyllic lifestyle with her.

Jack propped the padded envelope up against his in-tray. He'd take another look at the letters later — he couldn't explain it, but there was something about them that didn't quite sit right.

* * *

Time: 1.45 p.m.
Date: Sunday 28 August 1994
Location: Flat 3c Connaught Road, London

Narelle tucked her legs up beneath her and settled back against the pillows on the narrow single bed. She was sure she'd seen something scuttling across the floor yesterday, darting out from underneath the bed and then scampering over to the broken wardrobe opposite.

Had it been a mouse? A rat, even? She remembered being taught at school about the Great Plague that had hit London back in the seventeenth century. Wasn't it rats that'd spread the disease? The thought made her shiver. Pulling out the latest postcard she'd picked up from the newsagents on the way back from the café, she flipped it over to the front. It depicted the classic Changing of the Guard scene outside Buckingham Palace and had '*I love London*' stamped across the top corner.

I love London.

Did she love London? She liked the *idea* of London, and sometimes she really did feel as though she was enjoying herself. Sometimes. But the job at the café was hard work — on her feet from early in the morning, she often didn't finish until late in the afternoon. Most of the time it was so busy she didn't even have time for a proper break — maybe a quick fifteen minutes when they were quiet, which wasn't often.

And then she went to work at the pub, and she could easily be there until midnight. Sunday was the only day she had off, and she usually spent the majority of that sleeping.

The woman who ran the café was all right, but she could get quite irritated if Narelle made even the simplest of mistakes. When she first started, she sometimes got mixed up with the money — getting confused with British Pounds and Australian Dollars. The customers often found it amusing, endearing even, but not so Brenda White.

If she could get more hours at the pub, she would happily jack the café job in. The people were friendlier there, and she loved it when she was working a shift with Gina.

Flipping the postcard over, she tapped the biro against her chin and thought about what to write this time. How many different ways was there to say she was having an amazing time? She had already used most of them she was sure — probably more than once. She didn't want Mum or Dad thinking she was unhappy and not enjoying her travels as much as she'd thought she would. It had been a real wrench for them to let her go in the first place — Dad had loaned her some of the cash for the airfare for the first leg of her journey, even though she knew money was tight. It would break their hearts if they knew she was feeling so homesick. Dad would no doubt stump up the necessary cash to fly her home — money troubles or no money troubles — but she didn't want to admit defeat.

With a sigh Narelle put the pen to the card and scribbled '*AWESOME!*' in big letters.

* * *

Time: 5.00 p.m.
Date: Sunday 25 May 2014
Location: Metropolitan Police HQ, London

"Sorry for bothering you again . . . so soon." Mrs Williams' voice sounded faint, even though she couldn't have been more than a couple of miles away. "I just thought of a couple more questions."

"Not at all." Jack leaned back in his chair, telephone receiver in hand, his eyes still resting on the padded envelope containing Narelle's letters home. "How can I help?"

"We were just wondering — about the newspaper reports. That little girl that was found . . ." Mrs Williams' voice cracked, her words tailing off.

Jack nodded, slowly. "Maisie. Maisie Lancaster."

"Yes. Well, we wondered — with the body being found so close to our Narelle . . ." Again, her words withered like a wilted flower in the sun. "We wondered if there was any link?"

Jack's eyes strayed to his in-tray and the copy of yesterday's *Daily Courier* that was still folded up on top. He hoped neither of them had managed to get hold of a copy.

"I'm sorry," he replied. "I wish I had something concrete I could tell you. But at this stage we just don't know the relevance. We're keeping an open mind — but I wouldn't always believe everything you read in the papers." Jack kept his eyes on the folded copy of the *Daily Courier*.

"We're well aware of how the press work — but we also know that sometimes things are kept out of the media."

Jack nodded to himself. He'd read somewhere in Narelle's file that her father had worked for one of the main Brisbane newspapers around the time of his daughter's disappearance. "We honestly don't have any firm leads as to a connection between the two girls." And that part was true; they didn't. All they had was supposition and suggestion, and a feeling that something wasn't quite right — but at the end of the day that counted for nothing.

Nothing except the fact that both victims had been dismembered in a similar fashion. And being found metres away from each other, decades apart, crushed the notion of it being an unhappy coincidence — at least, it did in Jack's view.

But he needed proof — something he didn't quite have.

Not yet.

"We want to take her home." Christine Williams' voice was barely audible, and Jack needed to press the receiver close to his ear to catch her faint words. "When can we have her back?"

Jack sighed. "I'm sorry — that will take some time. There has to be a formal inquest — and the criminal investigation will delay that a little. But we'll do everything we can to hurry it along." He tried to sound encouraging but he knew that, as far as the inquest process went, his hands were tied.

There was silence on the other end of the line and Jack wondered if the call had been disconnected, but then Mrs Williams' faint voice crackled into life once more.

"In that case, we want to go and see her. Will you come?"

CHAPTER THIRTY-ONE

Time: 5.55 p.m.
Date: Sunday 25 May 2014
Location: Westminster Mortuary, London

Jack had been to the viewing room only once before. Highly trained in dealing with relatives coming to view their loved ones, the mortuary staff would usually take care of that side of things. But, this time, he felt an almost inexplicable need to be present. Mr and Mrs Williams were due in at six o'clock and he knew, beyond a shadow of a doubt, that they would be punctual.

The room itself was fairly small but tastefully decorated. Pale, warm hues replaced the impersonal, sterile coldness of the rest of the building. There were no stainless-steel trolleys or harsh overhead lights in here.

Also gone was the familiar cloying smell of the mortuary. Instead, no doubt assisted by an abundance of air fresheners and an efficient air conditioning system, the room smelled sweet and fresh. Close your eyes and you could fool yourself into thinking you were in a meadow full of blossoming spring flowers.

A bed — the size of a traditional single bed — was positioned in the centre of the room. Ordinarily, a purple velvet throw would shroud the body being viewed, with the deceased's head resting on a soft, ivory-coloured pillow. To all intents and purposes, they would look as though they were asleep.

But today's viewing wasn't like any other.

Today there was no body to lie peacefully beneath the velvet throw. Instead, the mortuary staff had laid Narelle's skull on the ivory pillow, with the rest of her remains on a crisp, white sheet. The purple throw was neatly folded at one end of the bed, not needed this time.

Bereaved relatives could request a favourite piece of music to be played in the background, but Mr and Mrs Williams had requested nothing: nothing but silence and time alone with their daughter.

Dr Matthews had kindly offered to be on hand to answer any questions Narelle's parents may have, and in the meantime had retreated to the sanctuary of his office.

Jack stood in the corner of the viewing room as the door opened. Christine Williams looked as though she'd aged fourfold in the few hours since Jack had last seen her. Bruise-like rings encased her sunken eyes, her face devoid of colour. Her husband, too, looked haggard and drawn, as if sleep was no longer his friend.

No words were exchanged — instead, both Mr and Mrs Williams simply went to Narelle's side and wept.

After a few minutes, Gregory Williams stepped to the side and turned his face towards Jack, his skin blotchy and red. Whoever said that real men don't cry had obviously never had to look upon their dead daughter's skeletal remains.

"Thank you for arranging this." The man's Australian drawl was thick with emotion. "It means a lot."

Jack merely nodded — his throat refusing to release any words; not that he really knew what to say. He caught Mrs Williams' eye. "I'm so sorry for your loss." Somehow, it didn't quite sound enough.

Christine Williams acknowledged Jack with a weak smile. She had one hand on Narelle's head and was gently caressing what would have been her daughter's cheek — a loving mother's touch. Jack looked away, feeling a lump constricting his throat.

He'd successfully convinced Maisie's parents that viewing her body wouldn't be the best way to remember their daughter. Initially they'd insisted they wanted to, but eventually succumbed to Jack's subtle suggestion that it might not be so wise. No parent should ever have to see their child's decapitated torso.

But Christine and Gregory Williams had been adamant that they needed to see what remained of Narelle — and then to take her home as soon as the inquest had concluded.

Jack cleared his throat. "Dr Matthews is more than happy to speak to you — if you have any questions at all."

Both Mr and Mrs Williams nodded, mouthing a 'thank you' before turning back to their daughter.

Jack decided to take his leave, and with a final sad smile he headed out into the corridor. He thought about calling in on Dr Matthews but felt that he needed the fresh air more. Pushing open the fire exit, he took in a lungful and closed his eyes. Although the sun was still warm, he felt chilled as he stood in the shadows of the mortuary building. As Cassidy often said, there was something about the place that just made you shiver.

Pulling his phone from his pocket, Jack noted a text message from DC Daniels. They'd found an address for a Gina Simmonds, and the café where she currently worked. With it still being relatively early, they would hopefully be able to catch up with her later. Realising that the working day showed no signs of being over just yet, Jack sighed and turned towards the car park. As he did so, the phone in his hand started to trill.

This time it was Dr Hunter.

"Dr Hunter," he greeted, reaching the side of the Mondeo.

"Oh, come on, Jack." Dr Hunter's voice was light. "I think we can dispense with the formalities — you've seen me kick off my high heels after one too many margaritas, remember?"

Jack swallowed a smile. "Rachel. You've managed to have a look at the papers I sent through?"

"I have. Most intriguing. And heartbreaking."

Jack's heartbeat accelerated a notch. "And what did you think?"

"I'm putting all this in an audio file, which I'll send over later today — but I'll give you the edited highlights now if you have time? Let's start with Maisie."

Jack heard the rustling of papers in the background and wondered where she was. It didn't sound like a restaurant or bar this time.

Dr Hunter cleared her throat and began. "The fact that Maisie disappeared without any fuss — without anybody seeing anything untoward — that leads me to surmise that Maisie knew or at least trusted her abductor. Your man will be a self-assured and confident person. He'll be calm, with an ability to think on his feet. Quick-witted. Cocky, even. And I say 'he' because I'm certain the person you're looking for is male.

"I would suggest an age range of between thirty-nine and fifty-nine. Research tells us most abductors are middle-aged or older. It's not a young person's crime. They will be local, or with at least a good working knowledge of the local area. If employed, they will hold down a low-skilled or manual job — but it's more than likely they will have had periods of unemployment. Research shows they will most likely have an average IQ. They will be a car driver — with either their own vehicle or access to one. Due to the nature of the offence, they will live alone. Their house or flat will have a rear entrance and will not be overlooked. They will have had relationships in the past, and may even have been married, but they will be living alone at present. It is likely the abducted child spent some time with the offender, possibly at their home address, and therefore unlikely anyone else lives at the property. This person is likely to have a criminal record, mostly involving violence."

Dr Hunter paused, and Jack heard more rustling of paperwork. "I'm assuming there were no witnesses to the dumping of the suitcase?"

Jack shook his head. "No, none. Just the chap who found it."

"It's a busy part of London, Jack — even in the middle of the night. With the tide times you supplied, and the forensic report confirming the suitcase had not been submerged in river water for any length of time, then it suggests your man was on the bridge after six o'clock the previous evening. This links back to him being a confident individual. Sunset wasn't until around nine — he could've been seen at any moment, but he still chose one of the busiest bridges in London to be his dumping ground. This says a lot about him. Have you established how he came to be on the bridge?"

Jack gave another shake of the head. "No. CCTV on the bridge itself was out of action. We've been checking out vehicles in the surrounding streets, eliminating drivers."

"He was on foot, Jack. He walked on to the bridge."

"I'm sorry." Jack's eyebrows shot up. "He *walked*?"

"A car stopping on the bridge would attract far more attention than a person — plus there's the potential for ANPR and other camera tracking. Your man's not stupid."

"We've been concentrating on vehicles," replied Jack. And one vehicle in particular, he thought, as the image of the silver Vauxhall parked close to Raymond Dixon's house flashed across his mind. "But you're saying he was on foot?"

"Almost certainly. Like I said — he may not be a criminal mastermind, but he's not stupid. Also, your man will have been resident in London in 1994." Jack heard more paper rustling in the background. "You'll need to cross-reference that with any suspects you might have."

Jack pulled his thoughts away from Dixon and swapped the phone to his other ear. "1994?"

Dr Hunter paused. "Your cases are linked, Jack — just as you suspected they might be. Maisie *and* Narelle — it's the same killer."

CHAPTER THIRTY-TWO

Time: 6.30 p.m.
Date: Sunday 25 May 2014
Location: Metropolitan Police HQ, London

"Tell me how it can be the same killer. The murders are . . ."

"Twenty years apart, I know."

"So, how come . . . ?" Jack rubbed his forehead, another headache starting to throb at the temples. He had raced back from the mortuary, his mind frantically trying to connect the dots. The idea that the cases were linked had gnawed away at him like a nasty toothache ever since he'd watched Professor Kaufman examine Narelle's remains. Common sense told him that it was implausible but if you ignored the time scale . . . it wasn't as crazy as it sounded.

"It's the location."

"The location?" Jack stopped massaging his forehead, his eyes narrowing. "You mean the river?"

"More so the bridge, I think." There was a pause. "Correct me if I'm wrong, but your working hypothesis is that the suitcase containing Maisie's remains was thrown from the bridge rather than it having been carried there by the tide from further upstream?"

"That's certainly how we're thinking, yes. The lab has a pretty high degree of certainty that neither the suitcase nor the body had been in the water for long. Probably not submerged at all. We think the killer tossed it over the side and it landed on the mud flats below at low tide."

He could hear the sound of rustling pages as Rachel flicked through her notes. "And Narelle's remains — all found close by?"

Jack gave another nod towards the phone's handset. "The skull was buried in the silt barely a few metres away from where the suitcase was found. The upper and lower limbs were found close by — again buried in the silt — as was the pelvis and the rest of her remains. We believe they've been *in situ* for some time, if not for the whole duration since she died."

"Is that likely?"

Jack gave a further nod. "I've spoken with the Port Authority. It's not common, but it's not exactly uncommon either. The tides and current would normally transport a body away from its dumping site, which might lead us to speculate that she'd entered the water someplace upstream. But . . ."

"The chains," finished Dr Hunter. "Then you have to consider the chains."

"Yes, the chains. Fragments of bone have been found in sections of the recovered chains. All linked to Narelle. And fragments of some kind of material or fabric were embedded in her skull. It's possible her head was inside a bag of some sort before being thrown into the river, and the rest of her encased in chains." Jack felt himself shudder — the thought of Narelle's decapitated head inside a bag chilled him.

"And both pathologists believe Narelle was dismembered in the same fashion as Maisie?"

"Yes — we're awaiting the formal report but that's essentially what they said."

"And no known connection between the families?"

"None that we can find so far."

"Then the only logical connection between them is the bridge."

"But why the bridge?"

"It's important to him. He chose it for a reason, Jack. Killers put a lot of thought into their dumping sites, more so than you might imagine. It's all part of the killing process for them. Killers, especially serial killers, go through various phases in their killing process — and choosing a dumping or disposal site is one of them. It won't be just some random choice. London Bridge means something to your killer — and to track him down, you need to find out what that is."

"Is he likely to do this again?" Jack knew he had to ask.

Dr Hunter hesitated briefly before replying. "Someone who can dismember a small child is always going to be a risk, Jack."

* * *

Time: 6.30 p.m.
Date: Sunday 25 May 2014
Location: Niko's Café, Sunderland Street, London

Gina eyed the tacky wall-mounted clock and willed the time to go backwards. The day had dragged like no other. Darren, thankfully, hadn't shown up for breakfast — but it did nothing to quell the nausea she felt inside.

The builders had eventually left around midday, giving Gina yet another rendition of their lurid singing, and would have attempted to smack her behind again if she hadn't kept out of the way of their straying hands. Mr Georgiades had found the whole encounter most amusing and spent the rest of the afternoon in an unnervingly hospitable mood.

At a little before four o'clock, as Gina stepped past him to head towards the kitchen with an order, he'd sidled up to her and pushed a handful of notes into her hand, letting his chubby fingers linger on her skin one or two seconds longer than necessary. She had felt herself recoil at his sweaty touch and the look that had crossed his face as he did so.

The notes in her hand amounted to a decent advance on her wages. And as much as it sickened her, she could put up with his roving eye and lurid comments if it meant she could escape going to Darren's tonight.

She'd texted Darren immediately, telling him that she'd managed to get some of the money together. Not all of it, but most of it. The message had gone unanswered, which had added to Gina's stress levels. Then, just half an hour ago, she'd felt the tell-tale vibration in her pocket. With a growing degree of trepidation, she'd pulled out her phone and tapped the message icon.

Her heart plummeted.

'I'll send someone to pick you up. Bring the cash as well.'

Gina took another glance up at the wall clock. Half an hour before the end of her shift and the beginning of her nightmare.

As she turned to continue scrubbing one of the plastic tables, trying to dislodge a deposit of congealed bacon fat encrusted in tomato sauce, she tried to convince herself that maybe this was the best way out of the unholy mess she was in. The thought of any number of men clawing at her, putting their hands where she definitely didn't want them to, and then . . . whatever it was she was expected to let them do to her . . . made her feel physically sick. But maybe she could tolerate it — just one more time. Maybe she could just shut her eyes and pretend she was somewhere else.

Maybe.

Despite willing the hands of the clock to go backwards, the end of her shift soon arrived and Gina could see the black BMW parked outside on a double yellow line. The car's windows were tinted, so she couldn't see which of Darren's henchmen he'd dispatched to round her up.

Resigning herself to her fate, she started peeling off her apron. She had brought her only decent outfit with her and left it hanging up by the fire exit — a short skirt, although probably not as short as Darren would like, which would by now reek of fried food and cooking fat.

Before moving off to retrieve her change of clothes, a movement outside caught her eye. As she turned to look through the floor to ceiling windows that flanked the front of the café, she saw the BMW had been joined by another car.

The occupants of the second car were standing by the BMW's passenger side window, in conversation with someone who Gina could now make out to be Marco — a little runt of a man who did all of Darren's dirty work for him. What looked to be a heated conversation was then terminated by the BMW suddenly gunning its engine and speeding away from the kerb.

Gina frowned and watched as the two men entered the café.

"Gina Simmonds?" The slightly taller of the two strode towards her. He had a kind, if slightly careworn, face, and held up a warrant card. "Detective Inspector Jack MacIntosh of the Metropolitan Police. This is DS Cooper. Could we have a word?"

* * *

Time: 7.00 p.m.
Date: Sunday 25 May 2014
Location: Metropolitan Police HQ, London

DS Cassidy drummed her fingers, impatiently, on the table as she clamped the phone receiver to her ear. It was the fourth time she'd tried to ring Brian Johnson, and again the call went straight to answerphone.

"Still not answering," she commented, terminating the call without leaving a message. "Do you think I should go round?"

Daniels looked up at the clock. "It's getting a bit late. Do you think they're not answering on purpose, or they're just not there?"

Cassidy shrugged and stifled a yawn. "No idea. I'll keep trying, but I might pop round in the morning."

"At least we've finally got Raymond Dixon's phone records in." Daniels tapped his computer screen. "I'm just collating them all. Doesn't look like he uses his phone all that much, so it shouldn't take long."

Cassidy pushed herself up from her chair and went over to the hot water urn. "Coffee?" She received a nod in response. "It'll have to be black. I'm not buying any more milk for it just to get swiped."

Depositing a mug of black coffee on Daniels' desk, she peered over his shoulder. "Anything useful on the car yet?"

Daniels shook his head. "I think we need to widen the parameters of the search. And maybe the timescale too. Like the boss said, it can't just have vanished."

Returning to her seat, Cassidy picked up the desk phone once again. "Good idea. While you're doing that, I'll try this number one more time."

* * *

Time: 7.05 p.m.
Date: Sunday 25 May 2014
Location: Niko's Café, Sunderland Street, London

Niko Georgiades had thankfully decided to keep out of the way, shutting himself in the kitchen and closing the dividing door. Gina offered the two detectives a cup of coffee, but both had declined — which was probably wise.

Her initial surprise, and then concern, at a detective wishing to speak to her had very quickly morphed into gratitude. Their appearance outside the café had clearly orchestrated Marco's hasty departure, no doubt returning to Darren's poky one-bedroom flat in Soho to relay the bad news. Tonight's soiree looked to be off the cards.

And Gina, for one, couldn't be more thankful.

But the relief didn't last long as the nature of the detectives' visit became apparent.

Narelle.

Gina hadn't heard that name in over two decades.

At this precise moment in time, she would have given anything to be nineteen again — but when she realised that the skeleton she'd been reading about in the newspapers actually belonged to her friend, her face visibly whitened.

"I'm sorry," Jack added. "This must come as a bit of a shock. Cooper, see if you can find some water behind that counter."

Cooper headed off towards the counter, spying a wide-doored drinks cooler standing behind the till. Pulling it open, he selected a bottle of Highland Spring.

"Did you know her well?" Jack placed a copy of Narelle's picture on the grease-topped table.

Gina's watery eyes lowered to the photograph of her friend and suddenly she was nineteen years old and 'Love is All Around' by Wet Wet Wet was playing on the radio. They were both dancing around in the kitchen of the pub, getting under the feet of the head chef. If only she could go back in time — she'd treasure that moment, and maybe not make the catalogue of horrendous mistakes that followed.

Through tear-filled eyes, Gina nodded. "Pretty well."

"I don't suppose you can remember the last time you saw her?"

Cooper arrived back at the table with the bottle of Highland Spring which Gina gratefully took hold of, immediately ripping the cap off and taking a large gulp. Returning her gaze to the picture of Narelle, she shook her head. "Not really — one minute she was there, the next . . . just gone. I remember everyone saying that she'd moved on — gone back on her travels."

"So, nobody was all that worried or concerned?"

Gina shook her head again. "No, not that I recall. People came and went all the time."

Just then, the door to the café opened and three taxi drivers shuffled in, leaving their cars parked outside on the double yellow lines. Jack ignored them and focused back on Gina. "How long did you work there? At the pub?"

Gina frowned as she forced her mind to think back. "Gosh, it's hard to remember. I started in the autumn of 1993 after I left college, and Narelle joined around April time the next year, I think. I must have stayed on for another couple of years after she disappeared."

"Did Narelle ever confide in you about her personal life? Any customers or acquaintances she was having trouble with? Anyone overstepping the mark?"

Another shake of the head was followed by another gulp from the water bottle. "Sorry, no. Nothing that sticks in my memory."

"Was she happy?"

Gina's eyes clouded over as images of nineteen-year-old Narelle flooded her head. That smile, that sun-kissed skin, that carefree attitude. "I guess so. She always seemed to be smiling, loving life. Travelling was her passion — I think that's why nobody thought anything of it when she didn't show up for work."

Jack nodded. That had been the distinct feeling he'd got from the scant paperwork on offer.

"Is it true?" Gina's voice cut into Jack's thoughts. "What they're saying in the papers?" Her eyes flickered towards the rack of newspapers on the wall that paying customers could read while dipping toast into their runny eggs. "That she was murdered?"

"Yes." Jack saw no sense in pretending. "There's evidence of several blows to the head which would've killed her."

Gina's face lost even more colour and she took another gulp of water.

"Did you ever meet Narelle's parents? Mr and Mrs Williams?"

"Not really. I saw them once, I think. They came into the pub when they were looking for Narelle. I think that was the first time any of us thought that maybe she hadn't gone off travelling like we'd been told. I always wanted to believe that she'd just run off — but in my heart I guess I knew that wouldn't be the case. Narelle wasn't really like that."

Jack's eyebrows hitched. "Like what?"

"Flighty. Rebellious. Narelle didn't like taking risks. And she loved her parents too much, and her brother. It never really sat right with me that she would up sticks so suddenly and not tell anyone where she was going." Gina paused and gave a half-hearted shrug. "But we were young. We believed what we were told. And as time went on, I'm ashamed to say that I forgot about her."

"Did she have any other friends? She had another job at a café not far from her flat. Did she ever mention anyone else?"

Gina shook her head. "Not that I remember, no. Narelle was quite shy. She didn't go out all that much — neither of us did. We worked most nights in the pub — that was our social life, really."

Jack placed the padded envelope containing Narelle's letters and postcards on top of the table. "Narelle wrote home fairly frequently." Dipping a hand inside, he pulled out the bundle of correspondence. "Do you know if she wrote to anyone else? Friends back home? Boyfriend, maybe?"

Gina shook her head once more, her eyes fixed on the letters in Jack's hand. "May I?" She nodded towards the bundle.

Jack handed the collection across the table and watched as Gina's trembling hands unwound the elastic band. Silently, she started to read each letter, tears dripping from her cheeks. She flipped the postcards over to see Narelle's trademark '*AWESOME!*' scribbled over the back. Her hands shook as she let the cards fall back on to the table.

"It's nice that she mentions you, though. When she wrote home." Cooper nodded towards the letters and postcards that Jack was starting to scoop up and slip back inside the padded envelope. "There's quite a few references to 'G' on her postcards."

Gina swallowed another mouthful of water, rubbing the tears from her cheeks. "We were good friends — but she never called me 'G'. She probably meant Gerard."

"Gerard?" Jack and Cooper exchanged a look. "Who's Gerard?"

"He worked with us at the pub. She always called him 'G'. Sometimes Gerry, but mostly just 'G'. They were inseparable — thick as thieves sometimes."

Jack eyed Cooper as the young sergeant took out his notebook. "You happen to have a surname for this Gerard?"

"Murray, I think." Gina nodded. "Yes. Gerard Murray."

"Thanks for your time, Gina." Jack flashed another look at Cooper, indicating that it was time to go. "I hope we didn't keep you from anything?"

Gina felt the familiar trembling in the pit of her stomach begin again. "No, nothing at all." She eyed the clock and then the road outside. Marco hadn't come back for her. Surely it was too late to go now?

Just as Jack got to his feet, Mr Georgiades bustled in from the kitchen, heading over to the table of taxi drivers, armed with three plates of all-day breakfasts. Once he'd deposited the plates, he waddled over in Jack's direction, noting the half-empty bottle of Highland Spring in Gina's hand.

"I hope you're going to pay for that," he grumbled, wiping the sweat from his brow with the edge of his grubby apron.

Gina's cheeks coloured. Just as she reached into her pocket for some change, Jack threw a five-pound note on to the table, narrowly missing a globule of something dark coloured — presumably brown sauce, but in a place like this it could be anything.

"For the water," he clipped, eyeing the fat café owner with a stony stare. "And any inconvenience caused."

Mr Georgiades merely grunted, swiped the note off the table and waddled back towards the kitchen.

Jack turned to Gina. "It's getting late. Can we drop you off anywhere?"

CHAPTER THIRTY-THREE

Time: 7.45 p.m.
Date: Sunday 25 May 2014
Location: 30 Lambert Grove, London EC1

Raymond Dixon squinted down at his phone screen, noting yet another message. He'd considered turning off the phone, getting rid of it even — but something stopped him. If he got rid of the phone, then he would have no idea what they were planning. And forewarned is forearmed . . .

He exited the screen without reading the message. He didn't have to. He knew what it would say. Slipping the phone back into his pocket, he nudged the edge of the net curtain to one side and peered out at the small section of Lambert Grove he called home. The sun would be setting soon and the light outside heading towards twilight — but he could see enough right now.

Naturally, his eyes came to rest on number 21. He'd watched the comings and goings over the last few days: mostly the police, with the occasional good-natured neighbour calling by to see if there was anything they could do.

Which, of course, there wasn't.

After a while, the Lancasters had stopped answering the door.

Right now, their house was shrouded in the failing light; curtains tightly drawn across each and every window.

Dixon let the net curtain fall back into place. He didn't need to wonder what was going on inside number 21 right now — he already knew. No doubt Russell and Sara would be dumbstruck, sitting in the same position for hours on end, feeling nothing but numbness. Each day would merge into the next, with people urging them to eat and sleep, but they would be wanting to do neither.

Stepping away from the window, he let his eyes fall on the battered sofa still sitting in the middle of his own front room. It was the same one they'd had when they'd moved here in 1987. Kelly had chosen it — set her heart on it from some fancy fashion magazine she'd read in the hairdressers. They hadn't been able to afford that one, instead getting one that looked similar from a cheap furniture store that was closing down. The sofa badly needed replacing now — he could feel the springs jabbing painfully into his skin whenever he sat down — but he just couldn't be bothered.

Without Kelly, he couldn't be bothered to do most things.

Despite the protruding springs, Dixon slumped down on to the sofa and closed his eyes. He could feel everything spinning out of control, but there was nothing he could do to stop it — not this time. He was at the mercy of others, and that irritated him. But it was his own fault — he should never have involved anyone else in his plan. That had been his first mistake. Well, maybe not his first — he'd made plenty of mistakes before this one.

As was usually the case when he was left to his own thoughts, Dixon's eyes opened and gravitated towards the ceiling.

Carrie-Ann had probably been his first and biggest mistake.

Sitting there in the half-light of the coming night, Raymond Dixon could almost see the sneering, condescending figure of DI Graham Hobbs sitting next to him. The man had been an idiot, that was plain for all to see — but his incompetence was something that had probably saved Ray's skin in the end.

If Hobbs had been on the ball, listened to that squealing runt of a detective constable by his side, then maybe they would have found Carrie-Ann a lot sooner than they did.

And Raymond Dixon wouldn't be the free man that he was today.

So, all things considered, Hobbs had done him a favour.

The phone in Dixon's pocket vibrated once more. Fishing it out, he pushed himself up out of the uncomfortable sofa and rammed the phone into one of the drawers in the nearby sideboard.

Out of sight, out of mind.

Just like Carrie-Ann.

Needing a drink, Dixon headed to the kitchen, slamming the door closed behind him.

* * *

Time: 7.55 p.m.
Date: Sunday 25 May 2014
Location: Ironbridge Buildings, Ironbridge Lane, London

"Are you thinking what I'm thinking, Cooper?"

Jack sat behind the wheel of the Mondeo looking out at the block of flats where Gina had entered just moments before. Run down, graffiti daubed on every available surface, and with the brickwork chipped and cracked — it wasn't the most desirable of addresses. In many ways, it reminded Jack of where Narelle had been living back in 94 — although those flats were long gone now.

He turned towards Cooper in the passenger seat. "About this 'G' fella?"

Cooper nodded. "I think he could be our Jerry, boss."

Jerry.

Gerry.

Jack shoved the keys into the ignition and gunned the engine. "I'm sure our friendly barman Steve didn't mean to mislead us on purpose — Gerry with a G is easy to confuse with a Jerry with a J, especially if you haven't worked there very long. We'll give him the benefit of the doubt — for now."

He pulled the car away from Gina's flat, taking one last look at the huddle of hoodie-wearing teenagers gathered on the corner. The defiant looks on their pale faces told him they were likely up to no good — but tonight they weren't his concern.

"But the man lied to us, Cooper. This *Gerry.* He swore blind he didn't know anyone called Narelle. And it's a pretty unusual name — certainly around these parts. An Australian backpacker would've stuck in his memory, don't you think? He remembered Gina, after all." Jack paused as he swung the Mondeo out on to the main carriageway back towards the station. "And according to Gina, they were bosom buddies. First thing tomorrow, see what you can find out about Gerard Murray — and then I think we need to pay him another visit. I'll head back to the station and get the ball rolling — shall I drop you off at home?"

"Shouldn't you be somewhere right about now, boss?"

Jack started to frown then looked at the dashboard clock. "Shit. Stu's stag night."

CHAPTER THIRTY-FOUR

Time: 8.25 p.m.
Date: Sunday 25 May 2014
Location: Kettle's Yard Mews, London

"Sorry!" Jack held both hands up as he entered the flat. "Got caught up at work." An open can of Budweiser was thrust into his hand while he slipped out of his jacket.

"You know, a lot of stags go away now. A week in Benidorm. A weekend in Amsterdam. They're all the rage . . ."

Jack managed a tired smile, loosening the tie around his neck. "Are you complaining again?" He took a sip from the can. "Anyhow, your passport's run out. Isabel told me. You're not going anywhere, sunshine."

Having already spent the best part of the afternoon at the pub with his workmates from the courier company, Mac was already a little unsteady on his feet. "I'm just saying. This is cool, though."

Jack saw that the flat had been transformed in his absence. An array of boxes, bottles and cans were stacked, one on top of the other, all along the kitchen worktop. More graced the surface of the coffee table. There was even an extra box of Corona on the kitchen floor by the fridge.

"I wasn't sure what to get, so . . ." Robert Carmichael stepped into view, giving a shrug. "So, I got it all."

"Jesus, Rob. We could start our own brewery in here. It's only us, remember." Jack took another grateful slug from his can. "We'll never get through this lot."

"I've a mate who uses a cash-and-carry." Carmichael whipped off the top of a bottle of Peroni and handed it to Jack. "I got really good deals on everything."

With two beers on the go already, Jack collapsed on to the sofa. Not usually one for a raucous boys' night out, he hadn't exactly been looking forward to his brother's stag-do — one of the reasons he had handed the reins of organising it over to Rob. And to be honest, the whole event had slipped his mind. But now it was here, there was a small part of him that was actually looking forward to it. It was a time to relax and push thoughts of work to the back of his mind — if he could.

Rob snapped the lids off two more bottles of Peroni, handing one to Mac and taking a sip from the other himself. "Everything all right, Jack?"

Jack knew part of Carmichael's question was in relation to James Quinn. He gave a discreet nod. "All good, Rob. All good." He glanced once more at the mountains of alcohol. "You've done us proud here, mate."

"And this is just for starters." Carmichael took another swig of his beer. "I've booked us into that curry house in Borough Market at half nine. You know — the good one that everyone's raving about."

Jack raised his bottle. "Good plan. I've a feeling we might need it to soak up all this." He gestured once again to the boxes of beer stacked up in his kitchen.

"Did I hear someone say curry?" Mac collapsed back on to the sofa next to Jack. "Great, I'm starving."

"Steady on, it's not for a while yet," grinned Carmichael. "I still need to get changed."

"I like your flat, Jack," slurred Mac, putting his feet up on to the laden coffee table, narrowly missing kicking over a bottle of single malt. "It's cool. A man-pad. But don't you get lonely in here, all by yourself?"

"I might be alone, Stu, but that doesn't make me lonely. There's a difference." Jack took several more swigs from his can, then crumpled it in his hand. "This flat suits me just fine."

"You need a pet," continued Mac. "How about a cat? They're great for company."

"And how am I meant to keep said cat fed and watered when I'm out of the house at all times of day and night?"

"Cats are resourceful — they can catch their own food. Like mice. Maybe birds."

"And how would said cat get outside to track down these elusive mice and birds? Abseil out the window?"

Mac paused, tapping the side of his bottle against his chin. "OK, so maybe not a cat. How about a fish?"

* * *

Time: 8.40 p.m.
Date: Sunday 25 May 2014
Location: Kettle's Yard Mews, London

It was time.

Quinn had again gone undetected as he parked up a few car lengths away from the entrance to Jack's flat. Londoners really didn't see beyond the ends of their own noses sometimes. Or maybe that was just detectives.

He felt a smile flicker. He couldn't wait to see the look on Jack's face — and that runt of a brother of his. He'd watched Jack arrive home not long ago, but the detective had again failed to notice the strange car parked with one wheel up on the kerb.

Peering through the tinted windows, he felt for the reassuring coolness of the gun in his pocket. Finally, Stella MacIntosh could be with her precious boys — but that wasn't quite why he was doing it. There was no compassion embedded in his motives.

Tonight was all about revenge. Forty years may have passed, but the desire to destroy the MacIntosh family hadn't dimmed. Stella's demise had begun the end to his empire — quickly he'd lost all his best punters, and once they'd jumped ship, the girls soon followed. Nobody saw James Quinn as a player anymore — not after Stella MacIntosh had swung from the light fitting at Old Mill Road. His standing and reputation had crumbled in the same way her bones would have done beneath the earth, decaying inside her cheap, council-funded grave.

And by the time the simple headstone had been erected, James Quinn was a nobody.

Until tonight.

Tonight he would become somebody once again. He might be pushing sixty-five, but he still had it.

Gripping the gun inside his pocket, he opened the car door and stepped out into the night. Nothing stirred as he made his way stealthily across the cobbled street and slunk unnoticed inside the unsecured communal door.

* * *

Time: 8.45 p.m.
Date: Sunday 25 May 2014
Location: Isabel's Café, Horseferry Road, London

"Close your eyes, and don't peek!" Smothering a grin, Sacha placed her surprise in front of Isabel and clapped her hands. "Open!"

Isabel's eyes snapped wide open. On her lap was a small, square box wrapped in silver paper. She glanced up at her friend, eyes shining. "What is it?"

"Open it and see!" Sacha resumed her seat on one of the café's sagging sofas, her excitement brimming. "I really hope you like it!"

Isabel ripped the paper off, her hands trembling. They'd managed to consume two bottles of Prosecco between them already, and they were well on the way through the third. She stifled a hiccup.

With the paper discarded, Isabel snapped open the lid, a breath catching in the back of her throat as she spied the contents of the velvet-lined box. Nestled inside was the most beautiful silver bracelet, with an abundance of tiny silver charms dangling from it. Isabel had never seen anything quite like it.

"Oh my goodness," she managed to stutter, taking the bracelet out of the box and turning it over in her hands. "It's beautiful."

"It belonged to my nana. And probably her nana before that." Sacha took the bracelet out of Isabel's hands and clasped it around her wrist. "No one's quite sure."

"It's so beautiful. Truly stunning. And heavy, too."

"Solid silver, I think," smiled Sacha. "The charms, too. My nana told me that each of the fifteen charms brought something different. Healing. Wealth. Protection from evil. She left it to me when she died. It's your 'something borrowed' — for the wedding."

Isabel looked up into her best friend's eyes. "Oh, but I couldn't. It looks so expensive. And means so much to you."

Sacha leaned forward and patted Isabel on the hand. "*You* mean a lot to me. It would make me so happy if you wore it on your big day."

Isabel choked back the tears that she knew were threatening to spill. Too much Prosecco always made her emotional. "I . . . I'd be honoured. Thank you."

Sacha topped up both their glasses with the remains of the bottle and raised a toast. "To the wedding!"

"To the wedding!" laughed Isabel, wiping her eyes and taking another sip. She would regret the third bottle in the morning, she knew that much. But right now, she was happier than she'd ever been.

"So what else have you got?" asked Sacha. "For the rest of it? The something old, something new. You've got the borrowed now. What about the blue? Please tell me you're going all traditional?"

Isabel giggled and put down her glass. "Well. Now you've lent me this gorgeous bracelet, I have to, don't I? For the something old . . ." Isabel hesitated and placed a hand on the pendant around her neck. "I'm not sure if it can be classed as old, but it's one of the oldest things I have."

Around Isabel's neck was a pendant in the shape of a heart. Made in two parts, each half slotted together perfectly. When Isabel was small, her mother gave her one half of the pendant, keeping the other half for herself — that way they were always connected. And now that her mother was dead, Isabel cherished both halves.

"It's lovely," smiled Sacha. "What about something new?"

"A new husband?" Isabel raised her eyebrows and shrugged. "But I expect I'll buy some new underwear or something."

"Too much information!" grinned Sacha, emptying her glass. "Let's move on! What about something blue? What colour is your dress?"

"Not blue!" replied Isabel. "I've gone for a peachy-ivory colour. I'm picking it up tomorrow."

"Maybe the underwear could be blue?" ventured Sacha.

Isabel laughed. "No way! But I think we'll have the blue covered if Mac gets up to do a speech . . ."

Just then, the bell over the café's front door sounded and Dominic, fresh from his night school classes, stepped inside.

"How was your evening, Dom?" Sacha placed her empty glass on the table in front of her. "What did you learn tonight?"

Dominic Greene placed his leather satchel down on one of the chairs. "Advertising and recruitment. And retention of employees."

"Sounds scintillating." Sacha made a face and pointed to the fourth bottle of Prosecco sitting on the table. "Shall we?"

Isabel smothered a grin. "I really shouldn't, Sacha. I'm already a bit squiffy and I've got to open up in the morning . . ."

"No you don't. Dom can do that." Sacha smiled over at her son, who was slipping off his jacket. "You'll open up for Isabel in the morning, won't you, Dom? Let her have a lie in? It is her hen night, after all!"

Dominic nodded, nudging his spectacles further up his nose. "Of course." He pulled out his notebook from his back pocket and made the relevant entry.

'*Open café 6.00am.*'

"Good, that's settled then." Sacha popped the cork off the fourth bottle.

"Did you say advertising and recruitment, Dom? At your evening class?" Isabel accepted the fresh glass from Sacha, knowing it was a bad idea and she would definitely regret it in the morning. But . . . it *was* her hen night . . .

Dominic slipped his notebook back in his pocket. "Yes. Advertising strategies. The process of recruitment. And how to retain employees."

"In that case, I have another job for you." Isabel took a sip of Prosecco. "I'd like to advertise for another member of the team. Part-time to begin with. How about you design an advert and take care of the interview selection?"

After only a few seconds consideration, Dominic nodded. "OK." He pulled the notebook back out of his pocket and made the additions.

Sacha beamed at Isabel, mouthing the words 'thank you' behind her glass. She then turned towards her son. "And while you're on your feet, Dom, be a love and slip a couple of pastries in the oven, will you? We need something to soak up all this Prosecco . . ."

CHAPTER THIRTY-FIVE

Time: 8.45 p.m.
Date: Sunday 25 May 2014
Location: Kettle's Yard Mews, London

"I'm going to get changed." Carmichael downed the remnants of his Peroni and headed towards Jack's bedroom door. "The taxi's coming in half an hour."

"Don't be long!" Mac got to his feet and grabbed a bottle of tequila from the coffee table. "I'm pouring shots!"

Jack groaned inwardly as his brother began lining up shot glasses on the table, while Carmichael disappeared into the bedroom.

Shots. He hadn't done shots since . . . so long ago he couldn't remember. Which made him feel each and every one of his forty-seven years. All he could remember was that it hadn't ended well. Accepting the shot glass, knowing he couldn't refuse, Jack downed its contents in one.

"Hey, steady on, bro!" Mac turned and chugged down his own shot. "I wasn't ready!"

Jack screwed his eyes up tight as the neat alcohol hit his bloodstream. He now remembered why he didn't do shots.

Almost before he'd managed to prise his eyes open again, Mac had topped up his glass.

"Down the hatch!" slurred Mac, slugging another serving of tequila down his throat. "Hurry up, Rob. You're getting left behind!"

Whether it was the alcohol coursing through his veins, or his brother's incessant chatter about how great everything was, Jack didn't hear the door to his flat creak open. With both their backs to it, and the tequila flowing, the sound went unnoticed.

The first inkling that something wasn't quite right was when Jack sensed a movement behind him. The alcoholic haze that'd been quickly descending suddenly sharpened. Jack's veins instantly flooded with ice. Launching himself to his feet, he turned sharply, and found himself facing the man who had haunted his dreams ever since that fateful hypnotherapy session with Dr Riches some two years ago.

James Quinn.

"Hello, son."

* * *

Time: 8.47 p.m.
Date: Sunday 25 May 2014
Location: Kettle's Yard Mews, London

Carmichael pulled on a fresh shirt and doused himself with a liberal spraying from the deodorant can sitting on Jack's bedside table. There wasn't much else on the table — a glass of water and a small, silver-framed photograph of Jack's mother. Jack kept a lot of his past to himself, a private man with his own private thoughts, but Carmichael knew the history surrounding his mother's death — and then both boys' subsequent paths through the care system. As he began to button up his shirt, Carmichael couldn't help thinking that Stella MacIntosh would have been proud of how her two boys had eventually turned out.

Pulling on a fresh pair of jeans, Carmichael sat down on the edge of the bed to lace up his shoes. Out of the corner of his eye he spied Mac's tatty old teddy bear, still sitting propped up on the chair in the corner of the room. Knowing what was hidden inside made the hairs on the back of his neck prickle. Jack sure knew how to complicate things — bringing the gun back into the flat hadn't been his best idea. But so long as it stayed hidden . . .

Getting to his feet, Carmichael looked into the small mirror above the bedside table. The tiredness was showing in his eyes, but he'd do. After another liberal spray from the deodorant can, he turned towards the door, his stomach beginning to rumble in anticipation of a decent curry.

After just one step, he froze — holding his breath and straining his ears. He could hear voices. Inching closer towards the door, taking care not to make a sound, he pressed himself up against the wood and listened.

There it was again.

Voices.

Or, more accurately, *a* voice.

And it wasn't Jack or Mac speaking.

No, this voice was different.

This voice was deeper — and something within Carmichael convinced him that the owner of the voice hadn't come to join in the stag night's festivities.

* * *

Time: 8.47 p.m.
Date: Sunday 25 May 2014
Location: Kettle's Yard Mews, London

Son.

The man had called him *son.*

Jack felt himself bristle and, although frozen to the spot, his fists instinctively clenched into balls by his side.

All he could do was stare at the man's cruel smile and broken teeth.

James Quinn.

It was only then that he saw the gun.

"Jack? What . . . ?" Mac had by now turned towards the commotion and grabbed hold of Jack's arm. "Who's this?"

"No sudden movements." James Quinn waved the barrel of the gun towards them.

Jack didn't have a lot of experience with firearms. Was it real? Was it fake? Was it even loaded? Questions tumbled around inside his head, shunted back and forth like a pinball machine, and all the while he stared at the gun barrel. Whatever it was, real or not, it was pointing in his direction.

Quinn's eyes flashed with hot anger. "Come closer, where I can see you — but no sudden movements. Don't make me pull this trigger."

"What do you want?" Jack cautiously stepped forward, Mac by his side.

"All in good time." Quinn waved the gun once more. "Let's just have a little chat now, shall we?"

"Who is he, Jack?" Mac hung back, his eyes widening by the second.

Quinn flicked his gaze towards Mac, another smile stretching across his lips. "You don't remember me, do you, boy? But your brother here does." Quinn's sneering face turned back towards Jack. "Are you gonna tell him, or am I?"

It was then that Jack realised what Quinn was here for. In an instant, he felt four years old again, looking up to see his dead mother's body swinging from the light fitting. And all the while, James Quinn had been there — in the background, laughing and drinking. Repositioning the chair to make it look like poor Stella MacIntosh had decided to take her own life.

James Quinn.

Images tumbled through Jack's head like a raft on a white water rapid. His sessions with Dr Riches had partially unlocked that part of his inner subconscious — but now, standing here in his own living room, he felt the door fully open and reveal the full force of what had truly happened.

James Quinn had murdered their mother — stringing her up to make it look like a suicide.

Jack knew — because now he remembered.

Wrestling his thoughts back to the present, Jack stared back at the gun barrel.

"The lad's got a right to know, don't you think, Jack?" James Quinn's sneering voice cut through the silence of the room. "He needs to know the truth about your dear mummy."

Suddenly, Jack wished he'd had the chance to talk to Stu — had that conversation about Quinn that he had been putting off for so long. That he had finally had the guts to tell his brother that the man now standing before them was responsible for their mother's death, instead of letting him grow up believing that she had chosen to leave them behind.

But now it was too late. Stu was about to find out the truth in the rawest way possible — and Jack was powerless to stop it. He just hoped that one day his brother would forgive him.

"Well, if you're not going to tell him, then perhaps I will." Quinn's face contorted into another sneer.

Jack felt his stomach clench. He opened his mouth, but it was so dry that no words could even begin to form. Anger coursed through him as he flashed a look at the advancing Quinn. The barrel of the gun was now much closer: close enough to do significant damage. Jack was no firearms expert but knew the result wouldn't be pretty.

"Cat got your tongue, Jack?" Taking another taunting step forwards, Quinn began to laugh. "I'll tell him then, shall I?" He turned towards Mac. "Your brother here hasn't been entirely truthful with you, laddie. It's about that lovely mother of yours. He's let you go on thinking that she killed herself and left you two little toe rags behind on purpose." Quinn flashed a contemptuous and mocking look towards

Jack. "But we know that's not quite what happened, don't we, Jack?" Quinn waved the gun in the air. "Go on, tell him. I *dare* you."

Jack eyes were still glued to the gun barrel, his mouth too dry for words.

Quinn's taunting voice filled the silence. "Looks like it's down to me to spill the beans, eh?" Keeping the gun trained on Jack, he switched his gaze back towards Mac. "Your poor dear mummy didn't kill herself, sonny. *I did.* I killed her with my own bare hands and strung her up like a piece of meat in the butcher's shop."

Quinn broke off and started to cackle, his mouth opening wide to reveal the full extent of his uneven and broken teeth. "Like a piece of meat, she was — and a cheap cut at that!"

Jack closed his eyes, feeling his anger reach boiling point.

"I . . . I don't understand . . . Jack?" Mac tore his eyes away from the gun. "Jack? What does he mean?"

It was then that Jack made a decision.

Whether it would be a good decision remained to be seen.

Lunging forwards, he made a grab for the barrel of Quinn's gun.

* * *

Time: 8.49 p.m.
Date: Sunday 25 May 2014
Location: Kettle's Yard Mews, London

Within a split second of hearing the gunshot, Carmichael wrenched Jack's bedroom door open and hurled himself head first into the living room. Confusion attacked his senses from every possible angle. Both Jack and his brother were on the floor, and the man Carmichael recognised as being the fugitive James Quinn, was standing over them with a gun held loosely by his side.

After what felt like an eternity, Carmichael lunged towards Quinn brandishing the gun he had removed from Mac's childhood teddy bear only moments before. He'd considered loading the gun, but that would have cost him vital seconds. And he was no crack shot, either — AFO material he most definitely was not. If he missed — the thought didn't bear thinking about.

So, instead, he struck the back of Quinn's skull as hard as he could with the butt of the gun.

The resulting crack floored Quinn in an instant. His once muscular frame, now mostly fat and flab, slumped to the floor. Carmichael flung the gun on to the sofa and went to Jack's motionless body.

Carmichael couldn't be sure where the bullet had hit — if, indeed, it'd hit anything. But Jack's shirt was starting to turn red at the shoulder and his face was deathly white.

With his phone already out to call 999, Carmichael got to his feet and went to retrieve the gun from the sofa — intending to ram it back inside the teddy bear before anybody arrived. Nobody needed to see the gun. Too many awkward questions would follow.

In hindsight, that was his first mistake.

His second was turning his back on the incapacitated James Quinn.

CHAPTER THIRTY-SIX

Time: 7.15 a.m.
Date: Monday 26 May 2014
Location: Metropolitan Police HQ, London

Jack's early morning call to Darsten's head office hadn't been met with much enthusiasm. And this time there was no pleasant-sounding Scottish voice on the other end of the line, either. Instead, a rather harsh and clipped tone filled Jack's ears.

"You'll need to give me a moment to check the records." More tinny-sounding music burst from the receiver.

Serves you right for advertising your opening hours from 7 a.m., mused Jack as he impatiently tapped his desk with his pen. The pain from his shoulder was knocking on the door of excruciating — although he wasn't due more painkillers for another two hours. A lack of sleep was also adding to his crabbiness. He'd discharged himself from A&E at five o'clock that morning — not long after his dislocated shoulder had been successfully relocated, and his superficial graze from Quinn's bullet dressed. They had wanted to admit him, keep him in for observation and pain relief, but Jack flashed his warrant card with his good hand and walked.

A quick change of clothes back at the flat, and he was back at his desk not long after six.

Gina's revelation about Gerry had left him chasing each and every loose end, trying to knit them together into some sort of coherent logic.

Gerry.

The man had lied about knowing Narelle — and innocent people, as a rule, didn't feel the need to lie. And the fact that the pub was merely a stone's throw away from the dumping site of both bodies, hers and Maisie's, added to the sense of disquiet.

'He chose it for a reason, Jack.'

'The bridge means something to your killer.'

Dr Hunter's light voice filled his head.

And if the bridge meant something to the killer, maybe the pub did, too.

Jack's thoughts were interrupted by the return of the brusque-accented call handler. "We have a Gerard Murray working at that particular public house from June 1992 until mid-1996. And he was re-employed from September 2008 to the present day."

"Can you confirm any reason for him leaving in 1996?"

There was a brief pause and Jack heard a keyboard tapping in the background, accompanied by a tut and a sigh. "It looks as though Mr Murray left our employment to join the Army. We have a reference request from HM Forces prior to his departure."

Jack nodded. The man had mentioned something about the Army so maybe he wasn't telling them a whole pack of lies.

Just some.

"And are you able to tell me if Mr Murray rented any of the rooms above the pub, between 1992 and 1996?" Jack couldn't help but think of Carrie-Ann lying dead upstairs in the attic of number 30 Lambert Grove.

Another tut and sigh assaulted Jack's ears. He bit his tongue.

"I can see here that Mr Murray rented a room from February 1993 until his departure in 1996. Will that be all?"

Jack ignored the question. "Do you happen to have an up-to-date address for him? I take it he isn't living above the pub anymore?" Jack remembered the barman saying that the rooms above were used for storage now.

"The rooms above the pub are no longer used by employees. According to the records they haven't been since 2002."

"And an address for Mr Murray?" repeated Jack, any patience he'd had waning by the second.

"I'll need to speak to my supervisor before handing out personal information on current employees. If I can take your number, I'll get someone to call you back."

Jack left his number and cut the call. Just as he returned the receiver to its cradle, there was a brief knock at the door before DC Daniels' head appeared around the door frame.

"Boss — I've been looking into Gerard Murray, like you asked. I've asked for his Army records — assuming he was telling us the truth about joining up."

"Well, I'm waiting on the pub's head office to ring me back about an address. But I'm not holding my breath that it'll be anytime soon. While we're waiting, we'll have a briefing — there's quite a lot we need to catch up on — and then we'll find out all we can about Murray's stint in the Army."

Daniels scurried along in Jack's wake and, just as they approached the incident room, DS Cassidy came charging along the corridor, her face flushed.

"What are you doing here? You look awful!"

"Thanks, Amanda, just what I need to hear." Jack tried a smile but it turned into a wince.

"You know what I mean." She nodded towards Jack's shoulder strapping and sling. "Should you even be here after what happened?"

"Where else am I going to be, Amanda?" Daniels held the incident room door open and Jack stepped inside. "I'm fine — I can barely feel a thing."

Cassidy followed, heading straight towards the white-boards, passing DS Cooper who was sitting at his computer monitor unwrapping a bacon sandwich.

"In that case — you need to see this. It's about Maisie. Last night, Trevor and myself put the car Darren Hughes said he no longer owns into the ANPR system — the silver Vauxhall — but we widened the parameters and the dates. We already know it's pinged at various locations around the time Maisie went missing and although there aren't any cameras on Lambert Grove itself, we've got a pretty good idea of the car's journey that afternoon." Pausing, Cassidy stepped across to where the map had been pinned to the wall. "To refresh our memories, the car is first picked up heading along Cranston Avenue, at just after five o'clock on 14 May. That's only four streets away from Maisie's house. The car then heads towards the South Bank." She pointed at the two locations on the map.

Jack eased himself into a chair, trying to hide his discomfort. "We really need to know who that new owner is, and where the car is now. Any more joy from that chap at number 32?"

"I tried his number most of yesterday evening, but no joy. However, I managed to track him down this morning."

Jack's tired eyebrows hitched. "And?" He noted Cassidy's excited smile was widening by the second.

"Brian Johnson has lived at number 32 Lambert Grove for the last thirty-five years. He confirmed what Rita Hamilton told me — that a silver Vauxhall was often parked in the street, and more often than not just outside his house. He doesn't own a car himself anymore, so wasn't too bothered with it taking up his parking space. He couldn't tell me the registration but did confirm what Rita said — that the passenger side door was a different colour." Cassidy paused and held Jack's gaze in hers. "And although he doesn't know who owns the car, he did tell me who he's seen driving it."

Jack's eyebrows hitched even higher. "Who?"

Cassidy's grin widened. "Your friend Raymond Dixon from number 30 — his next-door neighbour."

And there it was.

Raymond Dixon.

Jack let the information sink in before flicking his gaze to the photograph of Dixon still tacked to the cork pin board. "Remind me what Dixon said in his house-to-house statement?"

"Said he was home all day on the day Maisie disappeared. Didn't see anything unusual."

"Well, if he was home all day, this car certainly wasn't." Jack hauled himself out of his chair and pulled the photograph of Raymond Dixon from the cork pin board. He turned and tacked it to the first whiteboard, just beneath Maisie Lancaster's name. "The man's lying. I've said it before, and I'll say it again. He's a child killer. Where are we on Dixon's phone records?"

Daniels slipped into one of the vacant chairs and logged on to his computer. "These came in late last night. He's got just the one mobile phone registered in his name — and we've got details of the last three months' activity." Daniels navigated the screen and hit the print button. "Doesn't look like he uses it all that much."

Jack swiped the papers out of the printer tray, quickly scanning the pages before passing them to Daniels. "See how many of these numbers you can identify. I want to know who he's been talking to. In the meantime . . ."

Jack crossed back to the whiteboards and snatched up a marker pen with his good hand, using his teeth to pull off the cap. He wrote GERARD MURRAY in capital letters on the second whiteboard. "On the Narelle Williams case, Cooper and I went to see Gina Simmonds last night. She confirmed she did work at the pub — called the End of the Road, at the time — with Narelle, just before she disappeared. She also gave us the name, Gerard Murray. Now, Murray — or Gerry as he's known to some — is a person we've already spoken to. Albeit we thought he was a Jerry with a J at the time. Still works as a barman in the pub. He claimed not to recognise the name Narelle Williams when we asked, or indeed recall any young Australian girl working there in the summer of 94." Jack turned to face his team. "But we have it on good authority from Gina that he and Narelle were 'as thick as thieves', I think she called it. Something which is backed up to some extent in her letters and postcards home."

Jack perched on the edge of a nearby desk. "And the pub's head office have confirmed Gerry just so happened to rent a room above the pub in the summer of 1994. Something else he failed to disclose. For some reason this chap is lying to us — and I'd like to know why. Cooper?" Jack shot a look across at Cooper, who was wrapping his mouth around a second bacon roll. "When you're finished stuffing your face, see if you can find our Mr Murray at work. Take Daniels with you. If he's there, bring him in for questioning. And I want that pub searched."

"Onto it, boss," replied Cooper, ramming more of his breakfast into his mouth. "What about tracing the phone numbers from Dixon's phone?"

"Go and get Murray first. That's our priority right now. I want him where I can see him. Then we'll deal with the phone records. But before you go, I need to update you all on a conversation or two I've been having with Dr Hunter."

"You've got a forensic profile?" Cassidy was still hovering by the whiteboards. "What does it say?"

"Nothing too formal yet, but it's certainly interesting. According to Dr Hunter, we're looking for a male, aged between thirty-nine and fifty-nine, who lives alone, in a low-skilled job or unemployed, has access to a vehicle, and more than likely has a criminal record involving violence." Jack let the characteristics sink in before continuing. "And she's certain he's responsible for both murders."

"So, it *is* one killer." Cassidy's mouth dropped open. "Jeez . . ."

Just then, Daniels' computer beeped with an incoming email. Pulling his chair closer, he stared, wide-eyed, at the screen. "The lab just sent an update. More results on the suitcase."

"What kind of results?" Jack passed the marker pen to Cassidy to replace the lid.

Daniels hesitated. "I think you might want to take a look for yourself, boss. There's a link to a previous case."

Jack came to peer over Daniels' shoulder and, as soon as his eyes skimmed the contents of the email, he felt his mouth turn dry. "You're kidding me. Fibres found inside the suitcase, and trapped in the zip, give a 99.8 per cent match to fibres already on the system."

"A case already on the system?" Cooper pushed the remains of his bacon roll into his mouth and pulled his chair across. "What case would that be?"

Jack tried to keep his voice controlled, but his heart had started hammering ten to the dozen. "Fibres from the suitcase match those recovered from a duvet — a duvet that was found wrapped around the body of Carrie-Ann Dixon back in 1989."

The team sat in stunned silence until Jack pulled his car keys from his pocket. "Cooper. Go and find Gerard Murray at the pub." He threw his keys at Cassidy. "Amanda — you're with me. We're going after Dixon. You're driving."

CHAPTER THIRTY-SEVEN

Time: 8.30 a.m.
Date: Monday 26 May 2014
Location: 30 Lambert Grove, London EC1

Jack stood at the bottom of the short path that led up to the front door of number 30 Lambert Grove. Suddenly, he was a wet-behind-the-ears detective constable getting a stiff talking to from Hobbs for daring to step out of line and give his opinion.

Leading the short procession of officers up the garden path, he hammered briskly on the front door with his good hand. The vibrations sent a wave of pain coursing through his shoulder, quickly followed by a bout of nausea. He clenched his teeth and ignored both.

Acutely aware that, by now, a succession of net curtains would be twitching all along the street, Jack kept his eyes firmly fixed on the shabbily painted front door — and in particular to the tarnished number 30 in the centre.

It didn't take long for Raymond Dixon to appear, with a mug of tea in his hand and a drooping cigarette in his mouth.

"What do you lot want?" he grumbled, taking a slurp of his tea and suppressing a belch. His eyes flickered over the top of Jack's head to note the four uniformed officers behind him. Concern started to seep into his bloodshot eyes.

"Raymond Dixon. I'm arresting you on suspicion of the abduction and murder of Maisie Lancaster. You do not have to say anything, but it may harm your defence if you do not mention when questioned something which you later rely on in court. Anything you do say may be given in evidence. If you'd like to dispose of your cigarette and mug, we'll get you on your way." Jack stepped to the side to show Dixon the police van that had just parked up behind them.

"You've got to be kidding me!"

Dixon stood rooted to the spot in the doorway, his mouth agape — the cigarette falling to the floor at his feet. Jack eyed the man he suspected of killing his own daughter twenty-five years ago, seeing the same lies and deceit embedded in his pale grey eyes. The intervening years hadn't changed him one iota.

Leaning in, Jack pulled the mug from Dixon's grasp while two uniformed officers approached with handcuffs.

Relieved that the first stage had gone relatively smoothly, Jack watched as Raymond Dixon was bundled down the garden path towards the waiting police van. His attention then turned to the team of crime scene investigators that now filed up towards the front door, an outer cordon already being established around the perimeter of the house. Jack acknowledged Cassandra Newcombe, crime scene manager, and accepted his white protective suit.

Cassidy stepped forward to help Jack step into the paper suit, pulling the zip up and over his sling — then bent down to assist with the overshoes. If the crime scene manager found the performance amusing, it didn't show on her face. With a single protective glove on his good hand, Jack followed Cassandra and Cassidy across the threshold and into the hallway.

If déjà vu were a physical entity, then it knocked him sideways. The hallway looked exactly as it had done back on that summer's day in 1989 — even down to the pale green woodchip wallpaper.

Behind him, white-suited scene of crime investigators began to spread out. Jack edged forward, hovering at the threshold to the front room — immediately seeing his younger self sweating by the bay window.

The interior hadn't changed at all in the intervening decades. The same brown leather sofa, now somewhat worse for wear and sagging in the middle, sat in the centre of the room: the same sofa where he'd watched Hobbs force his condescending tone on the mother and father of missing eight-year-old Carrie-Ann.

Carrie-Ann.

Jack tore his eyes away from the sofa and glanced around the rest of the room. The same nauseating collection of Toby jugs sat in a double fronted display cabinet on the far side. All still there. All still grinning out at him. It made him shiver.

The crime scene investigators were already setting up — allocating specific jobs to each team member. Jack watched as the efficiency rolled out before him. A common pathway was established with a series of stepping plates, which Jack was kindly asked to adhere to when moving around the property. Jack nodded his understanding.

But he wasn't really sure what he was looking for.

This wasn't like the last time.

Last time they didn't have a body.

The thought that they might find poor Maisie's head somewhere in the house was at the forefront of everyone's mind.

"Guv?" Cassidy broke into Jack's thoughts. "Are we looking for anything in particular — apart from the obvious?"

Jack shook his head, as much in response to Cassidy's question as to rid himself of the memories of 1989. "Just the usual. I want to know if Maisie Lancaster has ever been inside these four walls." He paused and raised his eyes to the ceiling. "And then I want to look in that attic."

* * *

Time: 8.35 a.m.
Date: Monday 26 May 2014
Location: The Bridge Public House, London SE1

He knew he didn't have much time. Handing over the contact details for head office hadn't been his best move — but the detective had caught him off guard. And he would have found the details out for himself anyway, so there'd not been much point in lying.

Narelle.

He hadn't thought about her in many a year. Well, maybe that wasn't strictly true — sometimes her face floated in front of him when he was least expecting it. Memories were strange like that.

Gerry sat on the makeshift camp bed and pulled his holdall towards him. He wasn't meant to be sleeping up here — the current landlord had made various noises about renovating the upstairs rooms to eventually offer bed and breakfast, but it was an idea that hadn't yet got off the ground.

So, Gerry had taken advantage of a roof over his head. No one seemed to notice, or if they did, they didn't much care. He suspected the latter. It wasn't ideal, but it was better than the streets — which was the alternative. Getting his old job back at the pub had been a lifesaver.

He'd managed to move most of the storage boxes out of the way, making room for his fold-up camp bed and the rest of his meagre belongings. There was still running water in the bathroom — not exactly hot water, but it was better than nothing. Life on the outside was bad enough when you left the Armed Forces — everyone knew that. But it was even harder if you'd been kicked out.

Gerry flinched at the memory. Even after all these years, it still stung.

He'd been a good soldier — an *exceptional* soldier. The Army had been his life.

But then everything had gone wrong.

And there was only one person to blame for that.

But he didn't have the time to reminisce about how and why it had all gone so spectacularly wrong.

He needed to leave.

And fast.

He'd seen the newspapers over the last couple of days — first Maisie, and then Narelle. The past was coming back to haunt him, alongside the present.

As he rammed a change of clothing into the holdall, he couldn't help but see Narelle's beautiful face staring back out at him — her bright blue eyes, her pearly white teeth. It had been a bag not too dissimilar to this one, if he remembered rightly — maybe more of a rucksack than a holdall. But the purpose had been the same. Narelle's severed head had fitted quite nicely inside.

Glancing at his watch, he knew he needed to get going. There was still stuff here he should get rid of, destroy even — things belonging to Narelle that he hadn't quite wanted to part with. But now wasn't the time.

Grabbing the holdall, he swung it up on to his shoulder and headed for the door.

* * *

Time: 8.45 a.m.
Date: Monday 26 May 2014
Location: 30 Lambert Grove, London EC1

If déjà vu had hit him hard downstairs, it was nothing compared to what Jack felt on entering the attic. Reaching the roof space via the same set of wooden steps as two decades before, Jack instantly felt the chill as he entered. But it wasn't the cooler temperature that made him shiver.

Carrie-Ann had been found not six feet from where he now stood. She had been rolled tightly inside a duvet and wedged up against the water tank. The tiny attic window set into the roof above gave only a subdued light. Carrie-Ann's last known resting place was dull and lifeless.

Jack felt the hairs on the back of his neck bristle. Everything looked the same — and yet nothing really was. The duvet was no longer there — still in storage as part of the evidence in the flawed case against Dixon — but everything else was exactly as it had been. The water tank was still there, as were several stacking boxes rammed up against the wall behind the hatch. On the far side were a series of suitcases — Jack's stomach churned at the sight of them.

Not wanting to get too close in case of contamination, Jack could already see the same patterned suitcase as the one that had held Maisie's dismembered remains. A coincidence? Jack baulked at the idea.

"Guv?" Cassidy hovered behind Jack at the top of the steps. "Anything?"

Jack dragged himself back into the present. If the suitcase that contained Maisie's dismembered remains had been up here, then Jack needed to know when. Each and every inch of space needed to be combed. He turned back towards the wooden steps. "We'll get a team up here."

Jack didn't want to spend any more time inside number 30 than he needed to. If there was any trace of Maisie inside these walls, the investigators would find it. After leaving the attic, he made his way downstairs along the metal stepping plates and back towards the front door. "Let's get back to the station. There's not a lot else we can do here." Just then, he felt his mobile ring inside his pocket. Pulling it out he saw it was Cooper.

"Cooper? Anything at the pub?" Jack paused at the front door.

"Sorry, boss. Doesn't look like Murray's here. The pub's still locked up. No sign of life inside. What do you want us to do? We can't really force entry without a warrant, or until we track him down and arrest him."

Jack cursed under his breath. "Leave a uniform on site, in case he shows. But you and Daniels head back to the station. We'll meet you there."

Jack slipped the phone back inside his pocket and motioned to Cassidy to follow him outside. He had only managed to set one foot outside the Dixon's front door when he felt the fist connect with his chin.

CHAPTER THIRTY-EIGHT

Time: 10.05 a.m.
Date: Monday 26 May 2014
Location: Metropolitan Police HQ, London

Jack dabbed his lip with a tissue, wincing as the pain shot across his jaw. He had refused a trip to A&E — his second visit within twelve hours might raise a few eyebrows. And nothing was broken: the only real damage was to his pride. The force of Derek Foster's punch had sent him crashing to the ground, but thankfully he'd landed on his good side. He didn't fancy re-dislocating his shoulder — the pain from the first experience was still turning his stomach.

Foster was now languishing in a police cell, and Jack, for one, was in no hurry for him to be dealt with.

"You sure you don't need checking out?" Carmichael nodded towards Jack's sling. "You took a fair knock."

Jack shook his head and threw a packet of high-strength painkillers across his desk. "I'm fine. But get two of those son-of-a-bitches out for me. I can't do it one-handed."

Carmichael pressed two tablets from the blister pack and passed them over. Jack tossed them in his mouth and dry swallowed.

"Was he badly hurt? Quinn?"

"Well, he's not pretty, that's for sure. He's got a badly busted leg, fractured pelvis and depressed skull fracture." Carmichael ran a hand over his jaw where Quinn had landed his first punch. Quinn had managed to get to his feet while Carmichael's back was turned, and when he'd realised what was happening, it was too late — Quinn had cracked him around the jaw, sending him spiralling towards the floor. He'd hit the edge of the coffee table on his way down, winding him but causing no major damage.

"How come he ended up at the bottom of the stairs?"

"From what your brother told me, no sooner had Quinn laid me out, he headed for the door. Mac gave chase, but in the end — it was the cat."

Old Mrs Constantine from the flat below kept a sprightly ginger tabby cat called Marmaduke, and often the animal would make the trip upstairs to sit outside Jack's door. Many a time Jack would arrive home from work to find the tabby patiently waiting for him on the doormat. He didn't tell Mrs Constantine that he occasionally gave the moggy a titbit or two –leftover chicken seemed to be his favourite.

"Apparently, just as Quinn reached the landing, the cat ran across his path — sent him tumbling down to the landing below." Carmichael made no attempt to hide his grin. "Those concrete steps are pretty unforgiving — must've bounced a few times on his way down. Paramedics found him with a massive scalp laceration and one of his legs bent the wrong way."

"Good old Marmaduke."

"Mac told you you should get a cat."

Jack returned the grin. It was a bad move. Pain sliced through him with even the smallest of movements.

"What do you think he's told them?" Carmichael kept his voice low. "Quinn?"

Jack tried a shrug, instantly regretting it. "I doubt he's saying much. Looking at his previous cases, he likes to keep his mouth shut."

"And you?"

"I gave a short statement while I was in A&E. I didn't say I knew him. Said, as far as I knew, it was a total stranger in my flat."

Carmichael nodded. "I told them exactly what I saw. Which was a man with a gun in his hand, standing next to the body of my colleague. I grabbed the nearest thing from the table — a bottle — and swiped him over the back of the head." He paused and gave Jack a wink. "Well, it's nearly true."

Jack had to agree. Trying to explain why there was an unlicensed firearm hidden inside a teddy bear was probably best avoided — the bottle was a better idea. "I told them he stood there and confessed to killing my mother. Which means they should now look into the post-mortem again and find the evidence beneath her fingernails. And then the DNA. Quinn will have a hard time explaining that one away." Struggling to his feet, Jack eyed the time. "But right now, I've got bigger fish to fry."

"I'll leave you to it. Call me if you hear anything more about Quinn." With the promise of a fresh bottle of single malt and a punnet of grapes to aid his recovery, Carmichael left Jack alone.

Jack knew Dixon had been processed and was also now residing in the care of the custody suite, alongside his old friend Derek Foster. Jack was more than content to let the pair of them stew.

A uniformed officer had been left at the Bridge as instructed, but Jack wasn't pinning his hopes on Gerard Murray returning any time soon. With the hunt for Murray currently at deadlock, Jack decided to focus on Raymond Dixon, and whatever connection he had to Maisie. The clock was ticking and they couldn't get it wrong this time. How he'd been involved in the poor girl's disappearance and murder, Jack wasn't sure — but with the suitcase linked to 30 Lambert Grove, involved he surely had to be.

And then there was the car.

Deciding he needed a coffee to clear his head, Jack made his way out into the corridor — straight into the path of DI Jane Telford.

"I hear you've got Raymond Dixon in custody," she remarked, matching Jack's stride as they headed towards the stairs.

"Good news travels fast. We're letting him sweat a little before interviewing him."

"How's he connected to your murder?"

"Of that, I'm not entirely sure. He lives on the same street — knows the family. But the biggest connection so far is the suitcase Maisie was found in came from his attic. Or it's at least been in contact with the duvet Carrie-Ann was found in. Trace fibres have shown up to be a match."

DI Telford's eyebrows shot up as they headed upstairs and through the double doors to the canteen. "I see. Keep me up to speed. I'd like to know how things pan out."

"Of course." Jack led Telford towards the self-service coffee machine, glad to see that the milk thief hadn't made it upstairs. Needing the energy hit, he selected a white coffee with extra sugar. DI Telford chose a fruit tea.

"Did you have a chance to look over that summary I collated for you on Dixon?"

Jack picked up a packet of shortbread biscuits and shook his head. "Sorry, no. I'll take a look before we interview him."

"It's just a chronological summary of his convictions, time spent in custody — that sort of thing. Might not be of much use."

"I'm sure it will be. I'm about to discuss an interview strategy with Amanda."

DI Telford couldn't mask her smile any longer as she nodded towards Jack's split lip. "I see you've been in the wars . . . again. Anyone I know?"

The look on her face told Jack that the news of Derek Foster clumping him outside number 30 had already reached the subterranean depths of the Cold Case Unit. He grabbed another couple of sachets of sugar, ripping them open with his teeth.

"The man's a liability. I've given my statement, such as it is. I'm keeping out of it now."

"And the shoulder?" Telford nodded towards Jack's sling. "I heard you had a spot of trouble at home last night. You OK?"

Jack let the well-practised lie trip from his tongue. "I'm fine. Barely a bruise."

The look of concern in Telford's eyes told Jack she believed none of it. "Well, if you need anything. You know where I am."

They made their way out of the canteen and headed for the stairs. "Anything you particularly want me to ask Dixon?" Jack took a sip of his coffee as they negotiated the double doors. The hot liquid singed his split lip.

"I trust your judgement," replied DI Telford. "But if he starts looking like he might talk about Carrie-Ann, give me a shout."

* * *

Time: 10.15 a.m.
Date: Monday 26 May 2014
Location: Troughton Street, London

He'd opted not to use the Tube, although it would have been quicker. Now the police were sniffing around, he could do without making their job any easier by leaving a digital footprint wherever he went. He'd binned his Oyster card and taken to the streets.

Leaving the pub far behind, he'd quickly lost himself in the backstreets, keeping to the quieter parts of the capital. The less people saw him, the better. He doubted that he'd ever be able to go back to the Bridge now, and the thought saddened him. The pub had been there for him when everyone else had slammed the door in his face and shunned him. It had been there to pick up the pieces, giving him somewhere to rebuild his life once the Army and the prison system had spat him out.

He'd only intended to come back to the pub for six months, a year at most. Enough time to get back on his feet and move on. But six months had very quickly turned into six years.

Hoisting the holdall further up on to his shoulder, he turned down a side street.

Hearing Narelle's name, after all this time, had been the trigger. Giving him that final push to move on. The past was catching up with him.

Narelle.

Quickening his stride, he slipped safely out of sight along a narrow alleyway flanked with parked cars. He felt a smile twitch at the corner of his mouth.

Narelle.

She *had* been a stunner, of that there was no mistake.

* * *

Time: 3.30 p.m.
Date: Wednesday 31 August 1994
Location: The End of the Road Public House, London SE1

Balancing the tray of empty glasses in one hand, Narelle Williams slid behind the bar and made her way towards the kitchen. The temperature was soaring outside, which meant a rapid influx of customers in search of a cold drink. Wiping a hand across her brow, she deposited the tray next to the sink. Her hair clung damply to the back of her neck.

At least the kitchen was cool — with the back door wedged open, a welcome breeze rippled inside from the courtyard. *If* you could call it a courtyard. Really, it was just a paved area where the wheelie bins were stored, serving as an informal smoking area for staff.

The air was heavy with the growing stench of rotting vegetables and other fermenting rubbish from the bins, but Narelle didn't mind so much. She stepped out and took in a lungful of pure London air. The heat was stifling, even with the faint breeze, but it was nothing compared to the summer weather back home.

Home.

Narelle felt another twinge of homesickness. She smiled as she recalled spending the previous summer with her friends on the Gold Coast. They'd spent lazy afternoons sitting in beachfront cafés, watching the windsurfers tackling the waves, talking about the adventures that lay ahead. Their exams were over and they could, at last, kick back and relax. It'd been a wonderful six weeks of not worrying about anything except having a good time — and it had been Christmas, too. They'd all gathered on the beach for a barbeque: one last time together before they all went their separate ways.

It was only a few months ago, but it felt like a lifetime.

Summer in London was very different. The sun was hot, but the air felt uncomfortably heavy. There was no breeze coming in off the ocean like back home, and although the pub sat on the banks of the Thames, you couldn't really compare the brown, murky waters she saw every day with the cool, crisp blue of the Pacific Ocean.

Sometimes, Narelle asked herself what she was doing here. She swallowed back a small laugh as she batted away yet another fly, no doubt attracted by the decomposing contents of the bins. She was working her way around Europe, that was what she was doing. And if it meant she had to work long hours in a crappy pub, then that's what she'd do. It wasn't for much longer anyway — soon she was moving on to France. The thought excited her.

She'd enjoyed her time in London. She'd visited all the places her mother had earmarked for her in her pocket-sized travel guide before bidding her farewell at the airport — Buckingham Palace, the Houses of Parliament, Big Ben, the

Tower of London, the Royal Albert Hall, Harrods. The list was endless. So much culture packed into such a small space – small compared to back home, anyway.

But her time here was coming to an end, and she felt renewed excitement at what the next chapter in her travels could offer her.

Just then, a shadow crossed the courtyard and Narelle turned around. Colour flooded her cheeks that had nothing to do with the steamy temperature of the courtyard. She'd seen him the first day she'd started work, but it had been several weeks before she'd drummed up enough courage to actually speak to him. And even that had only been 'where's the wine list?'

He was good-looking in that dark and brooding type of way. His hair was longer than the Aussie beach boys back home, grazing the collar of his Oasis T-shirt, and he had that look of danger about him. She imagined he had a motorbike stashed away somewhere and would ride off into the sunset every night with a cigarette dangling from the corner of his mouth.

It was all in her head though.

In reality, he had a pushbike that he kept chained up in the courtyard, and as far as she knew he didn't smoke. But he was older than her; she knew that much for definite. Maybe only a few years, but definitely older. But sometimes older was good — it meant experienced. It meant dependable. It meant mature.

And his name suited him. Gerard. Gerry. It sounded very British.

"What time do you finish?"

And she loved his accent. She loved any British accent really, but his was exquisite. She felt her stomach flip. "In about an hour or so," she replied, trying to sound nonchalant. She could feel the colour in her cheeks deepening, and turned her head away to hide it. But that only meant she was staring directly into the searing afternoon rays flooding the courtyard. She squinted, holding up a hand to block out the afternoon sun.

"Cool, me too." A small smile swept on to Gerard's lips. "Why don't you come upstairs when you're done — I've got the new Oasis album we could listen to. And a bottle of whisky."

Narelle slipped back inside the pub, her eyes blinking rapidly from the harsh sunlight. "Great!"

Once they'd got to know each other, they started spending most of their free time together. Gerry had shown her around London — including the bits that weren't in the tourist books. Every time she saw him, her heart did a little jump. But she was never quite sure what he thought of her. Sometimes he had this odd look in his eyes. And once or twice he'd gripped her hand just that little bit too hard.

She felt his presence behind her as she crossed the tiled kitchen floor.

"See you later, then. Don't be late."

* * *

Time: 12.30 p.m.
Date: Monday 26 May 2014
Location: Metropolitan Police HQ, London

Jack had insisted on leading the interview, with Cassidy at his side. Although interviewing wasn't always part of his role anymore — experienced and highly trained interviewing officers usually taking the strain — this was one that he wanted to do. Because this one was personal.

The interview began in the usual fashion — Raymond Dixon had availed himself of the duty solicitor on-call for the day, and Jack had a feeling he wasn't going to get much past her. Cordelia Bannerman was well known in the station and the Magistrates Court circuit as being a no-nonsense, by-the-book lawyer. Jack despised her already.

After the standard introductions, Jack launched into the interview strategy he'd hurriedly set out with Cassidy only moments before.

After the first ten minutes, it was clear they were getting nowhere.

"How well did you know Maisie Lancaster, Mr Dixon?" Jack eyed Dixon across the narrow wooden table. "It is correct, is it not, that you did know her?"

Dixon's stony stare remained fixed on the burn marks seared into the table's surface, countless cigarettes marking the interview room's previous history. He'd spoken just twice since arriving at the station — once to request a solicitor, and once to confirm his name. Apart from that, he had been silent. At the mention of Maisie's name, he blinked. Once.

Jack's jaw clenched. "They live at 21 Lambert Grove, if that helps."

Again, Raymond Dixon remained silent.

"Where were you on Wednesday 14 May, Mr Dixon?"

More silence.

"The statement you gave says you were at home all day. Is that correct?"

More silence.

"Did you use your car at all that day, Mr Dixon? You do own a car — registration BM12 ONS — don't you?"

Jack felt the open wound on his lip sting as he spoke. And his shoulder ached with every passing second. "Mr Dixon — you're not helping yourself by remaining quiet for these simple questions. You do know that?"

"I think you'll find that my client is entitled to exercise his right to silence, Detective Inspector MacIntosh." Cordelia Bannerman's voice cut through the air, as sharp as the beak-like nose on her narrow, pinched face. "I'd appreciate it if you ceased badgering him."

Jack ignored her. Badgering? He'd barely started. "Where were you on the night of Tuesday 20 May, Mr Dixon?"

More silence flooded the room, the only sound being the rhythmic whirring of the tape recorder. Jack's eyes travelled up to the ceiling where the video recorder's red light blinked.

"What did you use to cut her up with, Mr Dixon?" Jack sensed Cassidy flinching in the seat next to him.

Still, Dixon remained tight-lipped and stony-faced.

To labour the point once again, which would no doubt earn him yet more disgruntled remarks from the duty solicitor opposite, Jack slid copies of the post-mortem photographs across the table. The graphic content of the images still elicited no response, so Jack left them in full view before embarking on his next line of questioning.

Resting his hand on top of the thick buff coloured folder he'd brought with him, Jack's gaze settled on Raymond Dixon. Little did Dixon know, but inside there was just reams of blank paper — it was a trick he'd learned from a fellow DI. '*Let them think you've got shed loads of evidence, Jack. It plays on their mind.*' Jack saw the man's eyes flicker towards the folder, just for a split second. But his blank expression remained.

"Do you like little girls, Mr Dixon?" That particular question earned the slightest of movements from across the table, a muscle twitching on the side of Dixon's neck. "You do know we'll be accessing your phone, laptop and any other pieces of electronic equipment we find at your house — pulling it all apart? Don't think you'll be able to hide anything from us this time."

Another muscle twitched, joined by a slow reddening of the skin — but Raymond Dixon's mouth remained clamped tightly shut.

Jack tapped the top of the thick folder once more. "Maisie was the right age for you though, wasn't she? The same age as Carrie-Ann?"

That did it.

Dixon erupted from his chair and lunged across the table. "You fitted me up for that, you know you did, you bastard! You and that Hobbs fella! I never touched Carrie-Ann!"

Jack pushed his chair back just in time to escape the somewhat feeble punch heading his way. "Whoa, careful there, Mr Dixon. Got a bit of a temper, I see."

Cassidy moved out of the way, while Cordelia Bannerman hauled her client back into his chair.

Jack fought to keep the smirk from his face, happy that the video recorder above was documenting every second of Dixon's outburst. "Was that what happened with your daughter, Mr Dixon? Did Carrie-Ann do something to make you angry? To make you snap?"

"You conniving little shit." Dixon shrugged off the vain attempt from the duty solicitor to placate him. "Are you gonna just sit there and let him do this to me?" He flashed the solicitor a thunderous look, spittle flying from the corners of his mouth. "Surely I have rights here?"

"Inspector," began Cordelia Bannerman, her lips pursed in annoyance. "My client was found not guilty of the offence I think you are referring to. Kindly desist from this line of questioning."

"Well, not exactly, Ms Bannerman. The case was thrown out before the jury even got to hear it. That's not quite the same thing — that's not quite the same thing at all."

"In any event, my client has been arrested in connection with the murder of Maisie Lancaster. Kindly limit your line of questioning to that."

Jack pulled his chair back towards the table and sat down. "As you wish." Pulling out DI Telford's summary from his pocket, he leaned forward, his elbows resting on top of the buff coloured folder. "On the subject of your temper, Mr Dixon — it says here that you were convicted of ABH in the year 2000. A fight outside a pub, no less. You served two years of a four-year sentence. Care to tell me what happened?"

Dixon reverted back to silence, his face reddened — anger still simmering in his eyes.

Jack lowered his eyes to DI Telford's summary and saw something that had escaped his attention earlier. Trying to mask the emerging frown on his brow, he got to his feet and sharply scooped up the buff coloured folder with one hand.

"Interview suspended at 1.05 p.m. Turn the tape off, Amanda. We're done for now." Jack paused and turned back round to face Raymond Dixon. "Don't get too comfortable. We'll be back."

CHAPTER THIRTY-NINE

Time: 1.10 p.m.
Date: Monday 26 May 2014
Location: Metropolitan Police HQ, London

Despite the pain raging in his shoulder, Jack took the stairs two at a time, while DI Telford's summary burned a hole in his pocket. Why hadn't he checked it more thoroughly before charging in like a bull in a china shop? He'd been so focused on finally getting Dixon into an interview room that he'd let his emotions take over — and he hadn't read the summary properly.

On entering the incident room, he caught DS Cooper's eye. "Cooper? Pull up what we have on Ray Dixon's arrest and conviction for an ABH in 2000. In particular, details of his co-defendants."

Cooper saw the urgency in Jack's eyes and instantly started tapping his keyboard.

"And what about his phone records? Any further forward on tracing those numbers?" Jack made his way over towards DC Daniels, tossing the buff coloured folder and DI Telford's summary on a desk as he passed.

"Full call history is now in, and we've also got the cell site information, too. According to triangulation, on both days — the fourteenth when Maisie goes missing, and night of the twentieth when the suitcase is dumped — his phone doesn't seem to leave Lambert Grove." Daniels angled his computer monitor towards Jack. "And as for the numbers on his phone, we've managed to identify and account for all but one."

Jack peered over Daniels' shoulder to see one mobile phone number highlighted on the itemised list.

"Appears to be an unregistered pay-as-you-go mobile," continued Daniels. "Untraceable. You want me to ring it and see if it's still active?"

Jack stared at the computer monitor. Ray Dixon had called the unknown number frequently up until about six weeks ago, often several times a day. Then the calls had petered out. In the last week they'd disappeared completely.

"What about incoming calls?"

"Same," replied Daniels. "The only number we can't account for is this unregistered pay-as-you-go."

Jack noticed the unknown number had been calling Dixon with increased frequency over the last two weeks, especially in the last couple of days. None of the calls had been answered.

Someone was clearly very keen to speak to Raymond Dixon.

"Messages?"

Daniels shook his head. "Not that many, it's mostly calls. We're obtaining transcripts of what messages there are."

"OK, good work. We've something else to ask him once he's had time to stew a little longer. What about news from his house? Anything from the search team yet?"

"Not yet," replied Daniels. "I'll give them another call."

Jack didn't hold out much hope of them finding anything linking Dixon to Maisie at 30 Lambert Grove. The man was too clever for that — he'd been through this once before and was unlikely to make the same mistake again.

"Boss? Case details here on Dixon's ABH conviction." Cooper scooted his chair to the side to make way for Jack and angled his computer monitor towards him. "Which is weird, because I've just been reading about the same case in relation to Gerard Murray."

Jack nodded. It was as he suspected. "Tell me what you know."

"Says here, in 2000, Raymond Dixon was involved in an altercation outside a pub. Witnesses report tempers flared after accusations were made by some of the pub goers in relation to Carrie-Ann's murder. Sounds like it started off as drunken banter, but then spilled out into the street and became a full-on brawl. From what I can gather, several other people got involved and it turned into a bit of a free-for-all."

"And his co-defendant?" Jack already knew the name that was about to spring out of Cooper's mouth but wanted to hear it for himself.

"None other than Gerard Murray, boss. Both ended up being charged with ABH."

Jack nodded.

Gerard Murray.

Jack had seen the same name listed on DI Telford's summary on Raymond Dixon. He again chastised himself for not spotting it before. He could blame the pain induced fog currently cluttering his brain, but he still should have seen it. He pulled the blister pack of painkillers from his pocket and threw them at Cooper. "Pop a couple of them out for me, Cooper."

Cooper did as he was told and Jack dry swallowed them in one. "Any information on how Murray got involved? He just so happened to be in the same place at the same time?"

"Well, here's the thing." Cooper couldn't help the smile emerging on his lips. "Guess which pub the fight broke out in?"

It took a few seconds for the penny to drop. "The Bridge?"

Cooper nodded. "Yup. See the summary, here. On the day in question, Dixon swaggers in, already having had one too many by all accounts. Upsets one of the regulars who then starts making accusations about his Carrie-Ann. More accusations start flying, followed by fists. Gerard was helping out behind the bar at the time and seemed to feel compelled to join in. Looks like he and Dixon set about the trouble-maker and got ABH charges for their trouble."

"They spend time together in prison?"

DS Cooper shook his head. "From what I can gather, both served their sentences at different prisons — which was probably just as well. Murray's army history came in while you were interviewing." Cooper clicked his mouse and brought up another document. "Joined up in 1996 as we thought, but he was dishonourably discharged after the fight in the Bridge in 2000 and the ABH conviction that followed. Understandably, that put paid to his army career. But his army record is littered with violent incidents — I think this was just the one that finally broke the camel's back, as they say. After his release from prison, it looks like he was unemployed for a while, until getting his job back at the Bridge in 2008."

Jack's mind started to whirr. "OK, so we have Dixon acquainted with Gerard Murray — and we're currently looking at Dixon in relation to Maisie's murder, and Murray in relation to Narelle's. The fact the pair know each other concerns me. Especially as we have Dr Hunter telling us we should be looking for one killer." Jack rubbed his temples — the painkillers had yet to kick in.

"And more sightings of the silver Vauxhall?"

Cooper shook his head. "Nothing for the fourteenth. Or the twentieth. And nothing since."

Jack heard Dr Hunter's words echo inside his head.

'He was on foot, Jack. He walked on to the bridge.'

"Do we have any idea where it is now?"

"Nothing so far, boss," replied Cooper.

"Run the plate again. This time, include the Soho area, around Darren Hughes' address. And all days in between the fourteenth and the twentieth. I want to find that car." Jack scooped up several images of the silver Vauxhall and placed them inside the folder.

Just then there was a knock at the incident room door and a PC's head appeared around the door frame.

"DI MacIntosh? A message from the custody suite. Raymond Dixon wants to talk."

CHAPTER FORTY

Time: 1.45 p.m.
Date: Monday 26 May 2014
Location: Metropolitan Police HQ, London

Jack once again took his seat opposite Raymond Dixon, the tape and video recorders already running. He placed the buff coloured folder of blank paper on the table, in full view of Dixon and his solicitor. Jack had even added a few more pages for good measure.

"Raymond Edward Dixon. You remain under arrest for the murder of Maisie Lancaster. You also remain under caution. The time is thirteen forty-five and the same persons are present in the room as before. I hear you wish to say something, Mr Dixon?"

Dixon nodded. "Aye, I do. I want it on record that I had nothing to do with this."

"Duly noted. Now that you seem to have found your tongue, maybe we can go back to some of the questions I asked earlier?" Jack received a shrug in response. "How well did you know Maisie Lancaster, Mr Dixon?" Jack looked up and held the man in a stony gaze.

"She's a neighbour. The daughter of some friends of mine."

"That would be Russell and Sara Lancaster?"

Dixon nodded. "Yes."

"When was the last time you saw Maisie, Mr Dixon?"

"I don't exactly remember. I don't see her very much. She's a kid."

"I thought you said the Lancasters were friends of yours?"

Dixon hesitated for a fraction of a second. "I'm more friends with the Fosters, really."

"And that would be Maggie and Derek Foster. Sara Lancaster's parents?"

Another nod. "That's right. But I haven't seen much of them lately, either."

"And why would that be?" Jack watched closely for any change in body language. All he got was another shrug.

"No reason."

"Enquiries tell us that the three of you regularly attend the Lambert Grove Working Men's Club. Namely on a Tuesday and Thursday evening — along with your neighbour, Mr Brian Johnson."

Raymond Dixon cautiously raised his eyebrows. "Aye. We do. They've got a pretty good pool table."

"That's as maybe, but our enquiries also tell us that you haven't been for the last six weeks. They have, but you haven't." Jack let the statement sink in. "Why would that be?"

Jack detected the smallest of flinches in Dixon's facial expression, watching the muscles at the side of the man's jaw momentarily clench.

"Well, with Maisie going missing, playing pool doesn't seem like the right thing to do."

"I'm talking about before Maisie went missing, Mr Dixon. Records show the last time you went was back in mid-April. That's some time before Maisie disappeared."

An uneasy silence filled the room as Raymond Dixon dropped his gaze to his lap. "Well, I don't rightly remember. Perhaps I just didn't feel like it."

"Have you fallen out with the Fosters, Mr Dixon?"

Dixon flashed a look of concern towards his solicitor but received nothing in response. "Not that I recall, no."

"Not that you recall?" Jack pretended to jot the response down on one of the blank pieces of paper inside the folder. "DS Cassidy? Make a note to ask Mr Foster when we speak with him next."

Jack waited for the penny to drop across the table — and a split second later, it did. Raymond Dixon's face turned a translucent shade of white. Jack did his best to smother the smile that threatened to break out on his face. "Oh, didn't you know? We have your good friend Derek Foster here with us, too. Maybe he'll be able to fill us in on the state of your friendship. Anyway, let's move on." Jack made a point of rummaging among the blank papers in the file. "Do you own a car, registration number BM12 ONS, Mr Dixon?"

Raymond Dixon hesitated, his mouth feeling dry. "You know I do."

"Well, I don't actually — seeing as the car hasn't been transferred into your ownership. But never mind that. We know it belongs to you. How do you know Darren Hughes?"

Dixon remained stony-faced and shrugged. "I don't."

"But you bought the car from him, did you not? Darren Hughes?"

Another shrug followed. "If that was his name, then yeah, I did."

Jack glanced sideways towards Cassidy, deciding to park that line of questioning for the time being. "Let's move on. What were your movements on the day Maisie Lancaster was last seen?" The uneasy silence continued. "It was Wednesday 14 May, if that helps."

"I was probably at home. I don't go many places these days. Only the bookies."

"Quite." Jack slipped a piece of paper out of the folder. "So, you believe that you were home all day, and didn't leave your house?"

Dixon nodded. "I think that's what I said when one of your lot came knocking at the door."

"Indeed, it was." Jack paused before continuing. "So, you wouldn't have gone out in your car at all that day?"

Dixon shrugged. "Not that I remember. No need to."

"That is, again, what you said in your statement to one of our officers, Mr Dixon."

"Well, there you go then."

Jack tapped the piece of paper he'd extracted from the pile. "So, would it surprise you if we had evidence suggesting the exact opposite?"

A fleeting look of something akin to panic crossed Raymond Dixon's face. "What do you mean?"

"Your car, Mr Dixon. The car you've just admitted to owning. We have it on camera being driven on the afternoon of 14 May. It's been picked up on various cameras, actually — one very close to where Maisie was last seen, and at about the right time, too." Jack watched as Dixon's look of panic turned into something else. Fear.

Dixon's mouth opened and closed several times before he managed to reply. "Ah, yes, I remember now. I lent the car to a friend."

"A friend?" Jack let his eyebrows hitch. "And who would that friend be?"

Dixon remained silent.

"What did this friend want your car for, Mr Dixon?"

Dixon shrugged. "I don't know. I didn't ask. If a friend wants my car, I lend them my car. I don't quiz them."

"Well maybe you should, Mr Dixon." Jack fixed Raymond Dixon with a hard stare. "I'll ask you again. Who was this friend? And where is the car now?"

Dixon returned the stare. "I've said all I want to say. I didn't kill Maisie Lancaster."

* * *

Time: 2.45 p.m.
Date: Monday 26 May 2014
Location: Metropolitan Police HQ, London

Jack had decided to keep his knowledge about Gerard Murray and Dixon being involved in the fight at the Bridge out of the interview for now — and the forensic evidence linking Carrie-Ann's duvet to the suitcase. There would be time enough to drip-feed those tasty morsels into a future session. Although Dixon had started to speak, he hadn't divulged anything of value to take the investigation much further.

But Jack knew he was definitely hiding something — and, subject to the custody clock counting down, he was prepared to bide his time.

Dr Hunter's voice floated into his head as he headed for the corridor leading to the incident room.

'*Your cases are linked, Jack. Just as you suspected. It's the same man.*'

Lost in his thoughts, Jack almost collided headlong into DS Cooper hurrying along in the opposite direction. The young detective's cheeks were flushed.

"Boss — you need to come and see this."

Jack followed Cooper back to the incident room, his interest piqued. Both Daniels and Cassidy were huddled around one of the computer monitors.

"It's definitely him," remarked Cassidy, leaning over Daniels' shoulder to get a closer look. "One hundred per cent."

Jack headed towards the gathering around Cooper's monitor — the ginger-haired detective sliding back into his seat.

"We've found an image of the silver Vauxhall — it's on CCTV from a garage forecourt in Soho." Cooper tapped the screen to enlarge the image. "Taken at 2.30 p.m. on Tuesday 20 May."

Jack leaned in close. The image on the screen was surprisingly clear — not one of the grainy black and white jobs that were of no use to man nor beast. The garage had clearly invested in some half decent security cameras.

And it was true. The silver Vauxhall, complete with the different coloured side panel, was parked on the forecourt and there was no mistaking who was sitting behind the wheel.

"Darren Hughes," muttered Jack, his frown deepening. "What the devil is he doing driving Dixon's car around, only hours before Maisie Lancaster's body is dumped?"

"Dixon did say he'd lent his car to a friend," added Cassidy, straightening up. "I guess that friend was Darren Hughes."

"But that's not all." Cooper angled the screen a little more towards Jack. "Look at what's on his front passenger seat."

Jack noted the gleam in Cooper's eyes, and when he saw the image he knew exactly why.

The image couldn't be any clearer.

A suitcase.

"We need to bring our friend Darren Hughes in. And quick." Jack straightened up. "Dixon can marinate for the rest of the day — I'm in no hurry to chat to him again. We've got more than enough to detain him longer than twenty-four hours."

Jack began to turn away but noticed the gleam in Cooper's eye was still there. "There's more?"

Cooper nodded. "Trevor's been looking into that ABH case involving Dixon and Gerard Murray."

Jack switched his attention to Daniels, who already had his notebook out. "Daniels?"

Daniels flipped over a page in his book. "I looked into the court papers and you'll never believe who was a witness for Gerard Murray's defence?"

Jack's eyes flicked back towards Cooper's computer monitor which was still showing the image of Darren Hughes behind the wheel of the silver Vauxhall. "Surely not?"

Daniels nodded. "The one and only Darren Hughes."

"But . . . why?" Each thread of information was tangling inside Jack's head, tying itself up in knots. Nothing made any sense. "Why was he called by Murray's defence?"

"The witness statement he gave at the time stated he was supporting his brother — Gerard Murray."

"They're brothers?" Jack failed to keep the incredulity out of his tone. "Gerard Murray and Darren Hughes?"

"Half-brothers, to be precise," corrected Daniels. "Same mother, different fathers. Hence the different surnames."

Jack ran his good hand through his hair.

Dixon. Murray. Hughes.

All three intertwined.

"And you wanted to know where Darren Hughes was in 1994?" Daniels flicked to another page in his notebook. "He was here in London."

"So, who do we think it is?" Cassidy mirrored Jack's own thoughts. "If Dr Hunter says we're looking for one killer for both Maisie and Narelle — is it Dixon, Murray or Hughes?"

It wasn't a question anyone could answer.

Jack turned on his heels. "Cooper — you're with me. Let's go and see if our friend Darren Hughes is at home."

CHAPTER FORTY-ONE

Time: 2.45 p.m.
Date: Monday 26 May 2014
Location: Flat 3a Ash Road, SE Soho, London

Gerard Murray kicked aside the upturned flower pot on the front doorstep outside Flat 3a and snatched up the key.

His brother was nothing if not predictable.

Ramming home the key in the lock, he shoved the door open and stepped inside. The hallway was dank and musty, in need of a good airing. He could already see the outline of his brother, slumped over the kitchen table at the end of the hall. The almost empty bottle of cheap vodka by his side told him all he needed to know.

Entering the kitchen, Gerard flung his hastily packed holdall across the tacky linoleum floor. It came to rest against the overflowing bin, knocking it over and sending a cascade of empty beer cans, bottles and takeaway food cartons across the floor.

Darren Hughes woke with a start. "Wha . . . ?" He rubbed his fingers across his eyelids and yawned.

"What the hell, Daz?" thundered Gerard. "What in God's name were you thinking?"

"What d'ya mean?" Darren Hughes had now prised open his eyes and frowned at the hulking figure towering over him. "Wha . . . ?"

Gerard slammed a fist down on to the sticky plastic table, sending his brother's tobacco tin flying.

"The kid, numb-nuts. The kid." Gerard's eyes blazed hot, spit flying from both corners of his mouth. "What was with the suitcase? And why there, goddammit? The bridge. Why there of all places?"

Darren straightened up, his alcoholic haze now clearing fast. "You told me to deal with it. So I did."

"I didn't mean like that! Shit, Daz, do you really only have the one brain cell?" Gerard ran a hand through his thinning hair. "Of all the places you choose to dump her, you choose to do it there. On the bridge? I literally live and work yards away."

Darren got to his feet, grabbing hold of the side of the table to steady himself. "You just said get rid of her! So I did! And I thought the suitcase was a nice touch! But I could hardly drag it through the streets, could I? It had to be somewhere close by and it suited you before — with that Australian bird."

Gerard's face was on the verge of turning purple. "Well, that was before! And I didn't know that was where you'd dumped her!" Veins started to pulsate at his temples.

Hughes merely shrugged and reached for the vodka bottle. There was just about enough left for another mouthful. Raising the bottle to his lips, he felt it fly from his grasp and saw it smash against the wall into tiny fragments. The smell of neat alcohol instantly mixed with the chip fat already clogging the air.

Gerard's fist hovered inches from his brother's face. "Well, thanks to you, they've now dug up that Australian girl — and it's only a matter of time before they link it back to me and rock up on my doorstep. Hell, I've already had the police sniffing round the pub. As soon as they get in touch with head office, I'm mincemeat."

Darren's face took on a defiant look. "Well, the Australian one was nothing to do with me! You did that all on your own . . ."

* * *

Time: 11.45 p.m.
Date: Wednesday 31 August 1994
Location: The End of the Road Public House, London SE1

He hadn't meant to kill her. Or, at least, he didn't think he had. To be fair, it was all a bit hazy.

He tried to think back to when it'd all gone wrong, but the memories were blurred and merged into one. She'd turned up at his door after her shift ended, he remembered that much. And he'd put on the new Oasis album just like they'd planned, and opened the whisky. How long ago had that been? He looked at his watch and saw it was nearly midnight. The time had passed so quickly.

When she had first started working at the pub, she had instantly caught his eye. Well, of course she did — she was beautiful. She had that natural golden tan that came only from living a life outdoors. And that accent . . . her voice was like sweet velvet.

Not that she'd be able to speak much now.

He placed the baseball bat by the side of the bed and considered his next move. Nobody really came up to the rooms above the pub, so he knew he was safe for a while. But she couldn't stay. He'd have to think of a way to get her out.

Pouring himself another glass of whisky, he felt his nerves steady. What was done was done – there was nothing he could do to change that now. The stupid bitch had brought it all on herself.

The alcohol was helping to sharpen his thoughts. She'd laughed at him — that's what she'd done. *Laughed* at him. And in that wonderful accent, too. The very voice that turned him on, had driven him to feel the sharpest, most intense hatred — to a level he hadn't experienced in a long time. Not since the last time, anyway.

And then it had happened — so very quickly. One minute she was sitting there, mouth open, laughing at him. Then the next . . .

When the baseball bat hit her skull, she hadn't laughed anymore.

Unsure what else to do, he wrapped her body up in the duvet from the bed and rolled her to the side of the cramped room.

He'd think about what to do with her later.

For now, he needed to sleep.

Killing was a tiring business.

* * *

Time: 2.55 p.m.
Date: Monday 26 May 2014
Location: Flat 3a Ash Road, SE Soho, London

Darren didn't see the punch coming before it landed on the side of his jaw. He tasted the blood almost immediately.

"You said it was the perfect place!" He spat a blood-spattered globule of phlegm on to the kitchen table. "All that stuff about the executions and the highwaymen. Tossing bodies over the side of the bridge. You were always so obsessed with it. You'd go on about it for days!" Darren stepped to the side to avoid yet another swipe from his brother's fist.

"I might like the history, Daz, but that doesn't mean you need to recreate it!" Gerard's wide eyes blazed like an inferno. "I thought you'd dumped the Australian miles away, or at least further downstream so she'd end up in the bloody sea! And the same with the kid — Jesus, Daz. What were you thinking?"

Darren shrugged and rubbed his jaw, feeling it begin to swell. "Well, I wasn't thinking, was I? You call me up out of the blue, to get you out of a bit of bother — yeah, I think that's what you called it. '*A bit of bother*'. And she was a bit of a looker, that Australian one — before you cut her up."

Gerard's jaw clenched. Narelle *had* been a bit of a looker, that was true. But what was done was done. "You still should've taken her further away. You don't shit on your own doorstep, Daz."

"I did the best I could at the time. And as for the kid — after you'd killed her, you wanted her gone fast. I did as I was told. I thought the touch with Dixon's suitcase was quite clever . . ."

* * *

Time: 11.30 a.m.
Date: Tuesday 20 May 2014
Location: 30 Lambert Grove, London EC1

Darren Hughes made sure no one saw him as he slipped down the back alley and let himself into the back garden of number 30. He knew Dixon was out — he'd already seen him leave. Looked like he might be heading off down to the bookies, the *Racing Post* folded up underneath his arm.

The back door was unlocked and he was soon inside heading towards the stairs, knowing exactly where he was going. He didn't want to stay inside any longer than necessary — he needed to get back to the pub and finish clearing up the mess his brother had made.

The Fixer — that's what you are, Darren.

He smothered a smile and climbed the stairs.

Well, let's see him try and wriggle out of this one.

And all that stuff about his daughter — no one really believed him. Everyone knew he'd done it.

Pulling himself up the wooden steps, he entered the attic space. With the hatch open, a light chill descended. A single light switch to the side flooded the area in a bright light. Hughes paused, cocking his head to the side and listening for any sounds of Dixon returning home. But there was only silence from beneath.

He spied the stack of suitcases next to the water tank. Without hesitation, he stepped carefully along the joists, ducking his head beneath the rafters.

With such a variety of sizes, which one should he choose?

Conscious that he didn't have a lot of time, Hughes pulled one of the smaller cases out of the towering pile and headed back towards the hatch.

This one would have to do.

She was only a kid, after all.

* * *

Time: 3.00 p.m.
Date: Monday 26 May 2014
Location: Flat 3a Ash Road, SE Soho, London

Gerard shook his head and slumped down on to one of the plastic chairs at the kitchen table. "You're an idiot, Daz, I've no idea how we can be related sometimes. Now you've landed me in it for both of them." His eyes fell on the shattered vodka bottle, shards of glass now decorating the table and floor beneath him. That'd been a poor decision — he could do with a drink right now.

Darren could feel his jaw throbbing. It was a wonder he still had all his teeth. Edging around the side of the kitchen, he pulled open the cupboard beneath the sink in search of another bottle of vodka — his emergency supply. If now wasn't an emergency, then he didn't know what was. He grabbed the familiar shape of the bottle and stood up.

Gerard grabbed the bottle out of his brother's hands and ripped off the cap.

He took a long slug straight from the bottle. His knuckles were smarting from the punch. He knew Darren had only been trying to help but . . . sometimes he just took it too far. Wiping his lips on his sleeve he leaned forward and handed the bottle across to his brother. "Here. You need it just as much as I do."

Darren hesitated before taking hold of the bottle. It was true, he did need it. He could feel the shakes coming on already. He sank a mouthful and welcomed the burn.

"So, where's the rest of her, Daz?"

With the neck of the vodka bottle hovering in front of his lips, Hughes frowned. "What do you mean?"

"You know what I mean — the kid's bloody head, that's what. I read the papers, you know."

Seeing that the fire inside his brother's eyes hadn't dimmed, Darren cautiously inched further away, his eyes flickering automatically towards the freezer.

Gerard's gaze followed. "You've got to be kidding me . . ."

CHAPTER FORTY-TWO

Time: 3.05 p.m.
Date: Monday 26 May 2014
Location: Flat 3a Ash Road, SE Soho, London

"This wasn't exactly the plan, Daz." Gerard had calmed down a little, taking some time to roll a cigarette from the tobacco tin he'd rescued from the floor. "When I said get rid of her, I meant all of her. Why the hell keep it?"

Darren shrugged. "Suitcase was too small. I should've got a bigger one, but I just grabbed the first one I saw. Dixon could've caught me at any minute, rummaging around in his attic."

Gerard felt a small smile tug at the corner of his mouth. He had to concede that the suitcase was a nice touch.

"You still should've tossed the head."

Darren gave another shrug. "I know."

"What do you plan to do with it now?" Gerard cast a sideways glance at the freezer. "It can't stay in there."

"I guess I'll wait for the heat to die down and then chuck it."

"I don't think this heat'll die down for a good while yet, Daz. Which is why I'm out of here." He nodded towards the holdall by the upturned bin. "I'm gonna disappear for a while . . ."

"You think they'll come for me?" A worried frown crossed Darren's forehead.

Gerard's jaw clenched again. "That all depends on what that prick Dixon says. I don't trust him." Gerard bit back the hostility in his voice, visualising Raymond Dixon's head in the freezer instead of Maisie's.

"I don't want to go down for this, Gerry. I didn't kill anyone. Take me with you?"

"It's too risky, Daz." Gerard got back to his feet, taking another slug of the vodka as he went to pick up his holdall. "I need to get away, and it's best I'm on my own. You'll be fine here — just keep your head down. Don't go outside unless you really have to. Here, take some cash." Gerard pulled a bundle of notes from his wallet and thrust them towards his brother. "After dark, go and stock up on essentials, then keep out of sight. Don't answer the door."

"But . . ." Darren stumbled backwards as his brother pushed past him. "How long will you be gone for?"

Hesitating in the kitchen doorway, Gerard hoisted the holdall up on to his shoulder. How long *would* he be gone? A week? A month? A year? Suddenly, everything from twenty years ago was catching up with him, and he wasn't sure how fast he could run.

Narelle. Narelle. Narelle.

If he hadn't met her, none of this would be happening.

He wasn't too sure when he'd decided to cut her up — part of it was logistical. Dead bodies were heavy and cumbersome things, especially when you had to negotiate a narrow set of stairs. And he hadn't got it completely right — he knew that.

It'd taken much of the night — dismembering a body was harder than it looked. He'd dragged her into a small tin bath, which helped to contain much of the mess, but at one point he'd gone back down to the pub kitchen to find the largest butcher-style meat cleaver.

He'd eventually found the whole experience strangely enjoyable — feeling curiously detached from the whole process, remembering staring into her ocean-blue lifeless eyes while detaching her head from her body.

He'd taken her downstairs, piece by piece, and out into the rear courtyard. Choosing the wheelie bin closest to the road, it didn't take long for the flies to start buzzing, sensing a new delicacy had arrived — different to the usual offerings of rotten vegetables and old meat bones.

Making a quick trip later to the dilapidated block of flats she called home, he'd grabbed her passport and rucksack. When she failed to turn up for her next shift, people would assume she'd got itchy feet and moved on.

It had worked. For twenty years it had worked.

"Don't go. Please? You can't leave me here on my own."

Gerard swung the holdall off his shoulder and dropped it at his feet, shaking his head to rid himself of images of Narelle. "I can't stay, Daz. If they haven't turned the pub upside down yet, they soon will. I need to go."

"But what if they come for me? I didn't kill anyone, Gerry! I'm not taking the rap for it all."

Gerard pulled his brother in for a hug, patting him on the back. "You'll be fine. Like you say, you didn't kill anyone."

"At least stay tonight?"

"I can't. It's too risky. I need to be gone before it gets dark. Just make sure you don't have anything else here that ties you to me — or Dixon. Or anyone."

Both their eyes strayed back towards the kitchen — and the freezer.

"Get rid of the head tonight. Burn it if you have to. And anything else it might have touched. Clothes. Bags. But I can't stay, Daz."

Darren's face paled.

Gerard bent down to pick up his holdall. "You'll be fine. Keep your head down, like I said. Get rid of anything you wore, anything you touched. Burn it out the back."

"You'll come back?" Darren stared wide-eyed at his brother. "You'll come back for me?"

"Sure," lied Gerard. "I'll be back before you know it." Stepping towards the door, his hand came to rest on the door handle at exactly the same time as the sound of heavy hammering filled their ears.

"Darren Hughes. Gerard Murray. Open up. It's the police. You have five seconds."

CHAPTER FORTY-THREE

Time: 3.25 p.m.
Date: Monday 26 May 2014
Location: Flat 3a Ash Road, SE Soho, London

"Going somewhere?" Jack nodded towards the holdall that Gerard Murray had slung over one shoulder.

The man's face was a picture.

Jack stood in the narrow hallway of Flat 3a Ash Road, the doorway blocked behind him with a wall of uniformed officers.

"How about we step back inside for a few minutes?" Jack gestured towards the kitchen.

Reluctantly, Gerard Murray and Darren Hughes backed away and retreated to the kitchen, the uniformed officers filing in behind and blocking any escape.

Jack cast his eyes around the greasy kitchen once more — remembering it from their earlier visit not three days before. If he wasn't much mistaken, the same pile of dirty dishes was still crowding the sink, and the same smell of stale chip fat clung to the air.

Beneath his feet, his shoes crunched on shards of glass with a whiff of neat alcohol reaching his nostrils. "Had a little accident, have we?"

The comment made no impression on either Gerard or Hughes, who were both standing silently by the kitchen table. "You not going too, Darren?" Jack caught the younger brother's eye. "I note you don't seem to have a bag packed."

Darren's mouth opened and closed like a fish, but no sound came out.

Jack continued to fix him with a cool stare. "Looks like your brother was about to run out on you."

Reaching into his pocket, Jack brought out DI Telford's summary on Raymond Dixon. He made a show of smoothing out the creases before looking back up. "Darren — you spent some time in Rushmore Prison last year, just before you were released. Remember that?"

Darren Hughes remained mute, his eyes widening by the second.

Jack continued. "You ever come across a man by the name of Ray Dixon while you were there?"

Jack detected a slight flinch in Gerard Murray's posture at the sound of Dixon's name. Darren continued to impersonate a goldfish.

"Well, I think you did. In fact, I *know* you did."

"I don't need to tell you anything," spluttered Darren, finally finding his voice. "You need to caution me. I know my rights."

Jack folded the piece of paper and slotted it back inside his pocket. "Quite right. How remiss of me. Darren Hughes. I'm arresting you on suspicion of murder. You do not have to say anything, but it may harm your defence if you do not mention when questioned something which you rely on in court. Anything you do say may be given in evidence. Happy?" Jack watched as Darren Hughes' eyeballs almost popped out of his head. "Cuff him."

Jack then turned to Gerard Murray, holding the man's cool gaze before reciting the same caution. "Gerard Murray. I'm arresting you on suspicion of murder. You do not have to say anything, but it may harm your defence if you do not mention when questioned something which you later rely on in court. Anything you do say may be given in evidence."

With both brothers handcuffed, Jack nodded towards the bank of uniformed officers standing by the door. "Take them away."

After watching Murray and Hughes being led out of the property towards the waiting police vans, Jack and Cooper hovered inside the kitchen for a moment or two.

"We'll let the forensic team get started, Cooper. Get ourselves back to the station." Jack gave the kitchen one last sweep, hearing the front door opening and closing again, followed by the murmurings of the crime scene investigators arriving. As he did so, he spied a mobile phone sitting on the draining board.

Without taking his eyes from the handset, Jack reached into his pocket and pulled out his own phone. "Cooper? You have that unregistered number from Dixon's phone log to hand?"

Cooper flicked through his notebook. "Yup. 07700 900449."

Jack tapped the number into his phone and pressed 'call'.

A split second later, the mobile phone on the draining board sprang into life. Jack cut the call.

"I think we've found our mystery caller, Cooper. Bag that phone up."

Cooper took a plastic evidence bag from one of the scene of crime officers who'd filed into the kitchen, securing the phone inside. As he did so, Jack's own phone began to trill.

"Amanda." Jack nodded at Cooper to follow him out into the hallway. "Glad you called. We've just arrested Murray and Hughes. They're on their way to the station now. Can you organise a team to search the pub? Especially the rooms above?"

"Of course, guv," replied Cassidy, sounding somewhat breathless. "I'll get on to that right away. But the reason I'm calling is that you've got a visitor."

"A visitor?" Jack frowned as he made his way outside towards the Mondeo. "What kind of visitor?"

"It's Mrs Foster. Maggie Foster?" Cassidy paused. "She says she needs to speak to you. It's about Maisie."

* * *

Time: 4.05 p.m.
Date: Monday 26 May 2014
Location: Metropolitan Police HQ, London

Jack sprinted up the stairs to meet Cassidy in the corridor outside his office. "Where is she?"

"Interview room one, boss." Cassidy hurried alongside as Jack made a beeline for the interview rooms at the far end of the corridor.

"Has she told you what this might be about?"

Cassidy shook her head. "No, guv. Nothing other than it's about Maisie. And she'll only speak to you."

"Does she know we've got Dixon in custody?"

Cassidy could only shrug. "I don't know. She's not mentioned him."

"Do we still have her husband? Derek Foster?"

"I think he's been let go, guv. Pending further investigations."

Before they reached the end of the corridor, DC Daniels came striding towards them from the other direction, waving a piece of paper in the air. "We've got the transcripts in from Dixon's phone. His text messages."

Jack came to a halt outside the interview room, eyebrows raised. "Anything interesting?"

Daniels handed over the sheet of paper. "Whoever was on the end of that unregistered phone has been asking for money."

Jack took the print-out and gave it a cursory glance. He already knew Darren Hughes owned the unregistered phone, having watched it merrily trilling on the draining board back at

Ash Road — but why was he asking Dixon for money? Slotting the paperwork into his jacket pocket, he nodded at Daniels.

"We'll tackle Dixon later. For now, we've got Maisie's grandmother in interview room one." Jack caught the young officer's eye. "Care to sit in?"

"Of course. Do you know why she's here?"

Jack reached for the door handle. "Not yet. But that family is hiding something. While we're in here, Amanda, can you make sure Murray and Hughes are booked in — might be a good idea to put them in cells as far away as possible from each other. And from Dixon. Things might get a little heated down there." Cassidy nodded and hurried away.

Maggie Foster was seated on the far side of a smooth, plastic-topped table. She nursed a polystyrene cup of what looked like coffee but could essentially be any number of things if it came from the vending machine outside. Jack sat opposite, the sound of his scraping chair echoing around the otherwise silent interview room.

"Mrs Foster." Jack took a moment to regard the woman sitting six feet away. If it were possible, she looked even more haunted than before. Her eyes had sunk even further into her skull, her skin looked pale and slack. "I hear you want to talk to us about the disappearance of your granddaughter, Maisie?"

Maggie Foster nodded, her eyes full of tears. "Yes . . . yes, I do."

"What is it you'd like to tell us, Mrs Foster?"

Jack flashed a look at the clock on the wall. With Gerard Murray and Darren Hughes now in custody, alongside Raymond Dixon, there wasn't a lot of time to waste. They had twenty-four hours to charge or release — if no extension was granted — and that time would disappear fast.

As Jack switched his gaze back to Maggie Foster, he saw a resoluteness fill her eyes that hadn't been there before. Taking in several shuddering breaths, she began.

"In 1989 I gave an alibi to Raymond Dixon in connection with the disappearance and death of his daughter Carrie-Ann." Mrs Foster paused and looked Jack squarely in the eye. "I wish to tell you now that that alibi was false."

CHAPTER FORTY-FOUR

Time: 4.15 p.m.
Date: Monday 26 May 2014
Location: Metropolitan Police HQ, London

Jack fetched a fresh vending machine coffee for Mrs Foster, replacing the muddy-looking version that had now gone cold in front of her, and resumed his seat.

"Mrs Foster. A few moments ago, you admitted to providing a false alibi to a suspect in a murder enquiry. Could you confirm to me once more that that is correct?"

Maggie Foster nodded, reaching for the cup of fresh coffee. "It is. I can't lie anymore. I need to tell the truth."

"In that case, Mrs Foster, before we go any further I must caution you. You do not have to say anything, but it may harm your defence if you do not mention when questioned something that you later rely on in court. Anything you do say may be given in evidence. It is for your own protection as much as anything else. This interview will now also be recorded." Jack nodded towards the tape and video recorders that were already running. "You are not under arrest at this time, and I must also remind you of your right to ask for legal representation. Is there anything about the caution that you do not understand?"

Maggie Foster shook her head and raised the polystyrene cup to her lips, her hand trembling. "No," she whispered. "I understand."

"And do you require legal representation at this time?"

Mrs Foster took a hesitant sip of the boiling hot drink, wincing as it hit her lips, but again shook her head. "No. I do not."

"So, Mrs Foster, would you please confirm, for the purposes of the tape, the reason why you have asked to see us today."

Maggie Foster placed the polystyrene cup down on the table. A steeliness entered her eyes, replacing the watery tears that had been present only minutes before. "I wish to confirm that an alibi I gave Raymond Dixon in 1989, in connection with the disappearance and murder of his daughter Carrie-Ann, was false."

Jack exchanged a subtle look with Daniels. Neither of them knew exactly where this conversation was headed. One minute, Maggie Foster was asking to speak to them about Maisie, and the next she was mentioning Dixon and the case that had been a thorn in Jack's side for quarter of a century. Jack was struggling to connect the dots.

Maggie Foster swallowed before continuing. "Please, Inspector. You have to do something. For my Maisie."

Jack frowned. "Are you sure I can't get the duty solicitor in here for you, Mrs Foster? I think that in the circumstances . . ."

Maggie Foster brushed the suggestion aside. "No. I want to do this, and I want to do this now."

Jack gave a slow nod. "In that case . . . in what way was the alibi false, Mrs Foster?"

Taking in a deep breath, Maggie Foster stared resolutely ahead and began. "After Carrie-Ann's body was discovered in the attic of number 30 Lambert Grove, I told the police that Ray was with me during the time she'd most likely been abducted. I said that he'd been doing some painting and decorating at our house, and because of the amount of work involved he'd been staying with us for the duration."

Jack nodded, remembering the alibi Dixon had put forward in interview at the time. The alibi had blown their case out of the water — and once the forensic evidence was thrown out of court, the case had collapsed. "And you're now suggesting that this wasn't true?"

Mrs Foster shook her head, vehemently. "I'm not suggesting it, Inspector. I'm *telling* you it wasn't true. He did do some decorating at our house, that part is correct. He'd often do odd jobs here and there for us — my husband had no interest or talent in that regard, so we were more than happy for him to help us out. But he wasn't there at the times we'd suggested to the police. And at no time did he stay over when his daughter disappeared."

Jack's mind started to race. "I must remind you of your caution at this stage, Mrs Foster, and also reiterate your right to legal advice."

Maggie Foster again shook her head, taking another sip of her coffee. It had cooled a little, but she still winced. "I provided Ray with an alibi because . . ." She broke off, her composure starting to falter, her face sagging. "Because we were having an affair," she finished in a whisper.

Jack's eyes widened as he frantically searched his own memory of the Carrie-Ann murder investigation. He remembered the young Maggie Foster — she'd been newly married and pregnant at the time, and good friends with the Dixon family. He could picture her sitting on the Dixons' sofa, clutching Kelly Dixon's hand and sobbing her heart out as she shared in the family's grief.

"And how long had the affair been going on?"

Maggie Foster cast her eyes down to the murky liquid in the coffee cup. "Quite a while. Well, long enough. Long enough for . . ." She broke off and Jack detected a shudder from her slightly-framed shoulders.

"When did Ray Dixon ask you to lie for him?"

"Two days before Carrie-Ann was found, Ray came to me and told me I had to help him. He was paranoid that you were going to pin it all on him. He'd seen it happen before, we all had. People locked up for years for something they didn't do. He wanted me to lie about where he was and I . . ." She broke off and swallowed again. "I agreed."

"Did he tell you why he needed an alibi? Did he tell you what he was really doing at that time? Where he really was?"

Mrs Foster gave a sad shake of the head. "No. No, he didn't. But . . ."

Jack's eyebrows hitched. "But what?"

"He gave me something. A bag. He told me I needed to hide it. Keep it safe. Put it somewhere that no one would ever look, somewhere it would never be found. And to keep to the story that he'd been with me the whole time."

"What was in the bag, Mrs Foster?" Another shudder from across the table made Jack's stomach tighten. "What was in the bag?" he repeated.

Maggie Foster's voice trembled. "Clothes. Carrie-Ann's clothes. Her summer dress — the one she was wearing in all the newspaper reports and TV appeals. The one she was wearing when she vanished. And . . ." Tears began to course down Maggie Foster's cheeks. "And her underwear. I . . . I only took a brief look inside, but I saw . . . I saw blood."

Jack saw Daniels pull out his notebook and gave a discreet nod in his direction.

"What did you do with the bag, Mrs Foster?"

"I hid it — like he told me to."

"And where was that?"

Maisie's grandmother took in a deep breath and exhaled, her eyes closing for a second before she responded. "At my house. I put it underneath the floorboards in the spare room. It was the room Ray was helping us to decorate. It was to be . . ." Mrs Foster shuddered again. "It was to be a nursery. I was pregnant with Sara at the time."

Daniels stood up and, after another brief nod from Jack, left the room.

"DC Daniels has left the interview room." Jack sighed and sought out Maggie Foster's watery gaze across the table. "Mrs Foster — I must stop you before you say anything further. I am arresting you on suspicion of perverting the course of justice and assisting an offender."

Maggie Foster gave another weak smile and nodded. "I understand." A silent tear trickled down her pallid cheek as she listened once again to the police caution.

* * *

Time: 5.15 p.m.
Date: Monday 26 May 2014
Location: 11 Hartington Crescent, London EC1

DC Trevor Daniels paced up and down the pavement outside the Fosters' family home. The search warrant had been authorised in record time but getting an investigation team mobilised had taken a while longer. The temptation to rush headlong inside was ever present, bubbling just beneath the surface. But Jack's instructions had been crystal clear. Procedure was to be followed to the letter this time — where Carrie-Ann was concerned, there was no room for any more mistakes.

Daniels waited patiently while the site was secured. He was already dressed head to toe in his white protective suit and overshoes, the late-spring sunshine had now dipped out of view but it was still making him sweat.

Maggie Foster had said the bag was in an upstairs bedroom, but the whole house would now be searched for any trace of Carrie-Ann.

Davina Stansfield was leading the investigation team today, a seasoned crime scene manager with over twenty years' experience. *Nothing* got past her. Making her way out of the front door, she gave Daniels the nod — and after taking in a deep breath behind his mask, he quickly strode through the open garden gate and followed her back inside.

The hallway was neat. A small telephone table sat by the base of the stairs — but instead of a telephone it housed a vase of wooden sunflowers. Even the Fosters had entered the twenty-first century and moved on to mobile phones, or so it seemed. A kitchen could be seen at the end of the hall, and beyond that a small, enclosed courtyard garden.

Daniels envisaged the garden would host an assortment of cottage-style wild flowers, with pots and planters creating a haven for bees and other insects. He also suspected there would be herbs — Mrs Foster looked the type to grow her own.

But he wasn't here to admire the garden, herbs or no herbs. Ducking his head inside the one room that opened out from the narrow hallway, he noted a front room with a similar layout to that of the Lancasters' house just a few minutes' walk away around the corner. Again, the Victorian-style high ceiling and large bay window dominated the room. A simple cream sofa hugged the rear wall, with a bookcase standing on either side. In front was a glass-topped, low-rise coffee table sitting on a deep-pile rug.

Another vase of wooden sunflowers sat on the windowsill.

Daniels withdrew from the front room. Davina was already standing at the bottom of the stairs, alongside two crime scene investigators. They all knew where they were heading.

Upstairs there were three bedrooms and a family bathroom. Mrs Foster had referred to the bag being concealed under the floorboards of the 'spare room'. But which of the three bedrooms this would be wasn't altogether clear. In his haste to leave the station, Daniels hadn't asked — or, if he had, he hadn't listened to the answer. He felt his cheeks begin to colour and more sweat gathered at the base of his spine.

One of the bedrooms was more spacious than the others and was clearly the main bedroom. Situated at the front of the house, it contained a large double bed and a set of built-in wardrobes. Light and airy, a large bay window let in an abundance of natural daylight.

Davina was hovering by the door, eyebrows raised. Daniels shook his head. He was pretty sure that twenty-five years ago this room wouldn't have been the Fosters' spare room.

Which meant one of the other two must have been.

They were both of similar size and layout — with single beds and simple furniture. Tastefully decorated in a range of pastel shades, there was nothing to suggest what macabre findings might lie hidden beneath the floorboards in one of them.

Both rooms were carpeted, so neither was going to be an easy job — the carpets and underlay would need to be ripped up before accessing the floorboards beneath.

He silently cursed himself again for not asking more questions, or maybe not listening to the answers given — Mrs Foster could very well have said which room it was, but the adrenaline surge he'd felt on arriving at the scene seemed to have blocked it out. He hadn't felt this wired since the hunt for the Bishop — and he didn't need reminding how that had ended. It would be sod's law that they started in one room, only to find nothing and have to repeat the whole process in the other. And it would all take time — time they just didn't have. Raymond Dixon's custody clock was ticking.

"Detective?" Davina startled Daniels out of his trance-like state, nodding towards one of the bedrooms. "Shall we start in this one?"

Daniels' eyes darted between the two bedroom doors. Did it really matter which one they started with? Time was ticking and he needed to make a decision. He was about to nod when something struck him. He wasn't a family man as such — he had no children of his own and didn't know if he ever would, much to his mother's constant disappointment. But one thing he did know — or at least he thought he did — was that if you were setting up a nursery, wouldn't you choose the room closest to your own? It made sense, didn't it?

His eyes flickered towards the room on the left, closest to the main bedroom. Stepping forward, he lightly ran a gloved finger over the door. Was that faint lettering he could see, beneath the many layers of gloss paint that'd since been applied? A faint outline beginning with an 'S' and ending in an 'A'?

SARA
"In here," he said, stepping back. "We start in here."

* * *

Time: 5.25 p.m.
Date: Monday 26 May 2014
Location: Metropolitan Police HQ, London

"Please continue, Mrs Foster. What happened after you hid the bag in your house?"

Fresh water had now replaced the coffee, and Maggie Foster gratefully drank a mouthful. They'd had a break for some food, an offer Mrs Foster had politely declined, as she'd similarly done with the repeated offer of legal advice. She drank another mouthful, then placed the cup down on the table with a shaky hand. "Nothing. Carrie-Ann's body was found the next day and I kept to the story, just as Ray told me to."

"Can I ask why, Mrs Foster? Why would you go to such lengths to conceal the truth about what'd happened to her? Why lie for him?"

Maggie Foster looked up with sad eyes. She gave Jack a half-smile and at that moment, he saw the exact same emotion in her eyes that he himself had carried around for two decades — a millstone around both their necks.

Guilt.

"I was in love, Inspector. Or at least I thought I was. And Ray assured me it wasn't him. That he just found her clothes but knew the police wouldn't believe him. I . . . I just wanted to help him. And once I'd said it — it couldn't be unsaid. I'd lied to the police and I knew I'd get into serious trouble. So, I just panicked. I kept quiet."

Jack let silence fill the interview room. What Maggie Foster was now saying could blow the whole cold case apart. Finally, Carrie-Ann could get the justice she deserved.

"We've requested a warrant to search your home address for the bag of clothing. If the same is located, I'll hand the matter over to a different investigative team. They'll most likely approach the CPS for authorisation to charge you. Is there anything else you wish to say at this point?"

Mrs Foster merely shook her head. Jack noted a lightening of her eyes, and a small amount of colour entering her cheeks. If Jack weren't mistaken, she looked relieved.

"In that case, I'll pause the interview here. Interview suspended at 5.30 p.m." Jack reached towards the tape recorder, but before he was able to flick the switch, Maggie Foster raised her hand.

"Not quite yet, Inspector. That's not the whole reason I'm here."

"I'm sorry?" Jack let his finger hover over the tape recorder. "What's not the whole reason you're here?"

Mrs Foster nodded towards the tape machine. "What I've just told you about Carrie-Ann. About Ray. And about the bag. That's not why I came — not entirely, anyway."

"It's not?" Jack settled back in his seat. "What else would you like to tell me, Mrs Foster?"

Maggie Foster took another fortifying mouthful of water. Her eyes remained red-rimmed and raw, but another emotion flickered. This time it was one of anger. "I came here to tell you about Maisie."

CHAPTER FORTY-FIVE

Time: 6.10 p.m.
Date: Monday 26 May 2014
Location: Metropolitan Police HQ, London

"Interview resumed at 6.10 p.m. What would you like to tell me about Maisie, Mrs Foster? And I must remind you, you are still under caution."

They'd taken a break for a fresh round of coffee — more for Jack's sake than anyone else's — and Maggie Foster had once again been urged to take advantage of the duty solicitor. Once again, she had declined. As far as Jack knew, the search at Hartington Crescent was still in the very early stages and he wasn't expecting any news for a while. DS Cassidy slipped into the vacant seat next to him.

A pained look returned to Maggie Foster's face. "I spoke to Ray sometime last year — I can't be too sure on the exact date. I told him that I couldn't live with myself. I couldn't lie anymore about what he'd done — about Carrie-Ann. It's eaten away at me for years. I've been on antidepressants and sleeping tablets ever since. My relationship with Derek is a sham. We argue constantly, and it's all because of this — because of the lies I told all those years ago." She paused to wipe away a tear trickling down her cheek. "Twenty-five years ago this summer, it'll be." Mrs Foster broke off and took a mouthful of weak coffee, her hand shaking so much she almost dropped the cup. "I told him I was going to the police."

Jack's eyes widened, his eyebrows hitching up yet another notch. "And what was his reaction to that?"

"He went ballistic. Shouting and screaming at me not to be such a fool. I'd been to visit him in Rushmore Prison — and he lost the plot in the visiting room. They had to pull him off me, he was that angry. He told me we'd both go to prison if I told anyone. He even threatened to tell Derek that Sara wasn't really his." Mrs Foster dropped her gaze to the polystyrene cup in her hands, a fresh flush of colour entering her cheeks. "Sara doesn't know. Neither does Derek. It would crucify them both." She brushed away a fresh trickle of tears and looked up. "But I told him I didn't care what happened to me. I didn't care what he told anyone about Sara. I couldn't carry on the way I was. My life was already disintegrating around me. Whatever punishment I was to face — it couldn't be any worse than what I was living through. What I *am* living through."

"And what happened after that?" Jack felt a wave of unease sweep through him. "After you told him you were going to the police?"

"He went quiet for a while. When he was released from Rushmore he started avoiding me. Stopped going to the Working Men's Club. I thought he'd forgotten about what I'd said, but then . . . but then he threatened me. He told me that if I said anything, if I went to the police, then I would be very sorry. My whole family would be sorry. He said he'd cause me insufferable pain that I couldn't even begin to imagine."

"And what did you take this threat to mean?"

"Maisie." Mrs Foster looked up, her eyes wide with horror. "He was threatening to harm Maisie."

Jack and Cassidy exchanged a look. "Did he mention her specifically?"

Mrs Foster shook her head. "No — but he was standing in my front room, pointing to a picture of Maisie when he said it. I was under no illusion as to what he meant."

"And when was this threat made?"

"It was three days before Maisie went missing."

* * *

Time: 6.25 p.m.
Date: Monday 26 May 2014
Location: 11 Hartington Crescent, London EC1

It took some time for the furniture to be moved and the carpet and underlay to be rolled back. DC Daniels watched from the doorway, his stomach clenching as each minute ticked by. He was acutely aware of Jack awaiting his call, but each painstaking step seemed to take forever.

With the floorboards now exposed, the sound of nails being wrenched from wood began. Daniels found his stomach tightening as each board was lifted, watching as the investigators peered into the exposed cavity beneath.

With every shake of the head, the process moved on.

It took another seven floorboards being removed, and another thirty minutes to tick by, before Daniels saw one of the investigators pause and raise his hand.

"Here." The investigator turned, squatting on his haunches by the edge of the gaping hole, and waved the detective towards him.

Daniels felt his heart shoot into his mouth as he crossed the floor, carefully placing his feet on the exposed joists. The only sound he could hear was his own heartbeat thudding inside his chest. Kneeling down by the investigator's side, he followed the man's gloved finger towards what was, even from this distance, clearly a rolled-up plastic carrier bag. Daniels cocked his head to the side — from this angle it looked like an old Budgens supermarket bag. Covered in dust and cobwebs, it had clearly lain undisturbed for a significant amount of time.

Daniels made way for the investigator to take a series of photographs of the bag *in situ* before they made any attempt to move it. Before placing it inside a transparent evidence bag, the investigator opened it up — the aged plastic already starting to disintegrate.

Daniels peered inside.

It only took a second, but there was no doubt what he was looking at.

Carrie-Ann's missing clothing.

* * *

Time: 6.55 p.m.
Date: Monday 26 May 2014
Location: Metropolitan Police HQ, London

"This is Raymond Edward Dixon. Lives at 30 Lambert Grove. Previously suspected of the abduction and murder of his own daughter Carrie-Ann back in 1989 — and we all know how spectacularly well that turned out." Jack tapped the photograph of Dixon now tacked to the whiteboard. "Now in the frame for the abduction and murder of Maisie Lancaster."

Jack paused, his jaw tightening. Even saying the man's name made his simmering anger resurface. "If we can get justice for Carrie-Ann as well as Maisie, then we'll work our socks off to do so — no matter how much time has passed. As he's now had a fair while to stew, I think we might have another little chat with him. I want to see how he reacts when he realises Maggie Foster's been talking."

"What if he says she's lying?" remarked Cassidy. "His word against hers? A woman scorned?"

"Which is why we need something to come out of the search at the house. Cooper — any updates yet from Daniels?"

Cooper shook his head. "Not yet, boss. But it took a while to get the forensic team together. I'll give him a call."

Jack nodded. "Keep me updated. As soon as they find something, I want to know."

"What are we doing about Mrs Foster?" Cassidy's face softened. "I really feel for her."

"I've briefed DI Telford on what she's told us so far. She'll no doubt want to interview her herself in due course, once the forensics are finished with the house."

"Will she be charged, guv?"

Jack nodded. "Almost certainly. She's lied to a police investigation and concealed evidence, and also assisted an offender. She knows what's coming. But that's all in DI Telford's hands. It's her case now. We need to focus on how the information assists us in the hunt for Maisie's killer. If Dixon made threats towards Maisie three days before she disappeared, then . . ." Jack left the rest of the sentence unfinished.

"What about his links to Murray and Hughes?" Cooper brought up the summary from DI Telford which had now been uploaded on to the system. "They all seem to know each other, one way or another. Hughes' mobile phone is now linked to Dixon — and he's been asking him for money. And we know they both spent time in Rushmore Prison last year. *And* Hughes sold Dixon his car."

Jack rubbed his eyes. The same question had been bouncing around inside his head. What was the link between Darren Hughes and Raymond Dixon? And what was the money for?

"Well, we've clearly got Darren Hughes driving the silver Vauxhall with the suitcase on the front passenger seat — on the same day Maisie's body was dumped. And we have Hughes calling and messaging Dixon's phone." Jack tapped the image of Darren Hughes. "And we've all heard about his violent tendencies."

"So, who killed Maisie? Dixon or Hughes?" asked Cooper. "And what about Murray? His links to Narelle Williams surely put him in the frame, too?"

Jack's temples throbbed as he stared at the whiteboards.

Raymond Dixon.

Darren Hughes.

Gerard Murray.

According to Dr Hunter, there was only one killer. The problem was, who?

Just then, he heard the tell-tale beep of an incoming message. Fishing his phone out of his pocket, he saw it was Daniels. It took him two seconds to read the message, a satisfied smile crossing his lips.

"A bag containing what looks like Carrie-Ann's clothing has been found at the Foster's family home." Jack turned towards his team. "Let's see what Dixon has to say about that."

CHAPTER FORTY-SIX

Time: 7.05 p.m.
Date: Monday 26 May 2014
Location: Metropolitan Police HQ, London

"What's the nature of your relationship with Maggie Foster?" Jack and Cassidy resumed their seats opposite Raymond Dixon. Cordelia Bannerman afforded them both a disdainful look which they ignored.

Dixon shrugged. "I don't have a relationship with her. I already told you — we're friends."

"How long have you known her?"

Dixon puffed out his cheeks and exhaled. "Ages. About thirty years, why?"

"I'm the one asking the questions, Mr Dixon. At the time of your daughter's murder in July 1989, what was the status of your relationship with Mrs Foster?"

What colour there was in Raymond Dixon's cheeks began to recede like an ebbing tide. "What's that got to do with Maisie?"

"If you could just answer the question, Mr Dixon?"

Dixon flashed a brief look towards his solicitor before replying. "Same as now. Friends."

"Are you sure it wasn't a little bit more than that? More than just friends?"

"Where are you going with this?"

"As I remember saying before, Mr Dixon, I'm the one asking the questions." Jack paused and hid the smile fighting to break out on his lips. "OK, maybe we'll come back to that one. Two days before your daughter's body was found in the attic of your home address, did you give anything to Mrs Foster?" Jack detected the muscles at the side of Dixon's jaw flinch and his eyes widen.

"No comment."

"Did you give her a plastic bag containing items of clothing?"

"No comment." Raymond Dixon's face was ashen, and Jack detected signs of agitation setting in. But Jack didn't care if the man never spoke again. He knew they'd got him this time.

"A search at 11 Hartington Crescent is being carried out as we speak, and a bag containing what we believe to be Carrie-Ann's clothing has been found. It's being sent for DNA testing, but I think we all know what those results will be, don't you, Mr Dixon?"

"No comment."

Jack continued. "We have it on reliable authority that you gave this bag to Maggie Foster and asked her to hide it for you. Is that correct, Mr Dixon?"

"No comment."

Jack sought out Dixon's steely grey eyes. "She won't lie for you any more, you do know that?"

"No comment."

"Three days before Maisie Lancaster went missing, did you threaten Maggie Foster?"

"No comment."

"Did you threaten to hurt Maisie if Maggie Foster told the truth about Carrie-Ann?"

"No comment."

Jack had brought DI Telford's summary of Dixon's previous convictions with him again, which he folded out on the table in front of him.

"In 2012 you were convicted of fraud and sentenced to two years in prison. I believe this concerned the fraudulent use of a credit card. You served a portion of your sentence at Rushmore Prison?"

"No comment."

"This is all a matter of public record, Mr Dixon." Jack saw Dixon's hard, stony face staring straight past him. "You're doing yourself no favours in refusing to answer." Jack glanced back down at the summary. "During which time, you get acquainted with another prisoner called Darren Hughes."

"No comment."

"You're telling me you don't know him?" Jack raised his eyebrows, quizzically, in Raymond Dixon's direction. "You don't remember Darren Hughes? The Fixer? I'm told he was quite well known within Rushmore Prison."

"No comment."

"No matter." Jack shrugged and dropped his eyes back down to the summary. "I'm told Mr Hughes can't wait to talk to us, so I'm sure we'll get to the bottom of your relationship with him before too long."

"Inspector," interjected Cordelia Bannerman, her voice so taut it sounded as though it could snap at any moment. "I must object to your line of questioning. Please keep to the facts if you wish to question my client."

Jack ignored the duty solicitor and flashed a look back towards Dixon. The man's pale face had drained of yet more colour. "Prior to your time in Rushmore, in 2000 you were convicted of ABH. A fight in a pub, no less, for which you received four years' imprisonment. Your co-defendant at that time was a Mr Gerard Murray. Do you recall that, Mr Dixon?"

"No comment."

"Do you lose your temper easily, Mr Dixon?" Jack's question was met with another wall of silence.

"No comment."

"Did you snap before you killed your daughter?"

"Inspector!" Cordelia Bannerman bristled, the chain from her wire-rimmed spectacles clinking as she raised her pinched face towards Jack. "Kindly keep your questions to the offence my client has been arrested for. Namely the murder of Maisie Lancaster. Otherwise, I am going to have to press for his release."

Jack directed his best condescending smile towards the duty solicitor. "As you wish. Raymond Edward Dixon, I'm arresting you on suspicion of the murder of Carrie-Ann Dixon in or around July 1989. You do not have to say anything, but it may harm your defence if you do not mention when questioned something which you later rely on in court. Anything you do say may be given in evidence. Do you understand?"

Raymond Dixon's face drained of all remaining colour.

"I expect you'll want a moment alone with your solicitor."

* * *

Time: 8.00 p.m.
Date: Monday 26 May 2014
Location: Metropolitan Police HQ, London

Although they'd managed to put Raymond Dixon in a cell at the far end of the corridor, there wasn't so much choice when it came to housing Gerard and Hughes. The only cells available were right next to each other. Booked in at a little after four o'clock, they'd been left alone in their cells ever since — just the offer of a bland, microwaved meal in the interim.

And Darren Hughes was beginning to sweat.

He was no stranger to a cell — police or prison — but that wasn't what was worrying him.

This was murder.

And the murder of a child, at that.

He'd put his hands up to trying to kill that idiot in the Ford who'd cut him up — part of him was disappointed he hadn't succeeded.

But this?

This was different.

If he went down for this, he'd never see the light of day again — not with his record. The thought of ending his days behind bars churned his insides.

"I did it for you, Gerry!"

Hughes knew his brother was in the next cell — he'd already heard him swearing at the poor sod who'd delivered their dinner.

"Gerry? I said — I did it for you."

"I heard you the first time, Daz." Gerard's voice was low but floated easily through the thick wall between them. "Just shut up."

"But I did! You've got to believe me!" Hughes paused, his heart hammering. He'd already bitten his nails to the quick in the four hours they'd been locked up, and they were beginning to bleed. "Dixon ruined your Army career — if he hadn't been mouthing off in that pub, then none of this would've happened, Gerry. You'd never have got into that fight, you'd never have been kicked out of the Army. And *this* wouldn't have happened. But he just couldn't keep his big, fat gob shut, could he? I had to do something."

A shout from further up the corridor told Hughes to stop making so much noise. He fell silent, eying the congealed lasagne that still sat on the tray on his mattress. Gerry would see how he did it all for him — how he'd set Dixon up to punish him. Surely Gerry would see that, wouldn't he?

Dixon had been serving time on a fraud charge in Rushmore Prison when he'd approached Hughes regarding a 'job'. Hughes' reputation as 'The Fixer' around Rushmore had clearly reached Dixon's ears.

It sounded like an odd plan — to kidnap Dixon's best mate's granddaughter. The man had said he wanted to teach someone a lesson — a lesson they'd never forget. But he was prepared to pay Hughes handsomely for his trouble. Kidnap the girl, keep her for a few days, then give her back when the message had sunk in.

"Why d'you kill her, Gerry?" Hughes scooted over to the wall that separated him from his brother. He tried to keep his voice low. "The kid — why d'you do it?"

"Jesus, Daz. Can't you keep your mouth shut for five minutes?"

Gerard Murray also hadn't eaten his lasagne, and it was currently decorating the floor of his urine-scented cell. Why had he killed her? It was a question he'd fleetingly asked himself in recent days. Veins began to pulsate at his temples.

He hadn't asked to get involved — not this time. This wasn't like Narelle. This wasn't planned. But when Daz had rocked up at the pub with a kid in tow, asking him to hide her upstairs, what was he supposed to do?

The kid had started screaming once she realised she wasn't going home — and after one night Gerard knew she had to go. Maybe killing her had been a bit extreme, but what was he meant to do? He couldn't keep her quiet, and he wasn't even supposed to be up there himself, anyway.

Images of Narelle flashed into his head, and Gerard sent the plastic mug of cold tea in the same direction as the lasagne.

Everything was unravelling.

But at least Dixon looked like he was up to his neck in it, too. He had to hand it to Daz — as thick as he was sometimes, the suitcase had been a nice touch. A small smile tugged at the corner of his mouth. He loathed Raymond Dixon just about as much as it was possible to loathe another human being. The man had ended his Army career that night in the Bridge — no question about that. Gerard knew his Army record wasn't exactly spotless, but he didn't deserve to be kicked out like that.

Dixon deserved everything that was coming to him. And if he could somehow blame him for killing the kid, he would.

Gerard could still hear his brother muttering and wailing next door. The lad needed to put a sock in it before he said something he shouldn't.

Gerard, for one, wasn't going to be saying anything when they finally got around to interviewing them. He knew the police tactics of letting them stew — thinking it would work to their advantage; make them start saying things they otherwise wouldn't.

Well, Gerard wasn't falling for that one.

His lips would remain tightly sealed.

"Gerry?" Hughes' voice filtered through the wall once more.

"Shut it, Daz. Just shut it."

* * *

Time: 8.35 p.m.
Date: Monday 26 May 2014
Location: Metropolitan Police HQ, London

Jack briefly closed his eyes and let the aroma of the Colombian coffee filter through his nostrils. When the chief superintendent told you to take a seat and offered to make you a cup of the good stuff, it was an indication that you weren't in too much trouble. Not a bollocking at any rate. If you were left standing and the coffee machine remained idle, you could be in for a rough ride.

Dragging his eyes open, he saw the mug had already landed on the desk in front of him. He'd swallowed a couple of painkillers not long before, and they were making him sleepy. Still in pain, but sleepy.

"You look like shit, Jack." A genuine look of concern flashed across Chief Superintendent King's face as he slipped his ample frame into the leather swivel chair behind his desk. He gave a nod towards Jack's arm, which was still strapped in a close-fitting sling across his chest. "How's the shoulder?"

Jack tried a shrug but wished he hadn't. "It's all good, sir. I can barely feel a thing."

"Hmmm." Dougie King's expression told Jack that he didn't believe a word of it. "Well, you make sure you take it easy at least. Get that team of yours to do the donkey work." He knew he could force Jack to take sick leave — being shot at certainly warranted it — but he also knew it would be futile. Jack would do just as Jack wanted, sick leave or no sick leave.

"I will," agreed Jack, reaching for the coffee cup with his one-remaining useful hand. "I'll sit behind the desk and lead from the back." The look on the chief superintendent's face told Jack that he'd believe it when he saw it.

"How's it looking in the cells? We close to charging anyone yet?"

Jack took a sip of the hot coffee, relishing the warmth. "I'm told it's all getting a bit fractious down there — give it time and they won't be able to snitch on each other fast enough. The CPS are looking at the evidence — I expect there'll be an authorisation to charge first thing in the morning."

"Good. You've done well to solve both the Maisie Lancaster and Narelle Williams murder cases. Not forgetting helping to breathe life back into a cold case. Take some time. Recharge your batteries."

"I will."

"I've also read the statements concerning what went on in your flat, Jack. Yours. Your brother's. DS Carmichael's." Dougie King fixed Jack with one of his knowing looks. "It makes for one hell of a story. This man — Quinn. You've no idea why he was in your flat that night?"

Jack hesitated, buying himself some more time by taking another sip of coffee. It was smooth and rich, as comforting as a velvet blanket. But he knew he couldn't hide behind his coffee cup for long — he could feel the chief superintendent's eyes boring into him.

"No, sir — other than confessing that he'd killed my mother. I've never seen him before." Jack swallowed the rich coffee along with the lie.

Dougie King reached for his own coffee cup. "Well, Quinn's been charged with your attempted murder — you probably already know that. And I'm sure an investigation will now be reopened by Dorset Police into the events surrounding your mother's death. How do you feel about that, Jack? Your mother's death being reopened?"

"It'd be a very welcome step, sir."

Chief Superintendent King nodded and turned his attention to the computer screen before him. "They'll be looking into the post-mortem again, and the inquest — and any other details they feel might be relevant." He paused, peering over the top of his spectacles. "It could be an unsettling time for you. But let them do their work, Jack. No more heroics. You've got more than enough on your plate here. If there's evidence to be found, they'll find it."

Jack nodded. He knew the evidence was there — they wouldn't have to look far.

Dougie King paused and eyed Jack across the desk. "If there's anything you haven't told me, Jack — any lines you may have inadvertently crossed — now's the time to say."

Jack remained mute behind his mug.

"In that case, I'll let you go. But no going off-piste, Jack. I need you where I can see you."

CHAPTER FORTY-SEVEN

Time: 7.30 p.m.
Date: Wednesday 28 May 2014
Location: The Duke of Wellington Public House, London

Carmichael brought the tray of drinks to the table by the dartboard. A pint of lager for himself and Jack, a half for DS Cooper, a slimline tonic water for DS Cassidy and an orange juice for DC Daniels. Not the most raucous of parties.

"We did it, guv." Cassidy held up her tonic water in salute. "Maisie. Narelle. Even Carrie-Ann."

Jack took a large gulp of his lager. "We did that, Amanda. We did that."

"And the milk thief finally owned up."

"Oh?" Jack's weary eyebrows hitched across the top of his pint glass. "Who was it?"

Cassidy made a zipping action across her mouth. "My lips are sealed, but let's just say there are two pints of semi-skimmed in the fridge as we speak, plus a box of doughnuts."

The mood around the table was one of quiet elation — *very* quiet elation. The events of the last week had taken their toll on them all — and the realisation that all three cases were now solved had yet to really filter through and raise their spirits. All that was left was tiredness; but it was a happy tiredness.

"You manage to speak to the Lancasters yet?" Carmichael knocked back half of his drink in one go. "About what was found in Hughes' freezer?"

Jack gave a slow nod. "They're receiving all the additional support we can offer."

When he'd informed Russell and Sara Lancaster that they'd found the rest of Maisie's body, he'd sensed a flicker of relief from the pair of them. They could now start to grieve properly over the loss of their daughter — but they faced a tricky time ahead. The involvement of Raymond Dixon, someone they'd classed as a family friend for more than three decades, was a wound that was unlikely to ever heal. Dixon's continued insistence that his only involvement was setting up her abduction by Hughes and that she was meant to be returned to her family, unharmed, wasn't washing with anyone.

And then there was Sara's mother.

Families had fallen apart in lesser circumstances, and Jack could already see the cracks starting to form. Maggie Foster had been true to her word and admitted her involvement in the cover-up of Carrie-Ann's death. She was ready to face the consequences, whatever they turned out to be — whether she would ever be able to mend the fractured relationship with her own daughter remained to be seen. Maisie would never have been placed in harm's way if Maggie Foster hadn't decided to tell the truth about Carrie-Ann.

Jack wasn't sure that Sara Lancaster would ever be able to come to terms with that.

Derek Foster had been charged with assaulting a police officer — Jack's lip would heal but Foster was going to have to live with his actions for a lot longer. But maybe the realisation that Sara Lancaster may not be his daughter was weighing more heavily on the man's mind.

"And Narelle?" Cassidy put her tonic water down, a shadow crossing her face.

"I filled them in on what we believe happened to her." Jack took another long sip from his pint glass. "Wrong time, wrong place."

Christine and Gregory Williams were now going to head back to Australia to await the return of their daughter's remains. It'd been an emotional conversation, and Jack was full of admiration for how well they'd coped with the news of what had befallen Narelle.

"What about the others?" Cooper wiped his mouth with the back of his hand. "Murray and Hughes?"

"Both charged. Both now on remand. They won't see the light of day for a long time."

Gerard had initially said nothing after his arrest — refusing to answer questions or cooperate in any way. But the evidence against the barman and ex-soldier for both Narelle's murder and Maisie's soon started to become overwhelming. The room above the pub where Murray had been staying was littered with forensic evidence linking him to Narelle and Maisie. Once the lab reports had started to come through, his mouth had loosened somewhat.

But whatever sentence he eventually received in court, it'd be nothing compared to the punishment he'd receive inside the prison walls. Child killers were as unwelcome within the prison system as they were outside. And Jack had no sympathy. It was at times like these that the unregistered vigilante justice handed out by convicts against their fellow cell mates made up for the inadequacies of the legal system. Jack, for one, was prepared to turn a blind eye.

Darren Hughes hadn't been quite so reticent during his interviews – he was soon singing like a canary to try and save his own skin. Denying any involvement in the murders of either Narelle or Maisie, he'd been charged with perverting the course of justice and assisting an offender. Both were punishable by lengthy prison terms. The Crown Prosecution Service hadn't ruled out further charges but, whatever happened, Darren Hughes wasn't going to see the light of day for some time. Nobody, it seemed, would miss him. He was a leech on society. A parasite. A patsy. The world was a better place without him in it.

And, with Raymond Dixon charged, for the second time, with the murder of his daughter — and about to spend the rest of his life behind bars — Jack began to feel the memories of the last twenty-five years start to subside. Justice was coming for Carrie-Ann. It might be twenty-five years too late, but it was better than nothing. Dixon wouldn't have an easy time of it on the inside, either.

Cassidy frowned. "Why did they go to such extraordinary lengths? The whole thing was so bizarre."

Jack placed his half-empty pint glass back down on the beer mat in front of him. "I guess Dixon could see the truth about Carrie-Ann coming out. He'd spent the best part of twenty-five years laughing at us, thinking he'd got away with it. Then Maggie Foster comes along and threatens to blow that sky high — so he threatened her, hoping to get her to keep her mouth shut. It was a stupid plan, but he's not exactly the brightest spark. Unfortunately for Maisie, he chose to involve Darren Hughes — and the whole thing backfired."

"Imagine if they all end up in the same prison," remarked Daniels, lifting his glass of orange juice. "There'd be carnage."

They sat in relative silence for a while, quietly sipping their drinks and trying to make sense of the last forty-eight hours. The only sound around them was the occasional bleeping from one of the games machines and low- level conversations from the early evening pub clientele.

It was Cassidy who made the first move, placing her empty glass down and getting to her feet. "Sorry, I've got to dash. Hot date with a hot yoga class! Anyone else fancy joining me?" She looked expectantly around the table.

Jack held up his one good hand. "I think you know my answer."

"And mine," replied Carmichael.

"Trev?" Cassidy glanced towards the detective constable who was attempting to hide behind his orange juice. "Might do wonders for your back?"

Daniels' eyes widened at the thought of discovering exactly what hot yoga might entail, before smiling and shaking his head. "Sorry, I've got an online chess game starting soon. After last year's shenanigans, I sort of got hooked on it."

Cassidy's eyes sparkled. "That just leaves you, Chris. Come on, I'm sure you don't have anything better to do tonight. I know for a fact Jenny's working late at the lab."

Cooper eyed his empty glass gloomily.

"Um . . ." he stumbled, clearly trying to think of an excuse and coming up with nothing.

"Great, that's settled then. Come on. We've just got time to nip back to yours and get your things." Before Cooper knew what was happening, he was being hauled out of his chair and dragged towards the door.

"Enjoy yourselves!" Jack raised his pint glass as they departed. Once they were out of sight, he turned towards Daniels. "Nicely swerved there, Daniels. You fancy another?" He nodded at the empty orange juice glass.

Daniels shook his head. "No, sorry. I really do have an online chess game to get to. I didn't just make that up." He started to get to his feet. "Quite glad too — not sure hot yoga is my thing."

"Nor me, Daniels. Nor me." Jack watched the young detective head for the door and drained his glass. "Another one, Rob?"

Carmichael was already on his feet, heading for the bar — soon arriving back with two fresh pints. He slipped back into his seat, loosening his tie. "You all set for the wedding? You'll cut a fine figure on the dance floor with that sling!"

Jack reached for his fresh drink with his good hand. "There'll be no dancing, Rob. Not for me. Even without the sling. You know that."

"Ah, never say never, Jack." Carmichael took a sip of his pint, his eyes sparking mischievously. "But more importantly, who are you taking as your plus-one?"

* * *

Time: 8.00 p.m.
Date: Wednesday 28 May 2014
Location: Isabel's Café, Horseferry Road, London

"Any questions, then Dominic's your man. There's nothing he doesn't know about this coffee machine!"

Isabel beamed at Gina, wiping her warm brow with a tea towel. "Sorry it's so hot in here today — we've got all the ovens on doing a batch bake in advance. I'm getting married at the weekend, so I need to get organised!"

"Oh, congratulations!" smiled Gina. "I hope you have a great day."

It had been a long day, but a million times better than Niko's. For one, there were no lurid comments or groping hands, and her clothes wouldn't smell of bacon grease at the end of the shift. All in all, Gina had loved her first day at Isabel's.

"I'm leaving the café in the capable hands of a catering firm — they're a tad expensive but I didn't want to shut up shop for a week." Isabel threw the tea towel down on the counter and flopped into a nearby armchair. "Plus, Livi needs feeding."

Right on cue, the tabby cat threaded her way through the café and jumped up on to Isabel's lap, purring contentedly.

"And you'll be OK to work the weekend? I'm sorry the three of us won't be here, and you've only just started." Isabel flashed a look of genuine concern at the newest member of her team. "It's not great timing, is it?"

Gina shook her head, animatedly. "No, no, really, it's fine. I'm good. I'm looking forward to it."

"Would you like to stay upstairs in the flat while I'm away? It would help in looking after Livi —you'd have to be on feeding and litter tray duties, though?!"

Gina couldn't help the smile on her face widening into a grin. "Really? That'd be fantastic! It would save me a lot in travel."

Isabel returned the smile. "That's settled then! One less thing for me to worry about!" All day she'd been worried about Mac. What had happened at Jack's flat with James

Quinn had rocked them both, and she'd noticed Mac withdrawing into himself once again. It concerned her.

"He'll be fine." Sacha squeezed her best friend's shoulders as she passed by, noticing the worried look in Isabel's eyes. "It'll be a combination of what happened and wedding jitters. He is a man, after all!"

Isabel tried a smile. "Maybe." Perhaps he *was* nervous about the wedding. But somehow she thought it went deeper than that. Finding out his mother might not have committed suicide had been a shock like no other.

"He'll be fine," repeated Sacha, ferrying yet more baking trays out into the kitchen. Her face was bright red and beads of sweat peppered her forehead. "You just concentrate on getting this place ship shape before you head off."

Isabel pushed herself up from the chair, much to Livi's disdain, and crossed over to the door. She turned the sign around to 'closed' and sighed. After tomorrow, the next time she'd be back in the café she'd be Mrs MacIntosh! The thought both pleased and terrified her at the same time.

"Is there anything else I can do?" Gina's voice cut through into Isabel's thoughts.

Isabel smiled warmly and shook her head. "No, not at all. You've done brilliantly today. It was a real baptism of fire! Thanks for staying on. Why don't you head off home and we'll see you in the morning?"

Gina said her goodbyes and stepped out into the cool evening air. The weather had changed over the last few days — there was a keenness to the wind and a nip in the air. Pulling her jacket around her, she made her way towards the Tube, and as she did so she couldn't help but grin. Goodness knows what everyone thought as they passed her on the pavement — but she didn't care. Suddenly, her life had been turned around — and this time, in a good way.

Just two days ago she'd been walking along the street, not really looking where she was going. She just wanted to get away from her flat — and Niko's. And, once again, she found herself outside Isabel's Café.

A young lad was busily washing the windows outside and, as she stepped around the bucket of soapy water, she spied the advert on the door.

'Assistant required — apply within. Hours to suit.'

A strange feeling rippled inside her as she remembered how welcoming and friendly the café had been — and how many coffees she'd been allowed to drink for free. She still didn't quite believe the story that she'd been doing them a favour — but she'd drunk them all the same.

The thought of working there every day made her stomach flip.

Could she?

Could she really?

Before she had a chance to decide one way or the other, the café door opened and the familiar warm smile of the café owner greeted her.

"It's Gina, isn't it?"

She remembered.

Gina's cheeks began to flush as Isabel stepped forwards.

And that had been that. The first step on the road to getting out of the rotten hole she called her life. The first step on getting Rosie back. Ditching her job at Niko's had been one of the best feelings she'd had in a long time. The look on his face this morning had been priceless. She didn't even give him any notice — just handed him her apron and turned her back on the grease and grime.

And today when she heard that Darren Hughes had been arrested, she could have danced in the street.

He was gone.

And so was her debt.

At long last, she was free.

And freedom felt good.

CHAPTER FORTY-EIGHT

Time: 11.45 p.m.
Date: Saturday 31 May 2014
Location: Tannochside B&B, Tannoch, Scotland.

"Good speech, Jack," Robert Carmichael resumed his seat next to Jack, handing him another tumbler of whisky. "Short and sweet. Just how I like them."

Jack managed a smile and accepted the drink. He hated weddings, and speeches even more so. But when duty called you had to step up. "Cheers, Rob."

But the speech had gone down well — with Jack having no intention of dragging it out any longer than absolutely necessary. There were no embarrassing stories of them as children or young adults, much to everyone's relief — none more so than to the groom himself. It had occurred to Jack, when finally sitting down to pen something coherent, that he knew very little about his brother's formative years, embarrassing or otherwise. And what he did know wasn't exactly wedding speech material. So, he'd kept it concise. Speeches only got in the way of decent drinking time. And Willie McArthur had got in some excellent whiskies for the occasion.

"You don't scrub up too bad, Jack," added Carmichael, sinking his whisky in one. "Even the sling looks quite smart."

Jack grinned. He'd tried wearing his shirt without his arm trussed up in the sling, but the pain had been excruciating. So, here he was, still incapacitated but at least his drinking arm was fine. He sank the rest of his whisky while watching a succession of bodies twirling around the makeshift dance floor.

Willie had done them proud by erecting a marquee outside the B&B, on the banks of the babbling brook that eventually led to the spectacular Loch Tannoch. It was the most beautiful setting. After the ceremony, Willie had piled the wedding party into the back of his Land Rover and driven them down to the banks of the Loch for photographs at the water's edge under the setting sun. Even Jack had to conclude that it was a stunning backdrop.

And then there was Stu. Jack couldn't remember ever seeing his brother looking so happy. Isabel had been fiercely protective of them both after the events in Jack's flat — hardly letting either of them out of her sight. They'd played down the whole incident, but Isabel wasn't stupid.

Jack noticed Willie's granddaughter, Lily McArthur, sidestepping her way around the edge of the dance floor, avoiding the various arms and legs as people attempted to dance to the Macarena. She was handing out fresh tumblers of Willie's famous whisky collection to anyone who wanted a taste of the 'good stuff'. She'd made the trip up from London especially for the wedding, and had exchanged a few brief words with Jack when he'd arrived yesterday. But he could see it in her eyes that she didn't want to revisit the events of last year — so Jack tactfully kept off the subject of the Bishop.

There'd been a touching reunion between Lily and DC Daniels — although *reunion* was an odd way to describe people who'd never really met. Not properly, anyway. Daniels had undoubtedly saved Lily's life last year, something that neither Willie, nor his wife, Margaret, would ever forget.

The hearty handshake and tearful welcome that they gave the newest member of Jack's team said it all.

So, all in all, it'd been a good wedding.

Lily deposited two fresh glasses in front of Jack and Carmichael and then turned away back towards the bar — which was when Rob spied DS Cassidy talking to Jane Telford.

"So, what's with the date, Jack? You kept that quiet. You asked her to dance, yet?" Carmichael gave a sly wink over the rim of his tumbler.

"There are two things wrong with that statement, Rob. Firstly, this isn't a date, it's a wedding. And secondly, you know I don't dance."

Carmichael's eyes continued to glint. "Yeah, but bringing someone to a wedding, mate. A *family* wedding. It's a statement."

Jack shook his head and downed the rest of his whisky. "There's no statement here at all. It was you and Amanda — badgering me to bring someone." Jack pushed himself up out of the plastic garden chair he'd been sitting in and felt his shoulder groan in protest at the sudden movement. Although slowly healing, the pain still lingered.

"I'm heading back inside. I need some painkillers and then probably my bed." Jack made to step around the table and head towards the entrance of the B&B when Carmichael's phone pinged with an incoming message. A split second later, so did Jack's.

Exchanging the briefest of looks, they both pulled out their phones and saw the same message displayed.

"James Quinn arrested for the murder of Stella MacIntosh. Denying any involvement."

Carmichael caught Jack's eye.

"This isn't the end, Jack. This is just the beginning."

THE END

MESSAGE FROM THE AUTHOR

Thank you for reading the fourth DI Jack MacIntosh novel, *Twenty Years Buried* — I hope you enjoyed it! I really loved writing it!

While most of the locations in this book are real — London Bridge is definitely real and hasn't yet fallen down (contrary to the popular nursery rhyme) — I have exercised some artistic licence here and there. The Legend of Hangman's End is purely a figment of my overactive imagination — something I conjured up while drafting the book. To my knowledge, highwaymen were not put to death on the bridge, and the Hangman's End tavern did not truly exist. I did, however, make many trips out to London Bridge and I have pictured in my mind's eye the exact location of where the Hangman's End tavern and End of the Road/the Bridge pub would have been located. In my writer's head, they are real! Tyburn Tree, however, did exist and was the favoured place for public hangings of highwaymen back in the day.

If you've enjoyed reading *Twenty Years Buried*, I'd be delighted if you could leave a review/rating on Amazon — and spread the word!

And please also keep in touch: www.michellekiddauthor.com — join my author newsletter for information on future releases and special offers.

www.facebook.com/michellekiddauthor

Twitter @AuthorKidd

Instagram @michellekiddauthor

ACKNOWLEDGEMENTS

There are a large number of people I need to thank for helping me get this far with the fourth DI Jack MacIntosh book. Firstly, I must thank PS Rebecca McCarthy of Suffolk Police who has always been happy to help me on police procedure. If there are any remaining inaccuracies, then I can assure you that they are mine and mine alone!

I also thank Tracey Proctor for being my 'go-to' person for anything to do with forensics.

I must then also thank my childhood Australian pen pal, Narelle, for the creation of the character of Narelle Williams. Back in 1982, when I was ten years old, Narelle and I started writing to each other. We lost touch when we were about sixteen or so but have recently found each other again — some thirty odd years later! It's amazing to be back in touch after all this time. Narelle kindly agreed for me to use her name for my Australian backpacker character in *Twenty Years Buried*!

In addition, I am forever grateful to my good friend Sarah Bezant for helping shape the book in its early stages. Also heartfelt thanks to everyone at Joffe Books — especially Kate Lyall Grant — for your unswerving support.

And, finally, it is you — the readers! Without you, none of these books would ever see the light of day. I thank each and every one of you.

THE JOFFE BOOKS STORY

We began in 2014 when Jasper agreed to publish his mum's much-rejected romance novel and it became a bestseller.

Since then we've grown into the largest independent publisher in the UK. We're extremely proud to publish some of the very best writers in the world, including Joy Ellis, Faith Martin, Caro Ramsay, Helen Forrester, Simon Brett and Robert Goddard. Everyone at Joffe Books loves reading and we never forget that it all begins with the magic of an author telling a story.

We are proud to publish talented first-time authors, as well as established writers whose books we love introducing to a new generation of readers.

We have been shortlisted for Independent Publisher of the Year at the British Book Awards three times, in 2020, 2021 and 2022, and for the Diversity and Inclusivity Award at the Independent Publishing Awards in 2022.

We built this company with your help, and we love to hear from you, so please email us about absolutely anything bookish at feedback@joffebooks.com

If you want to receive free books every Friday and hear about all our new releases, join our mailing list: www.joffebooks.com/contact

And when you tell your friends about us, just remember: it's pronounced Joffe as in coffee or toffee!

ALSO BY MICHELLE KIDD

DI JACK MACINTOSH MYSTERIES
Book 1: SEVEN DAYS TO DIE
Book 2: FIFTEEN REASONS TO KILL
Book 3: SIXTEEN CARVED PIECES
Book 4: TWENTY YEARS BURIED

Made in United States
Orlando, FL
26 April 2023

32482456R00214